Full of energy, history, romance, and a true sense of what it was like to be a trooper in the Seventh Cavalry in 1876. This book "Hoka- A- Hey" is an alluring look at our early years as a nation through the eyes of some of our great leaders, and what I found to be a marvelous addition brought in by fictitious characters such as "Oraland, Waynoka, and Charlie Goes Slow". Custer, like him or not, is still an icon in American Military history; whereas the simple Indian had to struggle his entire life for his rights. Great job Wayne Treptow in telling a riveting tale. I am looking forward to your next adventure in storytelling. David Nelson, Patriot

In writing "HOK-A-HEY"IT IS A GOOD DAY TO DIE, Author Wayne F. Treptow has delivered a fresh perspective on one of America's most compelling historical events. This well researched, and detailed history provides readers with new insights into the lives of characters on both sides of this ongoing debate. History tends to be written by the victors, not the vanquished. Gene Goerke   Early Americanist

"Hoka- A- Hey" "It Is a Good Day to Die" is without a doubt the most history packed book that I have ever read on the Battle of The Little Big Horn. Mr. Treptow has done his research and the reader will come away with a better understanding of what happened that dark day in American military history. His incorporating a fictitious story line with factual events is brazen. He brought out ones yearning to be living in that time period, but also made it clear that life wasn't so sublime. Three cheers for the men of the Seventh and a very somber look at the lives of the native American Indian of that time period. What a refreshing look into the life of the Indian perspective. Truly a great read.
Clark Davies, American Military Studies

Hok A Hey

© Copyright Wayne F. Treptow 2015
Published by Glorybound Publishing
SAN 256-4564
10 9 8 7 6 5 4 3 2 1
Printed in the United States of America
ISBN 978-1-60789-305-9   1-60789-305-3
Library of Congress Cataloging-in-Publication data is available on file.
Treptow, Wayne F, 1947-
     Hok A Hey/Wayne F. Treptow
     Includes biographical reference.
1. History   2. Historical Fiction
I. Title

www.gloryboundpublishing.com

The painting used for the cover of
Hok A Hey by Samantha Rapp.

Hok A Hey

'It is a Good Day to Die'

By
Wayne F. Treptow

Glorybound Publishing
Camp Verde, Arizona
Released 2018

Overview of Hok A Hey

    This book was written with the greatest regard and respect for the people you will find inside the cover. My format in writing is a little different than any other writer.
    The reader will find a story line, then a biography on all of the Characters.
    The book is full of factual events which I intertwined with fictitious events or occurrences, I made up, and the result may seem a little obscure, but it could have happened.
    Our young country back in the 1800's was changing, and each of the people inside this cover helped carve those changes for the good or bad of the nation. I grew up studying and reading about each individual, and I am continuing to learn new things about each every day. I have stated many times, that I was born one hundred years too late and that I would have fit into that time period very well.
    Life goes on and I still can dream, so I ask you, the reader, to sit back and enjoy the book and let your mind lead you on a fantastic ride in our nation's past. A ride that will lead you to the most famous battle in our nation's history,

"The Battle of the Little Big Horn"!

    Note: No one knows for certain what happened that day and the reader can go on forever reading material on the famous Event. Even though there were thousands of survivors (Indians) and many of those were interviewed by the government, to this day there is a big question mark as to what happened. In doing the research on the Little Big Horn battle I found Colonel W. A. Graham's book "The Custer Myth" to be very helpful in weeding my way up to the battle and after. All those interviews and inquiries dove into the minds of many who were involved.

In the last sixty years I've read hundreds of articles or books, but you and I still don't know what happened. Experts all over the world are still trying to find that one clue that will lead us to the real answer, but for now all is still up in the air on What really happened on that day of June the 25th, 1876.

Keep Digging,

Wayne F. Trepton

DEDICATED TO MY WIFE
MARJORIE GRACE TREPTOW

Chapters

Section / Pg # /   Title

Chapter 1: (29)   Story line
Chapter 2: (165) Lt. Col. George Armstrong Custer
Chapter 3: (183) Major Marcus Reno
Chapter 4: (191) Captain Frederick Benteen
Chapter 5: (201) Chief Sitting Bull
Chapter 6: (207) Chief Crazy Horse
Chapter 7: (215) Chief Gall
Chapter 8: (221) Chief Black Kettle
Chapter 9: (225) Norvell Francis Churchill
Chapter 10: (229) Captain Tom Custer
Chapter 11: (233) Boston Custer
Chapter 12: (235) Elizabeth Bacon Custer
Chapter 13: (239) 1st Lt. James Calhoun
Chapter 14: (241) Henry Armstrong Reed "Autie"
Chapter 15: (243) Oraland Churchill & Waynoka
Chapter 16: (245) Map of the battle of June 25-26th 1876
Chapter 17: (246) The 12 co.'s of the 7th on June 25th 1876
Chapter 18: (249) Roster of the 7th dead & wounded on
                  June 25th & 26th 1876
Chapter 19: (255) Medal of honor winners at the little big horn
                  battle June 25th & 26th 1876
Chapter 20: (257) Scouts of the 7th cavalry 25th & 26th of June
                  1876
Chapter 21: (265) Myths & Truths surrounding the battle on
                  the 25th & 26th of June 1876
Chapter 22: (271) Signs of the times in America in June of 1876
Chapter 23: (273) Weapons of the Battle of the Little Big Horn
Chapter 24: (287) Bows and Arrows and Other Weapons

Acknowledgments (296)
Bibliography (298)
Illustration & photo credits (307)
About the Author (308)

STATEMENT OF WORK

This book is a work of factual and fictitious events. All characters and incidents are of my imagination with the exception or mention of past notables that made their mark in history. The story line is of my own and all of the fiction based incidents in the book are mine alone.

Hok A Hey

'It is a Good Day to Die'

By
Wayne F. Treptow

Boots and saddles

Death is waiting
the bugle sounds the charge
the sound of the horse's hooves
the thoughts of eternal peace
calm and solace ever so take hold
men leaning forward in their ride
the dryness in one's mouth
flashing metal, now can be seen
yelling, screaming, tears abound
humanity takes a step to the side
cursed is the vision of loss
death becomes surreal, alive
it opens up its arms, and tempts us
then the quiet, the mundane silence
is it over, or is it not
one believes, and hopes never again

The Regimental Staff of the Seventh Cavalry in June of 1876

Colonel Samuel D. Sturgis (detached service to St. Louis, Missouri)
Lieutenant Colonel George A. Custer (acting commander)
Major Joseph Tilford (leave of absence)
Major Lewis Merrill (detached service to Washington DC)
Major Marcus Reno
Adjutant First Lieutenant William Cooke
Quartermaster First Lieutenant Henry Nowian
Assistant Surgeon Georger Lord
Acting Assistant Surgeon James DeWolf
Acting Assistant Surgeon Henry Porter
Veterinary Surgeon C. A. Stein
Sergeant Major William Sharrow
Quartermaster Sergeant Thomas Causby
Commissary Sergeant Henry E. Schreiner
Saddler Sergeant John Tritten
Chief Bugler Henry Voss
Chief Musician Felix Vinatieri
(over saw 16 privates in regimental band)

The regiment was comprised of twelve companies consisting of each company having:

Captain	Two Buglers
First Lieutenant	Two Ferrier's
Second Lieutenant	Two Blacksmiths
First Sergeant	One Saddler
Five Sergeants	One Wagoner
Four Corporals	Fifty-Four Privates

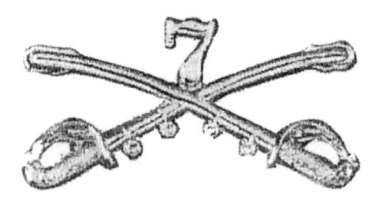

Total Roster Of The Seventh U.S. Cavalry in June Of 1876

PVT. ABBOTS, HENRY A.
PVT. ABOS, JAMES A.
SGT. ABRAMS, WILLIAM G.
PVT. ACHESON, THOMAS
PVT. ACKERMAN, CHARLES
PVT. ACKINSON, DAVID
PVT. ADAMS, GEORGE E.
PVT. ADAMS, JACOB
CPL. AKERS, JAMES
PVT. ALBERS, JAMES H.
SGT. ALCOTT, SAMUEL
CO. PACKER- ALEXANDER, WILLIAM
BLACKSMITH- ALLAN, FREDERICK
CPL. ALLER, CHARLES
PVT. ANDERSON, CHARLES
BUGLER- ANDERSON, GEORGE
SCOUT- APPEARING BEAR (SIOUX)
PVT. ANDREWS, WILLIAM
PVT. ARMSTRONG, JOHN E.
PVT, ARNDT, OTTO
PVT. ARNOLD, HERBERT H.
PVT. ASCOUGH, JOHN B.
PVT. ASSADALY, ANTHONY
PVT. AVERY, CHARLES E.
PVT. BABCOCK, ELMER
SGT. BAILEY, HEDNRY
PVT. BAILEY, JOHN A.
CO. INTERPRETER- BAILEY, WILLIAM J.
PVT. BAKER, WILLIAM H.
PVT. BANCROFT, NEIL
PVT. BANKS, CHARLES
REE SCOUT- BARKING WOLF
PVT. BARNETT, CHARLES C.

PVT. BARRY, JOHN
PVT. BARRY, PETER O.
PVT. BARSNTEE, JAMES F.
PVT. BARTH, ROBERT
PVT. BATES, JOSEPH
PVT. BAUER, JACOB
PVT. BAUMBACH, CONRAD
PVT. BAUMGARTNER, LOUIS
SCOUT- BEAR RUNNING IN THE TIMBER (SIOUX)
SCOUT- BEAR'S EYE (REE)
PVT. BECK, BENJAMIN
1ST LT. BELL, JAMES
SGT. BENDER, HENRY
SGT. BENNETT, JAMES
CPT. BENTEEN, FREDERICK
PVT. BERWALD, FRANK
SGT. BISCHOFF, CHARLES
PVT. BISHLEY, HENRY
CPL. BISHOP, ALEXANDER
PVT. BISHOP, CHARLES
CPL. BLACK, HENRY
SCOUT- BLACK FOX (REE)
SCOUT- BLACK PORCUPINE (REE)
1ST SGT. BLAIR, JAMES
PVT. BLAIR, THOMAS
COMPANY GUIDE- BLOODY KNIFE (SIOUX)
PVT.BLUNT, GEORGE
PVT. BOAM, WILLIAM
1ST SGT. BOBO, EDWIN
SCOUT- BOBTAIL BULL (REE)
PVT. BOCKERMAN, AUGUST
PVT. BOGGS, JAMES
BUGLER- BOHNER, ALOYS
SADDLER- BOISEN, CHRISTIAN
PVT. BONNER, HUGH

PVT. BOREN, ANSGARIU
PVT. BORTER, LUDWIG
PVT. BOTT, GEORGE
SGT. BOTZER, EDWARD
PVT. BOWERS, FRANK
C.GUIDE- BOUYER, MITCH
SCOUT- BOY CHIEF (REE)
PVT. BOYLE, JAMES
PVT. BOYLE, OWEN
PVT. BRADEN, CHARLES
PVT. BRADY, WILLIAM
PVT. BRAINARD, GEORGE
PVT. BRANDLE, WILLIAM
FARRIER- BRANDON, BENJAMIN
PVT. BRANT, ABRAM
PVT. BRAUN, FRANK
PVT. BRAUN, FRANZ
PVT. BRENNAN, JOHN
PVT. BRESNAHAN, CORNELIUS
PVT. BRIGHTFIELD, JOHN
FARRIER- BRINGES, JOHN
PVT. BRINKERHOFF, HENRY
CPL. BRIODY, JOHN
PVT. BROADHURST, JOSEPH
PVT. BROGAN, JAMES
SCOUT- BROKEN PENIS (SIOUX)
PVT. BROMWELL, LATROBE
SGT. BROWN, ALEXANDER
SGT. BROWN, BENJAMINE
COM-SGT. BROWN, CHARLES
CPL. BROWN, GEORGE
PVT. BROWN, HIRAM
PVT. BROWN, JAMES
PVT. BROWN, JOSEPH
PVT. BROWN, NATHAN
PVT. BROWN, WILLIAM
PVT. BRUCE, PATRICK
PVT. BRUNS, AUGUST
PVT. BUCKNELL, THOMAS
SCOUT- BULL (REE)
SCOUT- BULL IN THE WATER (REE)
PVT. BURDICK, BENJAMIN
PVT. BURDORF, CHARLES

BLACKSMITH- BURKE, EDMUND
PVT. BURKE, JOHN
PVT. BURKHARDT, CHARLES
PVT. BURKMAN, JOHN
PVT. BURLIS, EDMOND
PVT. BURNHAM, LUCIAN
PVT. BURNS, CHARLES
PVT. BUSTARD, JAMES
1ST SGT. BUTLER, JAMES
CPL. BUTLER, JAMES
SGT. CADDLE, MICHAEL
PVT. CAIN, MORRIS
SGT. CALDWELL, WILLIAM
1ST LT. CALHOUN, JAMES
BUGLER- CALLAHAN, JOHN
PVT. CALLAN, JAMES
PVT. CALLAN, THOMAS
PVT. CAMPBELL, CHARLES A.
CPL. CAMPBELL, CHARLES W.
SGT. CAMPBELL, JEREMIAH
PVT. CAPES, WILLIAM
SCOUT- CARDS (SIOUX)
PVT. CAREY, JOHN
SGT. CAREY, PATRICK
PVT. CARMODY, THOMAS
FARRIER- CARNEY, JAMES
SGT. CARROLL, DANIEL
PVT. CARROLL, JOSEPH
PVT. CARTER, ANDREW
BUGLER- CARTER, CASSIUS
PVT. CASHAN, WILLIAM
PVT. CATHER, ARMANTHEUS
SGT. CAUSBY, THOMAS
PVT. CHANNELL, WILLIAM
PVT. CHAPMAN, WILLIAM
SCOUT- CHARGING BULL (REE)
FARRIER- CHARLEY, VINCENT
PVT. CHEEVER, AMI
C. PACKER- CHURCHILL, BENJAMIN
SURGEON- CLARK, ELBERT
PVT. CLARK, FRANK
PVT. CLEAR, ELIHU
SCOUT- CLIMBS THE BLUFF (REE)

PVT. COAKLEY, PATRICK
CPL. CODY, HENRY
PVT. CODY, JOHN
BUGLER- COLEMAN, CHARLES
PVT. COLEMAN, THOMAS
PVT. COLLINS, JOHN
PVT. COLWELL. JOHN
PVT. CONLAN, THOMAS
PVT. CONLON, MICHAEL
PVT. CONELL, JOHN
SGT. CONNELLY, PATRICK
PVT. CONNER, ANDREW
PVT. CONNER, EDWARD
PVT. CONNORS, THOMAS
SGT. CONSIDINE, MARTIN
1ST LT. COOKE, WILLIAM
PVT. COONEY, DAVID
PVT. COOPER, EUGENE
PVT. COOPER, JOHN
PVT. CORCORAN, JOHN
PVT. CORCORAN, PATRICK
PVT. CORNWALL, MICHAEL
PVT. CORWINE, RICHARD
PVT. COVENEY, MICHAEL
PVT. COWLEY, CORNELIUS
PVT. COWLEY, STEPHEN
PVT. COX, THOMAS
CPL. CRANDALL, CHARLES
PVT. CRAWFORD, WILLIAM
1ST LT. CRAYCROFT, WILLIAM
PVT. CREIGHTON, JOHN
PVT. CRIDDLE, CHRISTOPHER
PVT. CRISFIELD, WILLIAM
CPL. CRISSY, MELANCHTON
PVT. CRISWELL, BENJAMINE
PVT. CRISWELL, HARRY
2ND LT. CRITTENDEN, JOHN
SCOUT- CROSS, WILLIAM
PVT. CROWE, MICHAEL
PVT. CROWLEY, JOHN
CROWLEY, PATRICK
BLACKSMITH- CRUMP, JOHN
SGT. CULBERTSON, FERDINAND
CPL. CUNNINGHAM, ALBERT
PVT. CUNNINGHAM, CHARLES

SCOUT- CURLY (REE)
SCOUT- CURLY HEAD (CROW)
SGT. CURTISS, WILLIAM
GUIDE- CUSTER, BOSTON
LT. COL. CUSTER, GEORGE A.
CPT. CUSTER, THOMAS
STEWARD- DALE, ALFRED
PVT. DALIOUS, JAMES
PVT. DANN, GEORGHE
PVT. DARRIS, JOHN
SGT. DAVENPORT, WILLIAM
PVT. DAVERN, EDWARD
PVT. DAVIS, HENRY
PVT. DAVIS, WILLIAM
PVT. DAWSEY, DAVID
PVT. DAY, CLARENCE
PVT. DAY, JOHN
PVT. DEETLINE, FREDERICK
PVT. DEIHLE, JACOB
SGT. DELACY, MILTON
PVT. DELANEY, MICHAEL
PVT. DEMOSS, CHARLES
1ST LT. DERUDIO, CHARLES
PVT. DETOURRIEL, LOUIS
PVT. DEVOTO, AUGUSTUS
PVT. DEWEY, GEORGE
SURGEON- DEWOLF, JAMES
PVT. DIAMOND, EDWARD
PVT. DOHMAN, ANTONIE
PVT. DOLAN, JOHN
PVT. DOLL, JACOB
SGT. DONAHOE, JOHN E.
CPL. DONAHUE, JOHN
PVT. DONNELLY, TIMOTHY
PVT. DOOLEY, PATRICK
C.INTERPRETER- DORMAN, ISAIAH
PVT. DORN, RICHARD
BUGLER- DOSE, HENRY
PVT. DOUGHERTY, JAMES
PVT. DOWNING, ALEXANDER
PVT. DOWNING, THOMAS
BUGLER- DRAGO, HENRY
PVT. DRINAN, JAMES
PVT. DRISCOLL, EDWARD
PVT. DURSELEW, OTTO

PVT. DWYER, EDMOND
PVT. DYE, WILLIAM
PVT. EADES, WILLIAM
CPL. EAGAN, THOMAS
CPL. EASLEY, JOHN
2ND LT. ECKERSON, EDWIN
2ND LT. EDGERLY, WINFIELD
TEAMSTER- EDWARDS, GEORGE
PVT. EDWARDS, GRANT
PVT. EISEMAN, GEORGE
PVT. EISENBERGER, PETER
PVT. ENGLE, GUSTAVE
PVT. ETZLER, WILLIAM
PVT. FARBER, CONRAD
PVT. FARLEY, WILLIAM
SGT. FARRAND, JAMES
PVT. FARRAR, MORRIS
PVT. FARRELL, RICHARD
PVT. FAY, JOHN
SGT. FEHLER, HENRY
SGT. FINCKLE, GEORGE
SGT. FINDEISEN, HUGO
SGT. FINLEY, JEREMIAH
PVT. FINNEGAN, THOMAS
BUGLER- FISCHER, CHARLES
PVT. FISHER, CHARLES
PVT. FITZGERALD
PVT. FLANAGAN, JAMES
C. PACKER FLINT, MOSES
PVT. FLOOD, PHILLIP
PVT. FOLEY, JOHN
CPL. FOLEY, JOHN
SCOUT-FOOLISH BEAR (REE)
SCOUT- FOOLISH RED BEAR (REE)
SCOUT- FORKED HORN (REE)
CPL. FOSTER, SAMUEL
PVT. FOWLER, ISSAC
PVT. FOX, FREDERICK
PVT. FOX, HARVEY
PVT. FOX, JOHN
PVT. FRANK, WILLIAM
PVT. FRANKLION, JIHN
SGT. FREDERICKS, ANDREW
CPL. FRENCH, HENRY

CPT. FRENCH, THOMAS
C. PACKER-FRETT, JOHN
CPL. GAFFNEY, GEORGE
PVT. GALLENE, JEAN BAPTISTE DESIRE
PVT. GALVAN, JAMES
SGT. GANNON, PETER
PVT. GARDNER, JOHN
PVT. GARLICK, EDWARD
2ND LT. GARLINGTON, ERNAST
PVT. GEBHART, JACOB
PVT. GEHRMANN, FREDERICK
CPL. GEIGER, GEORGE
1ST SGT. GEIST, FRANK
PVT. GEORGE, WILLIAM
C. INTERPRETER- GERARD, FREDERICK
PVT. GIBBS, WILLIAM
1ST LT GIBSON, FRANCIS
PVT. GILBERT, JOHN
PVT. GILBERT, JULIUS
PVT. GILBERT, WILLIAM
PVT. GILLETTE, DAVID
PVT. GLENN, GEORGE
1ST LT. GODFREY, EDWARD
SCOUT- GOES SLOW (SIOUX)
PVT. GOLDEN, BERNARD
PVT. GOLDEN, PATRICK
PVT. GOLDIN, THEODORE
SCOUT- GOOD FACED BEAR (REE)
SCOUT- GOSSE (REE)
SGT. GORDON, HENRY
PVT. GORDON, THOMAS
PVT. GRAHAM, CHARLES
PVT. GRAHAM, THOMAS
PVT. GRAY, JOHN
PVT. GRAY, WILLIAM
1ST SGT. GRAYSON, EDWARD
PVT. GREEN, JOHN
PVT. GREEN, JOSEPH
CPL. GREEN, THOMAS
PVT. GREGG, WILLIAM
PVT. GRIESNER, JULIUS
PVT. GRIFFIN, PATRICK
PVT. GRIMES, ANDREW

PVT. GROSS, GEORGE
PVT. GEESBACKER, GABRIEL
PVT. GUNTHER, JULIUS
PVT. HAACK, CHARLES
PVT. HAACK, HENRY
PVT. HACKETT, JOHN
CPL. HAGEMANN, OTTO
PVT. HAGER, JOHN
SCOUT- HAIRY MOCCASIN (CROW)
CPT. HALE, OWEN
PVT. HALEY, TIMOTHY
SCOUT- HALF YELLOW FACE (CROW)
PVT. HALL, EDWARD
PVT. HALL, PETER
BLACKSMITH- HAMILTON, ANDREW
PVT. HAMILTON, HENRY
PVT. HAMMON, GEORGE
PVT. HAMMON, JOHN
SGT. HANLEY, RICHARD
PVT. HARDDEN, WILLIAM
BUGLER- HARDY, WILLIAM
2ND LT. HARE, LUTHER
PVT. HARLFINGER, GUSTAV
2ND LT. HARRINGTON, HENRY
PVT. HARRINGTON, WESTON
PVT. HARRIS, DAVID
PVT. HARRIS, JAMES
PVT. HARRIS, LEONARD
BUGLER- HARRIS, WILLIAM
PVT. HARRISON, ALEXANDER
BUGLER- HARRISON, THOMAS
PVT. HARRISON, WILLIAM
PVT. HATHERSALL, JAMES
PVT. HAUGGI, LOUIS
PVT. HAVERSTICK, BENJAMINE
PVT. HAYER, JOHN
PVT. HAYT, WALTER
SADDLER- HAYWARD, GEORGE
PVT. HEATH, WILLIAM
PVT. HEGNER, FRANCIS
PVT. HEID, GEORGE
CPL. HEIM, JOHN
PVT. HELMER, JULIUS

SGT. HENDERSON, GEORGE
PVT. HENDERSON, JOHN
PVT. HENDERSON, SYKES
SCOUT-HERENDEEN, GEORGE
PVT. HETESIMER, ADAM
PVT. HETLER, JACOB
PVT. HEYN, WILLIAM
PVT. HEYWOOD, CHARLES
1ST SGT. HILL, JAMES
2ND LT. HODGSON, BENJAMINE
PVT. HOEHN, MAX
1ST SGT. HOHMEYER, FREDERICK
PVT. HOLAHAN, ANDREW
PVT. HOLCOMB, EDWARD
PVT. HOLDEN, HENRY
PVT. HOLMSTED, FREDERICK
PVT. HOOD, CHARLES
PVT. HOOK, STANTON
SGT. HORN, CHARLES
PVT. HORN, MARION
PVT. HORNER, JACOB
SCOUT- HORN IN FRONT (REE)
PVT. HOSE, GEORGE
PVT. HOUGHTALING, CHARLES
PVT. HOUSEN, EDUARD
PVT. HOWARD, FRANK
SADDLER- HOWELL, GEORGE
SCOUT- HOWLING WOLF (REE)
PVT. HOYT, WALTER
PVT. HUBER, WILLIAM
PVT. HUFF, JACOB
PVT. HUGHES, FRANCIS
SGT. HUGHES, ROBERT
PVT. HUGHES, THOMAS
SADDLER- HUNT, GEORGE
PVT. HUNT, JOHN
PVT. HUNTER, FRANK
PVT. HURD, JAMES
SGT. HUTCHINSON, RUFUS
PVT. HUTTER, ANTON
CPT. IISLEY, CHARLES
1ST LT. JACKSON, HENRY
SCOUT- JACKSON, ROBERT
SCOUT- JACKSON, WILLIAM
PVT. JAMES, JOHN

PVT. JAMES, WILLIAM
PVT. JENNYS, ALONZO
PVT. JOHNSON, EMIL
PVT. JOHNSON, PETER
PVT. JOHNSON, SAMUEL
PVT. JONES, HENRY
PVT. JONES, JULIEN
PVT. JORDAN, JOHN
PVT. JUNGESBLUTH, JULIUS
PVT. KANE, WILLIAM
SGT. KANIPE, DANIEL
PVT. KATZENMAIER, JACOB
PVT. KAVANAGH, CHARLES
PVT. KAVANAGH, JOHN
PVT. KAVANAUGH, THOMAS
PVT. KEEFE, JOHN
PVT. KEEGAN, MICHAEL
SGT. KELLER, JOHN
PVT. KELLEY, GEORGE
CORRESPONDENT- KELLOGG, MARCUS
BUGLER- KELLY, JAMES
PVT. KELLY, JAMES
PVT. KELLY, JOHN
PVT. KELLY, PATRICK
PVT. KENNEDY, FRANCIS
PVT. KENNEY, MICHAEL
CPT. KEOGH, MYLES
PVT. KERR, DENIS
PVT. KILFOYLE, MARTIN
PVT. KIMM, JOHN
CPL. KING, GEORGE
PVT. KING, JOHN
PVT. KIPP, FREMONT
PVT. KLAWITTER, FERDINAND
PVT. KLEIN, GUSTAV
PVT. KLEIN, NIKOLAUS
PVT. KLOTZBUCHER, HENRY
PVT. KNAPP, SAMUEL
PVT. KNAUTH, HERMAN
PVT. KNECHT, ANTHONY
PVT. KNEUBUHLER, JOSEPH
PVT. KORN, GUSTAVE
BUGLER- KRAMER, WILLIAM
PVT. KRETCHMER, JOSEPH
PVT. KUEHL, JESSE

PVT. LADEN, JOSEPH
C. PACKER-LAINPLOUGH, JOHN
CPL. LALOR, WILLIAM
PVT. LAMB, JOHN
PVT. LAMBERTIN, FRANK
PVT. LANG, HENRY
2ND LT. LARNED, CHARLES
FARRIER- LASLEY, WILLIAM
BLACKSMITH- LATTMAN, JOHN
PVT. LAUPER, FRANK
PVT. LAWHORN, THOMAS
BUGLER- LAWLER, JAMES
C. PACKER- LAWLESS, WILLIAM
SCOUT- LAYING DOWN (REE)
PVT. LEE, MARK
PVT. LEFLER, MEIG
SCOUT- LEFT HAND (SIOUX)
PVT. LEHMAN, FREDERICK
PVT. LEHMANN, HENRY
SGT. LELL, GEORGE
PVT. LEPPER, FREDERICK
PPVT. LEROCK, WILLIAM
PVT. LEWIS, DAVID
PVT. LEWIS, JOHN
PVT. LEWIS, URIAH
PVT. LIDDIARD, HEROD
PVT. LIEBERMAN, ANDREW
PVT. LIEMANN, WERNER
SCOUT- LITTLE BRAVE(REE)
SCOUT- LITTLE SIOUX(REE)
PVT. LITTLEFIELD, JOHN
PVT. LLOYD, EDWARD
PVT. LLOYD, FRANK
PVT. LOBERING, LOUIS
C.PACKER- LOESER, CHRISTAN
PVT. LOGUE, WILLIAM
PVT. LOMBARD, FRANCESCO
SCOUT- LONG BEAR (REE)
SURGEON- LORD, GEORGE
SADDLER- LORENTZ, GEORGE
SGT. MAJOR LOSSEE, WILLIAM
PVT. LOVETT, MEREDITH
CPL. LOYD, GEORGE
PVT. LYNCH, DENNIS
PVT. LYNCH, PATRICK
PVT. LYONS, BERNARD

PVT. LYONS, DANIEL
1ST SGT. MADDEN, MICHAEL
PVT. MADSEN, CHRISTIAN
PVT. MAHONEY, BARTHOLOMEW
PVT. MAHONEY, DANIEL
PVT. MAHONEY, JOHN
C. PACKER- MANN, FRANK
BUGLER- MANNING, DAVIV
PVT. MANNING, JAMES
SGT. MARONEY, MATTHEW
PVT. MARSHALL, JASPER
PVT. MARSHALL, JOHN
PVT. MARSHALL, WILLIAM
PVT. MARTIN, JAMES
1ST SGT. MARTIN, MICHAEL
PVT. MARTIN, WILLIAM
BUGLER- MARTIN, GIOVANNI
PVT. MASK, GEORGE
PVT. MASON, HENRY
1ST LT. MATHEY, EDWARD
PVT. MAXWELL, THOMAS
C.PACKER- MCBRATNEY, HENRY
PVT. MCCABE, JOHN
CPL. MCCALL, JOSEPH
PVT. MCCANN, PATRICK
PVT. MCCARTHY, CHARLES
PVT. MCCLURG, WILLIAM
PVT. MCCONNELL, WILSON
PVT. MCCORMICK, JAMES
PVT. MCCORMICK, SAMUEL
PVT. MCCREEDY, THOMAS
PVT. MCCUE, MARTIN
1ST SGT. MCCURRY, JOSEPH
CPL. MCDERMOTT, GEORGE
BUGLER- MCDERMOTT, THOMAS
CPL. MCDONALD, JAMES
BUGLER- MCDONNELL, JOHN
PVT. MCDONNELL, PATRICK
PVT. MCDONOUGH, JAMES
CPT. MCDOUGALL, THOMAS
PVT. MCEAGAN, JOHN
SGT. MCELROY, THOMAS
PVT. MCGINNIS, JOHN
PVT. MCGINNISS, JOHN
PVT. MCGLONE, JOHN
PVT. MCGONIGLE, HUGH
BUGLER- MCGUCKER, JOHN
PVT. MCGUE, PETER
BUGLER- MCGUIRE, JOHN
PVT.MCGURN, BERNARD
PVT. MCHUGH, PHILLIP
PVT. MCIIHARGEY, ARCHIBALD
1ST LT. MCINTOSH, DONALD
PVT. MCKAY, EDWARD
PVT. MCKEE, JOHN
PVT. MCKENNA, JOHN
PVT. MCLAUGHLIN, TERRENCE
SGT. MCLAUGHLIN, THOMAS
PVT. MCMASTERS, WILLIAM
PVT. MCNALLY, JAMES
PVT. MCNAMARA, JAMES
PVT. MCPEAKE, ALEXANDER
PVT. MCSHANE, JOHN
PVT. MCVAY, JOHN
BUGLER- MCVEIGH, DAVID
PVT. MCWILLIAMS, DAVID
PVT. MEADOR, THOMAS
PVT. MEADVILLE, JOHN
BLACKSMITH- MECHLING, HENRY
PVT. MEIER, FREDERICK
PVT. MEIER, JOHN
PVT. MEINIKE, ERNST
MAJ. MERILL, LEWIS
PVT. MERRITT, GEORGE
CPL. MEYER, ALBERT
PVT. MEYER, AUGUST
PVT. MEYER, WILLIAM
PVT. MEYERS, FRANK
PVT. MIELKE, MAX
PVT. MILES, JAMES
1ST SGT. MILLER, EDWIN
PVT. MILLER, JOHN
PVT. MILLER, WILLIAM
BLACKSMITH- MILLER, WILLIAM
PVT. MILTON, FRANCIS
PVT. MILTON, JOSEPH

PVT. MITCHELL, JOHN
PVT. MOLLER, JAN
PVT. MONROE, JOSEPH
BUGLER- MOODIE, WILLIAM
BUGLER- MOONIE, GEORGE
PVT. MOORE, ANDREW
C. PACKER- MOORE, EDWARD
PVT. MOORE, HUGH
FARRIER- MOORE, JAMES
PVT. MOORE, LANSING
PVT. MORRIS, WILLIAM
PVT. MORRISON, JOHN
CPL. MORROW, WILLIAM
CPT. MOYLAN, MYLES
PVT. MUELLER, WILLIAM
SADDLER- MUERING, JOHN
SGT. MULLEN, JOHN
PVT. MULLER, JOHN
PVT. MULLIN, MARTIN
SGT. MURPHY, LAWRENCE
PVT. MURPHY, MICHAEL
SGT. MURPHY, ROBERT
PVT. MURPHY, THOMAS
CPL. MURRAY, HENRY
PVT. MURRAY, THOMAS
PVT. MYERS, FRANK
PVT. MYERS, FREDERICK
SADDLER- MYERS, JOHN
2ND LT. NAVE, ANDREW
CPL. NEALON, DANIEL
PVT. NEELY, FRANK
PVT. NEES, EDLER
PVT. NEWELL, DANIEL
PVT. NICHOLAS, JOSHUA
PVT. NITSCHE, OTTOCAR
PVT. NIVER, GARRETT
CPL. NOLAN, JOHN
SGT. NORTHEG, OLANS
PVT. NOSHANG, JACOB
1ST LT. NOWLAN, HENRY
PVT. NUGENT, WILLIAM
CPL. NUNAN, JOHN
SGT. NURSEY, FREDERICK
PVT. O'BRIEN, THOMAS
PVT. O'BRYAN, JOHN
PVT. O'CONNELL, DAVID

PVT. O'CONNOR, PATRICK
PVT. OGDEN, JOHN
SGT. O'HARA, MILES
CPL. OMAN, WILLIAM
PVT. OMLING, SEBASTIAN
SCOUT- ONE FEATHER (REE)
SCOUT- ONE HORN (REE)
PVT. O'NEILL, BERNARD
PVT. O'NEILL, JAMES
SGT. O'NEILL, JOHN
PVT. O'NEILL, THOMAS
PVT. ORR, CHARLES
FARRIER- O'RYAN, WILLIAM
PVT. OSBORNE, AUGUSTUS
PVT. O'TOOLE, FRANCIS
PVT. OWENS, EUGENE
SCOUT- OWL (REE)
PVT. PAHL, JOHN
PVT. PARKER, JOHN
BUGLER- PATTON, JOHN
PVT. PENDLE, CHRISTOPHER
BUGLER- PENWELL, GEORGE
SADDLER-PERKINS, CHARLES
PVT. PERSONEUS, MARTIN
PVT. PETRING, HENRY
PVT. PHILLIPS, EDGAR
PVT. PHILLIPS, JOHN
PVT. PICKARD, EDWIN
PVT. PICKERING, RUFUS
PVT. PIGFORD, EDWARD
CPL. PILCHER, ALBERT
PVT. PINKSTON, JPHN
PVT. PITTER, FELIX
PVT. PITTET, FRANCIS
SURGEON- PORTER, HENRY
1ST LT. PORTER, JAMES
PVT. PORTER, JOHN
PVT. POST, GEORGE
PVT. PROCTOR, GEORGE
PVT. PYM, JAMES
PVT. QUINN, JAMES
PVT. QUINN, JOHN
SGT. RAFTER, JOHN
PVT. RAGSDALE, JOHN
PVT. RANDALL, GEORGE
CPL. RAICHEL, HENRY

BUGLER- RAMELL, WILLIAM
PVT. RAMSEY, CHARLES
PVT. RANDALL, WILLIAM
CPL. RANKIN, FRANKLIN
PVT. RAPP, JOHN
F.*.RRIER- RAUTER, JOHN
PVT. REAGAN, MICHAEL
SCOUT- RED BEAR (REE)
SCOUT- RED STAR (REE)
SCOUT- RED WOLF (REE)
CIVILIAN- REED, HARRY ARMSTRONG
1ST SGT. REED, JOHN
PVT. REED, WILLIAM
PVT. REES, WILLIAM
PVT. REESE, WILLIAM
PVT. REEVES, FRANCIS
PVT. REIBOLD, CHRISTIAN
PVT. REID, ELWYN
PVT. REILEY, MICHAEL
PVT.REILEY, MICHAEL
2ND LT. REILY, WILLIAM
SGT. RILEY, JAMES
MAJ. RENO, MARCUS
C. GUIDE- REYNOLDS, CHARLES
WAGONER- RICKETTS, JOSEPH
SCOUT- RING CLOUD (SIOUX)
PVT. RIVERS, JOHN
PVT. RIX, EDWARD
PVT. ROBB, ELDORADO
PVT. ROBERTS, JONATHAN
PVT. ROBERTS, HENRY
PVT. ROBINSON, WILLIAM
PVT. ROGERS, BENJAMINE
PVT. ROGERS, WALTER
PVT. ROLLINS, RICHARD
PVT. ROOD, EDWARD
PVT. ROONEY, JAMES
PVT. ROSE, PETER
SGT. ROSSBURY, JOHN
PVT. ROTH, FRANCIS
SGT. ROTT, LOUIS
PVT. ROWLAND, ROBERT
CPL. ROY, STANISLAS
PVT. RUDDEN, PATRICK
PVT.RUDOLPH, GEORGE
SCOUT- RUNNING WOLF (REE)
SGT. RUSH, THOMAS
BLACKSMITH- RUSSELL, JAMES
PVT.RUSSELL, THOMAS
PVT. RUTTEN, ROMAN
CPL. RYAN, DANIEL
PVT. RYAN, JOHN
PVT. RYAN, STEPHEN
PVT. RYDER, HOBART
PVT. RYE, WILLIAM
PVT. SAAS, WILLIAM
BUGLER- SADLER, WILLIAM
PVT. SAGER, HIRAM
PVT. SANDERS, CHARLES
PVT. SAUNDERS, RICHARD
PVT. SCHELE, HENRY
BUGLER- SCHLAFER, CHRISTIAN
PVT. SCHLEIFFORTH, PAUL
SADDLER-SCHLEIPER, CLAUS
PVT. SCHMIDT, CHARLES
PVT. SCHULTE, FREDERICK
PVT. SCHWERER, JOHN
PVT. SCOTT, CHARLES
PVT. SCOTT, GEORGE
CPL. SEAFFERMAN, HENRY
SGT. SEAMANS, JOHN
PVT. SEAYERS, THOMAS
PVT. SEIBELDER, ANTON
PVT. SEILER, JOHN
SADDLER- SELBY, CRAWFORD
PVT. SENN, ROBERT
PVT. SEVERS, JAMES
PVT. SEVERS, SAMUEL
PVT. SHADE, SAMUEL
PVT. SHANAHAN, JOHN
SGT. MAJOR SHARROW, WILLIAM
CPL. SHAUER, JOHN
PVT. SHEA, DANIEL
SHEA, JEREMIAH
PVT. SHERBORNE, THOMAS
CPT. SHERIDAN, MICHAEL
SCOUT- SHIELD (SIOUX)
SADDLER- SHIELDS, WILLIAM
PVT. SHORT, NATHAN
PVT. SICFOUS, FRANCIS

PVT. SIEFERT, AUGUST
BLACKSMITH- SIEMON, CHARLES
PVT. SIEMONSON, BENT
PVT. SIMONS, PATRICK
PVT. SIMS, JOHN
PVT. SIVERTSEN, JOHN
PVT. SLAPER, WILLIAM
PVT. SMALL, JOHN
PVT. SMALLWOOD, WILLIAM
PVT. SMITH, ALBERT
1ST LT. SMITH, ALGERNON
PVT. SMITH, FREDERICK
PVT. SMITH, GEORGE E.
PVT. SMITH, HENRY G.
PVT. SMITH, JAMES
PVT. SMITH, JAMES
PVT. SMITH, JAMES H.
PVT. SMITH, WILLIAM E.
PVT. SMITH, WILLIAM M.
PVT. SNIFFEN, FRANK
SNOW, ANDREW
SCOUT- SOLDIER (REE)
PVT. SORDEN, THOMAS
FARRIER- SPENCER, ABLE
PVT. SPINNER, PHILLIP
PVT. SPRAGUE, OTTO
PVT. ST. JOHN, LUDWICK
SCOUT- STAB (REE)
PVT. STAFFORD, BENJAMINE
PVT. STANLEY, EDWARD
PVT. STAPLES, SAMUEL
PVT. STARK, FRANK
PVT. STECK, CHARLES
VET. SURGEON-STEIN, CHARLES
FARRIER- STEINTKER, JOHN
PVT. STELLA, ALEXANDER
PVT. STEPHENS, GEORGE
PVT. STEPHENSON, THOMAS
PVT. STERLAND, WALTER
SCOUT- STICKING OUT (SIOUX)
PVT. STIVERS, THOMAS
PVT. STOFFEL, HENRY
PVT. STOUT, EDWARD
PVT. STOWERS, THOMAS
WAGONER- STRATTON, FRANK
CPL. STRESSINGER, FREDERICK
SCOUT- STRIKS THE LODGE (REE)
SCOUT- STRIKES TWO (REE)
PVT. STRODE, ELIJA
PVT. STUART, ALPHEUS
PVT. STUART- FORBES, JOHN
PVT. STUNGERWITZ, IGNATZ
2ND LT. STURGIS, JAMES
COL. STURGIS, SAMUEL
PVT. SULLIVAN, DANIEL
PVT. SULLIVAN, JOHN
PVT. SULLIVAN, TIMOTHY
PVT. SUMMERS, DAVID
SGT. SWEENEY, JOHN
PVT. SWEENEY, WILLIAM
PVT. SWEETSER, THOMAS
PVT. SYMMS, DARWIN
PVT. TAPLEY, DAVID
PVT. TARBOX, BYRON
PVT. TAUBE, EMIL
PVT. TAYLOR, WALTER
PVT. TAYLOR, WILLIAM
SADDLER- TEEMAN, WILLIAM
PVT. TESSIER, EDWARD
SGT. THADUS, JOHN
PVT. THOMAS, HERBERT
PVT. THOMPSON, MORRIS
PVT. THOMPSON, PETER
PVT. THORNBERRY, LEVI
PVT. THORP, MICHAEL
PVT. THORPE, ROLLINS
MAJ. TILFORD, JOSEPH
PVT. TINKHAM, HENRY
PVT. TOLAN, FRANK
PVT. TORREY, WILLIAM
CPT. TOURTELLOTTE, JOHN
SADDLER- TRITTEN, JOHN
PVT. TROY, JAMES
PVT. TRUMBLE, WILLIAM
PVT. TULO, JOSEPH
PVT. TURLEY, HENRY
PVT. TWEED, THOMAS
PVT. VAHLERT, JACOB
PVT. VAN BRAMER, CHARLES
PVT. VAN PELT, WILLIAM

PVT. VAN SANT, CORNELIUS
PVT. VARDEN, FRANK
SGT. VARNER, THOMAS
2ND LT. VARNUM, CHARLES
PVT. VETTER, JOHANN
SGT. VICKORY, JOHN
CHIEF MUSICIAN- VINATIERI, FELIX
CHIEF BUGLER- VOIGT, HENRY
SADDLER- VOIT, OTTO
PVT. VON ARNIM, JULIUS
CHIEF BUGLER- VOSS, HENRY
SCOUT- WAGON (REE)
CHIEF PACKER- WAGONER, JOHN
PVT. WALKER, GEORGE
PVT. WALKER, ROBERT
2ND LT. WALLACE, GEORGE
BUGLER- WALLACE, JOHN
SGT. WALLACE, RICHARD
BUGLER- WALSH, FREDERICK
PVT. WALSH, MICHAEL
PVT. WALSH, THOMAS
PVT. WALTER, ALOYSE
PVT. WARNER, OSCAR
SGT. WARREN, AMOS
CPL. WARREN, GEORGE
PVT. WASMUS, ERNEST
PVT. WATSON, JAMES
PVT. WAY, THOMAS
PVT. WEAVER, GEORGE
BUGLER- WEAVER, HENRY
PVT. WEAVER, HOWARD
PVT. WEEKS, JAMES
SGT. WEIHE, HENRY
CPT. WEIR, THOMAS
PVT. WEISS, JOHN
PVT. WEISS, MARKUS
PVT. WELCH, CHARLES
PVT. WELDON, GEORGE
FARRIER- WELLS, BENJAMINE
PVT. WELLS, JOHN
CPL. WETZEL, ADAM
PVT. WHALEY, WILLIAM
PVT. WHISTEN, JOHN
PVT. WHITAKER, ALFRED

SCOUT- WHITE CLOUD (SIOUX)
SCOUT- WHITE EAGLE (REE)
SCOUT- WHITE MAN RUNS HIM (CROW)
SCOUT- WHITE SWAN (CROW)
PVT. WHITLOW, WILLIAM
WAGONER- WHYTEFIELD, ALBERT
PVT. WIDMAYER, FERDINAND
SGT. WIEDMAN, CHARLES
SGT. WIGHT, EDWIN
PVT. WILBER, JAMES
PVT. WILD, JOHN
SGT. WILKINSON, JOHN
PVT. WILLIAMS, CHARLES
PVT. WILLIAMS, WILLIAM
PVT. WILLIAMSON, PASAVAN
PVT. WILSON, GEORGE
PVT. WINDOLPH, CHARLES
1ST SGT. WINNEY, DEWITT
PVT. WITT, HENRY
PVT. WOOD, WILLIAM
PVT. WOODRUFF, JERRY
PVT. WOODS, AARON
PVT. WRIGHT, WILLIS
CPL. WYLIE, GEORGE
PVT. WYMAN, HENRY
PVT. WYNN, JAMES
CPT. YATES, GEORGE
SCOUT- YOUNG HAWK (REE)
PVT. ZAMETZER, JOHN

General Custer's Dead
(Newspaper Headline July 6th, 1876)

GENERAL CUSTER DEAD INCLUDING FIVE COMPANIES OF HIS 7TH CALVARY REGIMENT

Those were the headlines in every newspaper throughout the country on July 6th, 1876. Our nation had just celebrated its 100th birthday two days earlier and this news of Custer's demise threw the nation into a whirl wind. The government took the news with a dismal and upsetting tone.

Calls rang out for revenge in every town, city, and most of all throughout Washington DC. Out of seven hundred troopers, Custer lost two hundred and eighty eight men, fourteen officers, two brothers, a brother- in- law and a nephew. They fell close to one another with the exception of Custer's brother-in-law.

Forty two men from Company E along with the Custer's died on the site now named Custer's hill. That day fifty two percent of Custer's command lost their lives. His scouts that morning came upon an Indian encampment with some have said totaled more than ten thousand Native Americans. Women and children were included in this number with the warrior number estimated at three to seven thousand. Warriors from the Sioux, Cheyenne, Arapahoe, Ogala, Brule, Sans Arc, and the Miniconjou nations had come together as one on the Little Big Horn River.

The Indians out numbered the Seventh Cavalry nine to one. The battle must have been reflective to Custer because thirteen years earlier he heard the yells and blood curdling screams of the Rebel yell at the battle of Gettysburg, Penn. during the Civil War. Now on this June twenty fifth, 1876 he heard different blood curdling screams coming in his direction, thousands of angry Indians converging on his position on top of that lowly hill. Custer and the Seventh lost the fight that day, but the battle immortalized him in the history books forever. Also on that day though, the way of life would be changed forever for the Indian tribes. The way of life as the Indian had known was dealt a death hand.

The "trail of tears" was just beginning for the red man, those two days in June of 1876.

....

Chapter 1

The life of the Seventh Cavalry was cut short in many respects. Some say the Seventh died with Custer at the Little Big Horn, but others say the regiment has lived on and never died on that horrific day in June of 1876. The Seventh has participated in every theater of operation from the Indian Wars to the battle for Kuwait in 1996. The Spanish American War, World War One, World War Two, Korea, Vietnam, Gulf War, and the Iraqi War. Custer drove the Seventh into the ground in 1876 maybe into glory, but the regiments soul rode on into some of our countries most trying times of war in the future of this nation.

AND SO, OUR STORY BEGINS: It's July the third, 1863 and a young (age twenty-three) Brevet Lieutenant General by the name of George Armstrong Custer (class of 1861 at West Point) who is the new Commander of the Michigan Cavalry Brigade. (a brigade consisted of two thousand to five thousand men) The Battle of Gettysburg has been going on now for two days and Confederate General of all the troops Robert E. Lee (class of 1829 at West Point) has been trying to pull the Union army apart at various positions on the battlefield, but has met tough resistance with each engagement. General George Meade (class of 1835 at West Point) commander of the Union forces on the field, is holding on, and is waiting for Lee to try and make another move against his defenses. Lee has chosen to make an all-out assault on Meade's entrenchments on an area called Seminary Ridge, right smack dab in the middle of the battlefield at Gettysburg. General George

Picket (class of 1846 at West Point) has been chosen to direct his Division of fifteen thousand troops to cross a three-mile field in direct line of the Union troops. Lee hopes this maneuver will unbuckle the Union lines and will claim victory for the south this day. Lee's executive officer General James Longstreet (class of 1842 at West Point) second in command of the Armies of The Confederacy sees Pickett's maneuver a failure. He is quoted as to saying to Lee that day: "General, I have been a soldier all my life. I have been with soldiers engaged in fights by couples, by squads, companies, regiments, divisions, and armies, and should know, as well as anyone, what soldiers can do. It is my opinion that no fifteen thousand men ever arranged for battle can take that position!" Lee won't hear of it, and summons Pickett to make his men ready. Meanwhile General Lee is waiting for field reports from his General of Cavalry, Jeb Stuart (class of 1854 at West Point) as to where the Union movements are being directed. Lee hasn't heard from Stuart in days and is fighting blind without reconnaissance information of the movements of Meade's troops.

Stuart finally shows up at Lee's headquarters and Lee goes off on a tirade with him. "General," Lee said "you are the Confederacy's eyes and ears, and you have let me down at this pivotal moment! He then orders Stuart back to the battle field east of the town to try and flank Meade's troops with a surprise attack from his cavalry. Stuart is Lee's best leader and knows the dashing cavalryman will not let the south down, or him this day. Stuarts maneuver will coincide with Pickett's charge that is going to commence, starting at noon. Not knowing to Stuart, a large contingency of Union cavalry is also north east of the battlefield, four miles from Gettysburg. A brigade of Michigan cavalry is scouting the areas east of Gettysburg for possible Confederate activity that might try to outflank the Union troops. Custer put out scouts earlier that day to search out any rebels that may be in the vicinity of his units. When they returned, they reported on observing Stuarts cavalry totaling over five thousand strong and heading his way. Custer now with his five Regiments (a regiment consisted of ten companies per regiment, a total of 80 - 250 men per company) of cavalry roughly twenty-five hundred men, orders a skirmish line, with the Fifth and Sixth Michigan holding the front with their new Spencer repeating rifles and uses the other regiments in reserve. The Spencer rifle could hold seven rounds of ammunition, and just one man had the fire power of seven men. These rifles would prove positive in the upcoming skirmish with Stuart's cavalry. Stuart's column is so large, that the dust the troopers kick up is hard not to see.

   Meanwhile back in Gettysburg General George Pickett was getting his troops of old Virginia ready for the most historic infantry charge in America's history to date. Before he gave orders for his brigade to advance towards the Union lines, General Lee had instructed his commander of Artillery, Colonel E.P. Alexander (class of 1857 at West Point) to commence with his artillery bombardment. This would be larger than any other artillery engagement recorded in war. One hundred and fifty to one hundred and seventy cannons were to open up on the Union defenses at Seminary Ridge. The purpose of this cannonade was to dislodge the Union lines on the battlefield for Pickett's men, when they made their assault on Meade's troops. Between both Armies, North and South there were over three hundred artillery pieces in use on this day of July third, 1863.
   Back to the north-east Stuart is engaged with the Fifth and Sixth Michigan who are dismounted and holding their own against the overwhelming confederate cavalry. Stuart had put his hopes on the Fourteenth, Sixteenth, and

Seventeenth Virginia Cavalry at the head of his first charge at the union troopers. Again, and again his cavalry charged the dug in Michigan regiments and each time the Rebs were pushed back. Custer now orders the Seventh Michigan into battle, and makes the charge at the head of troops. What a sight to see; this regiment of cavalry riding at a trot with sabres flashing in the sun light and riders stretching almost a quarter mile in length darting ahead shouting as they rode. Custer in front with his sabre held high, and the gold curly locks of his hair waving in the wind. What a sight it was, and he leading his men made their advance even more plausible.

While this action is being made Colonel Alexander's artillery starts his cannonade on the Union positions, with the Union artillery returning fire. The ground shakes with almost three hundred cannons going off simultaneously. The firing is so deafening and horrific that towns people in Harrisburg, Pennsylvania, some twenty miles north of Gettysburg can hear the noise of the guns which sounded like thunder. Custer still leading his Seventh Michigan boys in a charge against Stuarts cavalry is at a Gallup now and his adrenaline is flowing profusely. When they meet the enemy, his troopers start slashing and shooting every rebel they see and meet. Horses falling, men screaming, the sound of bugles, the charge, mass confusion everywhere. The carnage was unbelievable and the cry of battle was heard. Gun fire took over as troopers now had revolvers and carbines blazing all over the battlefield. Custer noticing, he is at a disadvantage in numbers has his bugler sound recall, and returns back to his field headquarters with the remaining survivors of the Michigan's Seventh. On returning, he finds the First Michigan already in position to make the next charge towards the Rebs. Custer immediately rides out in front of the First and draws his sabre once again, shouting at the top of his lungs, "come on, you Wolverines!" Stuart not expecting another charge so soon orders the First and Second North Carolina Cavalry into action, and mass confusion takes over. As Custer is advancing with the First, partial companies of the Fifth and Sixth Michigan also join in on the charge, but the confederates still have a five to one advantage. Again, man and horse clash, hitting one another head on, rubbing against one another in such a force as to cause legs to be crushed and even broken. Riders are being thrown from their mounts or trapped underneath the animals when they are shot. Screams of anger, of pain, and death are heard from the combatants.

Human suffering is everywhere. What a macabre sight, men fighting with such passion in a futile attempt to stay alive. Men are falling everywhere from sabre thrusts and the result of huge amounts of carbine and revolver fire. The rebel yell is deafened by the cannon firing going on in Gettysburg as Custer is having his glory day. As he slashes away at the enemy, the "Boy General" isn't aware that he has been spotted by a rebel officer who knows of him and wants Custer's blood on his blade.

The rider makes a dash at Custer, at a gallop with sabre held high, and is just about ready to swing at his prey, when out of nowhere a trooper from the First Michigan reaches out with his own sabre and deflects the Rebels sabre thrust. The Rebel officer, awestruck at what just happened turns around and starts for Custer again, but is struck down dead with one shot from the troopers Colt revolver before he could regain his balance on his horse. Custer now aware of what is going on smiles and tips his hat to the trooper and continues to fight.

Forty minutes into the fight Stuart finally has had enough and sees the battle not going in his favor, so he has his bugler sound recall and his troopers head in a western direction with what is left of his brigade. With the large numbers of troops involved this day the Union only suffered two hundred dead while Stuart suffered a total of two hundred and eighty-five dead. Custer has won the day and cheering springs up all over the battlefield. As Custer rides by his exhausted battle-weary troopers more cheering erupts, yes Custer has won the day and this victory will make a pivotal mark in his career.

Later that night back at field headquarters, Custer's orderly announces that there is a trooper outside to see the General. Here Custer meets the young trooper that saved his life a few hours earlier. "Private Norvell Churchill, Company L. First Michigan Cavalry reporting as ordered sir", are the first words that come out of the trooper's mouth. Custer stands up from his desk, with a smile gazing upon this true cavalryman.

"Churchill is it " says Custer, " sounds English, but I am sure you're a true blooded American," He notices Churchill stands at around five feet six inches, with broad shoulders, brown hair cut neatly, hazel eyes, weighs about one hundred and fifty pounds and every inch a true soldier. "At ease Churchill, or may I call you Norvell, that is your first name am I right" asks Custer? "Yes, sir I go by Norvell and you may call me that". "Well Norvell I have been shot off horse's numerous times and have always had the luck of getting out of those tricky situations. In the heat of battle, one's focal point is on his enemy and not his surroundings, and well you don't have the full jest of what is going on around you. "Today was a good example, and I am very appreciative of your actions for my safety today", remarks Custer. "It wasn't anything that I would not have done for any of my comrade's sir, I am just glad that you're alright." "Well please sit down Norvell and tell me a little about yourself over a cup of coffee won't you".

With that Custer calls his orderly and asks him to bring

him two cups of coffee. From Custer's initial information on Churchill when he sought him out after the battle, Churchill is the orderly for Captain George Horatio Nelson, Commander of Company L. First Michigan Cavalry.

Custer asks Churchill now, "how long have you been in the army"? I've been serving now, coming up on two years sir"." What was your profession before joining up may I ask"?

"I was a farmer in Berlin, Michigan sir with one hundred and sixty acres of the richest soil you would ever what to own". I grew corn and potatoes and made a good living from my crops", he said. Custer remarks, " I'm sure you did and what is important, you'll be back home in no time raising your crops again. With men like you on the firing line I see this war ending real soon", Custer now looking away at the side of his tent utters again, "real soon!"

Custer asks, "Are your folks still working the land while your away"? Churchill replies, "yes and my three brothers also". "Three brothers huh"? "yes sir, their all too young to join up and from what I've seen so far from this ugly war, I am glad they cannot".

Take my brother Oraland for instance. He's fifteen now, and I know from the letters I get from him, he's going to enlist as soon as he turns sixteen next month". "There's nothing I can do or say, and he's just as head strong as myself. So, I pray that he stays safe, and out of harm's way".

Custer is listening intently as his new friend goes on talking. "When I enlisted I had no idea of what to expect from army life, and I know I would not wish it on anyone. It came naturally for me because I've been around horses all my life and it was an easy fit. Some of these boys, hadn't rode a horse in their entire lives up to this point and some had, but the ones who hadn't, well you could see that there were going to be problems in the future for them especially when they have to do battle". Custer breaks in and says to Churchill "you would make a fine officer Norvell, you respect the men and I can hear it in your voice". Now there are two things on my mind at this moment, and both pertain to you. First, I'm going to reassign you to my staff as my personal orderly with a promotion to Sergeant, and second I want you to let me know about your brother, Oraland, that is his name isn't it he asks"?

Yes, sir that is his name. Well when he's ready to enlist, I want you to let me know and I'll pull some strings, that will keep him out of harm's way, I promise. "Why thank you sir Churchill responds". "You don't have to thank me, again I want to thank you! Now you'd better be off to your company and start packing your things, and I'll notify Captain Nelson in the morning of your reassignment and promotion". With that said, Churchill stands up and comes to attention and salutes his superior. Custer now standing salutes back and extends his hand to the private, they shake hands and Churchill exits the tent with a sense of euphoria going through his body.

The night went quick and the troopers awake to the news that Lee had turned tail and is heading back to Virginia. Pickett's charge was a failure and a waste of many men's lives. Custer has his bugler sound officers call and when assembled he tells his staff the casualty rate was enormous for both sides. For Pickett's charge the losses for the South were over sixty-five hundred dead and many more wounded, over fifty percent of Pickett's men, and for the Union defenses on Seminary Ridge they took a toll of fifteen hundred dead and many more wounded also. History will record the Battle of Gettysburg, not only as the turning point of the civil war, but the costliest in human lives on those three days in July of 1863. Total casualties for the three days of fighting, fifty-one thousand men. This battle proved to be the bloodiest ever fought on American soil. Custer's officers are jubilant, yet subdued over the news their commander just gave them.

"Gentlemen if the battles continue like the one we took part in over the last three days, I feel the war will be over soon". (NOTE) WRONG Call! There were to be many more battles on American soil in 1864 & 1865. The Wilderness, Cold Harbor, Fishers Hill, Cedar Creek, Five Forks, Salyers Creek, Winchester, Petersburg, and Appomattox, to name a few. Custer and his "Wolverines" were at every one of those battles and served with honor.

In the fall of 1863,Custer was notified by his now special orderly Norvell Churchill that his brother had enlisted in the army and was in the newly formed Tenth Michigan Cavalry Regiment and all that had volunteered were mustered into the Army of The Potomac a month earlier in Grand Rapids, Michigan. Custer taking no time when he heard this news contacted the commander of the Tenth, a Colonel Trowbridge and ordered that trooper Oraland Churchill be reassigned to his headquarters staff.

He was a man of his word and was going to make sure this young private was trained properly. Within hours the two brothers were again reunited and both were standing at attention in front of Custer sitting at his desk.

Custer observed the young man, sixteen years old decked out in a brand-new trooper's uniform. His cavalry shell jacket spotless, trimmed with yellow piping and eighteen bright new buttons. Sky blue riding pants and below the knee boots tops off his appearance. He was around six feet, and he probably weighed in at around one hundred and thirty pounds, Short blond hair, and blue eyes, rounded out this young trooper. "At ease troopers" barks Custer, "well trooper Churchill" begins Custer "I'm glad you're here with your brother, and I am personally going to do as much as I can in being your mentor" Both brothers now look at each other almost simultaneously, then back at Custer. Your brother, referring to Norvell, tells me you're a good horseman, is that so? addressing the young recruit. "Yes, sir I've been riding horses since I was old enough to remember, bare back or with a saddle, there is no difference to me". "Riding a horse is a big part of this job you've taken on here Churchill" remarks Custer. I'll take yours and your brothers word for it. Now what have they taught you in the last month since you've been in the army".

Well sir how to salute an officer sir, and the standard movements, such as coming to attention, rest, and about face. Also, the proper ways to behave when wearing the uniform of our country sir.

"Very good" replies Custer. Looks like your Colonel or Sergeant were on their toes when you experienced this training. "Have you been issued your side arm, carbine and sabre yet"? asks Custer. Yes, sir I was issued all three just as we were leaving Grand Rapids sir. "First lesson Churchill" barks Custer again,

"I see a trooper standing before me without his side arm on". The reason, I ask? Addressing the young recruit once more. Well sir, replies Churchill "I didn't think I needed to wear it since I was coming to see you". "Well my young friend, jumps in Custer, you always wear it", his voice getting a little more pronounced now. "You are in a battle area now and you never know what's going to happen where or when. You don't know how many times a soldier has been caught off guard not having the right protection to defend himself, because of plain laziness. I want you, from this moment on to have your side arm on at all times and if need be, sleep with it also, understood"? "I understand sir", remarks Churchill. Well it's getting late and tomorrow will be a new day for all of us. Report to me after roll call and we'll have some more things to talk about.

"Norvell", Custer addresses his orderly, when your

brother comes here in the morning bring him directly to me, understood? "Yes sir, General". Very well then good night gentlemen and I will see you at day break. Good night sir, is the response and with both coming to attention they salute and make an about face movement and exit the tent. Outside Norvell asks his brother what he thinks of Custer?

Well he asked a lot of questions, and I don't know what to make of this personal training thing, but don't worry big brother I won't let you or the General down. "Norvell", Oraland now looking at his brother addresses him in an apologetic tone. "I know you didn't want me to enlist, but I had to do the right thing for my country and myself, you can understand that can't you?" Yes, little brother and I'm very proud of you, was Norvell's answer and with that they both give each other a big hug and wished each other a good night.

Reveille sounded early at five A.M. next morning and the camp came to life once more. First on the docket was to make sure the horses are feed. Then chow down on whatever is available. Often a cup of black coffee and hardtack (hard bread). The army is always on the move rapidly and a soldier has to adapt to eating whatever when, and still replenish his body to have the strength to perform his duties of the day. Custer is walking around the camp area seeing that the men are satisfied and takes time to talk with one or two of his troopers. It's now seven AM and he has his bugler sound officers call. Within ten minutes all of his ranking officers are standing outside of his tent for their daily instructions. As he exits the tent one of them barks: "ATTENTION" Custer salutes them and they intern salute back. "At rest gentlemen, and good morning" he remarks. Good morning sir is said back by all. Now that the Gettysburg campaign is behind us I've been advised by General Pleasanton (class of 1844 at West Point) that the brigade should be getting ready for another go around with the rebels in the spring of the coming year. We will be bivouacked here for now, so I would recommend that you have your men dig in and get ready for winter quarters. Continue with your daily drills and have the men know their weapons inside and out. I'll set up a firing range somewhere around here, so you can train the men the right way in the use of their revolvers and carbines.

Sabre training will be every other day until further notice. The men must be comfortable on their horses when making charges at the enemy, and it's your duty to see to it. We're still vulnerable to enemy surprise attacks, so I want to increase the guard situation on our perimeter one thousand yards out. You must not let your, or your trooper's guards down at this time. I'll set up a larger medical tent area, because of our settling down here, and that should accommodate any large numbers of sick if need be. I figure seven to eight months here, unless we're moved on a minute's notice to someplace else.

It looks like both sides, we and the Rebs are going to take a little break in the fighting to build up our strength in numbers and war materials. "So, gentlemen are there any questions"? Asks Custer. There were no questions mainly because he had gone over everything with a fine comb, and Custer didn't expect any questions anyway. Fine gentlemen, now get back to your troopers, we have a lot of work to do. His staff comes to attention and salutes their commander and then walks back to their respective units.

Custer then summons Norvell Churchill and tells him to get his brother, and have him ready for a little ride in half an hour, also have my mount ready in front of my tent. "Yes sir" replies Churchill. Custer now goes back to his tent while Churchill is on his way to retrieve his little brother. Half an hour has gone by and young Oraland Churchill appears at Custer's tent as ordered. Custer comes out and gives him a salute which Churchill returns. Well my lad he says, let's see what kind of a horseman you say you are! Custer mounts his horse and commands Oraland to follow him. They ride two by two for a few miles chit chatting and Custer comes to a halt. They're on the edge of a field around three acres wide and four acres long. Custer gives the order to line up and get ready to charge the enemy which is dug in on the other side of the field.

"Take this seriously Churchill" says Custer, let's see who can reach the other side first. "Draw Sabre's is now the command, and both pull out their long knives shouldering the long blades. "Forward at the trot" is the command given and both start towards the other side of the field. Oraland is now taking a short glance at his leader and thinks Custer is what you read about in the dime novels back home on what is a true cavalryman should be.

"At the gallop" is the order now given and both increase in speed on their mounts. Then the order to "charge" is given and both almost at once extend their sabre's to their front and ride like the wind. Oraland gets a little carried away and whoops up a holler as he rides next to Custer. When both reached the other side of the field they came to a halt and laughed at one another. "You were not kidding when you told me you could ride Churchill", remarks Custer.

Now scabbard your sabre and let's get down off our mounts and see what kind of shot you are with a revolver. Custer picks a tree not more than thirty yards away and asks Churchill to hit the lowest branch hanging from it.

At thirty yards that would be some shooting, mainly because twenty to thirty yards is around the effective firing distance for a pistol. Churchill pulls out his Army Colt and aims it at the tree. He squeezes the trigger, POW! and the branch does a little dance after being hit. "Good shot", remarks Custer. Try it again, and once more the lad hits the branch. "Now retrieve your Sharps carbine and see what you can do to that branch. Oraland walks over to his horse and pulls out his carbine from its socket scabbard, and then walks ten feet from his horse.

He cocks the hammer and pulls up on the branch again this time cutting it from its tree trunk. "Nice shooting trooper" Custer remarks. Well I see you won't have any problems in the weapon department. "Thank you, sir, "is Oreland's reply. Now what do you say we get back to camp now and call it a day. "That suits me fine sir" remarks Churchill.

They arrive back at camp and all kinds of activity is going on. Men are being taught the art of marching, and riding, and how to care for their horses. They're also preparing their tents for the winter that is just around the corner. By placing logs three to four-foot-high around the tents, the cold weather during the day and night will be cut in half. Custer is smiling because he knows his officers took his speech this morning the right way.

Norvell Churchill is waiting at Custer's tent when the two returned, and takes hold of the reins of both Custer's horse and his brothers. "Churchill" remarks Custer, to Norvell, your brother is a true cavalryman!

Getting off his horse now Custer walks around to Oraland who is still sitting above on his mount and comments, "private I'm going to put you in charge of teaching the new or raw recruits on weapons instruction. "You're a dead shot such as myself and I want you to instruct your fellow troopers to be as efficient with their revolvers and carbines as you are. Think you can take on that task for me? ", he asks looking up at Oraland. Oraland looks over at his brother quickly and notices a slight grin on his face, and then looks back at Custer and replies, "Sir I can do that for you, and thank you for giving me the chance to prove myself. "Splendid then" remarks Custer. "I'll get you together with Sergeants Ryan and Maloney tomorrow. They are the best shots in the regiment, and the three of you can instruct the new men in marksmanship. Now get back to your company and I'll get the orders in motion. By the way stop over at the quartermaster's tent and pick up your Corporals chevrons. Oraland's face was a glow and Norvell stood there speechless. "Corporal sir" comes out of Churchill's mouth.

"By god yes lad" was Custer's reply. "How can I have two sergeants and one private instructing the men, it wouldn't look right! From what I've seen, you'll work out fine and being promoted is something that I am familiar with. I know how it feels to be recognized, and I feel good on my decision on promoting you. Oraland thanks Custer again and salutes him. Custer returns the salute, and the young trooper while pulling on the reins of his horse says good bye to his brother and rides off to his company.

Norvell now speaks up and says, "That was a fine thing you did there General, the boy won't let you down with his duties". "Not worried a bit on my decision Norvell. Looking at your brother and seeing a little bit of me in his demeanor and his attitude I know that I made the right decision. I know what drives men and I think I know your brother, he'll work out fine. Now stable my horse and I think I'll retire with a little sack time. Wake me up in an hour and I'll be ready for my supper"! "Yes sir", Norvell replies as he walks Custer's horse away.

The Virginia winter season has finally come and the brigade is settled in for the harsh weather that mother nature throws out each year. The men are sheltered in Sibley tents that can accommodate twelve troopers. The Sibley is a conical shaped tent that is twelve feet high and requires no guide ropes. They are pegged to the ground and have a pole extending up in the middle of the inside area. They are equipped with a stove and are very warm in cold weather. (They were invented in 1855 by Henry Sibley and patented in 1856. Thousands were used by the army up to the Korean war in 1950). Cooking tents are erected to feed the men, and a medical area has been set up to accommodate the sick. Sutler's who follow the troops around also have set up their tents to sell the troops their wares. Everything under the sun could be purchased through one of these Sutler's and I mean anything. The term "Red Virginia Clay" would haunt the regiment in the spring time after the snow has melted. The soil is very, very, very muddy, and is made up of clay which is reddish in color and, boy does it stick to you and discolors anything it comes in contact with. The troopers find the mud disheartening and tough to move around in, and the horses have a hard time maneuvering in the thick red muck! Photographers also now quite commonly seen in all camps and making themselves rich taking tin types (pictures) of individuals, and group pictures of men going through their daily drills and camp duties. There is plenty of cleaning going on in each regiment, ridding itself of the mud, and all have a sense of relief when the sun finally comes out and dries the ground hard again in late spring. Earlier in the year, February of 1864 Custer went back to his home town of Monroe, Michigan for a two week leave and is greeted, as the hero of Gettysburg. He also marries Elizabeth Bacon the daughter of a wealthy local judge. She would prove to be his love for the rest of his life. Late in the spring now of 1864 the army is on the move again when Custer receives his orders.

General Grant (class of 1843 at West Point) has been made commander of all the Union Armies and has ordered Custer's brigade to the move towards the town of Fredericksburg, Virginia. With the eighty-mile tract in front of them, he orders his officers to have their men break camp and be ready to move out in three hours. He figures they should make the Rapidan River by night fall and will be ten miles from where he was ordered to be. The troops are getting ready, and Custer asks Churchill to fetch his brother and to give his regimental commander a note he has written out.

"Yes sir" replies Norvell and mounts his horse, salutes and rides off. There is commotion coming from everywhere in the camp, and the men can't wait to get out of the hell hole they've been in for the last seven months. Custer feels for his troops, but he knows their trained and has no doubt that they will perform in battle like a precise working clock. Within the hour Norvell comes riding back with his brother. Sir the note you requested to be delivered has been served.

Custer has just finished talking with one of the troopers about the upcoming ride. They dismount and tie their horses up on a make shift rail that was built for Custer in the front of his tent. Both come to attention and salute which is returned by Custer. Are we already for this next adventure gentlemen he asks of the brothers.

"Yes sir" is the answer from both. I've been giving it a thought for a few days now Churchill, looking at Oraland. I'm going to have you out in front of the brigade with the other four scouts, to be our eyes and ears. "Do you think you can do the job", he asks? "Sir I have no problem with your wishes, I can do the job", remarks Oraland.

I know you can lad. Look at it as another training exercise. Just keep up with the other scouts and watch and listen to what they do. Being the brigade's eyes and ears is an important duty and I have all the faith in you just as your brother has. "Thank you sir" replies Oraland. Now get back on that horse of yours and report to Sergeant O'Hara with the other scouts. He's expecting you, and he is good at his job. Oraland then salutes Custer and says goodbye to his brother and rides off. Norvell asks Custer if he thinks he made the right decision, and Custer replies, "believe me Norvell when I say yes! Being a scout requires more than being a soldier.

You're at the point, sometimes miles in front of your column looking for any signs of the enemy and your always at risk of being caught or shot. You almost have to blend into the country side to be good at your job". Oraland was thankful to Custer for this duty because he had his eyes on the position for months now. He had talked to a few of the scouts in the previous months and decided, that he wanted this job over all others. Being a trooper is one thing, but being out front and in danger all the time really excited him. He had taken a liking to soldiering and thought maybe of making a career of it. He is his own man, and is going to show his brother he didn't need the farm to survive. The brigade was finally ready and the order was given, "by companies mount", and men mount their horses almost in unison. With the brigade mounted Custer rides to the front of the column and orders "scouts out!" As Oraland passes his commander he tips his hat and rides off with the others. Custer then gives the order "forward ho" to his troopers and all ride off headed south.

For an hour now, the brigade has moved at a constant pace and Oraland and the other scouts are at least ten miles ahead of the main column. They're getting deeper into rebel territory now, and Sergeant O'Hara tells Oraland to watch your sides and front for anything out of the normal.

"Don't do anything in haste Churchill", remarks O'Hara. Our job is to spot trouble and report back to the General. Your actions out here can cost a lot of men their lives if you don't do things right, so think first before you act. Oraland understands and tells O'Hara his message got through. O'Hara is a career army soldier. He served in the Mexican

War and has been in the cavalry for over twenty-three years, and is a stickler on army regulations. He's six feet tall, weighs about two hundred and ninety-five pounds with a balding hair line.

He also likes the liquor! As they ride on, very slowly in somewhat of a skirmish line, maybe fifty to seventy-five yards apart, Oraland suddenly stops abruptly! O'Hara notices the boy stopping and slowly rides over to him. Whispering, under his breath he asks Oraland what's up? Oraland replies that he saw the reflection of something shiny up in the hilly area ahead, pointing. The two are under cover in a wooded area, and just sit there watching and listening for any distracting noises or the sight of something moving around.

The other scouts have stopped also and know the routine. They too are just sitting in their saddles observing anything out of the ordinary. About fifteen minutes have gone by and Oraland gives O'Hara a nudge on his shoulder alerting the Sergeant that he has seen something again. Oraland points to his front and holds his hand up high in the direction of the hilly area he mentioned earlier to O'Hara. In less than a minute O'Hara grabs his hand and lets the boy know that he has seen what he is pointing at, Rebs!

"Good job Churchill", O'Hara tells Oraland very softly. He signals for the other scouts using sign language to slowly make their way over to his position. Very slowly the others make their way and now they are all together.

Whispering very softly they decide to advance a little closer to try and make out what is going on in the hills. They decide to double back and approach the hill from the other side. One of the scouts will remain where they are to keep an eye out on what is going on up ahead. If there are any signs of trouble, he is to double back and join the rest of the group a mile from where they are now to the rear. "No shooting unless it is necessary", remarks O'Hara. There could be a couple of Rebel foragers up there, or there could be a whole damn Reb Division, so be low keyed and stay alert. The one scout staying back now moves to his right a little next to a large tree, and gives O'Hara the 'OK' sign. The others now turn back to try and circle the hill ahead. They're about half a mile back now and they start to approach the hilly area on the other side from where they were earlier. O'Hara stops and tells all to be careful and to go very slowly. If you see something stop! We'll all try to keep a tight interval between us. "Alright let's advance and go very slowly as I said".

Oraland has been taking in all that has happened so far and his adrenalin is flowing fast through his body. Maybe one hundred yards up the hill Oraland stops, as do all the others. He points to his front again, and using sign language the best he can, signals that there is activity just ahead. He dismounts and ties his horse to a nearby tree. O'Hara is now next to him and cautions him to be very careful. The boy draws his revolver and starts to make his way forward, one step at a time very slowly. (its like deer hunting or tracking a prey) About forty yards from where he started he stops and immediately throws himself on the ground.

O'Hara is at the ready with his Sharps carbine now, watching what Oraland is doing in front of him. Churchill now raises his right arm and with his hand shows all five fingers and starts an up and down motion, meaning many men ahead. He now slowly makes his way back to O'Hara, and tells him there are a lot of Rebs up there. Infantry it looked like and they were digging trenches. "Alright lad", replies O'Hara let's get back a bit and we'll discuss what we're going to do. Custer is most likely four hours behind us now and the column is riding right into this Reb intrenchment. When all had rendezvoused back down the hill, it was agreed that two of the scouts would ride back and warn Custer, and the others would try and to find out how large of a force the enemy had up ahead. O'Hara wrote out a note for Custer stating that he (Custer) should remain where he is, and to set up a picket line just in case of a frontal attack, or flanking maneuver from the Rebs being so close by. Oraland was to remain with O'Hara and the other scout.

"Tell the General we'll get back to the column as soon as we make contact, and as to the size of the enemy's strength" The two scouts now ride in the direction of Custer's position, as Oraland and O'Hara and the other scout make their way back to the hill. O'Hara suggests that one of them stay with the horses so they won't spook, and the other two proceed on foot up the hill under cover to try and see what's going on. Scout John Duran volunteers to stay with the horses, so Oraland and O'Hara are elected to check out the enemy's movements.

O'Hara tells Duran that if he hears firing, be ready with the horses. With that the two starts to ascend the hill again crouching and moving very slowly forward, like bobcats on the prowl. They are about forty feet from one another, and make sure they have visual contact with one another as they climb the hill. It's now late afternoon and the sun is starting to go down. It will be getting dark pretty soon and they are almost to the top.

This will help Oraland and O'Hara as they creep ever so close to the enemy. As they near the top, voices can be heard and O'Hara makes his way over to where Churchill is. Both are crawling on their stomachs now and the talking is getting louder. As they reach the top they both notice Reb guards posted and lay still so as not to be seen. There is much activity coming from the other side of the hill and both O'Hara and Churchill watch as they witness the confederates moving into the area in great strength. Cavalry, Artillery, and at least two brigades of Infantry are making ready for an engagement. O'Hara motions to Oraland to move back down the hill slowly, and the two still on their stomachs make their way to where Duran is still waiting. Whispering, O'Hara tells the two to walk slowly back to their rear and to hold the horse's mouths, as to not letting them make any noise. "This place is swarming with Rebs and we have to get back to the General to warn him"! After a safe distance away from the hill they mount their horses and at a cantor, then Gallup head back to their regiment.

It's now six P.M. and when the three return, they find the entire brigade on sentry duty. The note that O'Hara wrote to Custer earlier put a warning light up in the Generals thinking, and he was going to make sure they we're well defended. Reporting to Custer was Churchill and himself(O'Hara). After coming to attention in Custer's presence, and saluting him, O'Hara tells Custer of the activity they had come upon. " It was Corporal Churchill that discovered the Rebel forces sir "remarks O'Hara." We counted a large force as big as our own digging in about two hours from here sir"! "Very good report O'Hara" says Custer "I'll see that it goes on your record".

Thank you, sir is, O'Hara's reply. Now as for you Corporal Churchill good job also! You have probably saved a lot of lives here today. Oraland gives his brother who is standing to the side a smile. Now if you two "scouts" would excuse me, I have battle plans to make.

Both salute and return to their posts, not before, Norvell shakes his brothers hand and says "great job Oraland, now get your self-something to eat, it might be awhile before you get another meal with the action coming up". Custer then orders Norvell to summon all his officers, without the bugle call. "Yes, sir General sir" replies Norval as he salutes Custer, and then does an about face and heads out to find each company commander. Night has already fallen on the weary cavalrymen, and the order has been given there is to be dead silence and no fires. With the Rebels so close Custer feels he may be able to surprise them early in the morning. The plan that he and his officers came up with was to hit the Rebs hard on all sides at sunrise.

The brigade is only ten miles from where they were supposed to be in the morning, and Custer feels this will go along with what General Grant expected from him and his brigade. Not knowing then, the battle to come in the morning will go down in history as the "Battle of The Wilderness". It would be a costly battle for both sides, but Custer's plan worked surprising the Rebel cavalry and dislodging the infantry in a route south.

Grant showed up during the battle and surprised the Confederates as well. Oraland preformed his duties and became a man that day experiencing the horrors of war. It would become his christening to all the battles that were to come. The suffering, the carnage, the moans of the wounded all buffered his feelings inside, and of the war. He would come out and prove not only to Custer, but to himself that he was a better person inside and out, and a leader.

The war goes on for another year and a half and when it ended, Custer was present along with Norvell and Oraland. On April ninth, 1865 Custer's brigade struck the Confederate cavalry at Appomattox, Virginia. The battle was a total disaster for the confederates and Lee had no choice but to surrender his troops. During that battle Oraland recovered the battle flag of the (oddly and ironically) enough, Seventh South Carolina Cavalry Regiment part of Holcombe's Legion.

Two weeks later he would be awarded the Congressional Medal of Honor for his heroism, and was also promoted to the rank of Sergeant. Custer himself took the white flag of surrender from the Rebels after the battle. Later that day after endless messages that where sent back and forth between Grant and Lee, they agreed to meet at the Appomattox Court House for a formal surrender.

Norvell and Oraland were outside while the surrender terms were discussed and signed. When over, General Lee exited the house and as he was walking down the side walk, he stopped and said something to Oraland who was standing next to his brother.

"Trooper, the war is ended here today, and I pray that you may return to your family. Where are you from he asked"? "From Berlin, Michigan sir" was Oralands answer to him, and I have my family here today pointing to Norval. "It has been a costly struggle these five years and I'm awfully glad you, (looking at Oraland) still have your brother with you. With that Lee salutes them both and walks over to his white horse, "Traveler," mounts and rides away saluting various men as he left. The war was over, and now men could go back to their homes and families to start the reconstruction process.

Both Churchill's were given a hero's welcome when they returned home to Michigan. Norvell's service to his country ran out and before leaving Custer, invited him and Libby to his farm for a visit anytime they wished. Oraland decided to stay in the army and was to report back to Custer when he returned from a thirty-day leave. It would take years for the country to bounce back from the ravages of war, but with the spirit of America and one nation in mind, the United States finally became whole again.

Custer went home for two weeks by order of General Sheridan and again was welcomed by the town folks as a hero. With Appomattox came peace and the Army didn't need hundreds of officers. So, the demoting commenced. Custer was looking for something to do after his five years in of service to his country. When he reported back to Washington he received his reassignment papers for duty in Texas as the new commander of the Second Division of Cavalry, Military Division of The Southwest. His new post was Fort Mason near Brownsville, Texas. He was to oversee the reconstruction process being sought out in Texas, and to try and keep peace with the Indian nations in the area. He found the troops in Texas to be untrained and unruly, basically because they were not close enough to the war at the time to receive proper training.

The officers on occasion fought an Indian or two, but for the most part daily training or maneuvers were far between. Custer changed that quickly and made many enemies. When Oraland came back from his long furlough Custer sent for him. Before Oraland left home Norvell reminded his brother to tell Custer that the invitation to visit the farm was still open.

Young Churchill met up with Custer in Texas a few days after getting back and their reunion was a happy affair. Custer asked on how his brother was and Oraland relayed Norvell's invitation. Look at those Sergeants stripes will you" remarks Custer. "Meet any young lasses while back on the farm Churchill", asked Custer? "You being a hero and such it comes with the territory you know". "Not really General, I have lady friends back home, but nothing serious". We'll, your young and time is on your side. I'm sure you'll meet that special one, who knows maybe she's out here in Texas country.

Now I want you to get settled and report back to me this afternoon. The army has provided me with Indian scouts also, and I want you to size them up for me. You'll be bunking with them, so have a keen ear to as what is going on with them. Life out here is a lot different than back east, so you have to be on guard all the time. You're going to hear a lot of grumbling from the other troopers. Most want to leave because the war is over, but they still have enlistments to serve out, so pick your friends carefully. There have been a lot of desertions and I may have to make an example out of one of them.

Shootings one thing, but your own men, it troubles me. So, get going and I'll see you later. Before Churchill gets completely out the door Custer remarks, "Oraland it's good to have you back", and Oraland replies, "It's good to be back sir" and exits. The boy leaves with a grin on his face after being called by his first name. Deep down he knows he has a true friend in Custer and respects the man and his ideals. He walks his horse over to his barracks and upon entering finds three Indians sitting at a table with two others, (white men) sitting there playing poker. He noticed as he was coming in, one of the white men has the rank of Sergeant on his uniform.

So, he starts off "Sergeant, I am Sergeant Oraland Churchill here to report for duty". Well Churchill, replies the burly man, welcome to Texas. I'm Sergeant John Griffin, and this is Corporal Henry Haun pointing to the other white man. The two-exchange hello's and shake hands. Then the Sergeant introduced the three Indian scouts present. Churchill this is Corporal "White Bird" from the Crow nation, they shake hands, then we have "Brave Bear", also from the Crow nation, again a hand shake, and last, we have "Charlie Goes Slow". Oraland is a little taken aback by the names of the three Crow scouts, especially Charlie's. Well it's good meeting all of you and I am looking forward to working with you. Corporal Haun then comments, "you're not working with us", which throws Oraland a for a loop," but you're working for Custer"!

The man is a slave driver and someday he'll get his due! Now remembering what Custer said Oraland plays coy, and replies "I've heard nothing but good things about the man, is there something I don't know" he asks Haun looking straight at him. "He may be a hero to some, but the man is a rouge! No feelings for no one, Indian or white man. He's had it in for me since he got here. Haun do this, Haun get that, Haun you take the point. I tell you he has it in for me". Sergeant Griffin pipes in now and tells Haun to stow it! " Custer is just being Custer, and you don't have to like the man, just do as he says"! "That's easy for you to say Griffin, you've got that extra stripe and he leaves you alone". "Well Corporal may be in another ten years, you'll earn that other stripe and then you'll be in my corner, replies Griffin. There is no war on now and promotions are very scarce. It'll take a Lieutenant twenty-five year now to make Captain and that's the way it is, so eat it, and shut up".

While Griffin is scolding Haun, Oraland is eyeing the Indians and you would think there was nothing going on in the room. They're just sitting there playing poker! Well if you fellows don't mind I'll bring my tact in and set up home. Oraland turns around and as he goes through the door, Haun throws out a question to him.

"You're not a Custer lover are you Churchill"? Oraland turns around and looks Haun right in the face and replies to him, "I keep my mind and my thoughts and feelings to my self Haun. If you have a problem with that, then we're going to have a problem between us. I like, Griffin here earned my stripes, doing things I didn't want to do and I don't take shit, so as Sergeant Griffin said it earlier, stow it"! With that Oraland walks out and retrieves his belongings off his horse and returns into the barracks. The five are playing poker again as he lays out his gear. He announces to the five I have to take care of my horse, I'll be back later. No reply as he walks out the door. Thinking to himself, "this is going to be interesting". He reports back to Custer as he was asked to do earlier, and when asked about the other scouts he replies what had happened. Corporal Haun has an attitude problem says Custer and someday it's going to kill him! "What do you think of the Indian scouts", was the next question? "unusual names, especially Charlies"! Custer snickers a little with Oraland"s answer. In my career so far says Custer I've had a few Corporal Haun's. One way or another their problem is taken care of, and life goes on. I'd rather have a whole division of Indians than a division of Haun's! Now my boy let me go over the reason I asked you to come back here. The Indians are simple people! All they want is what's theirs, and we have, I mean the government has taken, and taken, and taken, with no give backs!

We're here today to make peace with the Indian nations, and that's all. Peace? Well, we can make peace, but how long will It take those who don't care, to create problems? The United States is growing leaps and bounds, and the call for more room to build towns, and cities is a death cry to the Indians. I know your experience with the red man is zero, but I think with your will power and my leadership, we can make a difference in this god forsaken country.

As far as the men are concerned, well their enlistments give them sixteen dollars a month to serve the United States Army until the time to be mustered out. I want to keep their minds busy and the thought of deserting out of their heads. So, starting tomorrow morning, I'll be sending out patrols to to scour the area for any trouble. You and the other scouts will be sent out as the eyes and ears for these patrols. Being new I'll have Charlie Goes Slow paired up with you and maybe he can teach you a thing or two.

"Sounds alright General", replies Oraland. Now go back to your barracks and have all the scouts get themselves out fitted with their gear and rations, and have Sergeant Griffin report to me on the double. "Very well sir" remarks Oraland saluting and then exiting the room. (rations for a cavalry trooper consisted of, salt pork, or salted beef, hard tack, coffee, beans, peas, and rice). Custer then has his bugler sound officers call and prepares to tell them what is going to happen in the morning. This is a new kind of war for Custer and he wants to do it the right way. He depends on experienced people around him and from then draws his own conclusions on how things should be done. He used that method throughout the war and he'll continue to use it now. It's now July and the weather conditions won't create problems for his troops, just the heat! With the war over, new replacements come in every day and have to be trained.

War deserters from both sides, thieves, immigrants from foreign countries, the worst of the worst enlist to hide from the law or whatever their running away from. He'll break them, every last one of them and then and only they can be called cavalrymen. After an hour of going over his plan with his staff Custer calls it a day.

The regiment has ten companies which total more or less, eight hundred to one thousand troops. Two companies, a total of one hundred men each will leave the fort in the morning and head east and west, to patrol the plains. Oraland and Charlie Goes Slow will ride with the eastern bound patrol and Griffin and Brave Bear will accompany the western patrol. Custer will command a third company that will head north, with Corporal Haun and White Bird serving as scouts. The plan is that the patrols will do a one eighty-degree march and meet up with Custer near the Rio Grande river about eighty miles out. Morning comes and the patrols exit the fort with Custer's company going first followed by the other two.

The fort is well protected leaving some seven hundred men to guard it. Seven days out, the troopers return to the fort, only having contact with hostile Indians once. That was Oraland's company, and it was he who spotted the band of red men just after leaving Charlie Goes Slow half a mile to his right flank. Charlie felt it better to make a skirmish line between he and Oraland, as to scout the area more widely. Ten minutes hadn't gone by when Oraland almost ran into the Indians who were heading straight for him. Around one hundred he figured as he reared up his horse and galloped back to where Charlie was. The two then headed for the rest of the company that was one mile south of where they were firing their revolvers as they tried to outrun the attacking Indians. Upon hearing the shots, the Captain of the company, one Mark Nelson ordered his troopers to dismount and form a skirmish line (twenty-five yards apart) and prepare to engage the enemy that was coming.

Charlie and Oraland finally reached the companies defense line and without hesitation Captain Nelson yelled out "fire" to his troopers. One big volley of carbine fire was delivered and then the order to fire independently was given. The Indians made three charges into the company's lines and each time were repelled back to regroup. After the fighting was over the troopers counted twenty Indian dead and with only one trooper wounded. Thus, Oraland's baptism under Indian fire was consecrated. When the three companies returned to the fort, Custer called for another officers meeting, including all noncommissioned officers, and his scouts. He commended all on a good job done and that the patrols will continue throughout the next two months. With all present he asks Oraland, "Churchill now that you're a real Indian fighter what do you think of the red savages"?

"Well sir they have a strong drive to win. Charge after charge they came at us determined to break our lines. I would call them very brave men", he said. "Their fighting for their land gentlemen", remarks Custer. "We're trespassing on it and they don't like it. So, when you're out there on patrol, don't take anything for granted. Be on guard one hundred percent of the time". With that Custer dismisses everyone assembled, and asks for Oraland to remain. With every one gone, Custer walks over to Churchill and shakes his hand. "Well done my boy and well said". You get the right idea of these Indians and it's going to save your life someday. He then asks if Charlie was any help to him? 'Yes sir", he showed me a few things that saved our lives and I know that I'll learn a lot from him, I know it. Good, now go back to your barrack and rest up, you've got some tougher days ahead of you. "Yes sir", replies Oraland as he salutes Custer and exits the room. November came and went, and so did December. Sparse fire fights between the whites and Indians take place, but nothing major.

Spring finally comes to Texas and it finds Custer reassigned once again, now to the Fifth United States Cavalry at the rank of Captain. He is with the Fifth for a very short period and requests a leave of absence for one year. The prospects of a congressional job played in his head for a while and other numerous offers made their way to his door step. People wanted something from Custer, not his ability to lead, but only the use of his name to ramrod ideas and schemes.

Later that summer in 1866 he and Libby made their way to Michigan to visit Norvell and his family. Custer was surprised not only seeing his old friend Norvell, but Oraland, who was there also on furlough, and the three had a grand old time hashing over old times. Before leaving Michigan, Custer asked Oraland to stay in touch with him and maybe someday they could serve together again. After their visit they both went their separate ways and upon returning to duty in Texas Oraland received orders of reassignment to Fort Kearny, Nebraska as head scout. Getting away from the dry heat was a relief for him and he was looking forward to the change in climate and topography.

In late September,1866 Custer would take a big step into history. He is ordered to take command at the rank of Lieutenant Colonel, the newly commissioned Seventh United States Cavalry stationed at Fort Riley, Kansas. What a dream he thought. He had worked hard to get this promotion, and his thoughts of glory erupted in his head. He would be attached to the command of General Alfred Terry's division of Artillery, and Infantry. Terry was not a West Point graduate, he worked his way up throughout the ranks on his own leadership abilities.

Libby was so happy for her husband and was looking forward to finally being able to spend some real time with her "Autie".

The first order of business when he took command was to procure one Oraland Churchill to be his head scout for the regiment. This was no problem and Oraland had his reassignment papers within the week to report to the Seventh Cavalry. Old friends together again, Custer now feels secure with Oraland by his side. In the weeks that follow General Terry is called to Washington to meet with President Grant. Upon returning to the fort Terry had Custer in his office for over four hours going over the orders from the President. With all of Terry's orders understood Custer returns to his headquarters and summons his bugler, Private John Martin to sound officers call, and to retrieve his chief scout, Churchill. With all his staff present Custer discusses his orders with them.

"General Terry has authorized me to round up the Cheyenne and to sit down with their Chief, Black Kettle to enact a peace plan between us. Looking over to his second in command he says, "Major Reno I want you to take companies C, I, and G and head northeast to try to find Black Kettle and his tribe. Major Marcus Reno (class of 1857 at West Point). You and I will take companies D, H, and M and will try to do the same heading to the northwest territory. Looking at a map of the territory, he points out the area where Reno should try to locate the Indians and he (Custer) will search in an area forty miles to Reno's rear. Custer now looking at Oraland, gentlemen this is Sergeant Oraland Churchill. Medal of Honor Winner, and my Chief of Scouts. He knows the Indians and the way they think. I trust him with my life, so feel free to talk with him and get acquainted. The man has a lot of knowledge! Well that's all, back to your troops and prepare for the morning. All salute, and exit to their men as Custer ordered. Leaving the building a few of the officer's approach Oraland and strike up a conversation with him regarding his civil war exploits, and with his winning the Congressional Medal and his experiences with the Indians in Texas. Experienced Indian fighters are few in this newly formed regiment and he is a welcome sign to such.

Oraland is impressed by all of Custer staff, all but one! That's Major Marcus Reno. He comes across as snob and someone who doesn't like to be told what to do. Oraland thinks back in time when Custer said to him, that problem people will be taken care of, and most likely by themselves. Oraland overseeing the scouts goes back to the barracks and informs his men of the upcoming patrol. He has six Crow scouts under him, and one who is his most trusteed, "Charlie Goes Slow". When Custer asked for Oraland's reassignment to the Seventh, Oraland requested that Charlie be transferred also. He as well trusted the man with his life, and they have become good friends.

Charlie is an added asset to the regiments compliment of experience. Morning arrives and the troopers are formed and ready for duty. Libby and Custer say their goodbye's as well as all the other married men of the regiment. Custer mounts his horse and gives the order to his company commanders, "troopers mount", and you can hear the order being given all down the long line. In unison all mount. Next the order flows down to the six companies, "companies forward" and all start to exit the fort. Women are standing on the sides of the buildings waving to their loved ones and the Seventh's Regimental band is playing "Gary Owen". The six companies outside of the fort now separate, and the three companies under Reno head east and the three companies led by Custer head in a north westerly direction. Three days go by and no signs of the Cheyenne. On the fourth day near the Rio Grande, about ten miles from Custer's position, Oraland and Charlie make contact with a small party of Cheyenne camped near the area called the Rio Bravo.

****** (AT THIS PART IN THE BOOK, YOU THE READER WILL FIND INDIAN SPELLING NOW AND THEN PRECEDING A WORD IN ENGLISH) ********

    The scouts are riding the river, (o-hi-i) bank and stop when they hear faint noises of giggling and laughing coming from north of where they were. Getting a little closer they come in eye contact with four to five squaws washing their cloths in the water, (mahpe). Charlie says to Oraland in his broken English, that the squaws are talking about the braves in their village, and how they are more occupied by hunting and do not show them any attention. Hearing this, Oraland smirks a little and asks Charlie does he feel it safe to approach the women?
    Charlie does not think it would be a problem, so they start to ride in on the women who are now knee high in the water. They give the women a little scare, so Charlie holds up his hand in friendship and in his native Crow language says, hello (kahe'shodaa) showing they mean the women no harm.
    They do not understand Crow it seems, so Charlie tries, do you talk Cheyenne, (Ne'tse'he'sene'stsehe). With that the women understood. One of the women ask, what's your name? (Ne'to'ne's`eve) Charlie replies, is his name. He then asks of Chief Black Kettle? (Moketetauato). Pointing

to the east, one of the squaws responds over there (ha-taal.) Oraland in the meantime still has his right hand in the air as a sign of peace. As the two men sit there Oraland is taken back by the beauty of a young woman, (he'e) that is with the group. He asks Charlie to tell them that, we come in peace and are looking for the great Chief Black Kettle. Charlie responds to Oraland that he has already asked that question and the women say Black Kettle is in camp about a quarter of a mile, pointing to the west. As he is talking he still can't take his eyes off the young squaw that caught his attention earlier.

She stands around five feet eight, with long black hair hanging down her back, and has the brownest eyes that have a calm soothing look. She is also wearing a full leather dress which sets off her brown skin tones. Oraland then asks Charlie if the women would lead them back to their camp. One of the squaws who is a little older converse with Charlie and agrees they would lead the two.

Charlie replies thank you, (Ne'a'es'e) Then for a moment Oraland and this Indian squaw give each other a look. The glance puts a smile on his face which makes the boy feel all warm inside. Reality strikes back, and after picking up their clothing the women, (he'`e) ask the two to follow them to their village, (man`ah'eno). As they are riding behind the squaws Charlie turns to Oraland and comments on how he could not help but notice the way he (Oraland) was looking at the young woman, (k`ase''e'ehe). Why Charlie her beauty overwhelmed me and I have not seen a prettier face in my entire life. "I have to find out her name".

The group walks for about ten minutes, and upon entering the Cheyenne village, many Indians start to gather around them as they continue to walk thru the camp. The two men, (hetane) have set off quite a bit of commotion. Young braves now appear with battle lances and bows and arrows and a few start to taunt, (t'tsetan'o) the pair. Stopping now,

Charlie shouts out in the Cheyenne language that they come in peace and do not wish harm to anyone. He then asks for Chief Black Kettle, where is he? (To'sa'e e'hoo'e.) Before he could finish his sentence an older (hemehe) a man emerges from a tepee (m`heo'o) and all around there is silence. Charlie then turns to Oraland and says to him, Sergeant meet Chief, (v`h'oeso) Black Kettle"! The man they call Chief Black Kettle is courageous looking and carries himself as one who is in charge. As he approaches the two still on horseback, he to holds up his hand in friendship.

After dismounting and standing in front of one another Black Kettle asks why they are hear? Oraland asks Charlie to introduce him to the chief and to tell him they are here on behalf of their great white chief General Custer. He wishes to meet with the great leader Chief Black Kettle for the purpose of sitting down and discussing peace.

Black Kettle tells them that the white man, (vi-ho-i) is always welcome, but in the past month's many have come to do harm to his people. My great white chief Custer is troubled over the way your people have been treated and wants to right the wrongs. Chief Black Kettle responds that it is good that the long knives want peace, as does his people, and agrees to meet with this Chief Custer and smoke the peace pipe together. Oraland is smiling now and reaches out to the chief for a hand shake.

Black Kettle is an educated man and knows exactly what Oralands motions are and as well reaches out and shakes his hand. "It's good" (le'p'eva'e) replies Black Kettle as the two shake hands. Oraland couldn't help but to see the young squaw standing there and gave her another smile which she returned. Chief Black Kettle then invites the two to spend the night in his village, Charlie accepts and tells Oraland that it is a great thing to be invited to stay and part take of the Cheyenne festivities. Oraland then tells Charlie to tell Black Kettle that they are looking forward to the tribe's ritual, and would be happy to stay overnight. Black Kettle tells Charlie he and Oraland can sleep in a special tepee after the festivities are over. That night the Cheyennes treated the two with a feast of food and dance. While sitting and enjoying the dancing, Oraland notices the young squaw again, and turns to Charlie and asks if he would introduce him to her. Charlie remarks that women are trouble, and he should stay away from them! Oraland persists and Charlie finally gives in.

Getting up they walk over to the girl and both she and Oraland give one another a smile. Charlie asks, "what is your name", (ne'to'ne`s^eve'he) to the girl. She replies, "Waynoka". (sweet water). Oraland then reaches out with his hand and says pointing to himself, Oraland. Or-a-lan-d she replies with a smile. Both give a little laugh, (s'eh'atamano'o) and as both are staring at one another Chief Black Kettle walks over. The Chief asks Oraland through Charlie if he likes his daughter? (ni-ss-don-ni) Daughter, Oraland is taken aback by the chief's response. Collecting himself he tells Black Kettle "Your daughter is very beautiful Chief." Charlie translates.

"I have seven children" replies the Chief. He then introduces his wife "Medicine Woman". Oraland smiles at the chiefs wife and then Black Kettle turns and calls out for one of his sons to come over. Through Charlie the Chief says that this is his oldest son (hi-hau-ho) "tahkeome" (Little Robe). He is seventeen years now and is fast becoming a man, (hi-dan-ni). Oraland again points to himself and says his name and then extends his hand in friendship.

The young brave extends his hand also and they shake. All stand there for a few moments exchanging pleasantries and the word peace must have come up four or five times. Black Kettle expresses his want of a peace with the whites, for he saw the future of his people many moons ago in a dream. The whites will come in numbers he says and his people will be pushed outside of their hunting grounds. Oraland spoke up after the Chief had finished and promised that his great white chief Custer will not allow this to happen. Custer is a good man and wants all, the whites and the Cheyenne to live in peace. The festivities in the village lasts for hours and Waynoka and Oraland beamed at one another through out. The boy is captivated by Waynoka's beauty and tries to converse with her the best he can. Through the sign language lessons that he had been given by Charlie he is doing alright. He then asks Black Kettle through Charlie if he could walk with his daughter. Black Kettle gave his permission and the two wonder off towards the river, (s'eo'nea'hasene).

They are alone now and are standing quietly gazing into the river with the reflections of the moon hitting the ripples in the water. Oraland tries to tell Waynoka that the land that he comes from isn't as beautiful as the Cheyenne territory. She asks if he has a family back there and is there a woman in his life. A little stunned by her questions, he tells of Norvell and his parents, and no he does not have a woman friend.

He stands there looking her in the face with the light of the moon, (da-ii-sshi-i) hitting her body making her look like an angel, ('ehotse'o). He then asks her if there is someone special in her life, and she replies in the negative also. I would make a good wife and mother she says aloud, which again throws Oraland for a loop.

Without a word between them they take each other's hands and move ever so close to one another, looking into one anthers eyes. Oraland tells her that she is beautiful, and Waynoka replies, thank you (n'e'a''se). Then both move each other's heads gently and kiss (v`os'emoht'a). Waynoka moves even closer now and gently wrapping her arms around Oraland. He returns the motion and for a second which felt like eternity. Not a word is spoken for they know that a true love has been born. Oraland steps back a little now and tries to tell Waynoka about his feelings, (hom'oseh) for her, and she to talks of her feelings for him as well. After a while of talking Waynoka mentions that it is time to go back to the village now for it is getting late. They stroll back to the village hand in hand and when in sight of the others around the campfire they release their romantic grip. Oraland now stands facing Waynoka and tells her that tonight was the best night he had ever experienced in his life. She replies "I'm feeling good (Na'pe'vomo'htahe), thank you" (Nia'ish). With that they both go to their respective sleeping quarters, her to her tepee and he to his. Morning comes quickly and Charlie and Oraland have some lengthy ridding to do to get back to Custer.

Chief Black Kettle walks over to them both now on their horses and says "good morning" (P'evevo'ona'o). Both return the gesture. Oraland then tells Charlie to ask Black Kettle in the coming days to contact his Kiowa, Commanche, Apache, and Arapaho brothers and discuss with them of what they had talked about last night, peace! Black Kettle replies, "as the crow fly I will tell my brothers of the great white chief Custer and of his visions for peace. When I have reached out to all I will send a party of my people to your Fort and you can make arrangements for a treaty signing if all goes well.".

Oraland was glad to hear those words coming from this honorable man standing in front of him and knew he was a man of true vision also. As the two start to ride off, Oraland looks back and Waynoka is now standing next to her father. He wanted to say goodbye, but time isn't on his side. They must get back to Custer as soon as they can. Oraland stops a moment and turns around in his saddle and raises his arm to wave farewell. He can see Waynoka doing the same and a smile comes across his face. We will meet again he says softly to himself, but Charlie heard him mumble and asks if he had something to say? No Charlie, nothing at this time as they continue to ride off into the desert, (noo' `ohov'a). For one and half days the two ride hard to meet up with Custer and Reno who should have met up with one another three days earlier at their rendezvous point. It is late in the afternoon and after riding up over a large hill they finally see the large encampment of the Seventh down in a valley strung out for about half a mile.

After being stopped by a pair of sentries they make their way to the general's tent located in the middle of the encampment. As they ride closer to Custer's headquarters they can see him standing in front of his tent along with Major Reno with a big grin on his face. Getting down off their horses both come to attention in front of Custer and salute him. Oraland then reports "Sergeant Churchill, and Corporal Charlie Goes Slow reporting sir"! Glad to see you both, one more day and I was going to send the other scouts out to look for you. "Come on into my tent gentlemen", Custer replies. Have a seat and you can tell Major Reno and myself what you found out if anything.

"Well sir", replies Oraland, "we made contact with Chief Black Kettle and discussed the proposal for a peace treaty and he was all for the notion. When we left I asked him to get together with the other tribes and to talk to them about your peace plans. He said he would seek out the other's and would send a party of his followers to the fort when they had done so. So, sir, now we wait for his answer". "Were his young braves alright with his desire for peace", asks Custer? "The whole village seemed surreal about his wanting peace sir", replies Oraland.

They are a proud people and I found Black Kettle to be a great leader and human being. The man wants nothing more than peace for his people. Well, great job men and I'll see that this report goes on both of your records. Custer stands up from his desk and points to Oraland and Charlie and says, "now you two rest up a bit, grab a hot meal for we ride back to the fort tomorrow morning". Custer addressing Reno now, "Major Reno inform your scouts that they will be out in front of the regiment on the way back". "Very well sir" is the reply from Reno. All now stand to attention before Custer and salute him, then all exit the tent. Custer's job in securing a peace treaty with the Indians seems to be a sure thing now.

Another notch on his glory ride reflects Custer. The next couple of months were normal, patrols out and in. No major incidents have occurred. Maybe a raid here or there, but for the most part, quiet! Custer feels it may have something to do with Chief Black Kettles promise to parlay with the other Indian nations in the region. Winter is setting in now and the cool days are upon the Seventh. Time is spent around the forts ongoing training. Each company in the Seventh has orders to maintain a strict discipline level. Horsemanship, the use of the sabre, and marksmanship with both revolver and carbine are Custer's expectations.

He wants the Seventh fine-tuned for any problem that may arise in the future. West Point doctrine precludes everything else and he adheres to that principle with a strict focus on such training. It is now 1867 and the Indian situation is still ongoing. More settlers have moved into the western territories with the advent of the railroads expanding their boundaries. Raiding parties from the Apache, and Arapaho nations have struck out at survey companies working in conjunction with the railroads. The Seventh has been ordered to accompany the construction crews who are laying rails at a rate of two miles a day. Custer tried fighting the railroad companies with his superiors, but with no luck.

His promise to Black Kettle and the other tribes is being tested for, (as the government says,) prosperity! One company of the Seventh, Company B. under the command of a Captain Stephen Albers has the pleasure of doing this job and Oraland has been assigned as head scout for the detail. He along with Charlie Goes Slow will be the advance lookouts for any trouble that may occur. Irony has it that the railroad is just ten miles from where Black Kettles village was some five months earlier. Charlie, when asked by Oraland if there was a chance that the Cheyenne village could still be there he answered, he did not see why not. Chief Black Kettle probably has leading members of the village seeking out the other tribes with the peace invitation that Custer gave him, and I would say yes, their camp fires still burn there.

Plenty of water and good hunting grounds all around would keep the tribe there. Oraland's inquiry was twofold. First, he did want to know if Black Kettle was still there so he could maybe find out how the peace accord was coming along with the other tribes, and secondly there was Waynoka! He wanted to see her again in the most awful way. Charlie was on the same page as Oraland and said to the boy, you know my friend that squaw back in the village was very pretty and if I were a younger man now I would be on my way to find her. Oraland laughs at Charlies remark, and says "so you think it's the girl I am thinking about huh"?

Charlie comes back with, "you said it I didn't". Both look at one another and laugh some more. Well my red friend let's go tell Captain Albers that we are on a mission of peace for Colonel Custer. With Albers permission next morning Oraland and Charlie head out for the Cheyenne village which Oraland hopes will still be there. After three hours in the saddle the sight of smoke, (he'poht`otse) can be seen in the distance. They finally come up on the river and it takes only minutes to enter the Cheyenne village. Charlie was right and Oraland is looking everywhere for Waynoka. As they enter the camp a great commotion erupts. Squaws, young braves, children, and old people make their way towards the two troopers. Charlie raises his arm in friendship and proceeds to dismount, as Oraland is still leaning in his saddle to try and catch sight of Waynoka. He finally dismounts also and one of the elders starts to talk. "Welcome" (va'o`htama) my friends"(ni-viss-si-no). Charlie greets the elder, (h'aa' 'ehahe) with thank you (ne'a'es`e).

He goes on and asks where, (t`os'e) Chief Black Kettle is. The elder Cheyenne states that Black Kettle and his wife have gone north to the Comanche nation to talk, ('eese) with Chief Ten Bears (parry-wah-say-men) about the peace treaty. Oraland asks Charlie to question the elder if any of the other tribes have given positive reaction to a treaty. The elder continues and states that Black Kettle had also talked with the Arapaho Chief Little Raven and he too said peace would be a good thing amongst the whites and Indian nations. He also spoke with the Kiowa Chief Sitting Bear (satank) and he also agreed that peace would be good. The Ogala Chief Crazy Horse walked away from Chief Black Kettle and also the great Chief of the Lakota Sioux, Sitting Bull, when they were offered the talk of peace.

Both said they would fight to the death before kneeling to the long knives. Oraland has been standing next to Charlie and asked him if he had heard of this Chief Crazy Horse? "Yes, I have and he is bad medicine for the white man. This one will be trouble for the army in the future I regret to say.

Sitting Bull on the other hand is a great medicine man and a spiritual leader (n'esemoo'o) of the Lakota. He is well respected in all Indian circles and looked at as a spiritual leader and great fighter for the Indian cause. Oraland is taken aback by what Charlie just told him, but is pleased to know that Black Kettle has made progress with the other tribes.

He has a total of three Indian nations now that want peace. The Comanche and Apache tribes are the only two remaining nations that have to be contacted. Oraland stumbles a little with his Cheyenne and asks the elder how long Black Kettle has been gone? Two (ta li) weeks and his party of elders and young braves traveled West (Wu-de-li-gv). Charlie at this time asks the old man "what is your name"? (Ni-don-sshi-vi). The elder replies," they call me Running Deer". Well Running Deer, we thank you for your help and it looks like your Chief is trying to do what's good for your people.

Charlie adds, "My Sergeant and myself will report back to our chief and relay what you have told us". As Charlie is talking with Running Deer Oraland grabs Charlie's arm and when he turns to Oraland to see what's up he takes a glimpse of Waynoka walking straight for the two. Oraland excuses himself from Charlie and starts to walk towards, (neohn'e'e) the girl that he had hoped to see again. They meet in the middle of camp and have created a commotion with the rest of the village. Squaws are giggling and the elders are talking and pointing, (hets`eh'e'e) at the two.

A few young braves give Oraland a sneer or two before turning their backs and walking away. Oraland's smiling at Waynoka as she stands there looking into his eyes. Charlie shake his head and continues to talk with Running Deer. "Oh, how I have missed you Waynoka", he tells her. I to have missed you Or-a-lan-d she replies. He now turns to Charlie and says "Give me an hour Charlie and then we'll start back to the detail". Alright remarks Charlie, "but don't get yourself into trouble with that young squaw".

Don't worry, I'll be a true gentleman the entire time. Oraland now turns to Waynoka (v'eetomev) asking her to go for a walk with him. Yes, she says, let us go down to the river once again. With that both start to walk to the river. There is silence, ('emoos'o) between the two for a moment and then they start talking and laughing at one another. Once at the river, Oraland takes Waynoka into his arms and gives her a passionate kiss. She to returns his advances and kisses him back. They stand now embracing one another and both can feel the love coming from within their bodies, (mav'etove). "I want you as my wife", ('ev'a) Waynoka, he tells her. She is surprised and tells Oraland that she too wants him as her husband.

She tells him though I will have to get my father's approval and he is away. I know he will come back with good news relating to the other tribes, and my telling him how I feel about you will only make him happier. She then takes off from around her neck a beaded necklace, (vo'ota`oxa'sheone'vo) and puts it around Oraland's neck, ('enotov'ah(n)). Oraland in turn takes off his Saint Christopher medal he wears and puts it around her neck. Then they embrace again and give one another a deep kiss one more time.

My love will grow each day for you Waynoka, he tells her looking into her brown eyes. Now we must get back to the camp, (h'ev'en'ove) so Charlie and I can tell my chief what Running Deer told us earlier. Reluctantly, (v'ahpe) Waynoka agrees and both walk back to the camp. The next time we meet we will spend more time together I promise, (v'estom'osan'e) he tells her. They start to walk back holding hands again, and when in sight of the camp, stop and give one another a long last kiss. Charlie is standing there with a big grin on his face forcing Oraland to blush a bit. "

Finished", he asks Oraland? Alright Corporal let's get back to camp he says in an over bearing tone. Charlie was put in his place by his Sergeant and both mount their rides. Oraland now looking at Charlie tells him to tell Running Deer to have Black Kettle contact the fort when he returns from his peace mission. May it be good news for both whites and your people he says. He then looks over to Waynoka who is standing outside of her tepee staring at him. She has a big smile on her face and he gives a wave of his hand and smiles back. The two proceed to ride out of the village and all-around people chant as the they ride off. After Oraland and Charlie returned to the railway construction camp they informed Captain Albers of their talk with Running Deer and Black Kettles progress in the peace talks. Captain Albers suggests that Oraland return to Fort Riley and report to Custer directly on his findings. Oraland had no problem with that and left the next morning on his three-day trip for Fort Riley.

But before leaving he gave head scout duties to Charlie and told him that he would hook up with him down the road somewhere in time. Both shook hands and off goes Oraland into the desert plains headed for Custer. It's now the month of May and the signs of peace look good. On returning to the Fort, Oraland headed directly for Custer's Headquarters.

Upon entering the H.Q., the First Sergeant who was seated at his desk outside of Custer's room welcomed him. Small talk in sued for a moment between both and then the Sergeant got up and knocked on Custer's door. Opening he announced Oraland and was asked to come in. Custer got up out of his chair and walked over to Oraland and gave him a masculine handshake. "Did you have a good ride to the fort" asks Custer? "My ride was uneventful sir" is Oralands reply. Well my boy I sense you have news for me? "Yes sir", replies Oraland.

He told Custer that the rail crews were so close to the Cheyenne village that he felt he may be of help in trying to see if any progress had been made by Black Kettle with meeting with the other tribes. Black Kettle was not there in the village, but I did meet with one of the elders of the camp and he told me that Black Kettle had the pledge from the Chiefs of the Arapaho and Kiowa nations for a peace treaty. He was still talking with the Comanche and Apache Chiefs and it looked good for their approval also." Splendid" replies Custer as he is pacing the floor in front of Oraland. "Did he have any idea when Black Kettle would return to his village"? asks Custer. Maybe in two or three weeks I was told sir.

"The raids that happen now and then are probably from groups of Indians who do not want peace and are defying the other chief's desires", remarks Custer. "It's hard to let go of what is yours after all these years and these small groups of warriors will die for their beliefs before they sign any treaty. So, we must be on the ready at all times". "Sir if I may, there were two tribes that met with Black Kettle and would not have anything to do with the treaty. They are the Ogala and Lakota Sioux headed by a Chief Crazy Horse and from what I heard a great chief called Sitting Bull.

They both didn't want anything to do with a peace treaty. Their warriors I am sure are the ones creating the raiding problems for us". If this Crazy Horse and Sitting Bull continue to attack settlers, then I am sure we will meet someday on the field of battle. I have heard of this Sitting Bull and no, nothing of Crazy Horse. So, what do you want to do Sergeant, stay here or go back with Captain Albers? "If I may ask sir", replies Oraland I would like to go back to the Cheyenne village and wait for Black Kettle's return. The faster we know of the results of his peace initiative the better for us, plus I can increase my knowledge and language skills in the Indian culture.

True, remarks Custer, and we won't have to wait for a Cheyenne party to bring us the news. Good thinking Churchill. Now why don't you head for your barracks and rest up and plan on taking off in the morning for the Cheyenne village. "Very good sir", is Oraland's reply, as he stands at attention and gives Custer his military salute. Custer walks Oraland outside to the porch and wishes him well on his journey tomorrow. The gleam in Oraland's eyes could blind a man. So, he heads off to his barracks and prepares for another long ride back to the village, but he knows it will be worth it, for Waynoka will be there waiting for him. Four days have gone bye and Oraland finds himself just outside of the Cheyenne village. He decides to go to the river and wash up before making his way into the Indian camp.

He ties his horse, (m`ahe'o) to a mesquite tree in the shade and proceeds to take his clothes off and wades into the water that looks awfully inviting. The heat and dust of the desert have made their mark on him and the water in the river feels good, really good. While he is wading in the cool waters he feels that he is being watched by someone or something. He looks around trying not to look suspicious and then hears low, soft giggles.

Looking in the direction of the sounds he catches sight of someone hiding behind a large Texas Sage bush. He calls out, who's there, show yourself! To his surprise it is Waynoka and she is walking towards him smiling. As they look at one another she starts to disrobe, taking off her leather (v'e'ho'evoht'ahoots'ev`ohon`otse) dress and moccasins. She is completely naked, (v'vo'kahe) now and is walking into the water, (von'oovot) heading for him.

They're both standing waist high in the river just staring at one another. Oraland reaches out for her and she melts, (h'ohpe'h'a) in his arms (he-`'ahtsene). They embrace for a few minutes and then kiss. Waynoka starts to cry and Oraland asks, "why"? I don't want you to leave me again Or-a-lan-d, I love you. And I you, repeats Oraland as he kisses her again. They hold each other for a long time and then Oraland tells her of his reason for being here. "The joy in my heart is great" , comments Waynoka. Still embracing they softly feel each other's bodies under the cool(toot'om'o) rivers current.Before long they are on the edge of the river bank making love, and the moans coming from Waynoka stir Oraland's manly needs. Each love thrust sends shivers, (nonomose) through their bodies and catches them gasping for air every other moment. I love you Waynoka, Oraland softly whispers, ('emoosee'eeste) into her ear as she moans again and again. With the act of love over, they just remain in each other's arms lying there for a moment breathing heavily.Oraland has never felt this way before and pledges himself to her for always. It is getting late in the day now and Waynoka suggests they return to the village for something to eat, (m'esehe). I'm hungry, (n'ah'a'e'ana) replies Oraland after their little lovemaking session.

The people in the village were glad to see the young army trooper again and many hugs and soft kisses on the check were given and received. Running Deer came over and welcomed him as well and asked about Charlie. He seemed a little disappointed when told Charlie was not coming to the village this time.

Waynoka whispers to Oraland that she was going back to her tepee to cook, (t'onet`aho't'a)) up a meal for him and that he could stay with her if he wanted to. She was the only one in the tepee, and well it would be nice for him to stay there with her. He remarks to her that he has to put his horse up and collect his gear, and that he would not be too long. Thoughts of her are still going through his mind as he takes off his saddle and blanket. (hestana''ev'a) His horse will be well fed tonight and will remain with the other Indian ponies corralled. When he enters the tepee Waynoka remarks, "come eat", (h'em`eseeste) and gives Oraland a small plate of beef and corn she has prepared. He asks if she likes to cook and she answers in the positive. She tells him that her mother taught her how to cook and that to be a good wife a squaw must know how to prepare food. After taking out the small cooking pot, (hom-ssi-vi-do-o) that she used to make his meal she returns. Oraland walks over to her standing now next to the door and gives her a passionate kiss. Waynoka tells him to eat first and then they can lay, (n`oho'hon'a) with one another again later. He sits down, (hum-ssto-ss-zi) on a bear robe in the middle of the tepee and starts to eat the seasoned bison, (hotoa'e) she has just made for him. Chewing on a piece of meat he looks at her and says, good food making a rubbing motion with his hand on his (stomach, (ma'ese`sen'a). She smiles and joins him now, also taking a piece of meat and eating it. As they sit there on the floor he looks around her tepee and notices that she is a neat person and it looks as if she takes care of her belongings.

    They catch a glance, (he`sk`es'en'oo''o) of one another again and smile. When finished Oraland takes his plate and asks Waynoka if he can help her clean up. No, she replies it is good that the woman takes care of her man, just relax and I won't be long in cleaning up. So, he sits there watching her as she picks up, and his mind is wondering on what a wonderful woman she is. After a while she is finished and suggests that they stroll the village to walk off their meal. It's dark now and the many camp fires are projecting the silhouettes of the cactus and mesquite trees that are in the deserts foreground. Hand in hand they walk around and stop to say hello to people sitting around the fires that burn so brightly.

    Young braves seem to look at the couple in a negative way, but that doesn't bother Oraland a bit. Waynoka is her own person and she has chosen him as her mate which makes him feel very proud. Interracial couples were not common in these days and the love bond that has been created between the two is strong and solid. He has a lot of soul searching to do and he is aware of this. His love is true for Waynoka and culture traits are not a problem for him. Gee, a lad from Michigan here in an Indian village, who would have predicted it to happen. After a long walk the two go back to Waynoka's tepee and it doesn't take long for them to become intimate again. The kisses and embraces continue throughout the night and both fall into a deep sleep, (t'o'eva'o) after their marathon of love making. When Oraland awakes in the morning his eyes are set on Waynoka still sleeping next to him. Her warm body is nestled next to his and the sweet smell of love making is still present. Her dark black hair has a luster to it and her skin is as soft as a new baby, (mo'nnahe). Her facial features have a smile and he feels that she is having a beautiful dream. Again, he thinks to himself, what a pretty thing she is.

Laying there looking at her, a smile comes across his face when she opens her eyes and gazes right into his. He takes his hand and runs his fingers through her hair which causes her to close her eyes for a moment. Good morning (p'evev'oona'o) he whispers to her as she smiles looking at him and moves closer to give Oraland a passionate kiss. He embraces her again and they proceed to make love to one another gently ever gently again. There is a great love bond between the two. Later on, after their love making Oraland suggests they stroll down to the river and clean up. She agrees and as they walk through the camp he notices that many of the squaws are tending the fires and preparing meals for their loved ones.

He knows that when they return Waynoka will serve up something good for both of them and is looking forward to that. The river is cold, but Oraland finds it refreshing and with Waynoka there he doesn't care. For the next couple of weeks Oraland learns more of the Cheyenne ways and the language. Waynoka is also learning English as well as many of the villagers. Waynoka's brothers went with their father Chief Black Kettle so Orland learns how to hunt and fish, (no-ma-ni) with some of the other braves left in camp. They find him willing to learn their ways and they take a stronger liking to him now. They laughed at him when he first tried to spear fish in the river, but he is now skilled in that art form. The use of the bow and arrow and spear are also mastered by Oraland. A month has gone bye and one day while returning from hunting in the desert Oraland finds the village filled with excitement. Chief Black Kettle has arrived back from his peace mission. Waynoka meets Oraland as he enters the camp and she is so happy that her father is back. Come Or-a-lan-d she remarks, lets us visit my father.

Oraland wasn't too happy of the chief's return, not because he didn't like Black Kettle, but because he would have to leave Waynoka again and return to Fort Riley. He tries to act happy and upon seeing the chief and his thoughts of leaving diminish as he greets Black Kettle warmly. Black Kettle is surprised to find Oraland in camp and asks why he is here? Speaking, (h'ona'ovesta) in Cheyenne he tells the Chief of his motives and finds Black Kettle taken aback by his language skills. It is good that my friend speaks the language (he'ev`ahetan'eveneste) of my people," welcome my friend", (ni-hi-ni-hin--o-zi) he replies.

They shake hands and Oraland suggests that they sit down and smoke the peace pipe, (hehnove'ohko) and then they can talk about Black Kettles trip. Waynoka is standing to the side with her older brother Little Robe who has returned also. She walks over to Oraland with Little Robe and the two exchange words. As they are talking the young brave notices the necklace around Oraland's neck. He looks at Waynoka and asks why the white man has her necklace. She explains that it was a gift, (m'eaht`otse) from her to him and then she shows her brother Oraland's Saint Christopher Medal that Oraland gave to her. Little Robe looks a little puzzled after being told the story by his sister and remarks that the beaded necklace was made by him for her only. Meanwhile Black Kettle has returned with the peace pipe and is sitting on the ground now asking Oraland to join him. Oraland a little taken aback by Little Robe's remarks sits next to the Chief and asks that Little Robe to sit also so they all can smoke the peace pipe. Oraland notices that Waynoka doesn't look to happy, but he has to try and iron out his differences with her brother one way or another now. Little Robe sits next to his father as the elder lights the pipe.

He then lifts the pipe in the direction of the sky and chants, (mom`aht`ahe'este) a few words and then puts the pipe to his mouth and inhales the smoke. He then passes the pipe to Oraland who raises the pipe to the sky, but doesn't say anything, and proceeds to puff on the pipe. After taking a puff Oraland reaches over to Little Robe and hands him the pipe. He too goes thru the motions of puffing on the pipe and after finishing gives it back to his father. Now my brother, (hev'asem'e'tov) looking at Oraland I have returned here to my village with the good news of peace. My Indian brothers the Comanche's and the Apache's have given their word that they want to sit down, (h'am`estoo'e) with your great white chief Custer and discuss terms for a peace between our two peoples.

Also, my brothers the Kiowa's and Arapaho's also have given their words that they too want peace. Oraland is smiling now after hearing the words from the chief. It is good that the Indian nations want peace Oraland replies and my great white chief will be happy. Black Kettle continues to tell Oraland that there are a few warriors from the nations who still oppose a peace and will continue to act on their own in a hostile way. Oraland remarks that the great white chief has discussed this with him and is aware of these rouge warriors. Again, it is good that my brothers the Cheyenne's and the other tribes, (no-zi) want peace as a whole, and we all have to work for that goal. Where would you, Black Kettle like to have this treaty signed and when? We have chosen the Medicine Lodge Creek area for the signing, because of the multiple grass meadows and the water supply for ourselves and our horses. Five to six thousand people will converge on this area for the signing so we need plenty of room (no'keen`a). I would say next month as the full moon shows itself in the sky would be a good time to sit down with your great white Chief Custer. "Let it be then", replies Oraland. I will leave first thing in the morning for Fort Riley and tell my great white chief of your wishes.

All stand up now and Oraland walks over to Little Robe. "Little Robe I mean you no disrespect in the matter of the necklace. I'm deeply in love with your sister and would not do anything to create a problem between both of you and myself". Oraland holds out his hand, (na'ahtse) in a gesture of friendship and Little Robe reaches out also and they shake hands. Both are smiling including Waynoka and their father Black Kettle asks Oraland if he heard right that he, Oraland is in love with his daughter? "Yes, chief I am in love with Waynoka and I would like to have her for my wife".

The great spirit is looking down, (s'e'onoo'e) upon us today smiling remarks Black Kettle. You may have my daughter my friend, for I know that you are a good man. Thank you Black Kettle I will forever love her and no other. Waynoka now standing next to both men gives each a huge hug, but Oraland leaves in the morning and the inner smile she carries inside fades away.

The night went quickly and morning has arrived finding Oraland having saddled his horse is now going around saying his good byes. Peace be with you Black Kettle as he shakes the Chiefs hand, I will see you next month, (he'k'oovotom) at Medicine Lodge Creek. You can reach out to all the Indian nations now and tell them of the time and place where they can meet to sign the treaty of peace. Walking over to Little Robe Oraland asks the young brave to watch out for his sister and then too shakes his hand. Lastly there is Waynoka who is standing next to Oraland's horse. Before getting up on his mount he tells her good bye and that the month will pass quickly and they would be together again. He then takes her into his arms and embraces her and both kiss for what seemed like eternity. Riding away, he turned back once seeing her waving as he disappeared into the desert. Great news! That was Custer's reaction to Oraland's news that he had just presented to his commanding officer.

"Well done Oraland," was his next remark. "I am so delighted that your input on this peace treaty came to be, and I'll make sure that your deeds will pay off for you."

"Thank you sir" replied Oraland. Now my boy I must plan for this monumental moment and if you have any input on the situation please let me know. "Sir there is one thing you ought to know" remarks Oraland. "And that is what asks Custer? Well sir the area that Black Kettle asked to have the signing is quite a way off and I feel we should make haste in preparing for it now! He said there should be over five thousand people not excluding the horses at this signing and I feel we should be prepared for the numbers of people that are coming. Food, blankets, hay for the horses, gifts for the chiefs of each Indian nation, medical supervision if needed should be available, and countless other amenities for both the tribes and our people who attend.

Custer is sitting now at his desk and is taken aback by what Oraland just said. You're right Churchill there is going to be a lot of people and the peace process should run like clockwork both at the signing area, and in the villages. I'll see to it that there are enough amenities for the treaty signing. We will also set up a security perimeter just in case Crazy Horse and Sitting Bull show up. I don't want any problems during the peace process. "Now please call my orderly in here for a moment won't you". asking Oraland. The First Sergeant comes into the room and asks" what can I do for you sir" to Custer. Sergeant I want all my staff present before me in one hour, and that includes all noncommissioned officers as well. I also want Major Carton and his medical non-coms. present also. That's it Sergeant, now get going on what I just asked for. "Very good sir" replies the First Sergeant. Would you like me to stay? Sir, comments Oraland.?

Yes, Churchill I'll need your input when this room is filled with my staff. You know the lay of the land and your comments should help with the planning of this treaty. The hour is up and all are present. Major Reno Custer's second in command calls every one to attention when Custer makes his entrance. He has been with Libby, his wife for lunch accompanied by Oraland. Libby has taken a great liking to Oraland not only because of what his brother did during the war, but because he has made her husband's job a lot easier and he has remained on the post more frequently than in the past. Oraland's help with the Indian situation has taken a great burden off Custer's back and she is great full for that. As they walk in Custer salutes all and asks everyone to stand at ease. He begins, "In a month you are going to be witness to the largest coming together of Indian tribes in our nation's history. We expect over five thousand Indians, women, children, and warriors of the Cheyenne, Arapaho, Apache, Comanche, and Kiowa nations".

There is a sudden stillness in the room. The mention of at least one tribe would make the hairs of a soldier stand up, but thousands, well everyone in the room became a little uncomfortable. NOTE (Custer and the seventh in nine years would be battling even more Indians than what is expected at the treaty signing). Custer saw the unrest in his staff when he mentioned the number of Indians and quickly put it to rest. "Gentlemen these Indians are a people who have united with one another in an effort to secure peace for their tribes and to work side by side with us to make sure that we enforce that peace. They will come in peace and we have to treat them with respect and humility. One of the staff asks for a question: "Sir my brother was with Captain Fetterman last year when all eighty-one of his troops were massacred. Are you asking me to forget what those red savages did to my brother"? Captain Fredrick Frobrick commander of Company H. asked the damning question.

"Listen Frobrick", replies Custer these Indians want peace now. I'm well aware that the Cheyenne and Arapaho tribes were involved with the attack on Fetterman and that there were other tribes also, the Miniconjou and the Sioux. General Grant has ordered me specifically to bring these tribes together in an effort for peace. Now pointing at Oraland, Chief Sergeant of Scouts, Sergeant Churchill has risked his life, not only for the nation, but for the Seventh Cavalry. He has lived among your so called red savages and has found them as human as you and I.

Custer again looking at Oraland asks, "Sergeant you have risked your life in battle during our civil war, you're a Medal of Honor recipient and you have been a Chief Scout now for over two years. Can you tell me and my staff what your feelings are towards the Indian as a whole? Oraland steps to the front of the assembly and begins with, "honestly gentlemen if the white man had treated the Indian the way we treat our people I don't feel we would be here in this room today. There would be no need for a peace treaty if we all lived as friends. He goes on, I did a little study on my own and found that since the United States has existed we have had some one hundred treaties with the red man and how many do you think we've broken"? Major Reno interrupts and says aloud "probably four or five I'd guess".

Wrong, Major looking him in the face, all of them, not one or two, but all of them. Looking at Custer now Oraland goes on. Sir I am not a brave man, but I do take pride in what I do in my job. May be after the war I would have resigned and had gone back to farming. Army life agrees with me and I take it very seriously. I'm paid to protect our people, but after living with the Indians for a short while I've found they need protection also. I'm not saying our people are bad or have a vendetta against the Indians, all I am saying is they want to live like they always have, in peace! There are bad whites out there just as there are bad Indians, but all are not bad.

Reno interrupts once again and gives his two cents. "So, we have another peace treaty and according to the Sergeant here we haven't lived up to the expectations of the Indians, so we all put on this act of liking one another". Custer now breaks in. "Major Reno you will refrain from further talk such as I have heard from you in the last five minutes. I don't care how you feel about the Indians and treaties! We are going to have this peace treaty signing and you will conduct yourself as an officer and gentleman of the United States Army.

If I hear just one negative comment from any one concerning you and the treaty I will see to it personally that you are court marshaled from the service. Do I make myself perfectly clear sir"? Reno replies with a dead stare looking at Custer, "Yes Sir". Reno dislikes Custer so much and doesn't trust the man. He feels that he should not be in command of the Seventh Regiment and he, Reno should be.

During the war he held the rank of Lt. Colonel and was brevetted a Brigadier General. Now he is second in command of the Seventh Cavalry with the rank of Major, unfair he feels. "Now we have wasted enough precious time on trivial comments", remarks Custer. I want two companies ready to ride in the morning to scout out the area where Chief Black Kettle wants the treaty signing. I expect reports on the lay of the land, water supply, grazing facilities for all the horses, and I also want a report on the abundance of wood for fires. It will be getting colder at night at the time of the treaty and no one should suffer because we didn't think of fire wood. Looking at his subordinate again, Reno I want you in command of this endeavor and I am assigning Sergeant Churchill here to be your Chief scout along with Charlie Goes Slow. Reno twitched a bit when Custer made him in charge.

Captain Benteen you take your Company M, and Captain Moore you will take your Company F for this detail. I think two hundred men should be sufficient for this detail and don't see any need for more men. I want a full report on what you find when you get back Major. Also, Major Carton as you are the head of the medical staff I want you to assign one of your best non-coms. to accompany Major Reno and to have him locate an adequate field hospital site for all who attend this treaty, both Indians and our people. Now again, I want it understood that this peace treaty must go on without any flaws. We all have lost friends through the years due to the war with the Indian nations, but we're going to make history in a few months and this must come off without any hitches. My very good friend and fellow comrade General Sheridan said at one time and a I quote: "The only good Indian is a dead Indian"! Well the Seventh Regiment is going to bury that kind of thinking. Everyone wants peace and we're going to see that it comes true once and for all. Are there any questions gentleman? A Sergeant in the back of the group asks, "sir what about the mess facilities for the event"? "Good question Mess Sergeant Myers", replies Custer. There is no need for you to accompany Major Reno on this detail, but I do want you to figure out the amount of food you're going to need for the troops. Beef, flour, beans and the such. We won't be feeding the Indian tribes, so limit your cooking skills for just the men. "Very good sir", is the Sergeants reply. Any other questions gentlemen? No one had answered, so Custer ends the meeting with, ":Now ready your companies for tomorrows ride Major and the rest of you carry on with your daily duties. I don't see a need for the daily patrols, but be on guard if we are needed, that is all gentlemen"! Everyone in the room comes to attention and salutes their commander, and he in turn returns it. "Sergeant Churchill please stay for a moment", remarks Custer. With every one out of the room now Custer asks Oraland, to keep an eye on Reno. I don't trust the man and his dismal thoughts of the Indians, he could create a problem for us in the future. I know his type and I know what could happen if he should make the wrong decision, so just keep an eye out OK? Oraland replies " Not to worry sir, I'll keep an eye out on the Major".

Now you better get going and get ready for this detail tomorrow. Oraland comes to attention and salutes Custer and remarks "yes sir and thank you sir" then leaves the room for his barracks. He is looking forward to seeing Charlie again and will catch up on talk about his trip to the village. Custer is confident that his orders will be obeyed and that the meeting with the Indian nations in the coming month will go along smoothly. He would like to go, but promised Libby that he would spend more time with her, and he wants to keep his promise. Three and a half weeks have gone by and the detail finally returns back to the Fort. Reno and Oraland accompanied by Major Carton and Captains Benteen and Moore immediately report to Custer's headquarters. Custer greets them and asks what they have found? If I may sir, Reno places a map of the area on Custer's desk that he drew up while in the field and starts off with," the land has plenty of grazing grass for all horse's sir, pointing to a specific spot on the map, and there is enough area for all present to live. The water situation is excellent along with a great multitude of wooded areas to collect firewood. I picked out a good place to hold the treaty signing sir, and a place for your tent, or I should say your headquarters. There is plenty of room for every one and no one should feel hemmed in sir. Very good report Major, now Major Carton what did you find out? "Well sir I found a spot out of the way where I could work comfortably and I could handle any medical situation that might arise. "Great" remarks Custer. He now asks Oraland if there were any signs of trouble? No sir I found the area and surrounding areas peaceful and no signs of any trouble. Custer then remarks, "since I last had my meeting with you gentlemen I've done a little thinking and feel we should post sentries around the whole area to discourage any trouble makers from creating a problem". Oraland now speaks up and says he agrees with Custer's thoughts. "I would let the chiefs know that sentries are posted for the safety of all present sir". "We want them all to feel safe", replies Custer "and I think that's a good idea Sergeant".

Alright gentlemen we have a month to prepare and now is the time to get started. I am going to send out another detail to start setting up the site. Gathering wood and roping off the areas where the mess, medical, and treaty signing tent will be are going to be your main duties. Since you all know the area now you'll have the pleasure of returning there to get things ready. Gentlemen you'll have one week to achieve this. Major Reno, please inform Captain Wright of Company K that he will also accompany you on this detail. Captains Benteen and Moore have your men rest up for a day and be prepared to go out and accompany Major Reno again in two days' time. Major Carton get your medical supplies ready along with anything else you are going to need and be prepared to ride with the Major also in two days. Major Reno, also inform Mess Sergeant

Myers to have his cooking supplies together and relay the same message of being ready in two days. "Sir" Oraland speaks up, "while at the site did a little canvassing of the area also and there is plenty of game to be taken. In a good gesture to the Indians, it maybe to our advantage to offer the tribes meat for their villages as a sign of friendship and hospitality".

Custer, listening intently agrees to Oreland's suggestion and orders Major Reno to have the mess Sergeant equip his men with enough guns and ammo for hunting meat. "Great idea Churchill", is Custer reply. Singing a peace treaty on a full stomach would be a good thing. "I will join you in the field two weeks from today and by then we should be ready for the Indian tribes who start to converge on us early". Major looking at Reno, Mrs. Custer will be accompanying me so make sure that my larger tent is brought out with you. Also make plans for tents for Generals Sheridan (class of 1853 at West Point), Sherman (class of 1840 at West Point), Crook (class of 1852 at West Point), Gibbon (class of 1847 at West Point) and our brigade commander General Terry.

General Grant might show up as well so be on top of it. Now let's pull together and make history next month. Again, before leaving Custer asks Oraland to remain. With all the others gone now he asks Oraland if he noticed anything out of the ordinary while he was in the field with Reno?" Well sir the only thing that came up which I noticed right away was the Major's and Captain Benteen's drinking". Custer's eyes opened wider when hearing this. "Excessive drinking sir", Oraland reported. It started just out of the fort as we left and continued until we were on our way back here yesterday. Their little drunk really showed up clearly one night after supper when both were putting you down verbally. They didn't know I was listening and rant and raved about you and the army and your past exploits during the war. The air was full of hate and, well I think you should be aware that their not to fond of you. Drink my boy is the curse of all man, but it is not up to me to judge an individual for his faults. I'll have to keep a better eye on them with all these Indians coming. Thank you Oraland. The boy was struck cold that he referred to him by his first name again. Oraland replies "thank you sir". Now get your things together because I want you to be with the detail when it goes back out there. Just keep a keen eye open at all times. With that Oraland proceeds to his barracks again to make ready for another trip. Back in the barracks he and Charlie talk of the upcoming detail and how happy Charlie was for Oraland of his relationship with Waynoka. He said things will be tough for them both in the white man's world. Oraland agreed, but made reference the desire of staying with the Indians. "I felt calm and at ease with the Cheyenne Charlie, and would not think twice about living with them"." My brother you have chosen your road to go down, and I will be glad for you". Two weeks have gone by now and the camp at Medicine Creek Lodge has been set up.

    The Indian nations have been filtering in one by one and Custer has assigned Oraland and Charlie to be the interpreters for the affair. The villages get larger and longer, and squaws and children are everywhere. There is excitement in the air as each tribe makes it way into the lush green valley. Custer is sitting back watching the commotion, and he and Libby are amazed at the number of people that don't seem to stop pouring in. Oraland was right, thousands are coming. Before the Indians started to enter the camp, Custer pulled Reno and Benteen into his tent and read them the riot act as far as being officers and gentlemen. No liquor before the treaty was signed. Both reluctantly agreed and the hatred for Custer grows even more now. Benteen later tells Reno after the scolding that Custer gave them, that one-day I'll get back at that jackass! Chief Black Kettle and his village finally show up and Waynoka and Oraland find one another and embrace and kiss. Looking into his eyes Waynoka tells him that she missed him very much. Oraland tells the same to her and they stand there for a moment and just huge one another. Oraland welcomes, (m'asets`estov) Black Kettle and his wife Medicine Woman as does Charlie and tells him that they have picked out a special place for the Chiefs people. The Cheyenne are then guided by Oraland and Charlie to their area that has been provided for them and are thanked by the chief. "My great white chief Custer wants to meet, (m'oheeohts'e) with you after you set up your camp Black Kettle", remarks Oraland. I am looking forward to meeting your great white chief says Black Kettle. Oraland gives Waynoka another kiss and tells her that he has to report back to his chief now and that they will see each other later. He then heads back to Custer's camp while Charlie now finds an old friend, Running Deer and starts talking with him. Oraland tells Charlie that he can stay and catch up on old times with Running Deer, but he, Oraland has to report, (mom`axeoesem) to Custer that all the tribes have finally arrived. Riding a short distance Oraland finds Custer sitting outside of his tent with two other officers including General Terry. As he approaches, he wonders who they are?

Getting off his horse he comes to attention and salutes his commander. "At ease", remarks Custer. "Sergeant I want you to meet two old friends of mine, Generals Sherman, and Sheridan". Oraland shakes each hand and says good day to General Terry. General Terry, Custer's and Oreland's commanding officer has his tent set up next to the Custer's and has let Custer take rein of the whole peace process which is coming to be. Your commander, Sergeant just mentioned to us, remarks General Sheridan that you won the Medal of Honor during the war. "Yes sir" replies Oraland. Well I'd like to shake your hand one more time if you wouldn't mind my boy, remarks Sherman. With that Sherman extends his hand and Oraland shakes it again with a wide grin on his face. Custer remarks that they were watching the Indian tribes coming into the camp areas and that he, Oraland was right there were thousands. Chief Black Kettle just arrived sir and I mentioned that you wanted to meet with him personally after he sets up his village. I'm looking forward to it Churchill he says. Well sirs if you would excuse me I have to make my rounds to see that everything is going as planned. Mamm, he gestures to Libby tipping his kepi as he leaves. The huge camp is coming along just fine and Major Carton has already applied his medical skills on a young brave who had been bitten by a rattle snake, (sshshi-no-vo-zi) gathering fire wood and a few young children who had minor cuts on their hands and feet. The entire area should be set up by tomorrow and the peace treaty would take place in two more days. That night Oraland spent time with Waynoka.

They walked and walked and talked while holding hands. There is almost a full moon and when they stopped, you could make out their figures if far away. I love you very much Waynoka, very much. He proceeds to kiss her and she melts under his romantic spell. They sit and talk some more and he explains to her what he had told Charlie about leaving the army and living with her people. She is so happy and he knows it for the smile on her face shows it. Tomorrow, (m`ahv'oon'a'o) I will introduce my great white leader to your father and I would like you to be there when it happens. I'll do whatever you ask Oraland she replies, I love you. They do not sleep with one another that night for Waynoka is sharing her tepee with seven other squaws and it would be awkward for all if he was to try. They kiss one more time and say good night and Oraland heads for his sleeping area. Morning comes and it finds activity of every type going on in each camp. Oraland was up early checking on each tribe to make sure things were fine and going as scheduled. He meets with the chiefs of each tribe and welcomes them again as he passes through their confines, and lets them know that his great white chief is looking forward in meeting each one. When he reaches the Cheyenne camp Black Kettle is ready to meet with Custer. Waynoka comes out of her tepee dressed in a beaded buckskin dress and moccasins, (mo`k`ehan`otse) which makes the temperature of his body rise seeing this beautiful creature standing now in front of him. He reaches over and kisses her which puts a smile not only on her face, but also Black Kettles and his wife's. They walk now to the soldier's camp and all eyes are on them as they pass the many long knives camped. Soft whispers are heard by the four of them as they continue to head for Custer's tent.

Now standing in front of the tent Oraland announces himself to Custer. Custer walks out escorted by Libby and the introductions take place. "Sir it is with pleasure that I introduce to you the great Chief of the Cheyenne, Black Kettle, his daughter Waynoka, and her mother Medicine Woman". Custer gives them the sign of peace in sign language. Oraland then introduces his great white Chief Custer and his wife Mrs. Custer. Black Kettle then reaches forward to shake Custer's hand surprising Custer to no end. Libby then steps forward and extends her hand to Waynoka, and also to her mother accompanied by a large smile. The moment is golden for Custer for he knows this will only help his career in the future. Standing there now talking they are interrupted by General's Sherman, Sheridan, and Terry. Custer takes the stage and the introductions start all over again. Oraland remembers what Custer said about Sheridan and his ideas about "the only good Indian is a dead one" and watches the General's demeanor as he is shakes the hand of Black Kettle. Custer is astute of the General also and prays Sheridan doesn't say something stupid at this point. All to the surprise of both Oraland and Custer Sheridan was a complete officer and gentleman. After a cool glass of fresh lemonade that Libby made, the talk revolved around what a lovely daughter Medicine Woman had in Waynoka. Yes, Medicine Woman replied she is going to make this young man a fine wife. All just sat there and smiled looking around at just what was pronounced by Waynoka's mother. So, Custer remarks we're going to be a husband now looking over at Oraland? Without thinking he answers "yes sir, I've asked Waynoka to marry me". All is silent again until General Sheridan stands up and walks over to Oraland and asks if he could shake the grooms hand. Surprised Oraland stands up and shakes the Generals hand which leads everyone to stand up and congratulations were flowing all over. Libby gives Waynoka a kiss on the cheek and General Sherman is shaking the hand of Black Kettle. Custer is now shaking Oraland's hand and then proceeds to give Waynoka a kiss on the cheek also. He then to Oreland's surprise shakes hands with Black Kettle and gives Medicine Woman a hug with well wishes. "Whew "Oraland says to himself. All sit down and Libby brings out another glass of lemonade for every one and Custer makes a toast, "to these two-young people, may they have a healthy and happy life".

The atmosphere was delightful and the Generals, through Oraland asked Black Kettle his feeling of the treaty and what he felt about the white people. Black Kettle didn't take any prisoners with his answer. He stated that many years have come and gone and still there is blood being spilled. Our peoples should respect one another and after tomorrows signing, peace should remain solid. All present understood where Black Kettle was coming from and agreed. He wants peace and peace is what he'll get. Then Sheridan raised his glass once more and made a toast to peace, and all repeated, "to peace" Custer now moves over to Oraland and wishes him and Waynoka the best. "You know son the first time I laid eyes on Libby my heart took over and well I was doomed. Laughing Custer looks at Oraland and says only kidding my boy. She is the best thing that has happened to me in my life time. I know you and Waynoka feel the same way. I just want you to know that even though we're not related I feel you are my son and couldn't be prouder of you and what you have accomplished in the last four years. "Gee sir, I am awfully indebted to you and Mrs. Custer for your feelings towards me. I'll try to live up to your expectations". Just continue to do what you do Oraland and you'll be fine remarks Custer. Now let's mingle with our guests shall we! The group talked a while more and Oraland at one spot said, "I think we should make our way back to the village Black Kettle. It's starting to get late and I want to make sure you return while there is still light. Before they parted back to their camp Custer asked Black Kettle to his side. He told Black Kettle that if it wasn't for his hard work this treaty would not be happening, so to show his respect for him, Custer presents Black Kettle with a Spencer carbine. Black Kettle accepts the weapon and pledges never to use it against his now new-found friends.

 Custer said he didn't want the other chiefs present when he made the presentation for he respected the Cheyenne chief more. Good nights and farewells were said, and a long day was nearing its end. When Oraland got back to the Cheyenne camp Waynoka gave him a big kiss and told him to sit outside with the others while she fixed him something to eat. "Boy, am I in love with you woman"! He says to her. Sitting outside in front of a fire Little Robe approaches Oraland and sits down on the ground facing him. So, you want to marry my sister, why? "Well Little Robe I've fallen deeply in love with her and to do the right thing would be to marry her". "Little Robe knows that you are a good man, even if your white and I will honor my sisters wishes in accepting you into my family". Little Robe, Oraland continues all white men are not bad! There are those who would harm both my people and yours, but we must try and treat each other with respect and dignity. Are there no squaws out there for you Little Robe asks Oraland? There are, but I am still my own person and I like it that way for now. The elders are always pressuring the young into getting married, but I am my own person and I know what I want. "Well good for you and my getting to know you has seen what you are about. I envy you and your people for you do not ask for a lot, like the whites do.

Waynoka comes out of the tepee now and hands Oraland a plate of food and Little Robe also. She sits down next to both and they went on to talk about the meeting with Custer and the Generals. After eating Oraland asks Waynoka if she would like to take a walk." A walk sounds good Or-a-lan-d" she replies. They say good night to Little Robe and start to walk under the stars. What a day remarks Oraland. Waynoka, I have been thinking and want to talk to you about us. "Yes, she answers".

Well I still have one year left to serve out my enlistment in the army and I think we should wait to get married until I am out. "You do not love me Or-a-lan-d", she replies? I do love you very much and that is why I think we should wait. I don't know where I'll be day to day and the thought of you alone makes me feel sad. "I too am sad also when you are away Or-a-lan-d" she replies. Well my enlistment will go fast and I know we will see each other while I serve out my time. With this peace treaty being signed tomorrow things will change in the territories now and the need for the long knives will dwindle. They may even say, " Oraland Churchill we don't need your services any more"! What a great thought, but I am to valuable and that won't happen. We'll always be in love with each other and when we see one another special moments will be shared by us. "Can you understand what I am saying Waynoka"? he asks. "No Or-a-lan-d I do not understand "she says now starting to cry. "Oh, Waynoka please don't cry I didn't mean to upset you in this way". He then puts his arms around her and holds her real tight. "Can you feel the love in my embrace, I love you Waynoka and I am not trying to be selfish. He now kisses her and she returns his kiss with passion. They stand there for a few moments and then continue their walk. Now out of the camps sight they find a private spot in the woods and there they stop and feel each other's bodies and proceed to make beautiful love to one another. Waynoka's warm body calls for the need of love and with every thrust of Oraland's body she feels full filled.

They lay under a large evergreen now staring at the stars above. Embracing one another and not saying a word for they know what each other feels. Hours go by and when they return to the camp they find everyone had turned in and had gone to bed. Only a few have stayed up and are enjoying the warmth of the fire they sit next to. Oraland again faces Waynoka and assures her that she will always be in his heart. She concurs and they give each other one last kiss before retiring to their resting places. Next morning there is excitement all through the camps, both army and Indian. The treaty will be signed at noon in an area that Custer picked out and will be in sight of all who attend. Work is under way of setting up tables and make shift seats for the chiefs of the Indian nations and the armies general staff. Custer has just gone over the planned proceedings with Libby and she gives her approval of his hard work. Word came in to the camp last night that General Grant would not be able to attend the treaty, and this news was brought in by General's Gibbon and Crook who arrived late in the evening hours.

Custer knew both from the war and West Point and he and Sheridan and Sherman sat with the two hashing over the late war and the signing of peace tomorrow Two bottles of scotch and a short night made for an interesting folly. Custer wasn't a big drinker, but the generals made up for this. Next morning Custer asks his top Sergeant to have the bugler sound officers call and to fetch Sergeant Churchill. Within moments his staff is standing in front of his tent, including Oraland. Gentlemen you all know your commanding officer acknowledging General Terry to his left. It is my pleasure to introduce General's Sheridan, Sherman, Crook, and Gibbon to you this morning. Sir's, looking at the general staff let me introduce each of my staff to you. Now turning to his staff, he proceeds, may I introduce Major Reno my executive officer. Reno steps forward and gives a salute to the four generals and then steps back. Major Carton, Captain Benteen, Captain Albers, and so forth and finally ends with Oraland. Custer now remarks to the generals, "Sir's with a sense of pride the men of the Seventh United States Cavalry" welcome you. General Sheridan being the highest ranking General present now calls the other three generals to attention and commands all to salute the Seventh's staff in unison.

Sheridan then thanks Custer and his staff for a job well done on securing a peace between the whites and the Indians." You all will be in the history books in coming years for the work you have performed here today. Now let me turn you back to your commander and he will go over today's proceedings with you all, Colonel Custer please continue". Custer thanks the general and begins with, today is important to all, be you Indian or white. History will judge us on the job we do here today and mankind will look upon us as the makers of peace. A lot of hard work has gone into this venture and you all should be proud of what you have done. Now at noon the Indian chiefs will come one at a time with representatives of their individual tribes to the table we have set up and will sign the treaty. Then the general staff here will also sign the peace documents. We have secured gifts from the government for each signer of the treaty. It is a medallion with the inscription "Medicine Creek Lodge Treaty, October 1867" on each. We also have a large supply of blankets for each tribe if they want them, courtesy of the government from civil war surplus. There will be a lot of celebrating so be mindful of people not thinking straight. A rifle shot in the air is no cause for alarm. Let us show the Indians that all we want is peace also. Major Reno will give each company commander their orders after I am finished and we will then proceed to the signing area. Are there any questions gentlemen?

None, then you are dismissed and let's get this treaty signed. Reno then gives the order, "ATTENTION" and all salute Custer and the General staff, then he gives the order "DISMISSED" and all fall back for orders from him. The generals are now talking with Custer and give him accolades on his address to his staff. When Reno finished with all the Company Commanders it was Oraland's turn to receive his orders for the peace ceremony. Sergeant, I want you front and center at the signing to help with any language problems.

I have Charlie Goes Slow as an interpreter for the Kiowa nation and Apache nation, and two other scouts as interpreters for the Arapaho's, and Comanche's. "Yes sir" he replies and heads for the other scouts to talk with them about their duties. The morning goes fast and at noon we find all at the signing table. The Seventh's regimental band has just played "The Battle Hymn of The Republic" and a color guard made up of each regimental company rode in review in front of the dignitaries at the table. What a sight thought Oraland watching no fewer than one hundred riders carrying their company's colors, plus their individual company guidon, and the American flag. This sign of strength was done on purpose to show the Indians the great numbers of long knives and their will to defend their country. Each tribal chief sit opposite the army representatives with Custer in the middle. He begins the signing with a little speech and then asks each chief to sign the document in front of them. Not many Indians knew how to sign their names so the interpreters that were assigned to each helped them along. Charlie had to help the Apache chief (essaqueta) "Pacer" with some of the translations concerning the treaty. The chief expressed his feelings about the metal giants that carry whites over the land of his people. He wants assurances that the giants will not continue to cross the land of his fathers. The Kiowa chief and the Arapaho chief also agreed that the metal giant (trains) had to cease running through their land.

Custer now intercedes and promises the giants will stop their voyage through the Indian territories as a sign of peace in the treaty. The signing took all of one hour and at the end they all smoked the peace pipe. Custer then presented each chief with the silver medallion constituting the ceremony. Peace was present on the land and all could look to the future for long lasting relationships. "Peace", what a wonderful thing Black Kettle expressed. Hands were shook and a photographer was present to take pictures of the occasion. Oraland had his picture taken and gave it to Waynoka to keep. He told her that she could look at the picture when ever she wanted and it would let her know that his thoughts were with her. She told him that her father was going to have the tribe pack up everything in the morning and that they were going to head back to their village. They are now embracing one another and Waynoka doesn't want to let go. Oraland feels the same, but he has duties to preform and tells her that he will see her later tonight. Still holding hands Oraland softly let's go and their hands separate.

General Sheridan in the meantime is telling Custer that he and the other Generals will be pulling out in the morning and will be heading back to their posts. "Grant will be happy to hear of this day " he says to Custer. Major Reno standing with the two in a low voice remarks, "I wonder how long it will take to break this treaty". Custer not amused dismisses Reno to his duties and shakes his head as Reno leaves. "That's the kind of talk that will cause problems for us in the future general". "Just keep on him", replies Sheridan. After finishing his assigned duties Oraland makes his way to the Cheyenne camp and finds some of the people already packing up. He finds Black Kettle and talks with him for a while and tells him what he told Waynoka last night. My son, (nae'ha) you do what is right and all will come together for you was his response. My daughter will understand and I know your hearts will be empty, but will be full when you see one another again. She will be taken good care of and I know deep in my heart you will do the same for her when you are one. Thank you, Black Kettle, for your honesty and understanding. My woman he said is always there for me and I know my daughter will be there for you. At that moment Waynoka walks over and stands beside the two talking.

 Looking at Oraland she tells him that my father is at peace now. This treaty is a good thing and he knows you had a lot to do with it. He will ever be thankful to you for bringing it to reality. I want to thank your father for having the courage to help unite all the Indian nations to make it happen. He is a brave man and warrior, (n'otaxe) Medicine Woman's voice is heard and she wants the chief to come to his tepee. Before leaving he looks at Oraland and shakes his hand and says, "If I do not see you before I leave my son please know that you are in my thoughts, and I know it won't be long before we see each other again. "Good bye Black Kettle" replies Oraland. Now turning to Waynoka, he tells her that tonight will be short for us, but in future days they will be long for us. With that they walk hand in hand and talk about the future. The night did go quickly and more than ever did the two want it to last longer, but alas it was morning and every one was leaving and heading back towards their villages. Oraland tells her that he must report this morning, and that he'll have to say good bye now. He kisses her softly and long, and then embraces her with a tear in his eye. She to is crying and does not want this moment to end. But it has to and Oraland breaks his hold on her and starts to walk away turning once to wave. By the end of the day almost all the Indian tribes have left, and only a few remain still packing up to leave. Custer has just said good bye to the four generals who are escorted out of the valley by a company of the Seventh. With them goes the signed documents of the treaty which will be forwarded to Washington. He has given orders to Reno to break camp and when done to head back to Fort Riley where' he will be waiting for him. Custer asks Oraland to accompany he and Libby and soon they head out for the fort. So, the treaty has been signed!

There is peace in the land, but remember it is only on paper. News of the treaty travels throughout the Indian nations and the the white nation. Men will do what they do and for a while there is peace. The promise that was made about the metal giants not searching out more area in the Indian territories came to be a real problem for the government. Companies back east are promoting land opportunities in the west, and the call for more railroads are getting louder. Five months have gone and it is March of 1868. Throngs of settlers that have converged on the western plains and the Indian raids start up again. The call for help from the army is heard from all over the plains territories and the need for army intervention is the only answer. The Seventh Cavalry for the most part has been inactive in the Fort Riley area of the Kansas territory. Drilling, training, and other duties keep the troopers busy, and Custer takes up a lot of time hunting and reading books. Oraland has requested a leave of absence more than twice and both times turned down. Reason? He's more valuable for training new recruits. Not seeing or hearing from Waynoka is driving him crazy. Soon the Indian raids get closer to the fort and more and more settlers are being killed by raiding parties. Reports have it that the Apache's, Cheyenne, and Sioux tribes are doing most of killing. Oraland can't figure out why the Cheyenne is mentioned in these reports. Black Kettle was emphatic about peace and he knew that the reports had to be false. Again, he asked for leave, but Custer said no, his leadership abilities were more important now than ever. Patrols were sent out again and each experienced fire fights with both large and small groups of warriors. Now the Seventh has been ordered to pursue the hostile tribes, Custer tells his staff at their next meeting. "We will start patrolling the western edges of the territory and work ourselves back to the fort. Reno and Benteen I want you both to take your full companies strength on this detail. Engage the enemy if you must and destroy them. I will take companies I, K, C, M, and B with me and head south and will do a right flank action ending up west of the fort in or around in three weeks. Double the men's rations and each man will be supplied with one hundred rounds of carbine ammunition and eighty rounds of revolver ammunition. Let no hostile get away, understood? This is not going to be a picnic so relay my message that I have just given to each of you and pass it along to your troops".

After his staff was dismissed he motions for Oraland to stay. My boy I know these last few months have been rough on you, but now I need you more than ever. I want you to find Chief Black Kettle and find out what is going on in the Indian nations. Take Charlie with you and may god be with you. "Thank you sir", replies Oraland I'll find Black Kettle and hopefully I'll have good news for you when we meet up again. Now get back to your barracks and prepare for your journey. Custer then salutes Oraland and as he heads out the door he could hear Custer telling him to be careful. When Oraland told Charlie about their mission Charlie remarked that " It will be good to get out of this fort, we've sat to long." Morning came and both were off before mess call was heard. They both couldn't wait to get out of the fort. Charlie told Oraland that the Cheyenne have probably moved their camp with all the fuss that was going on. Their most likely in the southern part of the Oklahoma territory were the whites have not yet tried to settle. Three days have gone by and signs of war parties have Oraland on edge. Charlie feels if they travel by night their chances of encountering hostiles will be zero. There are many warriors with these signs that they have come across and Charlie senses that they are Sioux. Sleep by day and travel by night works, and on the fifth day Charlie sights the Cheyenne village set up in a gorge filled with plenty of grass and a stream running through it. As they approach, as always there is a great commotion in the camp. Both have their arms held high and the sense of personal harm evades both. Not more than three minutes into the camp and Oraland sights Waynoka.

   He dismounts and starts to run towards her. As they meet they hold one another closely and kiss. Joy is written on Waynoka's face as Oraland peers at her. I missed you my love he says to her, and steps back still holding her hands. Then he notices something! Waynoka is a little bigger than the last time they were together. His thoughts are erased when she tells him that they are going to have a child, (na't'ov'oh'eoohe). "A father" he says," I am going to be a father"! All around the onlookers start to laugh at the young couple which makes Oraland feel a little embarrassed. Wow, I am going to be a father, he repeats over and over. Charlie now, still on his horse dismounts and shakes Oraland's hand and congratulates him and Wayonoka. "Thank you my friend" remarks Oraland. When are you due Oraland asks Waynoka? "Three more months and I will present to you your child" she replies. He gives her another hug and whispers in her ear his love for her. Now let us find your father for I have to talk with him about serious matters. She takes Oraland's hand and asks him to walk with her. My father has been so upset and sick(h'otoan'avvom'ohtahe) over the rising warrior attacks on your people. (h'otoan'avvom'ohtahe) He is not the same man you saw last fall. As they enter the chief's tepee Oraland senses something strange. Waynoka was right, Black Kettle is a different man. He sits and greets Oraland and Charlie as though they have just met for the first time. "Chief Black Kettle" Oraland remarks," I have come here today with my great white father's question of who is causing all of the unrest in the territory?

My great white chief Custer is concerned that the Cheyenne has collaborated with the Apache and Sioux on their murder raids against the whites coming into the territory". "My son do you feel the same way as your great white father does", asks Black Kettle? Honorable chief I don't know what to think. I know deep down in my heart that you're a man of peace, but there have been signs of Cheyenne hostility in some of the raids that have taken place. My son and the younger Dog Soldiers grow impatient of the white man's movements into the Cheyenne territories, and those of the Apache and Sioux. I cannot control the will of the younger braves, for they have now look down at the peace treaty that we agreed to last year with disdain. Dignity is one's inner soul and the whites have treated that factor with disrespect. I told you my son a while back that I had a dream that the white man would walk over all the Indian tribes because of the want of land and it is coming true. I do not want war with the long knives and with you my son, but one must do what is right in one's heart. My daughter carries your baby and with that I feel proud, but your people may force me to act in a way that will cause bloodshed between our two peoples and that may affect your feelings for your family. Oraland responds, " Chief Black Kettle I hold the utmost respect for you and your people and especially for your daughter. I'm torn between right and wrong now and god will eventually show me the way, the right way to proceed with my heart. I know the white man's thinking, and no good can come out of this matter without blood. My people are wrong in what they are doing in regards to the railroad, but they have a higher authority in Washington that over sees everything. The politicians are being pushed and a conflict with your people and the other tribes is inevitable. As far as the land treaty now stands I wish I could do more, but I am a lowly Sergeant in the United States Cavalry, and no one is going the listen to me. Maybe my great white father can intercede, but I feel the people in the higher places will stand firm and his voice will even be silenced as well as all the others that want peace. It is with pain in my heart that I must report back to Custer, of what you have told me.

Now looking at Waynoka he addresses Black Kettle on marrying his daughter as the sun sets tomorrow night in the village. I will take care of her and your grandchild he explains to the Chief. Black Kettle replies that he would be happy over the marriage and that he would welcome Oraland into his family not as a long knife, but as a blood brother and as a son. After saying this, Black Kettle takes out his knife, (mochk) and makes a deep slit in the cup of his right hand. He then passes the knife to Oraland who makes a slit in his hand and both grab each other's in a sign of friend ship. As the two stand there, Little Robe steps forward and asks Oraland if he too could be a blood brother of the white man who will be the father of his sisters child. "Sure, Little Robe" remarks Oraland as he passes the knife to him. Without hesitation the young brave makes a slit in his hand and reaches out for Orland to shake. After this he tells Oraland that forever they will be brothers in life and death. A little unsettling, but Oraland accepts Little Robes premise. Waynoka is smiling at the outcome of her father's meeting with Oraland. Now looking at Black Kettle again he asks if the elder would marry them both before the day ends. My enlistment in the army is ending in one month and I have decided to live with my people, the Cheyenne. Everyone around is smiling and are showing their favor on the proposed marriage and of Oraland's decision to live within the village. Even Charlie gets caught up in the festivities.

    He shakes Oraland's hand and gives his approval. "You're doing the right thing my friend he exclaims. You being white and she being Cheyenne will be a test for you both, but I for see nothing but happiness in your future". "Thank you good friend", replies Oraland. Waynoka is now in Oraland's arms and kiss of true love is passed between both. Black Kettle remarks that he will perform the marriage ceremony before the sun goes down and then the village will celebrate into the wee hours of the morning. I must leave you now Or-a-lan-d and make ready for me to be your wife remarks Waynoka. I know you're going to look beautiful my love replies Oraland and gives her another kiss.

    The village all afternoon is very active in the preparing of the marriage. Oraland and Charlie go to the river to bathe and discuss what Black Kettle told Oraland earlier. Charlie now talking of Sitting Bull, says he is a great medicine man. All the tribes look upon him as a great god and his dislike of the whites will lead to more trouble for all sides in the future. Custer must act with caution when dealing with this great chief. He speaks with forked tongue, (v'etanove) and must be dealt with cautiously. "Now Crazy Horse is another matter", remarks Charlie.
    He is nothing but bad. He does not like the white man

and long knives at all. He is evil in every sense and his followers look to him as a warriors, warrior! He cannot be killed they feel. He is always in the thick of the fight they say, and always comes out of battle unhurt. "Somewhat like our commander General Custer "Oraland remarks." Yes, there is a similarity in both" One day I fear they will both be on the same battlefield and nothing but death will come from it. As Charlie is talking of this Oraland gets a strange tingle in his body and it lasts for a few moments. Well my friend looking at Charlie now, I am getting married tonight and nothing can, or no one can ruin my happiness. I wish my family back home could be here, but I know their thoughts are always with me. Norvell, my brother would be real proud right now. After washing up and shaving the two go back to camp and proceed to their tepee. Oraland has a pair of dress trousers, a vest and a white shirt that he had in his saddlebags. Charlie shows him how to get the wrinkles out and Oraland is very grateful. Both relax and take a nap for the rest of the afternoon. Awaking later it's now almost sunset and the village is in full festive mode.

Drums are being played, rattles can be heard, and the sounds of flutes and whistles are in the air. The sound of women and children chanting are also heard. The music is tense, pulsating, and forceful. The men are dancing and a good time is had by all. At the right time Oraland and Charlie come out of their tepee and proceed to the center of the camp where they find a large fire with Black Kettle standing there waiting for them. He has his tribal ceremonial cloths on and looks very distinguished. His wife Medicine Woman is by his side along with Little Robe and three more of his brothers. As Oraland approaches, Black Kettle directs him to stand on his right side, and all are now waiting for Waynoka's appearance. As Black Kettle raises his arms to the sky the music slowly and softly stops. All eyes are on Waynoka's tepee now as she starts to exit. Oraland is lost for words when he sees his future bride coming towards him dressed in a white wedding robe, white buckskin leggings, and white moccasins. She has a beaded headband across her forehead and a lone white feather stands erect from the back of her head from an eagle's wing. Charlie notices Oraland's trance that he's in and gives him a nudge to reawaken his friend. She is now standing next Oraland and both give each other a slight smile.

Black Kettle begins his duties as officiant.

O Great Spirit When you look down onto these two young souls Bless them, their children, through a happy life. May their trails lie straight and level before them. Let them live to be old. Great Spirit for we are all your children and ask these things with good hearts. May the two young hearts be given the ceremonial blankets at this moment. Waynoka's mother steps forward and wraps her daughter with a blue blanket and Little Robe does the same to Oraland. (the blue blankets represent the couples past lives that may have been filled with loneliness, weakness, failures, sorrow, and spiritual depression). Black Kettle now asks the couple to step towards the sacred ring of fire before them.

He then begins the vows of the two:

> May the moon softly restore you by night.
> May the rains wash away your worries
> And the breeze blow new strength into
> Your being and all the days of your life
> May you walk gently through the world
> And know it's beauty
> Now you will feel no rain for each of you
> Will be shelter to the other
> Now you will feel no cold for each of you
> Will be warmth to each other
> Now there will be no more loneliness
> For each of you will be a companion to the other
> Now you are two bodies
> But there is only one life before you
> Go now to your dwelling place to enter
> Into the days of your togetherness
> And may your days be good and long
> Upon the earth

Black Kettle now motions that the two blue blankets be removed from Waynoka and Oraland and one large, (ma'hao'o`) white blanket be wrapped around the two. Black Kettle now blesses the two and remarks that the white blanket represents the couples new way of happiness, fulfillment, and peace. At this point Oraland is dumb struck and Waynoka says to him under a soft voice that you may now embrace and kiss me. (the blanket will remain in their tepee to designate their love for one another when visited by other people). Oraland does kiss his new bride and everyone cheers.

There is great jubilation all around and the two are welcomed by all as they come near to wish the new couple well. Charlie shakes Oraland's hand and remarks, "now you are a true Indian". The village reveled all night enjoying bison, venison, corn, beans, and other Indian delights that Oraland will soon come to like living with the Cheyenne. The couples wedding night was something to be remembered and Oraland could not be any happier. A week has gone by and Charlie tells Oraland that the honeymoon must end and they have to report back to Custer. He's probably worn the planks down an inch in his office by walking back and forth waiting for us. "I know Charlie and we will leave soon", replies Oraland. "You know I am going to be a civilian in another month, how about joining me"? No can do my friend, I still have two years in my enlistment. Maybe I could talk, ('eese) with Custer and he might be able to pull some strings in Washington to get you out earlier, remarks Oraland. Thanks, my brother, but I'll sit it out till it's my time to leave. Oraland tells Waynoka that he must leave in a day and that he'll be back before the fall sets in. I'll be back for good my darling he tells her and we can enjoy the rest of our lives together. " I will wait patiently for you my husband", she remarks. I should be just about ready to have your child when you return and I will be here waiting for you. Soon it was time to leave and all the good byes were said. Little Robe wanted to ride along for protection, but Oraland asks him to watch over his wife. We will be riding by night again and sleeping during the day so as not to alarm any hostiles he remarked to Little Robe. He now embraces Waynoka one more time and kisses her gently and asks her to take care of their child with in her. "I will my love" she replies and with that Charlie and Oraland mount and ride off into the desert once again. This will be the last time I will leave Waynoka he says to himself as they head southeast for Fort Riley. One week goes by and no trouble except for a rattlesnake wanting to crawl into Charlie's bed roll one day when they were resting.

Soon they we're entering the fort and Oraland gave a sigh, longing for Waynoka. They immediately reported to Custer. Now in his presence, Custer tells them he started to worry a little about their safety. I can't afford to lose two of my best scouts. So, what do you have for me in the line of information on the Indian problem? "Well sir the Apache and Comanche are our main worries, but the Ogala's and Sioux are up in arms more so!

The Cheyenne, I should say Chief Black Kettle's group is not as involved as much as the others. This Ogala Chief Crazy Horse has his tribes up in arms over our people settling in his territory. He will stop at nothing to take the lives of innocent civilians to keep his land. He is a great warrior and some have remarked in his circles that he is your double when it comes to fighting and not getting hurt. He takes chances and wins". "My double you say" remarks Custer. This country doesn't need two Custer's and I'll have to see to it that Crazy Horse is stopped and stopped for good. Oraland continues, now this Chief Sitting Bull, well he's another story!

The Lakota Sioux regard him as their god. Their super leader that has big medicine that will destroy the white man. He doesn't like the whites no less the Cavalry and will fight till he's killed. He has charmed other tribes as well, and his aura is evil. "We'll will soon see what fighters these two trouble makers are", remarks Custer! Orders arrived yesterday from Washington and they want the Indian problem out here to go away! "Away sir", asks Oraland. Yes, away, gone, annihilated! "Sir you don't mean destroy the Indian nations do you"? Asks Oraland. "My hands are tied at this point Sergeant", replies Custer. But General the Cheyenne have done nothing wrong. All they want is peace! You met with Black Kettle last year and you knew he was a man of honor. You drank a toast with him, and so did the other Generals. I don't understand my governments thinking!

Sergeant we have been given orders and we must obey them. Now I suggest you and the Corporal here go back to your barracks and rest up, you're going to need it. "Begging the Generals pardon sir" remarks Oraland." My enlistment is up in twenty days and I have decided to leave the army". Churchill, I took you for a career man and you hit me with this resigning business. " I'm sorry sir, but I have my reasons, and in three weeks I'll be a civilian again. Custer now looks at Charlie and asks, "Corporal do you know what is going on here"?

Looking at Oraland now Charlie asks for his forgiveness on what he is about to say to Custer. General the Sergeant has gotten himself married. "Married" replies Custer. Well congratulations my boy who is the lucky girl? Oraland replies, my wife is Waynoka the daughter of Black Kettle. You met her last year at the treaty signing, and you and Mrs. Custer gave us your blessing. "I see, my young friend your dilemma now. I remember the young lady now, but you can't throw your life away on just a girl! "We're having a child in two months sir". Custer is still now, looking out the window at the parade grounds. A child, well that changes everything. I'll see that your transition from soldier to civilian is done very quickly. Now leave me and get your rest. Custer then walks out the rear door of the room and disappears. Charlie looks at Oraland again and says he's sorry for telling the General. Don't worry about it Charlie I am not mad. He would have found out sooner or later any way. I'm glad it happened this way. Now let's get back to the barracks and I think we both could use a little rest. With that they proceeded to their barracks for a long-deserved rest. Custer is now in his parlor at home and he has just told Libby about Oraland. "George their young and in love remember us a few years ago. We felt the same way and no one was going to keep us apart"! I remember Libby, and I still love you to this day.

My problem is that my orders from Washington were specific," ANNIHILATE" the Indians, even the Cheyenne. Oh, George maybe if you talk with Uncle Phil (General Philip Sheridan) he may be able to do something about your orders. "Yes, he may be able to offset the carnage that is coming", replies Custer. I'll telegraph him tomorrow and see if he can intercede with the White House. "See a woman can put worries off to the side if she feels enough love for her man", replies Libby. Custer after hearing this from his wife gets up off his chair and walks over to her and gives her a huge hug and whispers in her ear, I am in love with you madam.

Next day Custer wires Sheridan and waits all day for a reply. Finally, word comes and the White House has given him new orders. The Indians have thirty days to go back to their reservation sites and desist all hostilities. If they are not on their reservation lands at the end of May the army will use force to enact the order. Any Indian nation that does not obey the general orders by the grace period of thirty days will be subject to swift and hostile action by the cavalry. Custer holding the message sends for Oraland to tell him the news. Well Sergeant you can thank Mrs. Custer for Washington's thirty-day delay in the Sevenths orders. Now as I understand you still want out of the army? "I do sir, remarks Oraland.

Well you have a little over three weeks left in your enlistment and I am going to put that time to, I hope good work! I am going to send you and Charlie out again to the Cheyenne and want you to have Black Kettle send out emissaries to all the other Indian nations. You tell him he has been given a grace period of thirty days, give or take a few days because of the late arrival of this message (holding the telegraph message up) and let him know the severity of the consequences if the orders are not obeyed! I do have a heart my boy, but I am a soldier also and will act against any tribe that doesn't take this order seriously. Do I make myself clear? "Very clear sir", replies Oraland. I will on my end here send out also, patrols to the various tribes in the area so as to make sure all parties are on the same page. Now as for you and your new bride Mrs. Custer and I wish you all the best especially with the event of your first new born coming. Now out of character Custer confides with Oraland.

Son please heed the governments orders and my warning. I'll have to do what I am ordered and can't guarantee anything after that. Watch out for your family is what I am trying to say! We live in rough times and may be some day in the future there won't be problems such these. With our two peoples and we'll live together in harmony. So please watch out for yourself. "Thank you, sir, I will", remarks Oraland. Now get out of here, time is wasting and get the job done. Oraland makes his way to his barracks and tells Charlie of the orders given him and within the hour both are on the way for the Cheyenne village. Oraland knows Custer, and he meant what he told him earlier. Custer is a good man, but he still has that beastly side to him.

He will always be a glory hunter and will let nothing to come between him and his career. The Indian tribes must obey the governments orders or a blood bath will prevail on the plains. Custer in the meantime calls for a staff meeting and puts the whole fort on alert. He has put his troops on standby and to be ready to move out on a moment's notice if the tribes do not adhere to the official orders in thirty days. You have time to prepare for this detail he tells his staff, so keep on the men's backs and make sure, they are ready to move out against the Indians. Four days have gone by and Oraland and Charlie sight the Cheyenne encampment. The news of their arrival hit the village earlier and Waynoka and her brother are on the edge of the camp to welcome her husband and friend. Oraland jumps off his horse and takes Waynoka in his arms and embraces her ever so gently. They kiss and hug some more then Little Robe now present gives Oraland a friendly greeting. Charlie is now standing there talking with some of the other tribesmen. Orland then tells Waynoka that he must talk with her father right away. They walk to his tepee and enter. The old man is sitting in front of a small fire and gives the peace sign as Oraland and the others enter.

What a surprise to see you my son so soon after your last visit, I see there is something of importance you want to discuss? Yes, great one, I have orders from my great white chief Custer for you. The people of my country back in Washington want revenge for all the white deaths that have taken place in the last five months. But my son I told you that the Cheyenne have had no interactions with the other tribes when it came to those deaths. I understand great one, but my people don't want to hear that! They want the killing to stop, ('ene-) and have given a dead line to be followed and if not, more blood will be spilled. All tribes have thirty, (na'n'o'e) days to go back to their treaty lands and the raids and killing must stop. If not, my great white Chief Custer will come down hard on any tribe that has not adhered to the order. Black Kettle you must make hast with emissaries to all the tribes you can reach and tell them of the graveness of this order.

Time cannot be wasted in this matter and you must act right away. I hear it in your voice, ('enose'hane) my son that this is very important and I will act right away. Looking at his son Little Robe now, Black Kettle directs him to call all the elders and young braves to his tepee. He gets up and goes outside and waits for all to assemble.

With every one standing before him now he directs all to

search out their Indian brethren, the Apache, the Arapaho, the Comanche, the Sioux, and the Ogala and to tell them of the order to return to their reservation lands and to stop the killing raids on the whites. They have one full moon to do this, and if not, the long knives will come and force them back. Now go like the wind and tell all of this everyone. If they do not go back much blood will be spilled on both sides, so go now and warn everyone!

The camp is lively now and horsemen are heading out of camp in all directions. Oraland now looking at Black Kettle with Waynoka beside him asks that he take his people back to their reservation lands. I am afraid of what will happen to all my people if you do not act on this right away. My wife is expecting, (hom'oset`ano) and I do not want her in harm's way as well as all the village, so please I beg of you to return to treaty lands. My son I will do this for you and my daughter. My people will return to the treaty lands before the moon is full again and may this show your great white chief Custer that we want peace. "Good then", replies Oraland. Let your daughter and myself now enjoy a few moments together and then I will help you plan the return of your people. Charlie is now talking with the elder Running Deer and tells Oraland to go and spend some time with his wife.

We must get back to the fort in a day or so Charlie, so relax a bit. Alone now Oraland tells Waynoka that he missed her terribly and that his enlistment is almost up. I am worried about you though, he tells her. I want nothing awful to happen to you or our child when I return back to the fort, so please press your father to act quickly on returning to the treaty land. Nothing is going to happen to me or our child Or-a-lan-d so please don't worry. My father will take good care of us. I wish your bother could have stayed behind, but he was the first out of the camp when your father gave the order to seek out the other tribes. He'll be fine my husband she remarks. They kiss and talk about the baby inside of her. Will it be a boy or girl? It doesn't matter, he tells her as long as the child is as beautiful as his or her mother. They embrace again and hold each other tight. " Wild horses couldn't keep me away", replies Oraland. After a day has gone by Oraland, tells Waynoka that it was time to leave again. Both he and Charlie have to make haste back to the fort to tell Custer of Black Kettles efforts in talking with the other tribes.

With kisses now a few hours old, Oraland thinks only of returning back to the village in a few weeks free of the army and Custer. It's starting to get colder each night, and for Indians that means finding a place of refuge for the winter months is essential. Black Kettle has a lot on his mind in regards to his people and his feelings towards Oraland and his daughter. Yes, Custer was on his mind also, but he is not as important as his loved ones. This is going to prove to be bitter sweet in the coming months for the old warrior and his village.

The old man has family on his mind and without guidance, his decisions will be the death of him and his loved ones. Meanwhile Charlie and Oraland not two days out run into trouble on their way back to the fort. A war party from the Apache has been on their tail for a day now and the two decide to stand and fight. With a multitude of rocks around them they decide to fight it out. They dismount and take cover behind a group of large boulders and have the sun to their backs. As the Apache warriors approach both take a number count of at least thirty. As the Apache warriors grow closer Oraland and Charlie wait until they are with in seventy yards and open up with their Sharps carbines. Every time each puts a round in the chamber of the weapon and fires it, a warrior would fall. With the sun in their eyes the Indians were confused and disoriented and took heavy loses. It was like swatting flies Oraland commented to

Charlie after the fight. Wave after wave the Apache tried to breech the two troopers, but to no avail. Finally, they gave up and rode off to the west and were soon gone. Charlie counted over twenty dead and Oraland commented on the will power of the Apache. They don't like us Charlie said, and god help those settlers out there who don't know the right way to defend themselves.

Now they have to make up for lost time and again head out for Fort Riley. The rest of the ride was calm and they didn't run into any more trouble. Soon they spotted the fort in the distance and in another twenty minutes would find them in a safe haven. Oraland was exhausted as well as Charlie, but they both reported to Custer right away. Again, they were welcomed by their dashing commander and told him of their trip. "I hope Black Kettle can work his magic", remarks Custer. One of our patrols ran into some trouble last week about sixty miles out and came into contact with a large concentration of Apache, Comanche, and Cheyenne dog soldiers. I lost three good men to those red devils, but we managed to kill over thirty of their kind. "Cheyenne sir", asks Oraland? Yes, and they were out for blood as well as the two other tribes they were with. "They were probably from the southern Cheyenne nation that Black Kettle talked to me about. I would not blame him for the terror that this other group is creating sir! They are Indians son and to the government they're all the same! "Now we sit back and wait to see if the Indian has sense enough to obey the orders", remarks Custer. I put the fort on alert when you two left and the troops are prepared to ride at a moment's notice, so I suggest you two rest up and prepare your selves as well. "Sir my enlistment is up in eleven days, so may I prepare for my transition back into civilian life"? "Under any other circumstances I would say yes Churchill, but I'll need your help if a problem erupts"!

Disappointed Oraland replies "very good sir I am at your

disposal". Well rest up now and relax a bit. Custer now addressing Charlie, "Charlie I am going to promote you to a Sergeant at this point, because of the impending loss of Churchill here, so report to the quartermaster's headquarters and pick up your stripes, you've earned them two-fold".

Oraland congratulates Charlie as well as Custer and both exit Custer's quarters. "A Sergeant now, how about that", remarks Charlie as he and Oraland walk over to the quartermaster's quarters. Oraland's time in the army came due, and the Seventh would not be the same without him. Custer had him over for a quiet meal with Libby the night before his discharge and each company commander stopped in to say good bye. Major Reno and Captain Benteen had other ideas though, free liquor! Both were on their way to becoming class A drunks in their careers and enjoyed each other's company only when drinking. The seventh had its drinking problem, but these two officers took it to another level!

Oraland thanked each for their support during his service with the Seventh and gave them his respect even though he had warned Custer of their disapproval of him. Custer asked what plans he had, and Oraland answered the question straight forward. "I plan to spend the rest of my life with my wife's people and our child sir. I have been very fortunate in being welcomed into their culture and have been accepted as one of their own". Custer becomes a little uneasy when he heard this come out of Oraland's mouth, but he still has respect for this young lad. Please do me a very big favor Oraland he asks. "What is it sir" replies Oraland"?

Watch over your family and always be aware that things may occur that are out of our hands. With this Indian problem I won't say I am happy with your taking up with them, but all I ask is take care of yourself. Your brother saved my life and I feel powerless in trying to save yours. You're a good scout and I know you'll use your knowledge to watch over your family, so just beware in the coming months. Libby sitting there now interrupts and says to her husband, "George the boy will be fine, you took him under your wing and he has grown into a fine young man, so let him go now and don't worry"! Looking at Libby, Custer gives her a smile, and says, "your right my dear so be on your way my boy and good luck to you".

"I'll always remember the good times with the Seventh sir", comments Oraland. "You helped make the regiments history and I will always be indebted to you", remarks Custer. With that Oraland thanks both again and exits the home and heads for the barracks where he will sleep one last time. In the morning after saying good bye to Charlie he heads out in pursuit of his new life with his new family. He is lucky and doesn't run into any Indian trouble on the way and soon he is riding into the Cheyenne camp. Waynoka is there waiting for him as well as Black Kettle and Medicine Woman. After a loving kiss, he is welcomed by all around. He feels good, he feels important he feels alive!

Waking up next morning a strange feeling came over him. Now sitting up on his blanket, he thought to himself, why wasn't the camp packing up when he returned yesterday? He was so happy to be back that Custer's warning skipped his mind. After dressing he tells Waynoka he'll be back as soon as he talks with her father. Looking for Black Kettle now, Oraland is frantic and finally finds the old man standing at the river's edge. He approaches the chief and asks why the village hasn't started to pack up yet? My son do not worry the long knives won't attack us now because we have one of their own among us, you! You are good friends with your great white chief and he wouldn't do you no harm especially in our midst. "No great one" Oraland remarks! He will come with force to drive you to your reservation. Women and children are here amongst us and I don't think he would be that reckless to cause any harm to them. Your wrong great one, he will use force and many will suffer, maybe die because you do not heed his warnings. Why may I ask did you send out peace parties to the other tribes concerning Custer's orders? I did try to contact the other tribes and all feel the same way about the treaty that we signed. The white man's government lied and lied to everyone that was there that day of the signing. My son I know you are not like the others, but you must open your eyes to the truth. Your people lied to us and to you! We will move the village, but it won't be on reservation land. It will be the land of my fathers, and his father's father. We will hunt the buffalo and fish the streams, ('o'hek`eso) that the Great Spirit gave to us many moons ago. It is our land, and we will continue to be its protectors.

Oraland senses that his conversation isn't going anywhere at this point so he excuses himself and heads back to his tepee. "He won't listen" he tells Wayonka, "and all will pay for his foolish ideals". "I have tried to talk with him myself she says, but with no success. Then we, you and I have to leave. Custer will come and I don't want anything happening to you or our child. Our child will be with us in one month and maybe my father was right. Custer will not harm us with you here! You don't know the man I know Waynoka, he will. Orders are orders and he will not stray from them. He does everything by the book. Listen now, we will stay here until the baby is born, (hesta) and then we'll move back to the reservation land.

The army is going to be very busy with the other tribes also and maybe we'll be lucky and they will come much later down the road. Now what do say we take a walk. It will be good for you and the baby and maybe we can clear our heads. "I'd like that" Waynoka replies. In the coming days nothing is said of or mentioned about moving the village and life just keeps going on. The thirty-day order has passed and Custer has his hands full with Indians from the other tribes. The raids continue and more people are killed. The Seventh's full attachment is busy trying to push the Indians back on their reservations through brutal force and are being driven into exhaustion chasing the Indians around and around especially the Apache. Not a good sign for Custer and his career. It is late July now and one-week overdue Waynoka finally gives birth to a son. Oraland is ecstatic and is so happy. The proud father stands in front of his tepee and shows off the infant to all that come around. The proud parents have decided to name their son "Little George" His grandfather, (nam-shimi), Black Kettle has a grin on his face that his wife Medicine Woman has not seen in years. "What a happy day for the young people", remarks Medicine Woman.

"My grandson will grow up to be a great chief", replies Black Kettle. Oraland now returns to the tepee and Waynoka where he lays the infant down next to her. What a handsome son you have given me my love looking into her eyes. "He will grow up strong and smart like his father", replies Waynoka. Oraland has never been so happy. Being a father comes with a lot of responsibility and he wants ever so much to be the best at it. His dreams of a family have come true and nowhere in his mind are the thoughts of Custer. Four months have come and gone and the village is getting ready for the winter season. They have slowly walked and rode their way to a place called Washita. It has good running water and the grass lands for one thousand ponies is excellent. It's snowing, (`eho'e`eto) and the village inhabitants are trying to keep warm and comfortable in their tepees. Winter is here and so being with it, darkness and death! On a cold day's late afternoon Oraland has gone to the river, (s'e'onea'hasen'e) to see if he can catch a fish or two for supper that evening. He sits there by the river bank and senses something is not right. Someone or something is watching him. His being out of the army now for almost five months now hasn't cost him his training in knowing when something isn't right. Staring out and around ever so slowly he catches sight of a figure of a man to his right. He gets up and makes believe he has caught a large fish that is fighting its way downstream towards the unknown figure. When almost five feet from the stranger Oraland throws himself on the individual.

To his surprise he finds no other than Charlie Goes Slow. "Charlie why are you hiding like this", he asks of his old friend? Oraland I came to warn you and your family. "Warn me, warn me of what"? "Custer", is Charlie's answer. He's not more than ten miles away and plans on attacking your village within hours, as soon as the sun rises. "No, it can't be", a confused Oraland replies. Yes, he has five companies of troopers with him and they mean to destroy your village and take all who survive back to the reservation. "He would not attack this village knowing that I am here with my family", replies Oraland.

I tried to tell him Oraland, but he mistakes your village for the southern Cheyenne that have been doing all the raids. Their dog soldiers have been tracked this way and he has it in his mind that your village is what he's looking for. I came here to warn you and your family so you can flee, (h'om`estov) before his troopers come. They mean to kill Oraland, and I could not see that happen to my friend. "Thank you my brother", replies Oraland. Come with us and leave the insanity of Custer. No, my friend I must go back, but I will be out of the way when they attack. Now please go Oraland and save you hide and those you love, please go now. With that they shake hands and Oraland takes off running towards his tepee. Inside he tells Waynoka of Charlie's warning and within minutes they are ready to flee into the hills. We must try and to get your father and mother to come along, he remarks to her. In Black Kettles presence now, he begs the old man to follow him and Waynoka and to live another day." No, my son", he replies. "My people are here and I must be with them. Looking at Waynoka now holding his grandson, he says to her, go with your husband daughter and raise my only grandson to know that I was a great chief among his people. With Medicine Woman beside him now he tells Oraland to go and run like the deer from the long knives. Be safe and always remember the things that I have taught you. You will always be my blood brother.

Oraland turns to Waynoka now and says, "let us go now". They make their way up the side of a mountain that is half a mile from the camp. On foot and not horse, Oraland doesn't want to leave horse prints that the other Seventh's scouts can pick up. Several hours have passed and daylight is starting to come up. They have been traveling all night and Oraland feels their out of danger at this point. There is a strange stillness in the air and the village is quiet and people are still sleeping. The quiet is suddenly broken by the sounds of bugles sounding the charge.

Troopers ride into the village and converge on it from all sides. Black Kettle and his wife were already up and dressed and are seen trying to escape across the river, but both were shot down and killed in volley fire by a squad of troopers waiting for fleeing survivors. Their bodies hit the cold water and float downstream until they are snagged by a dead tree that had fallen in the water months earlier. Across, back and forth thru the camp troopers ride down women and children fleeing. Young braves who come out of their tepees with bows and arrows are shot down almost immediately as they come into view of the soldiers. There is screaming everywhere and the carnage quickens at a faster rate. Custer is leading the charges thru the village and at one point pulled his revolver and shot a brave who had just shot an arrow at another trooper. As the action continues one of Custer's Captains is seen chasing twelve to fifteen Indians down the river's edge out of camp. This is Major Elliott and he has ten men with him and they are in hot pursuit of the red savages. What he doesn't know though is that it is a trap and about two miles downstream the Indians turn and come at the detail with force from all sides.

The Major, one Joel Elliott is killed almost immediately and the other troopers are brought down one by one as they try to escape. The Indians do not lose any time in scalping the dead, or dying troopers and some mutilation of their bodies occurs. They look like porcupines lying down with twenty or so arrows sticking out of their bodies. Weeks later after the battle, the troopers remains will be found and the ungodly sight of Major Elliott's body. His head is bashed in so bad that even his closest friend, Captain Benteen could not identify him. This would prove later on in years to come for one of the suspected reasons of Benteen's not aiding Custer at the Little Big Horn. With the village brought to its knees now Custer collects all his prisoners, a total of fifty-one women and twenty children. More than one hundred braves were killed including Black Kettle and his wife.

When Custer found out that it was Black Kettles village his heart grew sullen. He immediately orders all to look for the remains of Oraland and his wife. He had been warned that the camp was a friendly village, and not that of the southern Cheyenne that he thought was occupying the area. He didn't heed the warnings, and his lust for glory proceeded his now mistaken actions of the friendly camp. He was troubled when he saw the bodies of Black Kettle and Medicine Woman. He had made a bad mistake, but his reputation and the need to wipe out the killers of innocent people would outweigh any one's ill thoughts of him. He felt relieved when Oraland's body was not found or Waynoka's, and guessed that they had escaped or maybe were not in camp when the attack was executed. Custer still not thinking rationally orders the killing of the over eight hundred ponies captured after the battle. He feels that the Indians will need horses and his killing these would put a hardship on future raids. The sound of death once more fills the air as the screaming ponies are shot in multitudes. In the valley where the camp is located, Oraland and Waynoka have been hearing echoes of gunfire for the last few hours. As they make their way through the gorges and hills the sound is constant, and then as it started there is stillness. They both know that something bad has happened back at their village and only know that they are safe and their child is safe as well. Custer in the meantime has ordered one of the scouts, to try and find Oraland.

The scout picks up the couple's trail quickly and starts to pursue ever so slowly. He's good at what he does and looks for every sign that could lead him to them. He has determined that there are only two people on foot and their trail is only a few hours old. Oraland thought he had hid their trail pretty good, but this scout was a little keener. Within an hour the scout was on their trail like a dog stalking a rabbit. Oraland had a weird feeling about the surroundings around him. He knew the area pretty well, but in the back of his mind something wasn't right. Oraland now thinking to himself, "Custer had to know it was Black Kettles village he was raiding, but why would he do such a thing knowing I was there"! Any way his family is safe and he would do anything to protect them. It is starting to snow a little heavier now because of the higher elevation and their tracks are becoming more visible as they continue to climb the mountain. Custer now is rounding up all the survivors of his reckless attack and both Reno and Benteen are giving him a hard time about the engagement. Benteen wanted permission to look for the detail that was observed during the battle chasing hostiles down the river. Custer's orders were no, and this left Benteen with a bad taste for his commander. He was ordered to burn all the tepees and to bury the dead Indians. Reno in the meantime was putting this disaster down on paper and later would bring it up in a court of inquiry against Custer. Meanwhile the scout pursuing Oraland now picks up the couples tracks and knows he's not too far from finding the couple. He has his revolver drawn and anticipates coming into contact with the couple any moment. Ever so slowly his movement becomes, and he is looking all around for any sign that would give them away. Passing thru a small gap, he now senses something is wrong!

Within a moment he is surprised by being jumped on by Oraland who was waiting for his stalker. The scout by the force of the impact drops his gun and the two begin to fight with great rage. The snow is now coming down heavier and the two figures can just about make each other out. Wrestling and hitting each other the scout now gets the upper hand and has found his pistol and points it at Oraland who is now getting up off the ground. "Haun", blurts out Oraland! "Yes, it is me Churchill, and I have been ordered to take you back, but I have other ideas for you my Medal of Honor friend! I never liked you from the day I met you back in Texas", he replies. "What are you going to shoot me, you low life", asks Oraland. "With pleasure my friend," now as he cocks the revolver hammer back! The air is still and the snow has let up a little and all of a sudden, a shot breaks the silence, POW!

Both men are facing one another when one body falls forward and hits the ground, (hoi-vi) dead. Oraland stunned, looks around and sees his wife holding his Sharps carbine with a little stream of smoke coming out of the barrel. He stands there a moment and then rushes over to her and takes her into his arms. She drops the weapon and embraces her husband back and kisses him. "Oh Waynoka" he remarks. "He was a bad man and I am glad he is dead", she replies.

"He was an angry man and he will not be missed by any one that I know", remarks Oraland. Let me now get rid of the body and collect all his personal gear. When it starts to get warm in the spring the wildlife will take care of the remains. You go back to Little George now and mother him while I do this deed. Waynoka layed the baby under an evergreen tree and made sure he was warm before she had helped Oraland out with Haun's body. The army may send out a search party looking for Haun, but all that's gone on down in the valley will take away from his missing. Custer's hands are full and looking for Haun won't be one of his priorities. After disposing of Haun's body the two now climb the mountain once more with a little more vigor.

Waynoka knows of an area north west of where they are that no white man has ever seen and both agree that is where they will live and bring up their child. The snow starts to come down a little more heavily, but the two slowly make their way without trouble. Two days have now passed and Oraland and his family finally reach the beautiful valley that Waynoka had talked about so much. Plenty of water and local game have been spotted, beavers, deer, rabbit, and elk, (mo-i) Oraland feels this is an ideal spot to live. They discuss on how they will construct a temporary living quarter for the time being and agree on using downed trees and branches. Timber is plentiful and it doesn't take the two long to put up a large hut that will comfort the three from natures elements. When spring sets in he plans on building a permanent cabin that will that will be more comfortable. He's sure they are safe and the use of a weapon doesn't bother him. Later he will construct a bow and arrow, (maahe) which Little Robe taught him how to build and he will primarily use those when he hunts. Meanwhile back at the village, Custer orders his troops out of the valley after receiving reports from his scouts of Indian movement to his right flank about ten miles out. He doesn't want to confront the red savages after what had transpired two days earlier in the camp. All the dead had been buried and all that was left was burnt tepees still allowing a small cinder to erupt in fire now and then. It would take a week to get back to Fort Riley and the troops were eager to start. Custer sent Reno and two companies ahead a day earlier to act as a point and has Benteen and two other companies follow him up from the rear. He is in the middle with six of the remaining companies along with all the captives from the village. It is told that, and believed that he took up a romance with one of the surviving squaws, and back at the fort month's later she gave birth to a boy of fair complexion. Custer was open with his antics and didn't seem to mind the rumors that spread thru his ranks.

Libby was also well aware of her husband's exploits and didn't seem to take them seriously. With the Cheyenne cut to pieces now, the army was able to focus on the Comanche nation. In the coming month's Custer's troops were seen all over the territory, but with little luck in coming in contact with any hostiles. Oraland and Waynoka by this time have made a comfortable home for themselves and are very happy. Little George is getting bigger each day and is starting to walk. Spring is almost over and Oraland has collected deer, (mehe) buffalo and bear hides and he and Waynoka have constructed a fine large cabin. There have been no signs of a living soul all these month's in the valley and life is good for the two. He doesn't miss his past life and his thoughts are only for his family. At one point he took a journey back down the mountain to the burnt-out village. He was angered at what he saw and vowed revenge in some way or another against the army for what they did. While there he almost came into contact with a small band of Arapaho dog soldiers, but evaded them. They didn't see him and they just kept on their way heading in a south west direction. After they had long been gone he found the large mass grave that the army constructed for the dead and stood there for a few moments and said a prayer or two over their remains. He knew that Black Kettle and Medicine Woman were buried there also because of the articles he noticed that were placed on the grave. He knew that Waynoka would want to know of the fate of her mother and father and his finding their resting place would give him a little more ease of telling her. What a crime he said to himself. All these innocent people dead, and for what? He now wondered what had happened to Little Robe and if he had survived the battle?

Anger grew every moment thinking about his blood brother, but now it was time to return to Waynoka, so he left the scared village with reverence. Climbing the mountain, he passed the location of his fight with Haun and he took a moment to try and locate his body, but he was right, the animals had found it and his remains were not to be found except for a bone or two strewn here and there. For a moment he thought of the first time they had met, and the unpleasant exchange they had, but god willed his soul and Oraland proved to be the better man. Back at his lodge now, Waynoka welcomed him with an embrace and kiss. "I missed you my husband", she tells him. Oraland tells her of her parent's fate and comforts her. She is a strong woman and take the news bravely and asks of her brother's fate as well. "I believe Little Robe escaped the fighting" he tells her and that there were no signs of his demise that he could find. He is a brave and strong warrior and I know in my heart that he lives. Now my beautiful wife, I to love you, and our son and we will make it through whatever comes our way. The great spirit will watch over our family and keep us all from harm. "How is Little George", he asks her staring at the infant. "He's fine", my husband. He slept, (s'ohpenome) all night and feed really good this morning. Let him sleep, (t'o'eva''o) my love, you'll have plenty of time to hold him later. You're a good woman Waynoka, and a good mother, I love you. "I too love you my husband ", she remarks. Winter came and the month's lingered on. Oraland became a trapper now and had acquired over one hundred animal pelts. When spring came he hoped to sell them for money at the annual hide auction held outside of one of the trading posts. The army in the meantime was bringing Custer up on charges of killing Indian men and women at Washita without due cause. The charges were brought forth by Captain Benteen, who wanted justice for his friend Major Elliott who died at the Washita. All accounts of the Battle of The Washita were recorded from survivors and troopers who were present that bloody day, and by Reno who had written down all of the battle actions in his note pad.

By the end of the hearings Custer was found not guilty of murder and was released, still as a Colonel in the Seventh Cavalry. During the trial when it was learned that this Cheyenne village was not responsible for all the killings in the territory, Custer reflected on Oraland and wondered what became of him? Did he survive or was he not in the camp when his troops attacked it? He missed his head scout, but friend and confident more.

For several years more, the Indian problem in the western territories continued and Custer and the Seventh got their fill of blood. The Indian was elusive to the troops sent after them, and the government was getting upset with the army not settling the situation. It was 1874 now and Custer is ordered by now elected President Grant, to head up an expedition in the Black Hills territories of South Dakota and Montana. The Seventh is ordered to Fort Abraham Lincoln, in the Dakota territory and will be stationed there permanently with one thousand troops strong, he was ordered to find "GOLD" in the Indian held territories and to report any other expeditionary finds to Washington.

This detail was a relief to the troops who had their fill off chasing Indians all over the country. Custer used this time to hunt and fish the lands of the Indian and raped the natural resources that belonged to the Indians. Hundreds of buffalo were killed and the spoils of war that belonged to the Indians were taken by the cavalry. Gold was found, but only a small amount that didn't mean much.

Greed was everywhere and the killing of innocent people still continued after Custer's return. Oraland, Waynoka, and eight-year-old Little George were now back with what was left of their Cheyenne tribe and tried to guide their village in the ways of the whites which resulted in many arguments. Many of the Indians could not forget what had happened at the Washita and were not happy with the whites. On many occasions Oraland came so close to Custer and was tempted to approach the once mentor of his life, but rebuffed the chance. Hatred for the long knives ran rampant throughout the Indian nations and things were not getting any better for them. The chiefs were weary of the conditions that followed them from the treaty signing to their now unlivable conditions. Broken promises were once again the main problem.

This all changed when gold was found in the back hills of Montana in January of 1876. Hordes of prospectors pounced upon the territory looking for the yellow stone that the Indian knew too well was on their land. Death and destruction followed each camp of these leaches who were driven to find the gold stone. Oraland tried to stay out of the politics of the white mans greed, but his village wanted more, revenge on the long knives. Little Robe who survived the Washita massacre wanted revenge for his parent's deaths and had the younger braves all up in arms with the army. Oraland couldn't change his mind, and blood revenge was all the young brave wanted. With the army once again called in to quell the problem, Oraland could not stay away and do nothing to help his people. He elected in early May of 1876 to go to Fort Lincoln to try and talk peace with Custer. When Custer heard that his old friend was inside the fort looking for him he was over joyed. It had been eight years since they were in each other's company and he couldn't wait to see his old friend.

Standing now in front of his old commander he felt contempt. Custer acted as if nothing had happened between the two and reached out to shake Oraland's hand. Oraland pulled back and asked Custer why he had whipped out his village eight years earlier. Trying to duck the question Custer again tried to talk with his friend. "I was ordered to do what I did and have regretted the battle each day since it took place", replied Custer. "Battle" Oraland shouts out," it was a massacre of women and children, and of old people. How dare you stand there and justify that day as a battle"! Custer comes back angry now and remarks, "don't you dare judge me you Indian lover. Your people won't and will not obey the governments orders and must be treated the way they act". It's their land General and they will fight for it with their last breath if it comes to that. "Black Kettle only wanted peace and your troopers shot him down like a dog. Shame on you and your government, and may you all go to hell where you belong", replies Orland. "Hell" remarks Custer! We're all going to hell and the day is getting closer". "It is General", Oraland replies, because the Indian nations have had enough of empty promises and have lost enough people due to your governments Ill disrespect for their lively hood. Treaty after treaty has been broken, not by my people, but by your damn government. I'm here today to warn you, that if you persist in hunting us down like animals you will bury yourselves. The nations of all tribes will gather and the long knives will be no more. "Are you threatening me Churchill", asks Custer? "General at this very moment all the great tribes of the plains are gathering as one. No army on earth can defeat them combined, so I warn you and your government, leave us alone and let us live in peace, take it any way you want General", replies Oraland. Major Reno who is present and getting more restless at this kind of talk tries to settle things down, but Custer tells him to be quiet. "Reno, I know how to handle the Indians and this so called civilian standing before us". Go back to your tribe and continue to live without harm on your reservation land. General I just told you that the Indian will not obey your orders, and are ready to die for their land and holy beliefs. The great spirit has told us that there will be much blood spilled and that your troopers will be destroyed if you come for us, so stay away. Custer now getting angrier, tells Oraland to go now. "I will be very upset if I find you, my friend on the field of battle", remarks Custer. I will go now, but with a warning General, don't step onto our land! It is ours and the great spirit will protect us from harm. Custer snaps back, "then go now and I hope our next meeting will be a more pleasant one". After Oraland leaves the room Reno looks at Custer and says," if I see that Indian lover on the field of battle, I'll kill him myself". With that Custer shouts at Reno to get out of his presence. Oraland now standing outside runs into his old friend Charlie.

They stand and talk for a while. Charlie reenlisted and has decided to make the army a career. Oraland tells Charlie of the conversation with Custer, but to no avail would he listen to his warnings of war. Charlie puts his hand on Oraland's shoulder and tells his friend that he should go back to his people and prepare them for the worst, if he feels that this is what the great spirit has in store for his Cheyenne brothers. "I must follow my destiny just as you must follow yours", replies Charlie. "I don't see any other way out of this situation, except for one last great battle between the long knives and our people. My friend if we should meet on the field of battle please know that I respect you and will always look upon our days together as happy days, there will be no sorrow", remarks Charlie. "Good bye my friend" replies Oraland as he now heads for his horse and rides out of the fort with a heavy heart. Two weeks have passed and on the eighteenth of May, 1876 General Terry has been ordered to leave Fort Lincoln to pursue the Indians.

Custer's whole Seventh Cavalry are riding with him as well as two regiments of infantry, two batteries of artillery, and a company of four Gatling guns, in all over two thousand strong. Terry's column will head northwest towards the Big Horn River some four hundred miles away. General George Crook's troops also totaling over one thousand troops will leave Fort Fetterman in the Dakota territory and head north towards the Big Horn along the Rose Bud Creek. Crook with five companies of infantry and fifteen companies of cavalry, along with two hundred Shoshone and Crow Indians felt well suited for the battles to come. General John Gibbon's will leave Fort Ellis in Montana and will head in an easterly route towards the Big Horn with the Seventh U.S. Infantry and four companies from the Second U. S. Cavalry. The plan is to have all three columns hook up at the Little Big Horn River around the twenty sixth or twenty seventh of June. From there they can converge on the Indians in a three-point attack and once and for all put the Indian problem to bed. President Grant with generals Sherman, and Sheridan came up with the idea of attacking the Indian gathering, which Oraland eluded to Custer weeks earlier and decided that they would once and for all crush the Indian spirit with all the western troops available. Another feather in my hat thought Custer as he rode out of Fort Lincoln on that day in May. Meanwhile Oraland, now at the Little Big Horn encampment has told the chiefs of all the tribes of his visit with Custer and all want war! In a combined council of all the great chiefs of the Arapahoes, Northern Cheyenne, Two Kettles, Washpekute, Brule', Ogala, Sans Arc, Minneconjou, Blackfoot, and the Hunkpapa Sioux, and, Lakota Sioux, war was voted on by all. The peace council was out numbered, and was helpless in procuring a peace settlement. The calls for revenge of Black Kettle and other notables of the Indian race echoed throughout the meeting. Sitting Bull, the great chief of the Lakota Sioux spoke up and talked of having a vision the night before where the long knives were all destroyed in one last great battle. All the whites died he told the other great chiefs with all the Indian nations doing the killing. Oraland stood fast in trying to sway the talk on war, but his calls fell on deaf ears.

   He had become respected throughout all the nations for his honesty and love for the Indian people. His words were passed from tribe to tribe by chief Black Kettle when he was alive and Oraland won the respect of all, even though he was white. So here he stands alone, even his blood brother Little Robe has fought against him. He, Little Robe most of all stood out amongst the others in wanting war. "My life will not be whole again, until I kill the long knives who murdered my father and mother". Chief Crazy Horse echoed his words and the vote as to whether war or peace was taken. WAR! (h'esem`ahoh'enoot`tse) was voted on and all were joyous, except a few. Oraland is back in his tepee with Waynoka when Little Robe entered and asked to be heard. He wanted revenge for the killings of his parents, that's all he said. Waynoka would not listen to him. "I loved our father and mother Little Robe with a strong heart, but they will not come back. My husband has tried to talk reason with the long knives, but his words have fallen on deaf ears such as yours and no good can come from war with the whites. Little Robe is now furious that his sister will not see his way. My sister I love you and I respect your husband, my blood brother on the way you feel, but I must go where my heart leads me. War is the only way, and I will gladly die in battle to revenge our parents. Oraland now speaks up, "Little Robe you are my brother and I pray to the great spirit that he will protect you in battle. I understand how you feel and I will always be your brother, whatever happens". Oraland is now standing by Waynoka and asks Little Robe one more time to reconsider. "No, my brother, my future has been cast and I must play out what the great spirit has instructed me to do". With that he gives both the peace sign and leaves the tepee. Looking now at Waynoka, Oraland takes her in his arms and says, "I did the best I could do, Waynoka".

I know you did she replies and holds his body tight. Little George meanwhile is taking this all in and asks if his father is going to kill the long knives with his uncle? Oraland has been so busy with talking peace and forgot about his son. "Little George listen to your father, war is not the right way to decide differences. Your grandfather was a great chief and was well respected, (e'hahtov) among all tribes. All he wanted was to live in peace and no more. You must find it in your heart to search out your feelings and not to hate, just for the sake of hating. No, I will not go with your uncle, (n`ax''ane) to kill the long knives. I will remain here to protect you and your mother from any one or thing that threatens our home. I too have peace in my heart and want peace for all also". Kneeling down now and with both hands on his son's shoulders and looking into his eyes, Oraland pleads with his son to find peace within himself, please understand! A week later on June the seventeenth, one thousand Indians from the Cheyenne, Ogala, and Lakota tribes came into contact with General Crook's column at the Rosebud Creek, just one hundred miles from the Little Big Horn. Crook held out attack, after attack from the Indians who were led by Chief Crazy Horse. Crook had his cavalry, along with the infantry spread out in a half mile skirmish line. The Indians were relentless in their charges on the positions of the soldiers, but never over took one. Crazy Horse finally withdrew from the battle and the out come was, the army lost forty-one men and the Indians lost thirty braves. As this battle was called "The Battle of The Rose Bud". Both sides claimed victory, but Crook during the siege had already started to with draw his troops before the Indians did. He retreated downstream and spent the next two weeks trying to recoup from the battle. So much for aiding the other regiments heading for the Little Big Horn! Meanwhile, Crazy Horse made his way back up to the Little Big Horn, and his so-called victory over the long knives was a driving force that instilled every young brave.

   The large encampment that numbered over ten thousand was now alive with activity preparing for war. Talks of war rumbled through the large village and the young were anxious to do battle with the long knives. Crazy Horse's talk of defeating Crook and his column only incited the masses. The next day scouts alerted the camp that a large column of long knives where headed their way from the northeast. This would-be Terry's and Custer's column's and the Indian chief's felt it would take Terry another three to four days to reach the river, so there wasn't much alarm in preparing for the long knives. Oraland was in the camp of Chief Sitting Bull when Crazy Horse returned from the Rose Bud and could see the contempt for the soldiers. They had now tasted blood and they wanted more. His only reaction was to see that Waynoka and Little George were safe from the now impending battle. Little Robe was standing at the tepee door, (vo-da-ma) when he came back from the Lakota Sioux camp and was talking with Waynoka. My brother I have returned from battle with great joy in my heart. The soldiers, (vov'oneots'e'tov) were driven back and we will do the same to the long knives that are headed our way. "No good can come from this Little Robe", explains Oraland.

The whites will come and come and come and we will have no choice but to surrender in the end. Little Robe I ask of you to take Waynoka and Little George out of the encampment and to head north away from the fight that is sure to happen. 'No, my brother I must stay and fight, and fight I will. Not one long knife will escape, (aseohov'ahe) us and they will all die". Looking at Waynoka now, Oraland asks her to pack and take their son north. I don't want you around here when this terrible thing occurs, he tells her. You must leave, and leave today. "But what of you my husband", Waynoka asks? I must stay and protect our village. It is my duty not only for the villagers, but for our future. I want our son to grow up not hating, but to be productive in his community, not only with his own people the Cheyenne, but with the whites also. I will not engage the long knives in battle, but will stay here and protect, (h'oom) our home. So please, (p`eh'evetanov) take Little George and go before it is too late. "I will do this thing for you my husband", replies Waynoka. Little Robe still standing there puts his hand on Oraland's shoulder and says to him, "I am honored to be your brother".

Oraland remarks, "I too am honored to be your brother and may the great spirit watch over you in battle". Waynoka does what Oraland requested and makes haste northward on horseback for safety with their child a few hours later. They kissed each other goodbye and promised each that they would be together soon. Watch out for yourself my husband, I love you, she said to him leaving. Walking through camp Oraland senses nothing but death. The young are eager for battle and the old wish they we're a little younger themselves so they could fight. He cannot help but to think of his old comrades in the Seventh that are making their way to his camp to do battle. "Custer" he says to himself. He'll have every one of his troopers killed just to get that glory he thirsts so badly for. He should be glad that they might all die especially after what happened eight years earlier at the Washita battle. But a sense of loyalty has sparked in his head. He owes so much to Custer on one hand, but on the other he despises him. If all the braves feel like Little Robe there is going to be a blood bath this day, Oraland is now torn between two ideals. June twenty third 1876, General Terry has just given Custer the go ahead to proceed towards the Little Big Horn ahead of him, but warned him that if he comes into contact with any hostiles he should save a few for the rest of the column. He tells Terry that he wants to opt out bringing the cannon and the Gatling guns with him. They will slow down the regiment and he wants no distractions on this movement. Custer is now on his way! He gives orders to his staff that they would be making a forced march towards the Big Horn and to be prepared to pull out at eleven o'clock that night. Being in the saddle for thirty some hours is tough, and each trooper suffers immensely. The regiment rides eighty miles in thirty-five hours and arrives at the Big Horn River worn and exhausted.

It's early in the morning on the twenty fifth of June and it's hot, very hot. Custer left his pack train under the command of Captain Thomas McDougall (promoted through the ranks during the civil war) along with Co. B ten miles to the rear as not to slow his column down. *(Remember, he had cannon with him and four new Gatling guns) which were left with General Terry. Custer wastes no time in committing his troops when he reaches the Little Big Horn. Again, scouts have warned him of a large village on the other side of the river, but he cannot see this first hand. For over three days now his scouts have reported the same information to him and he just ignores the warnings and treats each report as hogwash! Sitting in his saddle with his binoculars looking straight due west over the Big Horn River he sees nothing. He has his bugler John Martin sound officers call and when all are present he directs his orders. His staff includes his brother Captain Tom Custer, (promoted through the ranks during the civil war) brother Boston Custer, (civilian forager) brother -in-law Captain James Calhoun, (promoted through the ranks during the civil war) and nephew Autie Reed, (served as a forager and cow herder with the pack train). First, he addresses Reno. Major Reno I want you and three companies, Co. M, Co. A, and Co. G to attack the village from the southern end. Take scouts Gerard, Herendeen, Bloody Knife, Little Brave, Bobtail Bull, Reynolds, White Swan, and Isaiah Dorman with you and hit the village hard with heavy carbine fire.

This will be a diversion for my hitting the village from the north. From the start, show the red devils your strength, understood Major? "Yes sir", is Reno's reply. Now addressing Benteen, "Captain Benteen I want you and three companies, Co. D, Co. K, and Co. H. to head southwest and south of Major Reno and form a skirmish line to catch any escaping hostiles from getting away, understood? Benteen replies "yes sir".

I want you to take scouts Half Yellow Face, Hairy Moccasin, and White Man Runs Him with you also! Captain Keogh, (Miles Keogh promoted through the ranks during the civil war) you sir will take companies I, L, and C, and Captain Yates, (George Yates promoted through the ranks during the civil war) you will take companies E, and F and both of you will advance with me north along the river to the head of the snake! I will take scouts Curly, Mitch Boyer, and Charlie Goes Slow. Then gentlemen I will start to push the Indians down the river to your position, so Reno you be ready for us. We'll act like a hammer and anvil and take care of these Indians once and for all. Reno now asks permission to speak. No Major Reno you may not, we must not sit on this opportunity to surprise the savages. Sir, Captain Benteen interjects, our scouts have for days told us that the

Indians down there have been watching our every move since we left the fort. How can this be a surprise attack?

"Captain Benteen", Custer replies, with an antagonistic voice, I gave an order, now if you feel you cannot carry it out find yourself sir with the pack train ten miles to our rear and remain there. Benteen now perplexed replies, "very well sir" and asks if he can now take his companies to the position Custer requested earlier. Please do so Captain and don't foul this plan of attack up. With that Benteen rides off and orders his companies west. Reno sitting there snaps out of a trance when Custer asks, "well Major do you also have second thoughts of my order"? "No sir", is his reply and then turns his horse to ride back to his companies.

Custer sits there watching both of his subordinates executing their orders and then orders his command to follow him north along the river which will lead to the head of the village. This scenario is almost the same attack plans that he used eight years earlier at the Battle of The Washita.

The only difference is he is riding into a wasp's nest and was warned many times of the impending danger. As Custer rides the hilly terrain the Indian village is becoming more visible. "What the bye Jesus", he mutters as his eyes cannot believe the magnitude and size of the village.

He can faintly make out riders on the other side of the river and their numbers grow by the minute. The column is stopped now and Custer orders his bugler John Martin to find Benteen and to give him a message.

Custer's Adjutant Lieutenant W. Cooke writes out the message It reads:

> Benteen
> Come quick. Big village.
> Be quick. Bring packs.
> W.w. Cooke
> P.s. bring packs

Martin high tails it back to where Benteen had separated with the column earlier and finally found Benteen and gave him the message from Custer. Benteen reads it and asks what the situation was where Custer wrote the message? Martin replied that the General seemed to be in control and had not yet engaged the hostiles. Upon hearing this Benteen folded the message and put it in his coat pocket, smirked and forgot about it until two days later when General Terry finds out about the message after the battle. Oraland now is watching all the commotion in front of his tepee. Young braves are making ready for war as they paint their bodies, and ponies with different signs and pigments of colors. He's glad Waynoka listened to him and is by now in a safety zone outside the village.

Sioux braves riding by at a gallop send shivers down his back, but he is acquainted with a few of the braves and gives a yelp as he recognizes one or two. Dog soldiers from the southern Cheyenne are now passing by and he notices one who is leading the group, "Chief Crazy Horse". Oraland has met all of the chiefs that have come together at this gathering place along the Big Horn, but Crazy Horse seemed every time to elude him.

Even the great chief Sitting Bull seemed to wonder off when Crazy Horse came into the camp of the Lakota. Even if he was welcome by the other tribes, the mood became very tense in his presence. As the braves ride by, he bows his head and nods with sorrow when he sees Little Robe riding among them with the look of death in his eyes. Now looking north east over the river Oraland notices a faint but familiar item from his past, a swallow tail flag waving as it heads north along the river. "Custer", he mutters. A faint bugle call can now be heard and he notices six to eight figures on horses stopped on a hill looking into the village. Although a half a mile away, the horsemen stand out with the open blue sky to their backs. "Custer" he remarks again. He can almost make out the General on his black steed. Almost at the same time he noticed a few puffs of smoke coming from where the riders are sitting. Oraland surmises that it is Custer along with his brother Tom taking pot shots at the village with their long-range rifles that they always carried with them. Things are heating up even more now when shots are heard coming from the southern end of the village. Faint, but telling volley fire is coming from Major Reno's column breaking the silence of normal life in the camp. Reno is hitting the tail end of the village where the Hunkpapa Sioux and the Lakota are camped. Chiefs Gall and Sitting Bull are in the village, and are yelling out orders to their young braves.

Bullets from the volley fire are hitting everything in their way, and sound like bees buzzing as they pass through the air. Indians now are running towards the rifle fire and start to grow in numbers to attack back at Reno's men. Chief Gall is on his horse riding back and forth directing the women and children out of the village to the north of his camp to safety. His only weapon is his tomahawk. Sitting Bull is also seen heading north west outside of the camp with a large group of elderly and also women and children. When Reno entered the camp, he ordered his troopers to dismount and to form skirmish lines.

The command for volley fire was given and the first volley found Chief Galls family in the line of fire and five family members were killed including two of his wives and three of his children. When Gall found out about the killings he went crazy with madness. Along with five hundred other braves he charged Reno's position and routed the now confused troopers. Reno orders a retreat, but the Indians are like a swarm of bees and the soldiers have difficulty in retrieving their mounts and start to make their way to the river which is to their backs running on foot. Some of the men take refuge along the river in timber areas and continue to fight under the cover of brush and trees. The Indians lose no time in cutting down any individual that is trying to escape. Chief Gall leads attack after attack towards the now confused and scrambling troopers, and is reported to have split the skulls of seven troopers himself with his tomahawk as he ran them down with his horse. Oraland now hears gun fire coming from all positions in the village as braves start shooting across the river at the column of long knives now visible. Pandemonium ensues and Oraland starts to feel differently about the events that are unraveling before his eyes. Again, he feels a kinship with the men of the seventh and without rational thinking, jumps on his horse and darts for the river to try and warn Custer of what he's getting himself into and his troops.

Forgiveness was in his heart and his hatred for what happened at the Washita eight years earlier. He knows the Big Horn River pretty well and is aware of a shallow area next to the Sans Arc camp. He rides hard and fast and finds the crossing and in no time, is on the east side of the river. Crazy Horse and his followers earlier were heading north to cut Custer off and had to travel two miles out of their way to cross the river.

Oraland could be in Custer's presence in a few moments by taking this short cut he knew and could save minutes by fording the river where he did. A few minutes would be enough to warn the General and would give him that time to lead his troops back to safety. Now on the other side he is surprised and startled by two Indian scouts from Custer's command who he knew very well. It was Mitch Boyer' and Charlie Goes Slow. Boyer' has his carbine pointed at him ready to shoot. Charlie turns and pushes the barrel out of Oraland's way and tells Boyer' that it's Churchill his old friend. Together now Oraland tells the two that Custer's column is riding into a trap and they have to warn him. Boyer' said he had been telling Custer now for days of the large concentration of Indians here at the Little Big Horn, but his reports were ignored by him. Boyer' then comments on the large size of the Indian village, and had not witnessed in all his years the number of tribes that had come together. He then replies that they should ride to Custer's aid, but within a second after speaking Boyer' is shot and falls dead from his horse. Turning to the camp Oraland notices a mass of Ogala tribesmen firing their weapons in their direction. He turns to Charlie and both without saying a word dart up the river bank riding hard through a ravine which leads them to a clearing.

They now see Custer's column and at a gallop rush towards the long line of cavalry men now halted. Heading up the hill now known as "Custer Hill" both are noticed by Boston Custer who yells out to his brother "Tom there are two riders coming from the river this way fast" Tom Custer pulls his carbine from his scabbard and has Oraland in his gun sights now, but his Brother George yells out put the gun down, "they're our people". Gunfire is getting louder now and Reno has made it across the river to safety loosing twenty or so men and has taken up defensive position three miles to the south east of where Custer split up his command. Benteen upon hearing the heavy firing turned his companies around and headed towards the gun fire.

He found Reno's column on a large bluff overlooking the river and were defending their position under heavy enemy fire. After arriving he asked "where's Custer"? Reno said he didn't know and said he thought that he was still heading north to attack the village from the north. As he is talking with Reno, Benteen notices blood all over Reno's uniform and dried blood and other matter on his neck. What ever happened he figured it caused Reno to act dazed and irrationally. He later finds out that Reno's head scout Bloody Knife had been shot in the head while standing next to Reno down in the village and that the Indians brains were splattered all over the Reno's body. Three other scouts where killed including Little Brave, Dorman the black scout, and Bobtail Bull. Both are pinned down now by hundreds of braves and are fighting for their lives. Oraland and Charlie now ride up to Custer and Oraland shouts out, "you have to turn your troops around now General or you all are going to die"! "Churchill what the hell are you doing here, don't be a fool I have all the troops I need to defeat these red savages".

Custer is surprised to see his old friend especially here right now. "Your wrong sir, you're going to be killed and so are all these men if you don't turn back now". Gunfire is going off now in every direction. Black powder smoke is very heavy and horses are reacting irrationally. But Custer sensing the horror in Oraland's demeanor now orders Captain Keogh to take one company and set up a defense post to their left of where they were now, about a quarter of a mile east.

You'll set up a diversion as to split the hostiles concentration of fire in one area. Keogh replies "very good sir" and salutes Custer and rides back to his company where he leads Company I at a gallop on his heroic horse Comanche to the position Custer ordered him to occupy. Custer now looking at Oraland tells him that the regiment will stand and fight here on their own ground. Now looking straight into Oralands eyes he now asks, "well Churchill are you staying with us or are you going back to your people"? Oraland remarks that he'll stay, but they better get to higher ground before their locked in the low land where they stand now. "Very good Sergeant", turning Custer orders his command up this hill to the top for a better vantage and defensive point. Custer felt good calling his old friend "Sergeant", for a moment he thought of the good old days during the war. As they reach the top of the hill all hell starts to break loose. They are confronted by hundreds of Indians coming from the northwest on horseback and are also taking on fire from Indians from the northeast. The tall grass all around leads to from a protection barrier for the Indians on foot from being seen. Custer now seeing the danger in riding into the mass of red savages orders his men to dismount and take up a skirmish position. He then orders his men to commence firing on the Indians. The fighting is now gaining momentum and confusion has now taken over, the same confusion that had plagued Reno earlier down at the river.

Custer now orders the killing of the horses to make barriers for protection from the rain of bullets that are pinning his men down along with swarms of incoming arrows shot into the air by hundreds of Indians. No man could escape the barrage of arrows raining down on them. Thousands of Indians are yelling war cries and the soldiers are now acting like a disoriented crowd instead of U. S. soldiers. The hidden Indians in the grass stand up and fire into the now dismounted troopers and then fall to the ground as not to be a target for the long knives. Captain Keogh and his Company I are now under attack and Custer is second guessing himself on splitting his command the way he did. The air is filled with the sounds of gunfire and orders are being yelled out over the loud noise.

Some of the soldiers have sought refuge behind their dead horses to defend themselves, but find that the dead animals don't act as a shield as they thought they would. Oraland standing there now without a weapon has thoughts of Waynoka and what he had said to her when they last saw one another. He promised not to fight and now he finds himself in this awkward position. He wants so much to live and be with her now. Men are being shot all around him and total confusion has set in. Custer now standing and firing his revolver at any Indian that moves turns to Oraland and says "just like old times Churchill". Oraland just looked into his face and smiled and knew he saw the face of a doomed man. Bullets are flying everywhere and just as Custer finished his statement, Oraland is knocked to the ground by a bullet that finds its mark just under his right shoulder. As he lies there he is looked at by Charlie Goes Slow. Charlie cradles Oraland and yells out his name to see if his friend still is conscience.

He shouts out "Oraland" picking up the boy to see how bad the wound is. Oraland comes too for a moment and sees his friend holding him and tells him to save himself. Charlie has stripped off his army cloths and is now wearing his Crow war outfit as he told Custer "If I am to die today, I will die a Crow warrior not a soldier". "I will remain here with you my brother, he tells Oraland and we'll both go to the great spirit together". Hit right under the arm pit and bleeding a lot Oraland now loses consciousness from the loss of blood. Charlie lays his body down again and turns to warn Custer one more time, but is taken down by two arrows that hit him in the back.

He falls down dead lying next to Oraland. Taken that Oraland was dead, Custer wanted to come to his aid, but he is now confronted by hundreds of horsemen hitting his command from the northwest. It's Crazy Horse and Chief Two Moons form the Southern Cheyenne. There are also Ogala, and Sioux braves in the mix as well as San Arc and Arapaho braves. In the fury of the fight a few of the troopers try to mount a few of the horses that were not killed and are quickly cut down by sharp shooting Indians positioned nearby around their perimeter. Surviving horses are running around and a few troopers try to catch them for the ammunition that are in their saddlebags, but to no avail. Each trooper wears a cartridge belt containing fifty rounds of carbine ammo, and when that's gone, their out of luck. Keogh's command is now completely wiped out and the Indians that did this now concentrate on the rest of Custer's command hitting his defenses from the east and southern end. Custer's men fight bravely and there is mass confusion everywhere. Crazy Horse is seen riding in front of the dismounted troopers more than once in daring acts of bravery, taunting the troopers and each time retreats unhurt. Tom Custer goes down shot through the gut and dies in his brother's arms. The two-time Medal of Honor winner received during the civil war blurts out the word "AUTIE" before his eyes shut for the last time. Custer lies his brothers body down and now stands firing his revolver at the oncoming Indians. Looking briefly over at Oraland laying there on the ground he realizes that the boy was right and he should have listened to him and heeded his warning. Men now are screaming and yelling at the Indians and some even try to surrender, but are cut down like animals.

Crying men pleading for their lives are slain quickly and scalped just as fast. Some are even alive yet as the knife of a brave cuts through the skin above the hair line. Soldiers try to run down the hill in an attempt to escape in the river, but they too are cut down. The Indians are showing no mercy for the dazed troopers, for today is payback time. All the years of suffering and death will be revenged today with the lives of these pathetic men trying to save their lives. It's around three or four o'clock in the afternoon and the weather is very hot with the temperature in the nineties. The heat is unkind and most of the troopers are fighting now in their tee shirts. Custer had shed his buckskin shirt earlier and is wearing his famous blue fireman's shirt with sleeves rolled up.

Ammunition problems start to plague the troopers as the 45/70 cartridges the troopers were issued start to jam their Springfield carbines, and pen knives are now being used to pry out the fouled rounds. Years later in a court of inquiry in Washington it will brought out that the quartermaster division of the army issued inferior ammo to the seventh which also attributed to their demise. Custer's other brother Boston, now goes down dead, shot through the neck with an arrow. As it penetrated his body the arrow point severed his jugular vein and horror-stricken Custer now kneels next to the limp body realizing his own predicament. He's seen men many times before killed in action, but the death of his two brothers now hits him hard. With the battle now going on all around him the adrenaline in his body pumps even faster and his actions now become more erratic. Custer is now standing alone in the Custer clan.

His nephew Autie Reed also has been shot dead in front of him also, and desperation now takes over. The Indians are now also firing arrows into the air and soldier after soldier goes down looking like porcupines. In all the confusion in the soldiers ranks now, Crazy Horse makes a daring charge through the line of defenders and succeeds in splitting Custer's command in half. This forces Captain Yates and his troopers of Company F to take stand just south west of Custer Hill.

Within minutes every trooper is killed including Yates. Meanwhile Captain James Calhoun (Custer's brother-in law) has made a gallant route to the east end of the field with Company L, but he to finds himself surrounded, and his command is wiped out within minutes also. The trooper's weapons are no match to the Indians. If a soldier went down, his carbine is now the property of an Indian firing it at another soldier and so on. With only thirty to forty men left standing on that bloody hill, Custer makes his last stand. His regiment decimated, Custer had to know that the end was near. One after another, the troopers around him go down dead. Custer now the only combatant remaining, stands there with revolver in hand at the ready. He's ready to meet his maker. Out of the group of Indians on horseback, one rider is in the lead now heading towards the lone defender. Ironically, it's Little Robe and he is armed with his father's Spencer carbine which was presented to his father, Chief Black Kettle at the Medicine Lodge Creek Treaty eight years earlier, by Custer himself. As he rides closer Custer raises his pistol, aims and fires, but misses. Little Robe now aims the carbine and he too fires, and hits Custer in the chest and watches the last defender go down dead. Custer falls backwards and winds up laying on his back against two dead troopers with a smile on his face. CUSTER IS DEAD! Little Robe wasn't aware of who he had just slain, all he knew was that the long knives were all dead and that his parent's deaths had been revenged. Riding in on the dead lying all over, he now dismounts and reaching to the sky with his father's carbine extended in the air, he cries out "HOK-A-HEY"!

The whole battle lasted no more than one hour, and then it was over. He witnesses his brothers in arms striking the lifeless bodies of the dead with stone tomahawks, hitting them in the head so hard that the individual is left unidentifiable. Little Robe proceeds to take Custer's scalp, and while looking around him, noticing all the macabre acts being brought upon the dead troopers.

He stops short noticing something out of place on that hill of death. Lying next to the man he had just killed he glances at another body lying there, not more than four feet away donning a necklace just like the one he had given his sister and one that his blood brother Oraland had worn.

Now forgetting the scalping of this soldier, he reaches over turning the body, and his demeanor changes. Lying there he finds his brother -in -law, his blood brother, Oraland! Bending over Oraland's body now Little Robes starts to shake him to see if there was any life left in his body. To his surprise Oraland gives a moan and makes a slight coughing noise. Looking around him now again Little Robe witness even more of his fellow tribesmen including squaws now on the battlefield continuing to mutilate the dead bodies of the fallen troopers. Ears are cut off, fingers, legs, feet, hands, and private parts are defiled by the now crazed Indians. Lone Indians are going around to each soldier now and are shooting them in the head to make sure that they are dead. Little Robe knows he must move Oraland quickly before one of the other Indians finds out he is still alive, so he takes a blanket that he finds on a dead Sioux warrior near bye and wraps up Oraland's body in it. He proceeds to lay him over his horse, and as he is doing this he over hears one of the squaws tell the others that the man he killed was Yellow Hair, the great leader of the long knives and that his body is not to be mutilated like the others. One of the squaws shoves a sewing awl into one of Custer's ears so in the other world he would listen better. Little Robe now recognizes him and remembers last seeing him eight years ago at Medicine Lodge. "Custer" he mutters, as he stands there staring at the dead man. He then slowly heads down the hill towards his village with Oraland's body swaying on his horses back. The battlefield now is consumed with squaws and children who are removing boots and clothing from the dead troopers.

    Any thing that can be used for future use is taken. Personal items are pocketed by new owners and the field around is cluttered with paper money. The troopers were paid just before they left Fort Lincoln and many had a wad of cash on their person. Money meant nothing to the scavengers, so it was thrown in the wind as nothing valuable and the green paper littered the battlefield. Little Robe passed many dead soldiers that had tried to run for safety, but were cut down quickly. The route to the river was littered with bodies all the way down the hill and their white skin made the landscape look like white washed rocks. Crazy Horse now passes Little Robe on his way to engage Reno and Benteen to the east. Chief Gall, and Red Cloud were already engaged with the dug in defenders and had surrounded the over six hundred troopers pretty well. Indian snipers were picking off any trooper that raised his head higher than he should have and the field around the troops were filled with Indians on foot waiting for the chance to rush the horrified defenders. Nearly all the troopers from the six companies were new recruits and had no Indian fighting experience, and most had never shot their carbines before. Again, it was hot and miserable. Lack of water also created a real problem for the pinned down soldiers. Men put pebbles in their mouths to create saliva to form, but it wasn't enough. Nineteen men volunteered and made a chance run to the river to gather water in the empty canteens they carried. None was injured or wounded in their venture and fresh water was available again for the thirsty troopers. All that were involved in the water run would later be awarded the Congressional Medal of Honor for their actions on that hot day in June of 1876. Benteen at one turn during the engagement took two squads of troopers and charged a strong hold of Indians about two hundred yards to the west.

   The Indians were caught off guard and retreated back to the river dazed and surprised as to the bravery of the soldiers. Even though the long knives were enemies of the red man they were respected as great fighters. Crazy Horse now sees the meaningless of the fight and decides to return to the village to celebrate the victory of the long knives earlier. Reno and Benteen expected Custer's five companies at any time, but as the day drew on they gave up hope of seeing their comrades alive again. Custer had perished hours earlier, and now it was obvious he wasn't coming back. All day the Indians attacked the seventh on all sides. Captain Thomas Weir (promoted through the ranks during the civil war) attached to Reno's column made a break for an area west of Reno's position with two squads of men in a chance sighting of Custer's column. He made it to a grassy knoll that stood some ten feet high and from there he and his men could see smoke and faint figures in the area where Custer was supposed to be. He surmised that Custer was dead now and the red devils were doing their dirty work on the trooper's bodies. He made it back to his position with Reno and relayed what he had seen to his subordinate. Reno and Benteen didn't believe what Weir had just told them and ordered him back on the battle line with the rest of his company. They were outnumbered not only in man power, but also fire power.

The Indians were well equipped with over forty different types of weapons being used against the Seventh that day, including the famous Winchester rifle. The Seventh trooper's were still using the single shot Springfield carbines. Custer blundered in dividing his regiment that day and many lives paid the price for his glory ride. Meanwhile Little Robe is back in the village and heads for Oraland's tepee to care for him. One of the elders of the village noticed what was going on and asked Little Robe if he could help mend the wound. "Please help if you can great one", he replies. The elder stops the bleeding and wraps up the wound the best he can.

He should live he tells Little Robe, but he must rest now. Random gunfire is still being heard and the chance of the remaining long knives coming into the village is nil. Our people have destroyed the long knives and we don't have to worry about them. Have him rest now. An hour goes by and with it the return of Waynoka and Little George to the village. She had run into a war party earlier and they told her the long knives had been defeated and it would be safe for her to return back to the village. Upon arriving some of her people told her of what had happened to Oraland and with that news she became a little frantic. She quickly ran to the tepee crying and upon seeing Oraland lying their she let out a bloodcurdling scream thinking he was dead. Little Robe returned on hearing the scream and finds his sister crying out of control. He holds her tight and calms her down, telling her Oraland was going to live. He is only sleeping my sister and there is no need to worry. He must rest he told her. Waynoka sits there stroking Oraland's hair now as she is talking to him. He was still unconscious and breathing slowly, but had a slight smile on his face that gave her a sense of strength. She then proceeds to kiss his forehead. The sound of battle could still be heard faintly from where Reno and Benteen were pinned down. After the fifty or so bodies of Custer's men were stripped, scalped, and mutilated the squaws and elders returned back to the village to rejoice in the victory over the long knives. Some did not rejoice though, for their loved ones had also had been killed that day on the battlefield. The customs of each tribe were different when it came to dealing with the death a loved one. Some Squaws now were cutting off a finger or cutting a gash in their stomachs as a sign of grief for their loss.

 Indian customs were strange to the white man, and this defiling of their bodies wasn't understood. A band of Sans Arc scouts had sighed Terry's column coming in from the east still two days out and warned the chiefs still trying to disengage Reno and Benteen. It was decided that they return to the village and celebrate their victory. In the morning they would pick up the camp and head south, away from the long knives that were coming. Enough blood had been shed and a great victory over the whites had taken place, just as chief Sitting Bull had predicted days earlier in a vision preforming the traditional sun dance. The night would go by slowly for the remaining dug in troops. They waited all night and most did not sleep one second fearing a surprise attack from any vantage point around their perimeter. A few braves stayed on the hill and took pot shots at the troopers which kept them on their toes. Meanwhile in the camp giant bon fires were erected and dancing was going on in every tribe's camp. A great victory was had today and every camp was lit up brightly up and down the entire village. For Reno and Benteen's men, they could now see the magnitude of the size of the Indian camp. All night the dancing went on while Waynoka nursed Oraland's injury with Little George staying close to his father's side. During the night Oraland awoke in a sweat and was assured by his wife he was going to be alright. "Just rest my husband and get well because you are going to grow old and wise" she told him as he lied there looking up at her. The night dragged on and morning finally came. Oraland had made it through the night without complications and had a good night's rest.

Waynoka fixed him a small breakfast and he ate well. Sitting up now he talked with his son and told him how proud he was of him taking care of his mother. Oraland told Waynoka that Custer was dead along with Charlie Goes Slow. "I'm sorry for Charlie Waynoka commented". "He was a good friend of mine for a lot of years", replied Oraland, I'll miss him very much. What is all the commotion outside he asks her? All the tribes are breaking up their camps and are heading south away from the long knives that are heading this way from the northeast. "Terry's column", Oraland remarks. "We must start to get ready also my husband, can you stand up"? Where is Little Robe inquires Oraland?

He has chosen to follow Crazy Horse and they headed

West last night while you were sleeping. He told me that you would always be brothers and the great spirit would look out for you both. Oraland now leaning on a staff pulls himself up and slowly walks around the tepee for a moment. I'll be fine my wife he tells her, as he asks her now to get Little George in here so we can start packing for our journey. Meanwhile up on the bluff where Reno and Benteen defended themselves and their troopers, the two are on horseback watching the large mass of Indians exiting the village and heading south. The troopers are now walking around without fear of being shot at, and the doctor is mending the wounded in an isolated area outside of the breastworks. Although there has been no gun fire in the last five hours, the defenders are still on alert. Three of the Crow scouts have reported back that Terry's column is around eight hours away and should be there around noon the next day. The men are a little more at ease, and water has been brought up from the river which was a relief to all. Scouts had been sent out to the west of their defense area to look for Custer and returned with the bad news of the death and demise of all five companies, including Custer. Reno couldn't believe the news, and all Benteen remarked was that "he finally got his glory". Oraland, now walking slowly with Waynoka are making their way around the village to pay their respects to the squaws that had lost their loved ones in the battle.

When they reached the southern end of the village they found Chief's Gall and Sitting Bull directing their tribes for their long trip. Oraland spoke to Sitting Bull and told him that he respected him on not only being a great chief, but also for his vision of the end of Custer and his men. The great spirit has given you a great power Oraland tells the chief and he hopes it will guide his people in the true ways of their Indian heritage. Sitting Bull replied that all came together, (em-ho-hey-mohey hey ah) meaning the Indian nations, to be as one in the eyes of the great spirit, and helped us to defeat to the death, (wi-ca-te) the long knives.

Chief Gall tells Oraland that the two tribes, the Hunkpapa's and the Lakota Sioux will be heading north towards Canada for refuge and protection from the Canadian government. He also commented on Oraland's injury, and Churchill replied that his wound was from a stray bullet fired in the confusion of the battle in the Cheyenne camp. He didn't want Little Robes heroics to come out among the leaders. "Many have died and the army will come down hard on our people for what we did here yesterday. They will never understand that this land is our land and we will continue to fight for it", with his head looking down comments Sitting Bull. Peace be with you, Oraland comments to the Chiefs "may the great spirit protect you on your journey". Oraland now standing with Waynoka and Little George on the southern tip of the Little Big Horn River spend a moment to reflect on what had happened in the last two days. He then comes to attention, and in the direction of his former commander gives one last salute to Custer and the troopers of the Seventh.

At that very moment both Reno and Benteen are on horseback overlooking the river and are watching the multitudes of Indians heading south. Reno is looking through his binoculars and suddenly stands up in his saddle straining his eyes saying to Benteen, "look at what I just found, it can't be"! Puzzled at what Reno had just said, Benteen asks his comrade what are you talking about? "Look through your binoculars down at the river where it starts to elbow south. Who is that standing there with a squaw and a child"? Benteen now looking gasps a moment and replies, "It's Churchill", now turning and looking at Reno. When the two try to focus a little closer in on the three they found, to their amazement the trio has disappeared. Within a second the three are not there anymore. "They just vanished", remarks Reno. "Do you think we really saw Churchill or was it our imaginations"? "Who knows Benteen", replies Reno. "If it was Churchill may god watch over him".

Now we had better get back to our regiment, I would say that this great event is over now. Before riding back to the regiment Benteen looks at Reno and remarks to him "with Custer dead my friend Reno, you are now the new commander of the Seventh Cavalry, and I pray you don't have any ideas of taking us to glory"! Yes, their lives had been spared, but their careers would fall apart in the years ahead! Oraland and his family are now walking back to their Cheyenne camp to join the others heading south. Each day his wound will heal more, and he will become stronger and, this chapter in his life would end. He, Waynoka and Little George will follow the other tribes till they get to the Washita, and then they will head up into the hills to their promised land and live free for the rest of their lives. Little Robe would be hunted down in the coming months with a band of other dog soldiers of the Southern Cheyenne, and would die a true warrior's death. Little George will leave his parents on his nineteenth birthday in 1889 and will live with his father's friends the Miniconjou, Lakota Sioux. The following year, in 1890 on a cold and snowy morning of December the twenty ninth he will be killed along with one hundred and fifty other warriors, women, and children at "Wounded Knee" South Dakota. Called the Wounded Knee Massacre, the demise of the Indian nations would evolve and the "Trail of Tears" would commence.

    The End
    HENA'HAANEHE

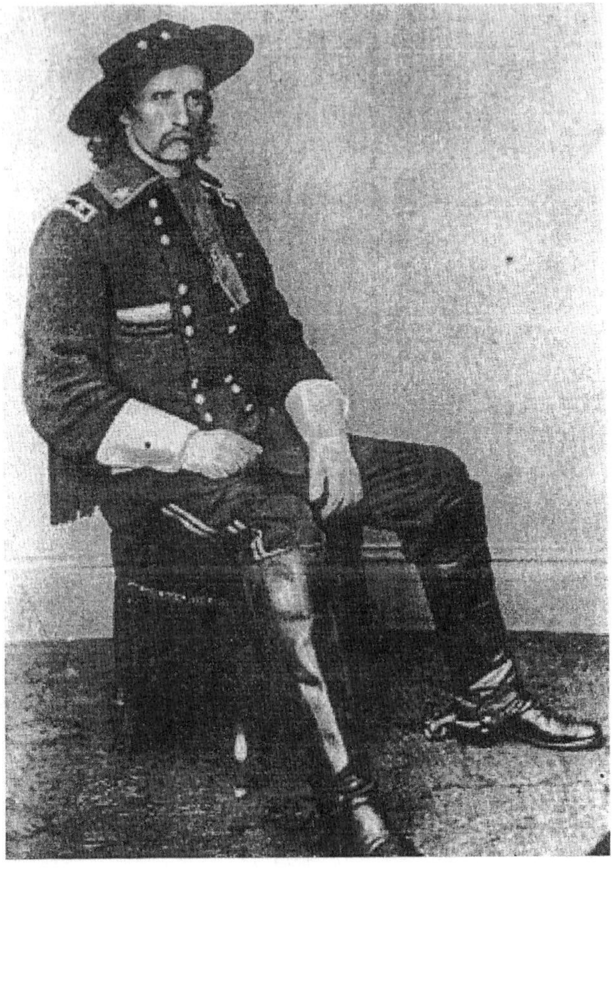

Chapter 2
Lt. Col. George Armstrong Custer

To understand Custer we must go back to December 5th, 1839. He was born in the town of New Rumley, Ohio. Emanuel Henry Custer was his father, and Marie Ward Kilpatrick was his mother. His father was a staunch old Jacksonian Democrat, a blacksmith, and farmer who was to become George's idol. George Armstrong Custer, as he was baptized grew up with quite a few siblings. His father had remarried and his step-mother had children of a previous marriage so the Custer clan was large.

The Custer's had Thomas, Boston, Margret, Nevin, and of course George the first born. Marie Kilpatrik's children included, Lydia, and David. The name Custer came from German descent, ("Kus'ter", or "coster". George went to school as did his brothers and sisters, and was always the wise guy in class. The schoolmaster was a harsh disciplinarian, and many times his brothers received the lash because George got away with another prank. He was lucky and would always go that extra distance for attention. This would prove to be self-evident all thru his life. He eventually moved out of the house in Rumley and went to Monroe, Michigan to live with his stepsister Lydia and brother-in-law John Reed. There George entered the Stebbians Academy, a local school at the age of twelve years. He was there for two years and went back to New Rumley at fourteen. Two months later he returned to Monroe, and his step sister sent him to the "Seminary" to finish out his education. While attending the school Custer would do odd jobs around the campus and nearby neighborhood to pay for room and board. In 1856 at the age of sixteen, George graduated and returned to New Rumley and applied for a job as a teacher in nearby Hopedale, Ohio. Teaching wasn't George's forte and after a year he wanted to pursue his only love, a military career.

He again moved back to Harrison County, Ohio. In his spare time, he would drill with the local militia and at this time in his life, found the calling to be a career military man. "Autie" was a nickname given to him by his family when he was real young, mainly because he couldn't pronounce Armstrong, and he would come out saying "Autie. "All through life he had many nicknames some including: "Fanny" given to him by his peers at West Point, "the boy general" given to him by the press during the civil war, or "Iron Butt," "Hard Ass," and "Ringlets" all given to him by his troopers. "Ringlets" was given because of his long blond hair which the Indians later would refer to him as "Yellow hair" or "Son of Morning Star" There was one more name given to him while attending West Point, and that was "Cinnamon", which was given to him by the other cadets.

This was because he use to put a scented pomade in his hair to smell better. Custer wanted it all and the only way to make that happen was to be a commissioned officer. There were already officers in his militia unit in New Rumley, so George being the one who always went the extra distance for something approached his local congressman, Representative John Bingham and asked for his help to be appointed to the United States Military Academy at West Point. Thru a little politics Bingham got Custer his appointment and he was enrolled at West Point in the fall of 1857 and became a plebe at the age of seventeen. Custer turned out to be an awful student. His attention span was that of a gnat. He played pranks on non-suspecting classmates and was always diverting his energy away from his studies.

George wanted attention and, got it! He had more demerits than any other cadet, and had no will to learn what the academy expected of him in his studies. His only savior while at the Point, was his ability to ride a horse like a professional, handle a sword expertly, shoot like a marksman and, had some knowledge of the art of battle. It was now 1859 and the nation was being pulled apart because of the slavery issue, and the fight over states' rights. The south wanted to succeed from the Union and blood had already been spilt in Kansas, Nebraska, and Ohio. The cadets at the academy were already called up to help put down the riots in New York City and the mood of the nation was changing each and every day towards succession.

April 12, 1861 WAR!!!!!!!!!!!!!!!!!!!

Yes, war had come to America on her own soil. Fort Sumpter was fired upon by confederate artillery batteries set up in Charleston Harbor, South Carolina. The class of 1861 at the academy was graduated a year early, because the army needed trained officers in the field. Custer graduated #34 out of a class of 34. His demerit record while at the academy was terrible. Some examples: talking in ranks, talking in class, dirty weapon, not clean shaven, day dreaming in class, nonmilitary items found in room, sneaking liquor into room, and the list would go on and on. Because of these demerits he should have been assigned to an obscure post out west after graduating, but his luck found him in Washington, DC as a Second Lieutenant assigned to the Second United States Cavalry. So here is Custer six-foot-tall, broad shoulders, one hundred and seventy pounds, blue eyes, and hair as golden as a new baby. His first action was at the First Battle of Bull Run named by the Union, or the battle of First Manassas as it was referred to by the Confederates.

He came through the battle untouched by gun fire and lived up to the training he received at West point. Riding a horse and charging an enemy was a natural for Custer and his whole demeanor was circled around action. Even though the union forces were driven back to Washington in a great route, his ability as a leader of men was born and noticed by several superiors. He thrived for the kill, which he would see more of in the next four years. The army reorganizing itself after their defeat assigned Custer to General George McClellan's staff and he was promoted to the rank of Captain; thus, Custer was on his way towards his boyish dream.

His next battle would be in August of 1862 at the battle of "Antietam" as the union called it or the battle of "Sharpsburg" as the rebels called it. Nearly 20,000 men lost their lives in this engagement, and both north and south claimed victory. Even though General Robert E. Lee ordered his troops to pull back, McClellan also called it a day and pulled his troops back also. "Lil Mac" as he was referred to by his troops could have cut the war by three years if he had pursued Lee after the battle, but he didn't and lost his job a month later when President Lincoln relived him of his command. Lincoln said "McClellan had the slows" so Custer again was reassigned and this time wound up on General Alfred Pleasanton's staff and soon became a favorite of the General.

In short time Custer was again promoted and in 1863 now held the rank of Breveted Major General of Michigan volunteers. Custer at this point in time was the youngest

General in the union army at the ripe old age of 23 years old. The war had been going on now for 3 years and Lincoln couldn't find a commander that had the guts or the nerve to face the rebels and defeat them. Custer meanwhile has been very active with his Brigade of Michigan cavalry and in July of 1863 his need for glory comes to him in the name of Confederate General Jeb Stuart.

The place Gettysburg, Pa. where Custer kept Stuarts cavalry at bay and Lee is found blind without Stuarts reconnaissance patrols around the surrounding area. Because of Custer, the Battle of Gettysburg was won by the Union and the confederate army was in retreat. During the battle when Custer engaged Stuart's troops he almost found himself a fatality. While in the heat of battle with clashing sabres and riders shooting one another at close range, a Confederate officer noticed the boy general and galloped within striking distance of Custer.

He raised his sabre and was going to cut the general in half, when out of nowhere one of Custer's one Sgt. Norvell Churchill of the First Michigan Brigade came riding in and proceeded to raise his own sabre and blocked the officers swipe saving his commanders life and then sent the Johnny Reb to his maker with a shot from his colt revolver. Throughout the four years of war Custer had eleven horses shot from under him during battle. Again, Custer's luck! After the war the Custer's, George and his future bride Elizabeth Bacon were invited to the home of Norvell Churchill and spent two weeks visiting. Custer was very appreciative of Churchills saving his life and never forgot him. Custer served out the war and was present at every major battle during the four-year conflict.

Even at the close of the war near Appomattox, Virginia he made his last cavalry charge and had routed the Rebs a day before. Lee surrendered his army at the Appomattox Court house on April ninth, 1865, on Palm Sunday. Custer was a witness to Lee's surrender being a member of General Ulysses S. Grants staff. George Custer did marry the love of his life Elizabeth Bacon the daughter of judge Danial Bacon of Monroe, Michigan. Elizabeth was born on April 8, 1842 and was the daughter of Danial and Elenore. Elizabeth's mother passed away in 1854 and she was raised by her father.

Custer took a liking to "Libby" as she was referred to, at first glance. Both wanted to get married, but her father wouldn't have it, because Custer was from a poor family and he wanted Libby to marry into prominence. Custer swore that someday he would be a hero and her father would have to give his blessings to them. So be it, in 1863 after the great battle of Gettysburg, Custer was a national hero and was also a General in the Union Army so the judge had to give in to their love pact.

The judge passed away in 1866. After the war General Sheridan gave Custer command of the 5th United States Cavalry Military Division of The Southwest in Texas. He was demoted to the rank of Captain because the war was over and the army didn't need a handful of high ranking officers, so his rank from General went down to Captain. After several months the unit was disbanded and mustered out of the army. He took an extended leave of absence and contemplated over various job offers that had been extended to him. Custer was a military man and no job offer was tempting enough for him to leave the army. Running for congress wasn't in his makeup and, working for someone else wasn't in his future also.

In October of 1866 Custer was appointed Lieutenant Colonel of the newly formed Seventh Cavalry Regiment headquartered at Fort Riley, Kansas. Later that year he took part in an expedition that was aimed at the Southern plains Cheyenne tribes. The Indians seemed to always be ahead of the seventh and the daily duties of a trooper became dull very quickly. During the campaign he went AWOL, abandoning his post to see his wife Libby and was brought up on charges, court-martialed and suspended for one year without pay. He would wait out his suspension in Monroe, Michigan while he was on administrative leave. Meanwhile the war department sent out another detachment of troops from Fort Larned to try and persuade the Indians to sign a peace treaty.

The Indian tribes said yes to what looked like a peace offering, and met at a place called "Medicine Lodge Creek" because the Indians wanted a place where there was plenty of water and grass for their horses. The first counsel was held on the nineteenth and twentieth of October 1867. The Comanches and Kiowas signed their treaties the next day, and the Plains Apache signed their treaty on the twenty fifth. Finally, the Cheyenne and Arapaho tribes signed their treaties on the twenty eighth of October, it was done! There would be peace, and all the Indians asked for was to return to their hunting grounds and the promise that the whites would keep the railroads from crossing their land.

SIMPLE!

Things were good for a while, but sooner than later the government did not live up to their promises and the Indians became nomadic once more and fighting ensued all over the plains. The Indians didn't take any prisoners and the army was bent on ending the problem once and forever. Custer now seven months into his suspension was approached by General Sheridan and was asked to command a campaign against the Cheyenne's. Later that year he led the Seventh Cavalry on a winter campaign and tracked the Cheyenne's to a place called Washita, which is located near what is now Cheyenne, Oklahoma. The Indians didn't think that the army would attack in the winter time, so they set up their camp along the Washita River. On November the twenty seventh 1868 Custer attacked the village in the early morning. Chief

Black Kettle and his wife were the first to be killed as they were leaving the camp on horseback for a ride. Custer had split up his Regiment into four attacking columns and surprised the camp as they rode thru it, shooting anything that moved. After the smoke had cleared dead warriors, squaws, children, dogs, and ponies were laying everywhere. Accounts of the battle were completely different from the view of both the army and the Cheyenne's. The dead numbers of the Indians were given at one hundred and twenty by the army, but the Indians said thru eye witnesses the dead numbered not more than fifty warriors including some women and children.

It wasn't a battle, it was a "massacre" referred to by some. After the action (as we will call it) Custer ordered eight hundred and seventy-five Indian ponies to be put to death. He felt that they may fall into Indian hands down the road, so he ordered their demise. This was the first significant action against the Cheyenne and a large portion of the tribe was placed on U.S. reservations. The death of Chief Black Kettle including his wife Medicine Woman at the Washita didn't sit very well with other members of the Cheyenne nation, and eight years down the line they would get back at the long knives at the Little Big Horn being led by the great Ogala Chief Crazy Horse.

Custer of course came out of the victory smelling like a rose and his luck was another notch up on his glory path, but history would be the ultimate enemy for him eight years later, because he used the almost, to detail battle plan that he used that day at the Washita. He split his regiment into four groups that would attack the Cheyenne encampment on four different sides. Yes, it worked, but the numbers of Indians wouldn't be the same in 1876. During the battle Major Joel Elliott a civil war survivor and eighteen of his detachment were ambushed and killed. They were seen by other troopers from Custer's company and reported to their leader that they saw Elliott and his men chasing Indian braves downstream on the Washita. Custer felt Elliott was correct in his actions and when the seventh pulled out of the defeated village the next day Custer made no effort in sending out a party of men to find Elliott and his men. Custer's thoughts were on the rest of his regiment because there were signs that the Indians that had escaped would be back with a stronger strength of warriors. If the Indians did attack, he felt the troopers would kill all the prisoners that they had taken and there would be more bloodletting. So, he left Elliott and his men on their own.

A month later a detachment from Fort Riley was sent back to the Washita to find the missing troopers. All were found dead! Being December, all the bodies were frozen stiff and the Indians made sure they were dead by cutting each man's throat. Elliott's body was found with two bullets in the skull and one in his left cheek. His right hand was cut off and his penis was missing. I could go into more detail on each trooper's demise, but I'll leave that for another time. People were brutal back then and on both sides. There were no angels amongst the Indians nor the army.

Elliott was a close friend of then Captain Frederick Benteen of Company H in Elliott's command and Benteen never forgave Custer for leaving Elliott and his men after the fight. This relationship between Benteen and Custer would work its way to the Little Big Horn. A grudge?

It's still one of the mysteries of June 25th, 1876. There is one other interesting fact concerning the battle of the Washita, and that concerns Custer and one William Babcock Hazen. Hazen in 1868 during the Washita campaign was the Indian agent for the U.S. Government at Fort Cobb, located in Oklahoma. Years earlier at the West Point Academy Custer and Hazen knew each other. Hazen had graduated in 1855 and now was on the academy's staff in 1861. It was Hazen who had Custer brought up on charges of not stopping a fight on the academy grounds a few days after graduation. The fight was between two cadets and Custer was the officer on duty that day, saw the brawl and did not try to stop it. Custer being Custer said something like "come on boys let's fight a fair fight". That's all it took to get Custer in trouble with Lt. Col. John Reynolds class of 1841 at the academy now superintendent of cadets. It was Hazen who brought up the charges.

Reynolds would later become the commanding general for the Union forces at the Battle of Gettysburg and would lose his life on the first day of the battle. General George Mead, class of 1835 at West Point replaced him for the duration of the battle. So, Custer is going to be court-martialed again, but with civil war on the horizon the court turned their heads and let Custer graduate.

Hazen never forgot that incident and in 1868 warned Chief Black Kettle about Custer's off hand wild behavior. Hazen referred to Custer as "the best hated man I ever knew" The Indians did not take heed of the Indian agent's warnings and thus history was born on the Washita River. In 1873 Custer was in the Dakota territory with the Seventh protecting a railroad survey crew from the Indians. The Seventh had a clash with the Lakota Sioux in August of that year, but no one on either side came out a victor. In 1874 Custer led the now famous "Black Hills Expedition".

Numbering over a thousand troopers, Custer was a on a big camping trip which it turned out to be. Hunting, fishing, hiking and the kind. He was also under orders to find gold if it existed in the Black Hills. Well Custer made the most of everything, including finding gold. This find could open the doors for thousands of people to migrate to the area, but it was Indian land, and there was a treaty! Well word got out about the find and soon there was another gold rush. The government warned any one going into the Black Hills did so at their own risk, which for many proved true. The new hordes of settlers demanded that the army protect them from the Indians, and the outcry for protection finally made its way to the White House where President Grant weighed the matter. Custer being Custer again, had to get involved with politics and was summoned to Washington.

There he accused the Secretary of State William Belkanap along with President Grants brother, Orville of issuing the army defective weapons and selling the Indians superior guns at many army trading posts. This accusation hit Grant the wrong way and Custer now finds himself at war with the President. He was slammed by the press; Secretary Belknap was impeached by the senate and Grant had decided to go after the Indian nations in the Black Hills. When Custer found out about Grants orders he went to the press and said that this action wasn't justified. The government had gone back on their words as spelled in the treaty of 1867. He testified that if the army got involved, then all the Indian nations would rise up to fight.

Now Custer was a career military man, a fighter, and yes, a glory hunter, but he also had in him compassion. The Indians had been given the word of peace and he felt the government should abide by that treaty. Grant was furious, and Custer found that a few of his army friends were against him on his thoughts and feelings. Now he finds himself again reprimanded in Washington, and cannot get anyone, except General Sheridan to listen to him. Grant orders the North Western Military posts to set out and find the hostile Indians and to correct the problem once and forever.

The Seventh Cavalry was part of that order and when Custer found out that his command was marching without him he went ballistic. No one wanted to hear anything from him. Sheridan told him that the only person that could get back his command was Ulysses S. Grant, the President of The United States. That was not going to happen anywhere in the near future he told himself. So, he tried and tried to make an appointment to see Grant, but hit a dead end each time. Meanwhile back at Fort Lincoln, Major Marcus Reno was in charge of the Seventh and was preparing the regiment for action. Reno was another civil war survivor and the class of 1857 at West Point. Custer had his dislike for Reno and made it very clear on how he felt about the man on many occasions.

He was not like Custer, he was cautious and reserved. The plan proposed by the war department was to have General Alfred Terry, Reno's subordinate leave Fort Lincoln and move north west towards the Big Horn River. Colonel John Gibbon would approach the Big Horn River from the west and General George Crook would approach the Big Horn River coming in from the south. Custer didn't give up on his trying to be reinstated to his command and the press started to taunt the government on his actions. The public started to get involved also and the pressure grew each day to reinstate "The Boy General".

General Crook and also Colonel Gibbon, including General Terry wanted him back also, because he had the experience not only to lead his men, but he knew the country and had some good contact with the Indians in the past. Grant could not take the relentless pressure from all sides and finally gave in, Custer was ordered back to Fort Lincoln to take command his fighting Seventh once again. In May of 1876 the Seventh Left Fort Lincoln and proceeded on the four-hundred-mile tract to the Big Horn River. It was estimated that the detachment should make the trip in around forty-five days. General Crook and Colonel Gibbon left around the same time at their respective posts and were to link up with Custer and General Terry on or about the twenty sixth or twenty seventh of June. Combined they would be a force of strength that the Indians could not defeat. On June the seventeenth Crooks army encountered a large contingent of Indians numbering over one thousand at the Rosebud

Creek. As Custer decried in Washington a month earlier, every tribe you could think of attacked Crook's flanks. The Ogala, Miniconjoux, Blackfeet, Unkpapas, the Sans Arcs, Cheyenne, and the Lakota Sioux. All these tribes were encamped a few miles upstream from the Rosebud on the Little Big Horn River.

Their scouts had sited Cooks column a few days earlier which gave them plenty of time for an all-out attack. The older Chiefs didn't want war, but the younger braves wanted to fight, especially the young warriors of the Cheyenne clan. "WASHITA" was on their minds, and revenge for their loved ones was the only thing that mattered. The battle lasted all day and finally the Indians fell back and retreated back upstream to their main village. It was a draw and no one side came out a winner. Crook pulled back down stream and couldn't understand why the Indians abruptly ceased fire and left, not knowing to him the Indians had bigger fish to fry, Custer and Terry! A little information on Crook and his command after the battle. Crook's regiment bivouacked in one of the most beautiful areas in the territory. It was referred to as "Goose Creek".

For the next two or three days the group hunted, deer, elk, mountain sheep accompanied by fine fishing.

It was reported by one of the officer's years later that Crook and his men had caught more than fifteen thousand trout and the campaign looked more like a "sporting club" than an Indian campaign. Now back to Custer and Terry. It was now June the twenty second and Terry called Custer to his tent. He told Custer to take his Seventh Regiment and proceed to the Little Big Horn on a scouting mission. He was ordered not to engage the enemy unless provoked and that he (Terry) would take up the rear position if Custer needed him. The last words that Terry spoke to Custer was "don't kill all the Indians Custer, leave some for us" Custer pulled out of camp and on the twenty fourth of June had them in a forced march toward the Little Big Horn River. His Crow scouts were sent out ahead of the column to try and find the Indian encampment. They came back on the evening of the twenty fourth and reported to Custer that they had found the Indian village, and that there were thousands of teepees set up along the Little Big Horn River.

Custer in the meantime had heard about Crook's encounter with the Indians a week before and wondered about Colonel Gibbon's regiment coming in from the west. Gibbon had infantry with him and Custer knew that the Indians would massacre the whole lot, just as they tried to do with Crook's regiments. That night the Seventh rode hard to the Little Big Horn and when they arrived all were "exhausted". Custer split his command into three columns. Major Reno with Companies M, A, and G totaling around one hundred and forty two men was to attack the village from the south end of the encampment, and Captain Benteen with Companies D, K, and H totaling around a hundred men was to circle around the south end of Reno's company and scout the southern end of the area and catch any fleeing warriors that try to flank Reno. Custer's five companies consisting of Companies C,F,I,E, and L totaling over two hundred troopers would head north along the river and attack the village at the north end of the camp. That was the last time Custer was seen alive, along with his troopers.

Washita was on Custer's mind and he felt he could catch the Indians by surprise as he had in 1868 and could win the day. Only one thing was wrong as I stipulated earlier, "THOUSANDS OF INDIANS"! Never has there been a larger encampment of Indians in the whole history of the native Americans. The pushing off their hunting grounds ended here today when all the tribes of the plains came together for one last battle with the long knives. The night before the battle Chief Sitting Bull over seer of all the Indian tribes told of having a dream about his warriors killing all the long knives and wiping them off the face of the earth. A great victory for all the tribes, but deep down he knew that it would be the last great battle of his people against the whites. So, on June twenty fifth around three o'clock in the afternoon the famous battle of The Little Big Horn commenced. Reno's men did attack the village and caught the Indians by surprise, but the troopers were soon over run by hundreds of very mad Indians. One Indian participant years later remarked that it looked like an ant hill going after their prey. Benteen heard the shooting and came back to find Reno's men in plenty of trouble with Indians attacking them from all sides from the river up to a nearby hill. Asked what about Custer Reno answered, he didn't know where he was.

It's around four o'clock in the afternoon now, and around this time during the battle Custer along with the five companies of troops that followed him were all dead. The Indians continued to try to pierce Reno's and Benteen's defenses all day and night, but to no avail. Next day, June twenty sixth both Reno and Benteen watched as the tribes started to leave their camps and make their way south. The fleeing Indians was said to have stretched for miles. One of the reasons for the retreat was tribal scouts had spotted General Terry's force that was coming in from the east. The warriors had experienced enough blood letting the day before, so they withdrew.

Custer was dead, including his two brothers, Captain Tom Custer of C Company and Boston, a civilian contractor, also his brother-in-law First Lieutenant James Calhoun who commanded L Company and his eighteen-year-old nephew Autie Reed. Two hundred and eighty of his men also died that day and seventy troopers wounded. The wounded were from Reno's and Benteen's commands. The Indian casualties numbered anywhere from eighty to three hundred. The Indian dead has always been up for question.

Fifty two percent of Custer's command met their deaths that day at the Battle Of The Little Big Horn. It not only changed the way the government dealt with the Indians in the future, it changed America as a whole. Yes, the civil war " Boy General" was dead. Hero or villain? You have to decide on that question. In short; Custer is a hero to some, and a glory hunter to others. His actions and decisions
   In battle and in civilian life molded the man, and speak for themselves. Was he a hero or that gusty glory hunter? In one man's opinion both, but to understand the man you must understand the man and what circumvented his life.

   This being the second chapter of this book, I hope that you, the reader has a better idea on Custer the man. The following chapters are on individuals that had an important part on that day on June twenty fifth, 1876. Their life stories also give you a better idea of who they were and what happened, or what went wrong on that day.

****

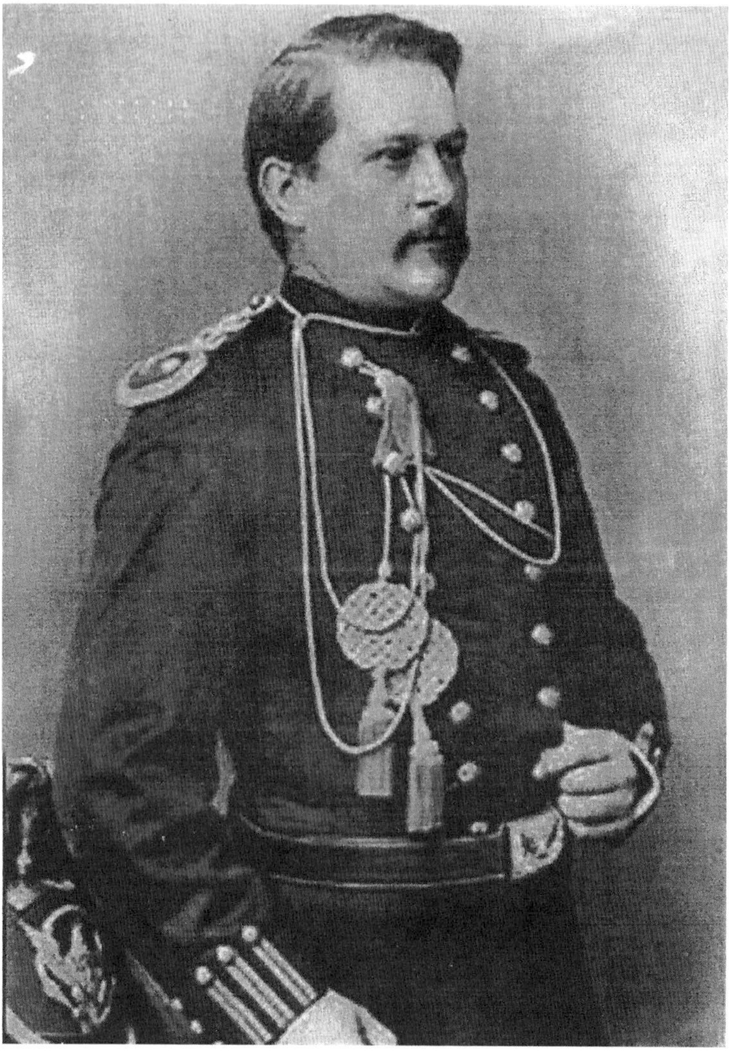

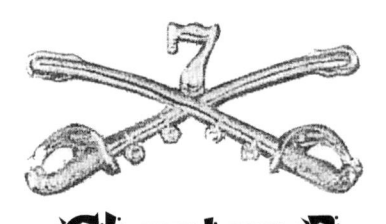

Chapter 13
Major Marcus Albert Reno

Marcus Albert Reno was born on November fifteenth, 1834 in Carrollto, Illinois. His parents were James Reno and Charlotte Reno. His father was a farmer and also in the mercantile trade. Later in life he purchased twelve real estate lots in town and built a tavern and a hotel, named the Red Hotel in the year 1831.

The hotel also served as a stagecoach stop and is still standing today. Reno had a step sister Harriet, belonging to his mother from a previous marriage and five brothers and sisters by his father and mother. There was Eliza, Cornelia, Leonard, then Marcus, followed by Sophronia, and Henry. The family name dated back to the ages in France and it was told that his great ancestor Phillippe Renault who came over from France with the "Marquis De La Lafayette" in 1777 and took part in the American Revolution.

It was said that the nation was so honored that he had helped out the colonists in their time of need, that they rewarded him with a land grant that was worth millions. Needless to say, Marcus Reno, nor his parents never saw any of the land. At the age of fifteen, Reno wrote a letter to the Honorable William Learned Marcy who at the time was the Secretary of State under President James K. Polk, requesting information on the qualifications needed to be admitted to the United States Military Academy at West Point in New York in 1851.

Two years later he was admitted to the academy. He had

to serve out two extra years at West Point, so instead of graduating in 1855, he graduated in 1857. This was all due to the number of demerits he had obtained throughout his first four years. The academy called them "EXCESSIVE". He graduated number twenty in a class of thirty-eight and was commissioned a Second Lieutenant in the First United States Dragoons in July of 1857 and assigned to the Pacific Northwest Territory in Oregon.

    When the civil war broke out in 1861 Reno was promoted the rank of Captain and later put in command of the First United States Cavalry. In August of 1862 at the battle of, "Antietam "again named by the Union, and "Sharpsburg" named by the Confederates. In the following year of 1863 Reno had his horse shot dead from under him, and the animal landed and pinned him down. This was at the battle of Kelly's Ford near Culpeper, Virginia. He received internal injuries from the fall and was out of commission for three months.

    For his actions at the battle he was given the rank of Major for his meritorious service. Four months later Reno was on the battle field again in 1863 at Gettysburg, Pennsylvania. Later that year he married Mary Ross of Harrisburg, Pennsylvania. In 1864 he took part in the battles of Cedar Creek, and Cold Harbor. Again, for his actions he was breveted a Lieutenant Colonel in late December of that same year and was put in command of the Twelfth Pennsylvania Cavalry. A year later in 1865 he was given the rank of Breveted Brigadier General. NOTE: When an officer was breveted he obtained a higher rank than what he had at the time, and holding that brevet temporarily. He was not paid for the brevet rank either, except when serving in that role. As noted in chapter one with Custer, he was breveted a Major General.

    After the war Reno and Mary bought a farm in

Cumberland, Pennsylvania and had a son Robert Ross Reno. This is where they wanted to retire after Reno's twenty years of service was up. But the army had different ideas for Reno and assigned him to Fort Vancouver, located in the North-West Washington territory. While there he became a Freemason in the local town and was initiated in 1867. In 1868 the army moved him again to Fort Hays, Kansas and promoted him to the rank of Major assigned to the Seventh Cavalry which later would be transferred to Fort Lincoln, North Dakota. As life dictates, Mary passed away suddenly in 1874 while Reno was in Montana on patrol.

When the word came about his wife Reno rode back to Fort Benton where he was assigned and asked for a furlough to go back east to attend to his late wife's funeral. The army turned down his request and it may have sparked ill feelings towards the army in future decisions handed him. He started to drink more heavily now and this would after time prove to be the main reason for his downfall that would ruin his career and his self-respect. He simply became a drunkard! When Custer left Fort Lincoln, Reno was second in command of the Seventh and Custer had his doubts about his executive officer.

Custer thought Reno was to slow in addressing situations that could be handled in a timelier fashion, but he went along with Reno's actions. Reno had never been in an Indian fight before and this was the main worry of his superior. On the night of the twenty fourth of June 1876 Custer summoned all of his officers to his tent. There he told them that their Indian scouts had sighted the Indian camp on the Big Horn and that the regiment would march in one hour. They would be at the River first thing in the morning and would surprise the Indians. Reno was the only officer that gave Custer any gruff on the matter. "A forced march all night would take any fight out of the men", he remarked. "General we would be better off moving at a slower pace and we still could surprise the savages next day". Custer wouldn't hear of it and the orders were to be obeyed. He also told his staff that the scouts let him know that the Indians had been observing the column for days and they knew we were coming to the Little Big Horn. To Reno's surprise Custer asked his officers assembled "would the person who has been in the back round since we left the Fort second guessing all of my commands and talking behind my back please come forward and expose you self like a gentleman".

It was said by Captain Benteen years later that if there had been a wood floor in that tent, that you could have heard a pin hit it if it had been dropped. To every one's surprise or maybe not, Major Reno stepped forward and told Custer that it was he who doing the talking. Custer at that point gave the order to be ready in one hour to march and excused everyone, but Reno. Benteen again years later said that "Custer was yelling at the top of his lungs" and after a few minutes Reno exited the tent and headed for his command in a hurry. Within the hour the regiment was on the move, and you could hear griping up and down the column. On the morning of June twenty fifth 1876, after traveling all night the Indian scouts again reported to Custer and said that they had never seen such a large Indian encampment as the one they reported earlier.

Bloody Knife one of Reno's scouts told Custer that if the regiment engaged the village, "we will all die". Custer wouldn't hear of it. He ordered Reno and his three companies to attack the south end of the village with Benteen and his three companies covering Reno's rear in case any Indians try to escape. Custer said he would attack the north end of the village and force the Indians south towards Reno. Sounds good huh? Well history wrote another story of how that day in June would play out. Reno and his three companies charged the camp which was the Hunpapas encampment where Chief Gall and Sitting Bull were, and for some reason after crossing the Big Horn River gave the order to dismount and fight on foot. Within twenty minutes Reno found out what it's like to swat a bee's nest, for within minutes there were hundreds of Indians counter attacking his command. Panic, confusion hit his troopers and a free for all to escape erupted. Many troopers were killed trying to reach the river.

Higher ground was on the other side, but the water level was high and each had trouble getting across. Reno himself went a little crazy when the Indian scout who told Custer they would all die today (Bloody Knife) was shot in the head standing next to him. The Indians brains were all over Reno's face, and Reno's uniform was soaked with the scout's blood. Reno escaped and made it back over the river with hundreds of Indians now on his tail.

Benteen two miles to the south heard the commotion and hurried back and set up a line of defense when he arrived. With his columns aid Reno and Benteen both held out for two days not knowing that Custer had died with his five company's hours earlier. The area now known as Reno Hill was only four miles from where Custer made his stand, and troopers from Reno's companies said that they could hear horrific gun fire coming from the west of their position. Reno said in later testimony he heard nothing coming from that area that day. After the fight, and it would go on for years, Reno tried to clear his name after he was accused of not aiding Custer during the battle.

Even Libby Custer who was Reno's biggest foe for years wanted the "coward" as she called him punished. Reno was put in command of the Seventh after Custer's death and remained its leader until they reached Fort Lincoln. There the army moved him to command post thirty miles away called Fort Abercrombie. He was drinking heavily now and made a pass at one of his officer's wives while her husband was away. The matter was resolved, but his drinking got worse. At a poker table one night he struck one of his subordinates after losing a large hand of money and was put under arrest. He was let go after a few hours and hit the bottle heavy again. This time around as he stumbled along the side walk of the officers' quarters, stopped and looked through the window of the daughter of the commanding officer of the post who was undressing in her room. Reno stood there mesmerized at what he saw, until the girl noticed him there and let out a loud scream which brought in her mother. Reno managed to continue on, but his peeping tom antics through him into a major court martial proceeding a month later in 1879.

He was brought up on two counts of actions unbecoming an officer. On the first count, of striking a subordinate Reno was found guilty, and on the second count of being drunk and conducting improper actions on spying on the commanding officer's daughter he was found guilty. The court had no other recourse that to dishonorably discharge Reno. So, after twenty-three years of service in the United States Army, he was through. After this disgusting and degrading event, he didn't know what to do. Reno went to Washington D.C. to try and find a job, but had no luck. He borrowed money to live on, and in the interim dated a woman, and in 1884 they were married, but the marriage only lasted a few months and ended up in divorce because of his drinking problem.

Reno finally landed a job with the Bureau of Pensions as an examiner and while there contacted several newspapers on the pretense of giving them his notes and diary on the "Battle of The Little Big Horn" which he said he wrote as he was defending his position that fateful day in 1876. No one wanted it, and that brought Reno down for ever. On March twenty ninth, 1889 Marcus Reno died at Providence Hospital in Washington after undergoing an operation for cancer of the tongue. Thus, Reno would join Custer again. It was said that Reno was brave, but not rash, and that Custer was both!

****

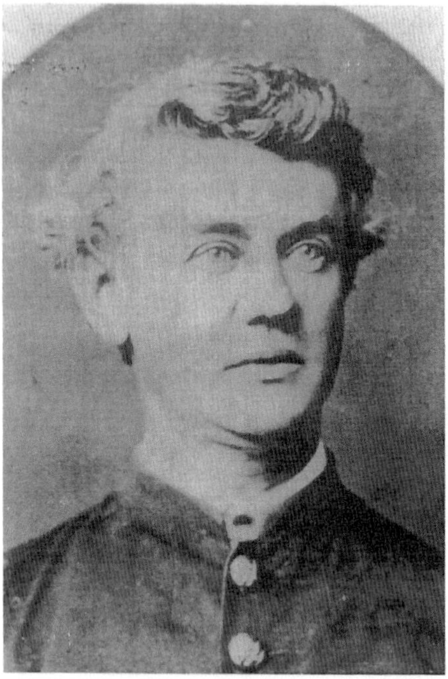

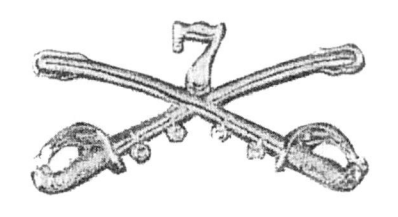

Chapter 4
Captain Frederick Benteen

Frederick Benteen was born in Petersburg, Virginia on august twenty fourth, 1834 to Theodore C. Benteen, and Caroline Hargrove Benteen. His ancestors came from Holland and settled in the Baltimore, Maryland area. During the American revolution their allegiance was to the "crown" (Great Britain). Benteen's father moved to Virginia in the 1830's where he painted houses, worked as a store keeper where he sold hardware glass, and paint. Benteen was educated at the Petersburg classical institute where he learned the ways of war and military drill. In 1849 Benteen's father moved to Saint Louis, Missouri where Benteen began working with him painting houses and signs.

He was tall, broad shouldered, had a large torso, and muscular arms. He had huge hands, was always clean shaven, and had deep blue eyes. Some remarked that the youthful Frederick looked like a small "cherub". When the civil war broke out he joined the union army, and on September first, 1861 he became a first lieutenant in Bowen's battalion which evolved into the tenth Missouri cavalry. In October of 1861 he was promoted to the rank of captain. Throughout the war he showed great leadership and took part in many engagements. His father didn't take to his son serving the union trash and disinherited him for not fighting for the southern cause. He said: "I hope the first god damned bullet gets you". His father was a stern secessionist and could not see any of his sons views on the war. In 1862, two things happened to young Benteen. First, he was married to a Miss Catharine Louis Norman in Saint Louis, and secondly, he saved the fate of his father. In 1862 his father was working on a Confederate steamboat called the "Fair play" Benteen had orders, not knowing his father was on board to seize the boat and destroy all the supplies. The act went well until Benteen saw his father amongst the rebel prisoners. Luckily, he knew a few higher ups in the chain of command, and they allowed his father to be jailed instead of being sent to prison for the duration of the war. After the war ended in 1865 he was promoted to the rank of Colonel of the One Hundred and Thirty-Eight Colored Infantry. Within the year of 1865 he was promoted again to the rank of Brigadier General of the Missouri Militia. His career was taking off now in the direction he had worked so hard for. Benteen served throughout the war with distinction and was cited for gallantry many times leading to these steady promotions. Then in July of 1866 he was assigned to a new duty roster to full fill, the "Seventh Cavalry".

The Seventh had just been formed and they needed officers with experience. He was made Captain and was to serve under the regiments new Lieutenant Colonel, George Armstrong Custer. Well they didn't hit it off right and that relationship would remain frayed throughout their tenure with the Seventh. Benteen didn't like Custer and was disgusted with him. He didn't like Custer's pretense and thought the man was a braggart.

Benteen was five years older than the young commandant, and he took it to heart, knowing he had more experience than his commander. "Custer the glory hunter wasn't going to ruin my career" he said and went about second guessing his subordinate. Then came the Indian wars! The Seventh was the eyes and ears of the army in the western territory which was on the verge of exploding. The treaties of 1867 and 1868 were falling apart, due greatly to the white mans need for more territory to settle, and the Seventh was there to protect the throngs of people migrating on treaty land. The Battle of the Washita in1868 was the way of things to come to the Indian people in the future. 1876 brought in a new year, and more troubles for the settlers of the west and also to Benteen's commander. Gold was discovered in the Black Hills of the Dakota Territory and a new gold rush followed suit. Benteen in the meanwhile had written a letter to the war department, accusing Custer's handling of land claims in the Black Hills as a money-making venture for him, and a few other prominent people up the food chain in Washington, DC. One which included the president "Ulysses S. Grant's brother, Orville. Custer was summoned to DC and reprimanded, and lost his command, but due to pressure from people all over the country finally got his regiment back.

Benteen caught hell when Custer returned, but the Seventh was ordered to move on the Indians right away and both didn't have time for grudges at that moment. We're at the Little Big Horn now and after an all-night, forced march which all objected to, here was the Seventh Cavalry ready to do battle, "EXHAUSTED".

Custer ordered Benteen with his three companies of troopers, Co. D, Co. K, and Co. H. to the south west of the Indian village, to support Reno's flank in case of any Indians. Reno with his troopers of Co. M, Co. A, and Co.G would hit the Indian village from the southern end of the encampment. Custer would take Co.C, Co.F, Co. I, Co. L, and Co. E and would hit the village from the north and drive the Indians south towards both Reno and Benteens troops. Benteen objected strongly after hearing the scouts report on the number of Indians that they had seen, and so did Reno. No good, Custer had his way and Benteen's place in history was about to be written. After the order was given he rode back to his companies and they galloped towards the south west just as Custer ordered. After Benteen, Custer took off with his companies never to be seen again alive and Reno headed towards the Big Horn River as ordered. Ten miles had gone by and Benteen hadn't run into hostile Indians. He had a strange feeling about the whole matter of scouting the area where they were, and gave the order to head back to the ridge where they had departed an hour before.

About five miles out Benteen halted his troops when he saw a rider coming at a gallop towards them. It was Bugler John Martin. Martin was instructed by Custer an hour earlier to locate Benteen and to give him a note that was written out by Lieutenant William Cooke the Seventh's Adjutant. Addressing the Captain Martin said: "sir a message from Colonel Custer. He handed the note to Benteen and sat in his saddle as Benteen peered over it. It read:

Benteen
Come on. Big village.
Be quick. Bring packs
W. W. Cooke
P.S. Bring packs

Benteen looked up at Martin and asked what Custer's situation was when he left the Colonel. "He was fine sir" answered Martin. "The Colonel was about to head down into the village, and all we're fired up over the upcoming fight with the Indians." Martin had made it sound like a picnic for Custer's men, so Benteen decided to continue to head for Reno's position. The pack train that Custer left back earlier was another five miles south of where Benteen was and he felt it would be a waste of time to do what Custer had requested. It's now around three p.m. in the afternoon and just around two miles from where they were headed, Benteen's scouts came back and told him of a great battle that was ragging as they spoke. Benteen gave the order to make hast and they headed for the ridge where Reno now was fighting for his life. The closer they got, the louder the gun fire was. Men screaming could be heard now, and again the gun fire was intense it brought memories of the civil war battles that Benteen was in.

With Reno in sight now he ordered his troopers to dismount and set up a perimeter with Reno's companies. Reno had a defense position that was holding back the advancing Indians, and Benteen's troopers added to the strength of those defenses. The Hill or knoll that they chose to defend would later be called Reno Hill. There were hundreds of Indians attacking the defenses now and their fire power was relentless. Reno had just got back up the hill in the chase of his life, and when he saw Benteen he had a sigh of relief.

Benteen rushed over to him and at once noticed the blood from the killing of the scout Bloody Knife all over his upper shoulder area. What happened he asked Reno as they both are now firing their revolvers at the Indians who had them pinned down. Reno was shaken badly and Benteen thought that he was lucky not to have been put in that position before. Benteen was a lucky soul also when it came to being shot. He seemed oblivious to bullets as they were being fired at the troopers in great multitude. He would stand up almost inviting the Indians to shoot at him. Later survivors would testify that Benteen was all over the defense area directing his men and Reno's to stand their ground. He felt later that when asked about Reno and his poor judgements on the hill, the man just went nuts and lost his sense of leadership after Bloody Knife's brains wound up all over him down in the village when the battle started. Benteen asked "where was Custer"? Reno just looked at him and shook his head. Reno said they heard volley firing coming from the position where Custer was supposed to be, earlier, but the firing dwindled down and things started to get hotter around his position. Benteen surmised that Custer was probably still north of the village and was handling the Indians on his terms.

His companies and Reno's are now being fired upon at a greater pace and both cannot figure where all the firearms came from. Bows and arrows weren't the choice of weapons being used by the tribes today. Again, years later he was quoted as saying "I state, but the facts when I say, that we had a fairly warm time with those red men". The six companies of Reno and Benteen held out all night and when morning came they could see this great movement of Indians heading south. Benteen said the line had to be at least ten miles long and three to four miles wide.

They later learned the Indian tribes turned their backs when scouts told them of more blue coats heading west and should arrive shortly. The fighting was over, and the war was or wasn't won on both sides. Benteen still wondered where Custer was and put his thoughts aside and took care of his troops. Reno was better this morning, but was still shook up.

Later that day General Terry's regiment showed up and Benteen asked him if he had seen Custer as they came in from the north west? "I haven't seen him, he isn't here" was Terry's response. "No" Benteen said, "but I figure he is just north of here waiting for the rest of us so he can claim his great victory over the Indians". Terry then told Benteen to ride the west and see if you can find him, and tell him to get his "sorry ass" back here. Benteen took another officer with him and within ten minutes out they started to see bodies all over the area stripped, and mutilated. They found Captain Keogh and his company all dead maybe a mile out, and then came upon the body of Captain Yates and his men a little further to the southwest, all dead also, I troop was no more! Now, almost four miles out the two came upon a ghastly sight, they had found Custer. Both rode around the defense perimeter very slowly taking in what they saw. Dead troopers all around, naked, and also mutilated.

Heads cut off, arms, legs, private parts missing all scalped and many with their heads bashed in. Arrows sticking out of every orifice you could imagine, and then finally they find Custer. He's in a sitting position lying with his back against a dead horse," smiling". Dead yes, but smiling. He has a bullet wound to his left side and a bullet wound to his skull. He wasn't naked as the others and not mutilated. His men were all around him in different positions of death. Benteen noticed Custer's brothers Tom, and Boston dead within five yards of him and his nephew Autie Reed dead also within the same distance from his uncle George. Around fifty in all Benteen counted, and there were more as they headed down towards the Big Horn. When they got back to Reno Hill they reported to Terry on what they had encountered. No one could believe it, Custer dead with all of his five companies! Benteen was pale as a ghost reported Reno, and he was disturbed. The officer that went with him said upon seeing Custer, Benteen muttered "There he is, god damn him, he will never fight anymore"

After the Little Big Horn battle Benteen became vindictive and held a cancerous bitterness towards his fellow comrades. In 1877 he was present at the Battle of Canyon Creek that was against the Nez Perce, and in 1879 he was summoned to testify at the court martial of his fellow officer, Marcus Reno who was brought up on charges of not taking the right actions at the Little Big Horn battle. For a short time in 1880 he was a Cavalry Recruiter for the army and in 1882 he received a promotion to the rank of Major with the Ninth United States Cavalry. He stayed with the Ninth for five years, and then in 1887 was brought up on charges of actions not becoming an officer. The Ninth wasn't like the old Seventh and the drinking problems weren't as numerous as the latter had. Benteen followed the footsteps of Reno and became a heavy drinker.

His attitude finally got the best of him and he was found guilty of obscene and offensive behavior, on one count, and being drunk on duty three times on the second count. He was ordered to be dismissed from the army and military service to the United States. He appealed and because of his non-tarnished record during the civil war, and because of his actions at the Little Big Horn, his sentence was reversed and he went walking with only a reduction in rank and half pay for a year. Benteen returned to duty on April twenty seventh, 1888, but only for three weeks where at that time he put in for a medical discharge due to a bad back.

He retired in Atlanta, Georgia in 1888 and he and his wife and son worked a little farm outside the city. He also started to write his memoirs about his life in the army and his reflections of what happened that day in June of 1876. In 1898 Benteen suffered a major stroke and died five days later on June twenty second. He once told a trooper from the old Seventh that was with him at the Little Big Horn "I've been a loser in a way all my life, by rubbing a bit against the angles or hair of folks, instead of going with their whims: but couldn't go otherwise, it would be against the grain of myself". Why Benteen and Reno never got along is puzzling? Their tarnished relationship with Custer created a wall that would not allow them to penetrate through it. All three, Custer, Reno, and Benteen knocked one another, and they could not help it. The Seventh's three ranking officers had a huge problem with one another. It was like the three were on a twenty foot fence with Reno and Benteen on the ground and Custer on top with the chances for the two to climb it also, was nil!

****

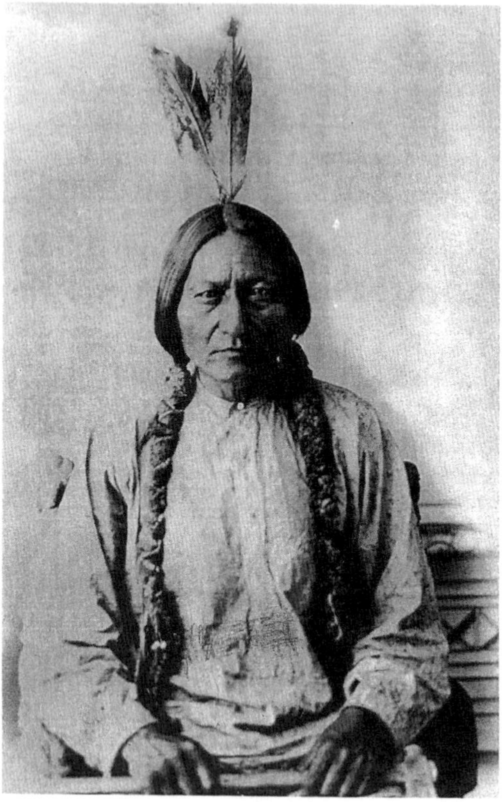

Chapter 5
Chief Sitting Bull

Sitting Bull was born between 1830 and 1837 no one knows for sure, along a tributary of the Missouri River in what was then South Dakota Territory. His father's name was "Jumping Bear" and his mother's name was "Her Holly Door". Both were full blooded Lakota Sioux from the Hunkpapa tribe. At birth he was named "Hoka Psice". Later on, in life he would be called names such as "Bull or "Bison." He was also referred to as "Jumping Badger." His mother called him "Slow" (Slon-Ha) for his lack of skills. At the age of ten he killed his first buffalo, and at age fourteen he counted his first coup on a slain Crow warrior while on a horse stealing mission.

For this brave action his people gave him the name "Sitting Bull" (Hunkesni) which would follow him for the rest of his life. The name given was to pay tribute to the buffalo, respect, and great wisdom and strength. All were what Sitting Bull was all about throughout his life. When he grew up and in his twenty's, we see a warrior about six-foot-tall, big head, and a large nose.

Pale brown skin that was scared by smallpox. He also was a little bow legged and acquired a limp due to being shot in the foot in 1865 by a Crow warrior while on a raiding party. He was a fierce warrior who would return from battle or raiding parties with scalps, ears, fingers, and hands of a warrior that he had killed. He was said to have had sixty-three battle coups during his life time.

Sitting Bull was as consistent and inflexible as a man could be. He was known to the Hunkpapa as a man of both worlds, earthly and spiritually. Growing up in the village he participated in every aspect of the life of the Sioux. He acquired great authority and many of his fellow tribesmen disliked him for this, but a great many others found him affectionate and considerate. He had a resonate voice and became a singer of tribal songs and courted away from the usual chants mouthed around the tribal fires at night. Sitting Bull was sort of a mystic to his people.

He was one of only two sash-wearers inducted into the "Strong Hearts Warrior Society" that entitled him to wear the famed buffalo horn war bonnet covered with crow feathers into battle. He did not speak until he thought through what he was going to say. At first, he was courteous, but developed a great dislike for white people. Sitting Bull felt the only way to negotiate with the "WHITES" was to avoid them entirely.

He spoke very little English and the only words you would hear him say were "hello, you be, and his name seed-a-boo", (Sitting Bull). He, like Custer and Chief Crazy Horse was seldom hurt. The "great spirit" (Wakan Tanka) was always looking after him he felt. He excelled in the virtues admired by the Sioux people, bravery, wisdom, generosity, and fortitude a true holy man. Sitting Bull signified a wise and powerful being and would become the most famous Indian in history a major spiritual, military, and political leader of the Indian movement.

So, the stage was set! Sitting Bull was the one the tribes listened to and who's visions of victory against the long knives took stock. On that day in June, 25th 1876 he and every warrior from the village took out their anger on Custer's regiment with fast and furious swiftness. In an interview given in 1877 he stated that another Indian spoke of long hairs death to him after the battle and the Indian said "long hair stood like a sheaf of corn with all ears fallen around him. He, Sitting Bull also stated that the soldiers who came with long hair were as good men as any other man who ever fought. They were at the time of the battle tired, exhausted from their ride, their horses were exhausted and their physical conditioned played a great roll in their defeat. Poor Custer and his men didn't have a chance in hell against the thousands of Indian warriors who had assembled along the Big Horn.

Years later people would ask of him what he thought that day about the battle? Sitting Bull would respond every time with "let no man say that this was a massacre, they came to kill us and killed themselves". But deep down when he had the vision of killing all the long knives and he knew in his heart the Indian way of life was lost forever. After he defeated Custer, he took his tribe to Canada and lived there for five years. The Canadian government gave them shelter, but that was about the extent of their hospitality. Sitting Bull in 1882 gave up and moved back to the United States and surrendered. In the coming years he would go through life at peace with the whites. He was hired by Buffalo Bill Cody to travel with him with his wild west show and became very popular.

After Cody's employment Sitting Bull was seen as the one who had stirred up the Indians once again, and the army caught wind that he had participated in a sun dance. He denied the charges, but the cards were not in his favor this time and the army was out to get him. On December 5th,1890 the army surrounded his cabin with at least three hundred troopers, including a battery of artillery, and forced him out in the open. Bad mistake, for that was when he was shot down and killed along with one of his sons. The great leader of the Lakota people was dead and his memory still lingers on. Today, in this year 2018 there have been since the early years of this great nation over five hundred and thirty treaties broken with the Indian people.

Here is a quote from Sitting Bull:

" WARRIORS ARE NOT WHAT YOU THINK OF AS WARRIORS THE WARRIOR IS NOT SOMEONE WHO FIGHTS BECAUSE NO ONE HAS THE RIGHT TO TAKE ANOTHER LIFE THE WARRIOR FOR US IS ONE WHO SACRIFICES HIMSELF FOR THE GOOD OF OTHERS HIS TASK IS TO TAKE CARE OF THE ELDERLY, THE DEFENSELESS AND THOSE WHO CANNOT PROVIDE FOR THEMSELVES, AND ABOVE ALL THE CHILDREN, THE FUTURE OF HUMANITY"

SITTING BULL

Have we as a people learned anything from what we have done in the past?

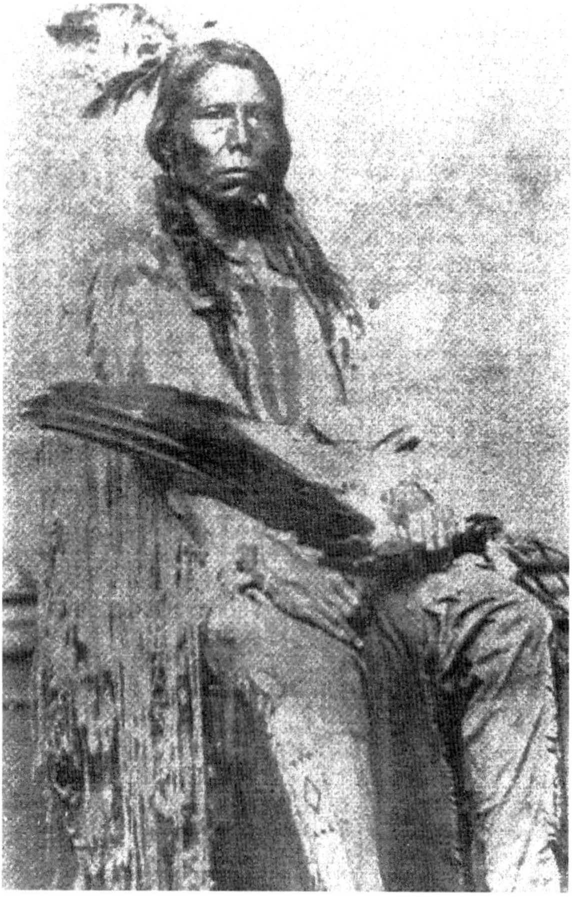

Chapter 6
Chief Crazy Horse

Crazy Horse was born in the fall of 1840 near present day Rapid City, South Dakota south of the Belle Fourche River. At birth he was named 'In the Wilderness Among the Trees"(CHA-O-HA). His name could also refer to "one of nature". His father named "Crazy Horse" was a medicine man of the Lakota Sioux. His mother's name was "Rattle Blanket Woman" a Miniconjou Sioux with Brule' Sioux blood lines. The word Lakota also known as "Teton" referred to the seven tribes of the "prairie dwellers" as they were known. The great people of the plains, who were part of a confederation from different tribes.

The Brule', Oglala, Sans Arc, Hunkpapa, the Miniconjou, Blackfeet, and finally the Two Kettles. He had sandy hair, and his mother always called him "Curly" and "Light Hair" until he was around ten years old. Growing up, he would go out into the wilderness for days without food or water and reflect on his life and the things to come in his future. At the age of fifteen or sixteen, he had experienced many episodes of war and violence. At age eighteen he lived with the Brule' Sioux and continued his education in the ways of a warrior. He attracted attention, was a good hunter, and was courageous in battle. Embracing death was a basic trait of a Sioux warrior, and dying in battle was appealing.

Around 1855 or 1856, he took the name "Crazy Horse"

after returning from a raiding party, and having two scalps of dead Crow warriors that he had killed. His father is said that he felt proud of his son's deeds, and that is when he gave him his name "Crazy Horse" His father would go thru life from then on, known as "Worm. "Indians of every tribe on the plains stole horses from other tribes as a manly thing and a warrior element. Crazy Horse grew up thinking of war and counting coup. "Fame" is what he sought! To be talked about and being respected with and having a place of position, he wanted the highest recognition. He was always the first into battle and his name was known by all, and people talked about what a great warrior he was. NOTE: (sounds a lot like Custer). He was of mid height and light frame. Had a light complexion, and didn't have high cheek bones as did other Indians, and he had hazel eyes. He also had powder burns on his face from an enemy that tried to shoot him at close range with a pistol later on in his late teens. Crazy Horse didn't talk too much, and he was a man of few words at counsel and usually had someone else speak for him.

Being older now Crazy Horse's feeling changed. Fighting was an important part of growing up and being a warrior, but he did not claim glory in war. Most Sioux would bring home scalps or other trophies after a battle, but he did not. When in his early twenty's he had a dream of meeting a man and having a conversation with him that changed his outlook on life. The man talked to him about not taking scalps or wearing war paint into battle, or even tying his horses tail in braids. These things Crazy Horse did for the rest of his short life. This dream he had with the man prepared him for the future, for the man told him he wouldn't die from a bullet, but he would meet his death by being held and stabbed.

In 1866 he led the attack on Captain John Fetterman and his brigade of eighty men near Fort Kearny in the Northwest Wyoming territory. All were killed and it sent a message to Washington. The "Fetterman Massacre" as the battle was referred to sent smoke signals that the Indian problem was getting larger. The Lakota Sioux referred to the fight as "The Battle of The Hundred in The Hand". In 1867 Crazy Horse led his braves totaling three hundred to one thousand strong in a fight, again near Fort Kearny in Wyoming, against a wood cutting crew from the fort totaling only twenty-six troopers and eight civilians.

Crazy Horse thought this was going to be an easy "coup" and didn't expect the final results. The troopers were issued the new breech loading rifles that could fire three rounds a minute, and the Indians thought they had their clumsy single shot muskets. The troopers surprised Crazy Horse after their first volley and when the Indians attacked thinking that the soldiers had to reload their muskets. Well they were surprised when the troopers almost immediately opened on them again and again and with no lull in their deadly volley fire. Crazy Horse had had enough and retreated off the battle field leaving over one hundred dead warriors. The soldiers suffered only two dead that day. In 1868 he was made a "Shirt Wearer." which meant that you as a warrior think of your responsibilities to the people and to rise above all ordinary or personal concerns. In battle he never wore a feathered war bonnet, and had one maybe two tail feathers from a spotted eagle tied to his hair including one or two blades of grass. The grass he felt was good luck and would always include them. Men married in their twenties to women who were young the squaws ranged from fifteen to sixteen years old. Crazy Horse was not the norm, he married in his thirties in 1870. He had three wives, Black Buffalo Woman, Black Shawl, and Nellie Larrabee. With Black Shawl he had a daughter born in 1874 by the name of

"They Are Afraid of Her," who died at an early age. Crazy Horse was a war leader, (blota hunka). He was the one who owned the peace pipe, (canumpa yuha). In May of 1876 he led the charge against General Crook and his regiment at the "Battle of The Rosebud" just south of the Little Big Horn River in Montana territory. He inflicted great destruction on Crook and his command which forced Crook to head south after the battle. Crazy Horse lost a lot of braves and he to back stepped off the battle field, but only upon hearing there were more blue coats coming from the north heading in line for the Little Big Horn where his, and the other tribes were encamped. Both sides in history called it a draw year later, but as in war there were no winners.

A week later on June twenty fifth, 1876 in the late afternoon, Custer along with eleven companies of troopers met Crazy Horse on the battle field. He split his regiment into three commands and attacked the Indian village. Crazy Horse had just returned from swimming in the Big Horn River when he heard the gun fire coming from the south end of the camp. (Remember there was an estimated ten thousand Indians encamped there now and the teepee's stretched for one or two miles long and one mile wide.) He had heard Reno's men attacking Chief Sitting Bull's Hunkpapa village.

There was commotion coming out in every direction of the camp an adrenalin was flowing in the bodies of every warrior. From his camp he could see the long knives coming from the north west now (this had to be Custer with his five companies) heading for the river. He quickly went into his teepee and returned with his medicine bag around his neck. He then asked for spiritual guidance from his parents and proceeded to apply a maroon pigment to his hands. The gun fire now was louder and every tribe was getting ready for battle. With the paint on his hands he put a hand print on each hind quarter of his horse and then drew an arrow down the animal's neck with a scalp on the end.

He had prepared for this day for all of his life, and with that he led a great number of Cheyenne Oglala and Brule' warriors and attacked Custer's main defense now called Custer Hill from the north and west in flanking moves that broke the soldier's lines. Chief Gall led the Miniconjou, the Sans Arc, and the Black Feet with the same effect hitting the soldiers from the east and south. It was reported by many Indian survivors later, that Crazy Horse taunted the soldiers with numerous charges and didn't even receive a scratch. This was his day and the great spirit was with him. It took two desperate attacks by Crazy Horses warriors to divide Custer's men into small fighting units. Custer was left with forty or fifty men around him, and the rest fought down the hill towards the river. No one got away that day. Crazy Horse was riding back and forth yelling "HO'KA-HE'Y (it's a good day to die). The battle was over in less than an hour, but still ragged to the south east four miles with Reno and Benteen;s companies still under attack. Crazy Horse along with Sitting Bull decided that their forces had made a statement to the whites that day and pulled out of their camps

The next day leaving the rest of Reno's and Benteen's men alone. Some of the survivors from Reno's company said later in statements that the Indian pull out looked like a giant snake. Miles and miles of Indians heading south. Crazy Horse would become a house hold name back east in another two weeks when the word of Custer's demise hit the newspapers. He was hated along with all the other red savages and would, the following year search his soul for peace with the white man. Later that year through a spokesman in an interview Crazy Horse stated that there were over eighteen hundred lodges (tepee's) in the Indian camp and at least four hundred or more wickiup's (rude huts built hastily for shelter half round). He said that there were over eight thousand old men, women, and children, in the camp with over three to six thousand warriors. Many of the young men also took part in the battle along with men from other tribes who were referred to as "hangers on". These were brought the total warrior count up to over seven thousand strong. Experts put the camp at over three miles long and one and a half miles wide. On May sixth, 1877 Crazy Horse gave himself up at Fort Robinson in Nebraska territory and surrendered. He was told to stay on the reservation, but left and was put under arrest. He was returned to the fort where a fight broke out as the soldiers were leading him to the guard house. He struggled and was bayoneted by trooper William Gentles in the kidneys, twice.

His parents were notified and Crazy Horse died in his father's arms the next day. So was the life of a great warrior Chief of the Sioux nation, "Hokahey"

Hokahey
It was a good day to die!

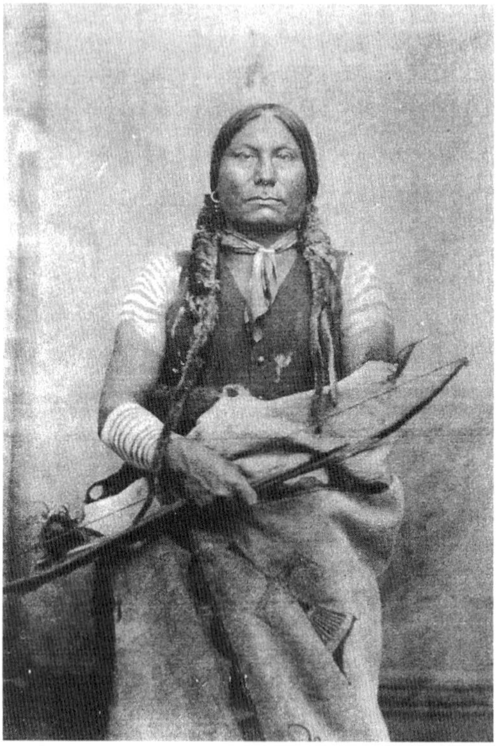

Chapter 7
Chief Gall

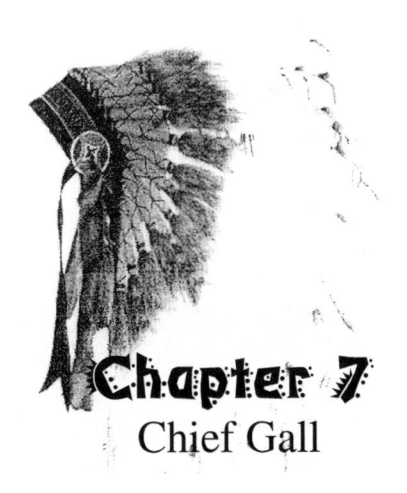

" Chief Gall" as he was referred to was born along the Moreau river in South Dakota territory around 1840. His father died early in his life and was regarded with more of sympathy than respect. His mother's name was "Cajeojowin" (walks- with-many-names). Both Gall's parents were from the Lakota Hunkpapa tribe. The first name that his mother gave to him was "Matohinsa" (bear shedding his hair). Later on, when he was around five or six he adopted the name "Gall", because he was found one day eating the gall bladder of an animal. All through his early life, he roamed the prairies with his tribe in pursuit of the buffalo. He had a great physique, stood around five feet seven inches, and had dark black eyes. Gall was very athletic and had much self-confidence. He was very strong in sporting events such as wrestling, throwing the javelin, and riding ponies. Much later in life he would weigh over three hundred pounds.

Gall was an accomplished warrior in his teens, and became a Chief in his early twenty's. He was a man of great power and spoke with respect and understanding. Gall had many coups in battle, and was brought into the prestigious "Strong Heart Society", which was a secret warrior policy making unit of the Hunkpapa's. He was a band leader or headman in the tribe responsible for caring for members of the tribe or "Tospaye". He was also a tribal peace leader, master, and ruler "Itancan" Chief Sitting Bull was his mentor all thru his life, and Gall became one of Sitting Bulls most trusted Lieutenants. Gall fought with Sitting Bull at the battle of Killdeer Mountain in 1864, and proved to be a natural leader of men in that fight. All throughout his life time Gall would be bayoneted, shot, stabbed, but always found a way to beat death. In battle he was also referred to as "Red Walker"

In 1868 a major problem plagued Gall steaming from the Treaty of Fort Laramie. The treaty gave the five northern nations of the Lakota, the Hunkpapa, Blackfeet, Sans Arcs, Two Kettles, and the Miniconjou's a vast partial of land which encompassed half of the southern South Dakota Territory. Gall took to the treaty, along with Sitting Bull, Red Cloud, and Red Horse. Crazy Horse and a few of the other Chiefs walked away from the treaty and didn't want anything to do with the whites. Things were fine for a while until gold was discovered in the Black Hills and the killing started again. The Treaty of 1868 was defied and more and more Indians wondered off their reservations because of double talk from the United States Government. In January of 1876 the tribes were given an ultimatum, and were told to return to their reservations by the end of that month. Many Indians never received that order and didn't find out about it until they heard the sounds of charge coming from a cavalry bugle later on.

Gall believed that the white man wanted peace, but in the end, he saw the light. The Battle of The Rosebud and the Battle of The Little Big Horn which were to follow in the coming months, would prove that the white man wanted and wanted, and wanted. On the morning of June twenty fifth 1876, Gall slept late in his tepee along side the Little

Big Horn River. Just weeks earlier he and Crazy Horse with a thousand other warriors did battle with General Crook at the Rosebud Creek. The night before, the Indian encampment was celebrating and the young (teca) braves from every tribe were involved with the war dance. Sitting Bull had spoken about his dream of destroying all the long knives in a great battle that was coming, which heightened the warrior's expectations. Gall was tired and felt it was the young men's turn at war. Only thirty-six years old, Gall retired early. His camp was set up on the south end of the Little Big Horn River to act as a sentry post for the rest of the camp. Again, some estimates put the entire Indian camp at over ten thousand, so the Hunkpapa's guarded the south end, the Miniconjou's guarded the middle, and the Northern Cheyenne guarded the northern end.

The Brule's, Ogala's, Sans Arcs, and Blackfeet were encamped in the middle. Each camp was put in a circle and it stretched four miles long. Around one o'clock in the afternoon Gall was woken by rifle shots (scisci) outside south of his teepee. He rushed outside and there saw cavalry soldiers dismounted, and shooting at fleeing women and children who had been down by the river swimming or doing laundry. These troopers proved to be part of Reno's detachment. He could see now young warriors challenging the troopers and were forcing the soldiers back. Gall put on his war gear, painted his arms with white stripes and grabbed his only weapon of war, a tomahawk!

Later that day, he would tell reporters years later that he found out that the troopers had killed two of his wives and three(ya<mni) of his children. This made him very sad and the anger stirred inside of him. It was reported by other survivors of the battle years later also that Gall was all over the battlefield that day. Attacking Reno's and Benteen's men on the south to leading at least one charge into Custer's main line of defense on Last Stand Hill. He rode out among the

soldiers and split (kaslece) their heads with his tomahawk. Later he would say "I killed a great many." He galloped through Custer's line like a wolf through a flock of sheep.

After the battle he returned to his camp and mourned his losses. Sitting Bull tried to console him, but the loss was too great for him to grasp. Next day Gall and the other Chiefs pulled up camp and headed south. A great victory they thought, but didn't want any part of another encounter with the long knives that were approaching from the west, and soon would be at the river. In 1886 ten years after the Battle of The Big Horn, Gall gave an account of the battle on the battlefield with government representatives. Present also was "Curley," Custer's favorite scout and numerous other Indians who had taken part in the battle. Standing where Custer fell, Gall presented the story of the Seventh's demise. Turning to Curley, Gall accused him of not being the sole survivor of the battle and accused him of running fast when the battle started.

He stated that the Indian scouts were watching the Seventh for hours before they separated. He told those present that Custer's men were killed off first, and then the Indians gave way to Calhoun's men, and then onto Keogh's troops. After they were defeated his warriors concentrated on Reno's position, until he saw dust coming in from the west (Gibbon's troops). Sitting Bull all this time was in camp making strong medicine in his tepee. Libby Custer was quoted as saying years later about a photograph she had seen of Chief Gall, "It is painful to look upon the picture of Gall, but I honestly never dreamed there could be in all the Indian tribes so fine a specimen of a warrior, as Gall".

Gall escaped to Canada with Sitting Bull and stayed there for five years. Finally, in 1881 he surrendered to troops of the United States. There he was put on a reservation, took up farming and in 1889 he was appointed a judge of Indian affairs. For the rest of his life he would act as an envoy for his people and made Indian relations a priority. All he ever wanted was peace, and peace finally came to him when he passed away at age fifty-four in 1895.

****

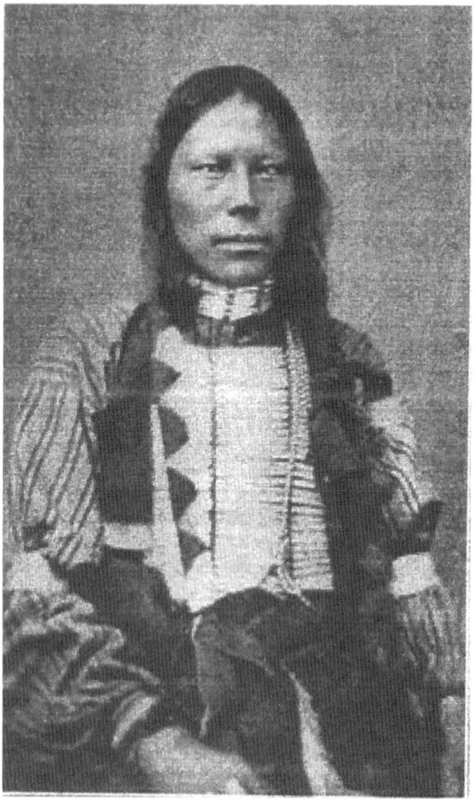

Chapter 8
Chief Black Kettle

Black kettle was born in 1803. Not much is known for the man until the year 1854 when he was made a chief at the forties chief ceremony. All through his life, his people were driven off their lands by the white people, simply because they wanted it. There were many treaties and his people were displaced onto reservation lands, but with the infiltration of white settlers there became a competition of hunting game, and the use of water and grazing grounds for their horses.

The whites kept coming and the Cheyenne were pushed all over the territories. In 1864 the army sent john Chivington with his third cavalry to put an end to the Indian raids that sprouted up after Indian resentment. Chivington had 700 men and attacked the Cheyenne village early in the morning on the banks of the sand creek. Black kettle was present and from his tepee he flew the American flag and a white flag of peace.

He was told by the local Indian agent that these symbols would protect his village from any hostilities from the army. Not so for that morning 163 men, women, and children were killed when Chivington's cavalry attacked. Black kettle escaped. He wanted nothing but peace. He was quoted as saying: "although wrongs have been done to me, i live in hope. I do not have two hearts. I once thought I was the only man that perceived to be a friend of the white man, but since they have come and cleared out our lodges, horses, and everything else, it's hard for me to believe the white man's lies anymore"

In 1865 he achieved the treaty of the little Arkansas river and the united states gave the Cheyenne people in reparation for the sands creek massacre lands in the Indian territory now (Oklahoma). The Indians didn't want this and the Cheyenne dog soldiers started to attack the whites and this went on for three years. Finally, the government was pressured by the public and the seventh cavalry under the command of George Custer was ordered in to quell the problem. On the morning of the twenty seventh of November 1868 Custer attacked the Cheyenne village at the Washita river and killed chief black kettle and his wife along with many women and children. Bad move by Custer for it will haunt him some eight years later at the little big horn.

Chief black kettle has always been looked at by his peoples a man of vision, and who only wanted peace for his nation. He was a great peacemaker in their eyes.

****

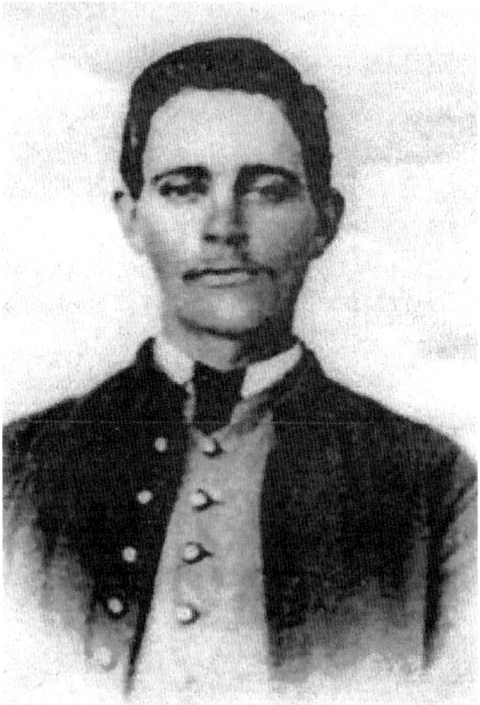

Chapter 9
Norvell Francis Churchill

Norvell Francis Churchill was born on June 11th, in 1840 to David and Zoa Churchill. They lived in Berlin, Michigan and in the county of St. Clair. Norvell grew up with seven other brothers and sisters and was well liked in the Berlin community. His father was a farmer and owened over 160 acres of prime farm land. Norvell was raised and educated well and was an expert horseman, very athletic, and loved to hunt.

When the Civil War broke out he volunteered and enlisted in the Army. He was assigned to the cavalry and was made an orderly for the 1st. Michigan Cavalry, Company L. Throughout his military career he served as an orderly for General's Nathaniel bank, General Joseph Mansfield, General William T. Sherman. In 1863 his regiment was re-assigned and put in the command of one General George Armstrong Custer. On July 2nd, 1863 the regiment saw action at the Battle of Gettysburg and that's where the two men's lives would cross each other. It happened four miles Northeast of Gettysburg in a small sleepy town called Huntertown. Confederate Brigadier General Wade Hampton was ordered by Major General Jeb Stuart to take up position near the left rear of the Confederate battle lines. There Hampton was to set up a defense around Huntertown road. During the large cavalry battle that would take place, Norvell would sweep down on a confederate officer who was about to swing his sword into Custer's chest. Norvell thwarted the thrust of the officer's blade and sent him to his grave with a shot from his colt revolver. For this Custer, made Norvell his special orderly. He was put on detached service training new recruits after the army felt he had seen enough battles. He was also offered battlefield promotions, but turned them down saying it was because of his lack of education and paperwork that would be a problem for him.

He was discharged from service On February 25th 1865 in Grand Rapids Michigan and returned home to work the family farm once more. Custer visited Norvell for three days in 1866 on the farm and is said to have asked Churchill to join him with his new assigned command of the 7th Cavalry in the west. Norvell declined for he had seen enough killing during the war and wanted to live his life out on the farm, but the two remained great friends for life. Norvell married one Hanna Savage from Berlin and the two-bought land in Antrim County where they lived out their lives.

Norvell Churchill taken around 1863.
(Photo courtesy of Pat Churchill Hedgecoth.)

They had seven children during their marriage and on June 25th, 1905 Norvell passed away at the age of 65. His valor during the war won him everlasting praise from his community, and from his country, and from George Armstrong Custer who had died thirty-nine years earlier at the Little Big Horn on June 25th 1876.

On July 2nd, 2008 there was a dedication of a monument in Huntertown depicting one Norvell F. Churchill's heroics during the battle. The monument tells the story of Norvell "saving" the life of Brigadier General George A. Custer on that 2nd of July in 1863. Present that day was Pat Churchill Hedgecoth great granddaughter of Norvell. Also attending were other Churchill descendants who had brought along with them the sword carried by Norvell Churchill throughout the war and is retained by the Churchill family.

Norvell and Hanna Churchill taken around 1870.
(Photo courtesy of Pat Churchill Hedgecoth.)

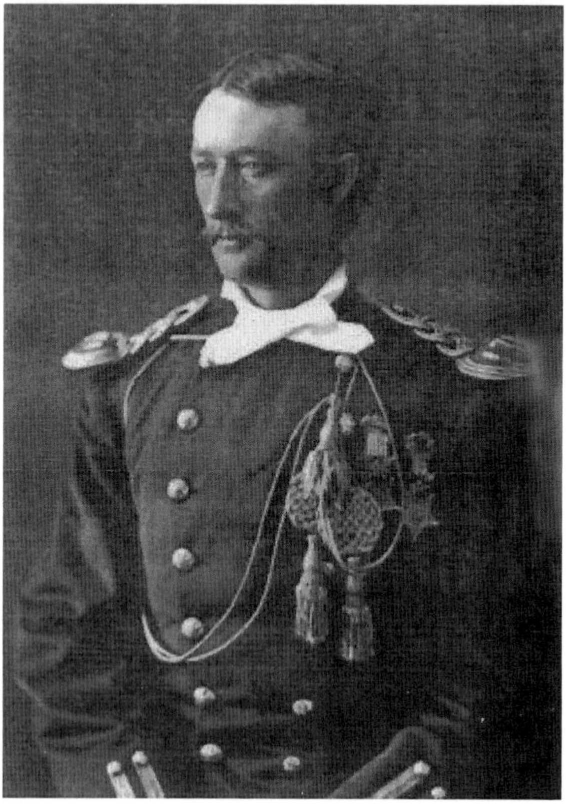

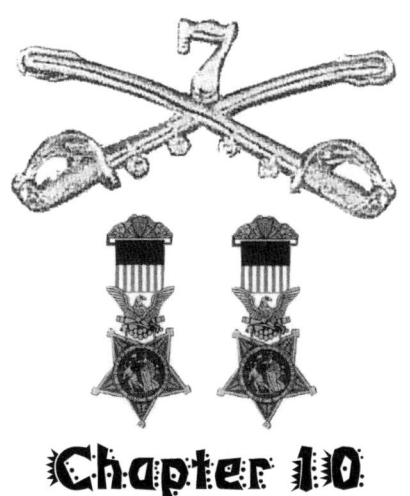

Chapter 10
Thomas Ward Custer

Born in march of 1845 and the younger brother of George Custer. Tom idolized his older sibling. Joined the union army in 1861 at the age of sixteen years and served in the twenty first Ohio volunteer infantry as a private. He participated in the battles of Stone's river, Chickamauga, Jonesboro, Missionary Ridge, and Kennesaw mountain. Mustard out in 1864 at the rank of corporal. In 1864 he served under general Sherman and saw action from Chattanooga to Atlanta. In October of that year he was appointed a second lieutenant in the sixth Michigan cavalry and served as an aide- camp to his brother George. During his service in the sixth he distinguished himself by winning the nation's highest medal, the Congressional Medal of Honor twice for bravery in the battles.

At Namozine church, and Saylor's creek in 1865. Both actions saw Custer capturing confederate regimental flags, one from the second North Carolina cavalry, and the second from the hands of a flag bearer of the army of northern Virginia under the command of general Ewell. Tom was only twenty years of age at the time, battle hardened in every respect in 1866 he was commissioned a first lieutenant in the newly formed seventh cavalry. He was wounded in the hand at the Washita incident in 1868 and participated in the Yellowstone expedition of 1873. Tom was a fierce fighter and made no friends among the Indians, and for his bravery in battle was much loathed. In 1874 tom participated in the capture of the Lakota warrior, "Rain-In-The-Face" who was thrown in the guardhouse at fort Lincoln. He escaped shortly after that and was said to have threatened the life of Custer. In 1875 he was promoted to the rank of captain in the seventh and was given command of Company C in the regiment.

He served as aid- de- camp to his brother George at the battle of the little big horn and was killed alongside him, in the area known as last stand hill. He was only thirty-one years of age. On finding his body after the battle, little of his body was recognizable. The only true identification was made by a tattoo that he was known to have on his right arm. Tom was buried were he fell and a year later in 1877 his remains were exhumed and his body was laid to rest at the national cemetery at fort Leavenworth, Kansas. On last stand hill a solid memorial slab now marks the place were Thomas Custer fell on that fait full day in 1876 next to his older brother George.

****

Guide- Forager- Packer-Scout

Chapter 11
Boston Custer

Youngest brother of Tom and George a. Custer. George gave him the nickname of "boss." Born in 1848 and died June of 1876. He was in poor health during his younger years which kept him out from serving in the union army during the civil war. He worked on a farm that his brother Nevin owned. In 1874, now healthier he served as a forager with his brothers on the black hills expedition with the seventh cavalry. He also served as a guide, packer and scout during the same time period. Custer after the campaign, wrote a letter of intent to Washington asking that Boston be promoted to the rank of second lieutenant in the seventh cavalry. Even though he wasn't enlisted in the army and only a civilian contractor, the war department declined Custer's request. In 1876 at the battle of The Little Big Horn, he was assigned to Company B with the pack train in the rear of the action. After hearing a message that was sent to the company's commander requesting more ammo, he rushed to the front to join up with his brothers. On the way he caught up with bugler John Martin who carried the famous message from Custer to captain Benteen, "bring packs".

Boston ended up dying some 200 yards south from last stand hill near the big horn river. It isn't clear if his brothers knew of his demise or not. His body was removed from the battlefield two years later and reburied in 1878 at the woodland cemetery in Monroe, Michigan. He was only twenty-seven years old.

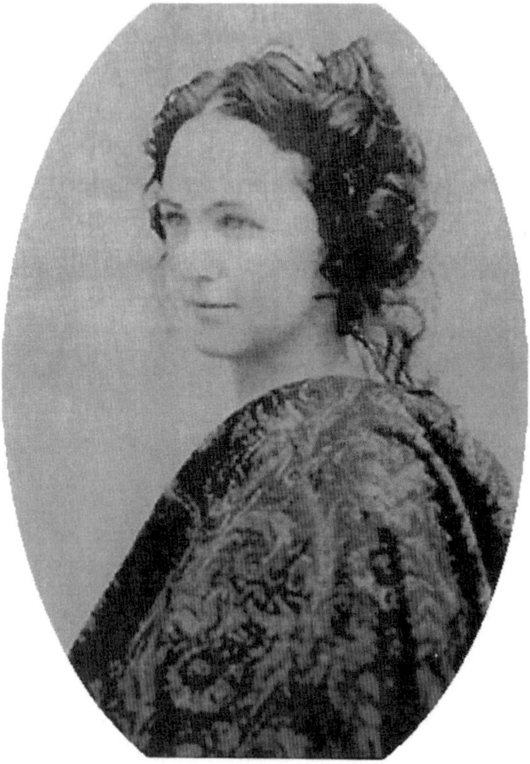

Chapter 12
Elizabeth Bacon Custer

Born in Monroe, Michigan in 1842 to her parents, Daniel Bacon and Eleanor Sophia Bacon. She had three other siblings who all perished within their first year of life. A tragic blow hit the Bacon Family in 1846 when Elizabeth's mother passed away. She now would go through woman hood with her father who was a very strict on the way she should handle herself around others. He wanted her to get involved in the inner circles of his rich friends and hoped someday she would marry a well to do gentleman.

She attended an all-girls school, (the young ladies' seminary and collegiate institute) in Monroe. Elizabeth was not only intelligent, but also talented, and beautiful. In 1862 she graduated first in her class and at a holiday social she met a young man who would change her life forever, George Armstrong Custer. Elizabeth's father didn't think too much of Custer and pushed "Libby" away from him, both at home and outside of the home.

After hearing of her husband's death at the little big horn she struck up a campaign to squash all the foil rumors that were going around the country, that her husband had taken all of his men to their deaths because of his need for glory. President Grant along with a few politicians and former officers of Custer's rode the line to disgrace the general. For fifty-eight years she fought to keep his name alive in the spot light and to keep it clean. She wrote three books, "Boots and Saddles" in 1885, "following the guidon" in 1890, and "tenting on the plains" in 1893. All these books pertained to Custer. She spoke at all sorts of functions where her husband's record was going to be discussed. Finally, in 1933 in New York city at the age of ninety years "Libbie Custer" passed away. She was buried next to her husband at West Point, N.Y. and this frail, little lady was finally again with her "Autie", her love.

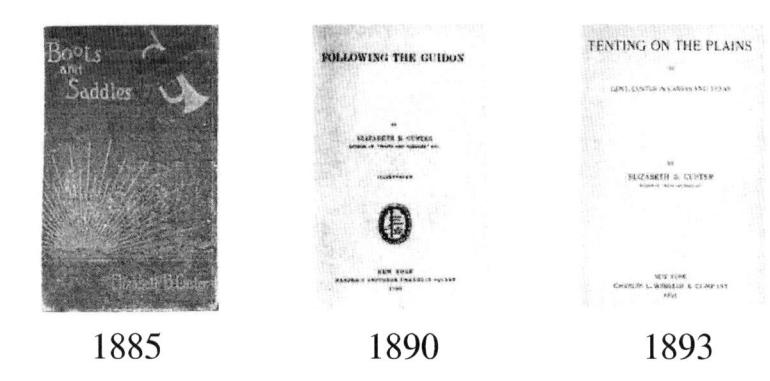

1885   1890   1893

**George and Elizabeth Custer
Circa: 1864**

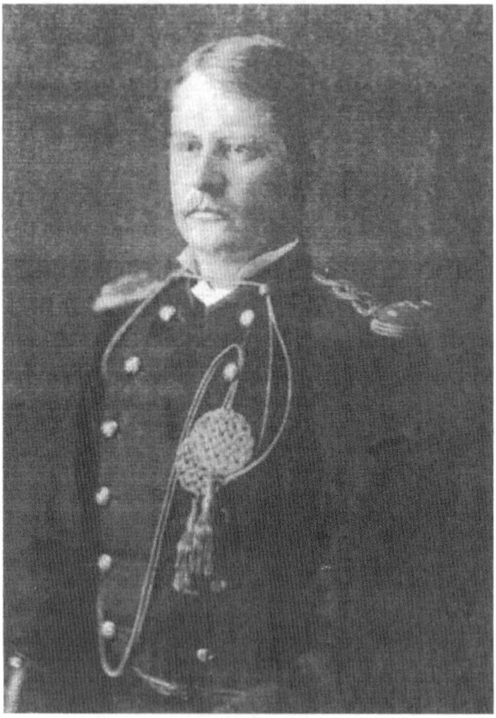

Chapter 13
James Calhoun

Born in 1845, and died on June of 1876. He was from a wealthy family and traveled all over Europe for the first two years of the civil war. In 1864 upon returning to the United States he enlisted in the union army. By the wars end he held the rank of Sergeant. In 1867 he was commissioned a lieutenant in the infantry and served out west until 1870. That year he met his future wife, Margaret Custer. Her brother George now commanding officer of the seventh cavalry re-assigned Calhoun to his regiment with the rank of first lieutenant and assigned him to Company C. He married "Maggie" in 1872 and was now a part of the Custer clan as they were called. In 1876 at The Battle of the Little Big Horn he was commanding Company L of the seventh when he was killed. The area where he died was given the name Calhoun hill because of the strong evidence that his troopers fought bravely and with fierce determination.

He was only thirty years old when he gave up his life along with his brothers - in - laws George, tom, Boston and his nephew Autie reed. His remains were later reburied at the Leavenworth national cemetery in Kansas.

****

Autie Reed
Heerder

Chapter 14

Henry Armstrong Reed
"Autie"

Born in April of 1858 in Monroe Michigan, Monroe county. He died in June of 1876 at the battle of the little big horn along with his uncles George, Boston, Thomas and his uncle-in law James Calhoun. Reed was raised with seven sisters and was the only son of David Reed and Lydia Ann Kirkpatrick Reed. He was given the nickname "Autie" by his mother and held the middle name Armstrong like his uncle George.

In early 1876 he was hired at fort Lincoln as a civilian cow herder for the seventh cavalry which used the beef for food along the way. When the regiment traveled in June of that year, "Autie" was in the rear of the regiment serving with Company B and the pack train. On that day of the battle when told that his uncles were ready to engage the Indians, reed climbed a mount and galloped forward to meet his uncles in the upcoming battle. He died some two hundred yards from last stand hill and was found near the body of his uncle Boston. His body was mutilated like everyone else's that day. The next year, in 1877 his body was exhumed from the battlefield and reinterred in the woodland cemetery, located in his hometown of Monroe, Michigan. He was only eighteen years old.

****

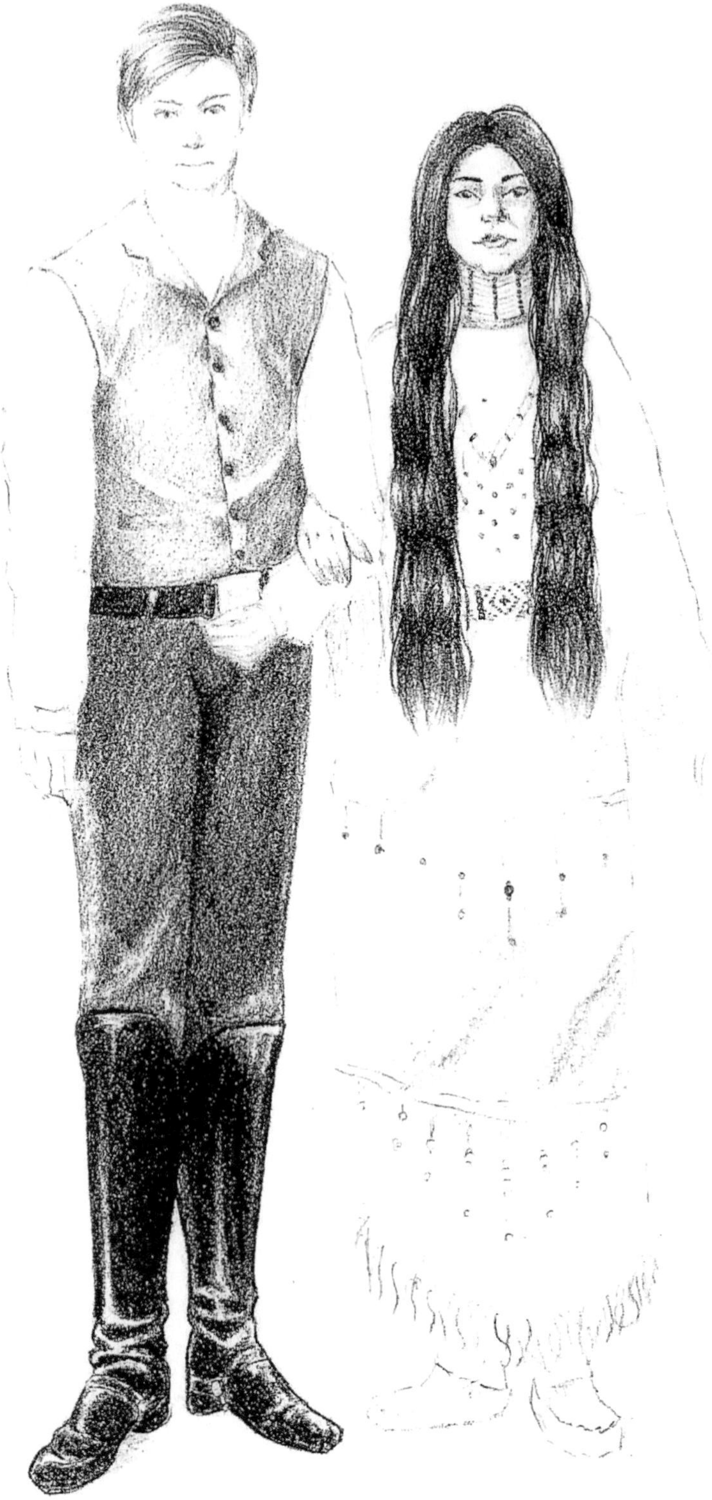

Chapter 15

Oraland Churchill & Waynoka

When I started this story it just ran with itself. The characters, well they came alive! Oraland was Oraland and Waynoka was Waynoka! Each had their own direction in the way they interacted throughout the story. I think there is a little bit of Oraland in me, for I have always felt that I was born one hundred years too late. He was confident, smooth, down to earth, and he believed in his convictions.

Waynoka was also sure of herself. She was understanding, sympathetic, loving, and a true woman. The people around them also helped mold their characters. I pictured Oraland to be a look alike to Robert Redford, blond, blue eyes, and manly. Waynoka was molded after donna reed, or Natale wood beautiful, always full of life, and a sensible woman. She was a wife and partner, and someone who had high values and ideals.

Oraland wasn't going to let anyone push him around, because he had principles and courage, and strong convictions, one is lead to believe that strong characters in a story can take that story anywhere. Although they were not real, both drove my mind in putting them in real situations. A long time ago, someone told me that I had a clear head for writing. Viewing their sketch of what I felt they looked like, I can pause and smile knowing that I brought them both to life, and brought them together, for you the reader!

CUSTER BATTLEFIELD

TWO MOONS

LAST STAND HILL
CUSTER 5 PM

CO. I KEOGH

CO. C T. CUSTER

CO. F YATES

CO. E SMITH

CUSTER

RAVINE

CRAZY HORSE

RED CLOUD

GALL

LITTLE BIG HORN

SANS ARC

NORTHERN CHEYENNE

BRULE

OGALA

Chapter 16

Map of the Battle June 25th, 26th 1876

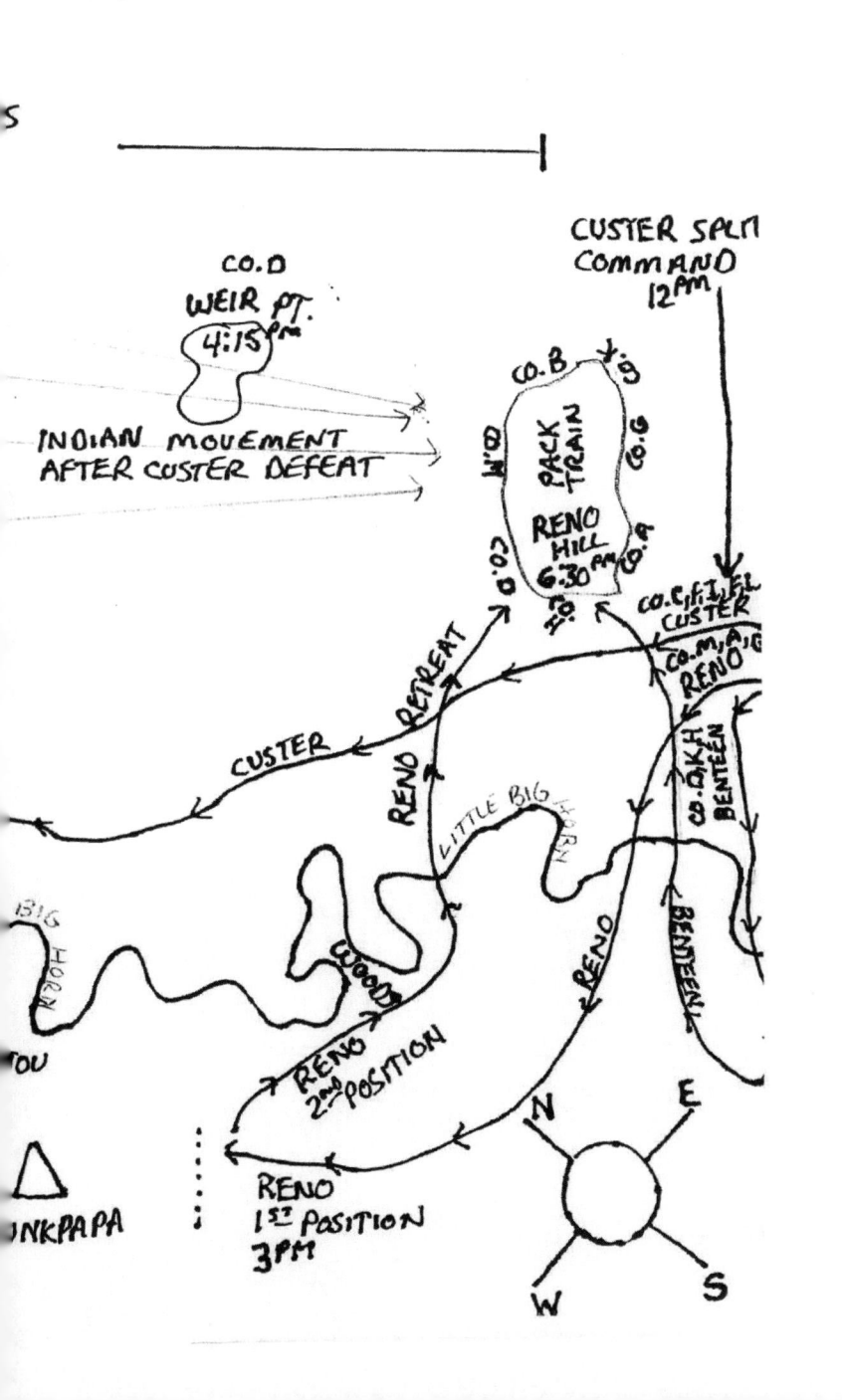

Before the Battle
Custer's command at the Little Big Horn split into three Battalions on June 25th, 1876.

Custer's Battalion (215 Men Total)
Regimental Staff: Lieutenant George A, Custer
Company C: Captain Thomas Custer
Company E: First Lieutenant Algernon Smith
Company F: Captain George Yates
Company I: Captain Myles Keogh
Company L: First Lieutenant James Calhoun

Reno's Battalion (131 Men Total)
Battalion Staff: Major Marcus Reno
Company A: Captain Myles Moylan
Company G: First Lieutenant Donald McIntosh
Company M: Captain Thomas French

Benteen's Battalion (113 Men Total)
Battalion Staff: Captain Frederick Benteen
Company D: Captain Thomas Wier
Company H: First Lieutenant Francis Gibson
Company K: First Lieutenant Edward Godfrey

Pack Train Escort (120 Men + 11 Citizen Packers)
Commanding officer: First Lieutenant Edward Mathey
Company B: Captain Thomas McDougall (detachment of one NCO and six enlisted men from each company)

Scouts/ Guides/ Interpreters (35 Total Men)
Commanding officer: Second Lieutenant Charles Varum

CHAPTER 17

After the Battle
The Twelve Companies of The Seventh Cavalry on June 25th 1876

Company A: Captain Thomas Moylan; one officer killed, one officer wounded, eight enlisted men killed, six enlisted men wounded, total = ten killed, six wounded out of fifty-five men on the roster

Company B: Captain Thomas McDougall; one officer killed, two enlisted men killed, five enlisted men wounded, total= three killed, five wounded out of seventy-one men on the roster

Company C: Captain Thomas Custer was made aid-de-camp under his brother and the command of C Company was commanded by Captain Myles Keough; three officers killed, thirty-six enlisted men killed, total= forty killed, three wounded out of a roster of sixty-six men

Company D: Captain Thomas Weir; three enlisted men killed, three enlisted men wounded, total= three killed, three wounded out of sixty-four men on roster

Company E: Captain Charles Ilsley; one officer killed, thirty-seven enlisted men killed, two enlisted men wounded, total= thirty-eight killed, one wounded out of a roster of sixty-one men

Company F: Captain George Yates; one officer killed, thirty-six enlisted men killed, total= thirty-seven killed out of sixty-eight men on the roster

Company G: First lieutenant Donald McIntosh; one officer killed, thirteen enlisted men killed, six enlisted men wounded total= fourteen killed, six wounded totals=sixty nine men on the roster

Company H: Captain Frederick Benteen; one officer killed, two enlisted men killed, twenty enlisted men wounded total= fifty-five men on the roster

Company I: Captain Myles Keough; two officers killed, thirty-six enlisted men killed, one wounded total= thirty-nine killed on the roster

Company K: First Lieutenant Edward Godfrey; five enlisted men killed, three enlisted men wounded total= five killed, three wounded on the roster

Company L: First Lieutenant James Calhoun; one officer killed, forty-four enlisted men killed total= forty-five killed, one wounded out of sixty-nine on the roster

Company M: Captain Thomas French; one officer killed, twelve enlisted men killed, one enlisted man wounded total= fourteen killed, thirteen wounded on a roster of sixty-three men

CHAPTER 18

Seventh U.S. Cavalry roster of the dead and wounded little big horn 1876

Ackison, D. Pvt. Co. E survivor admitted to field hospital
Adams, G. Pvt. Co. L - killed
Allen, F. Pvt. Co. C - killed
Andrews, W. Pvt. Co. L - killed
Armstrong, J. Pvt. Co. A - killed
Assdely, A. Pvt. Co. L - killed
Atchison, T. Pvt. Co. F - killed
Baba, E. 1st Sgt. Co. C - killed
Babcock, E. Pvt. Co. L- killed
Bailey, H. Blacksmith Co. I - killed
Baker, W. Pvt. Co. E - killed
Barry, J. Pvt. Co. I - killed
Bauth, R. Pvt. Co. E - killed
Benett, J. Pvt. Co. C - died of wounds afterwards
Benteen, F. Capt. Co. H - wounded
Bishley, H. Pvt. Co. H - wounded
Bishop, A. Cpl. Co. H - wounded
Bishop, C. Co. H - wounded
Black, H. Co. H - wounded
Bloody Knife, Indian Scout - killed
Blorm, Pvt. Co. I - killed
Bobtail Bull, Indian Scout - killed
Botzer, E. Sgt. Co. G - killed
Boyce, O. Pvt. Co. E - killed
Bouyer', M. Indian Interpreter - killed
Boyle, J. Pvt. Co. G - wounded
Brady, W. Pvt. Co. F - killed
Bragew, Pvt. Co. I - killed
Brandon, B. Farrier Co. F - killed
Braun, F. Pvt. Co. E - wounded
Brightfield, J. Pvt. Co. C - killed
Briody, Cpl. Co. F - killed

Broadhurst, J. Pvt. Co. I - killed
Brogan, J. Pvt. Co. E - killed
Brown, B. 1st Pvt. Co. F - killed
Brown, W, 2nd Pvt. Co. F - killed
Brown, G. Pvt. Co. E - killed
Bruce, P. Pvt. Co. F - killed
Brunn, F. Co. M - wounded
Bucknell, T. Bugler Co. C - killed
Burke, Pvt. Co. L - killed
Burnham, L. Pvt. Co. F - killed
Burtard, J. 1st Sgt. Co. I - killed
Butler, J. 1st Sgt. Co. L - killed
Calhoun, J. 1st Lt. Co. L - killed---Custer's brother-in-law
Callahn, J. Cpl. Co. K - killed
Campbell, C. Co. C - wounded
Carey, P. Sgt. Co. M - wounded
Carney, J. Pvct. Co. F - killed
Cashan, W. Sgt. Co. L - killed
Cather, A. Pvt. Co. F - killed
Charley, V. Farrier Co. D - killed
Cheever, A. Pvt. Co. L - killed
Clair, E. Pvt. Co. K - killed
Cody, H. Cpl. Co. M - killed
Coleman, K. Cpl. Co. F - killed
Conner, E. Pvt. Co. E - killed
Connelly, P. Sgt. Co. H - wounded
Conners, T.. Pvt. Co. I - killed
Considine, M. Sgt. Co. G - killed
Cooke, W. Brevet -Lt. Col. - killed
Cooper, J. Pvt. Co. H - wounded
Corcoran, P. Pvt. Co. K - wounded
Corey, D. Pvt. Co. I - wounded
Criddle, C. Pvt. Co. C - killed

Crowley, J. Pvt. Co. L - killed
Crisfield, W. Pvt. Co. L - killed
Criswell, B. Sgt. Co. B - wounded
Crittenden, J. 2nd Lt. Co. L - killed
Cunningham, C. Cpl. Co. E - wounded
Curley, Indian Scout - Survivor of the Battle
Custer, Boston - Civilian - killed
Custer, George - Brevet Maj. Gen. - killed
Custer, Thomas - Brevet Lt. Col. Co. C - killed
Dallious, J. Cpl. Co. A - killed
Darcy, J. Pvt. Co. M - wounded
Daring, PVT. Co. I - killed
Darris, J. Pvt. Co. B - killed
Davern, E. Pvt. Co. F - wounded
Davis, W. Pvt. Co. E - killed
Deal, J. Pvt. Co. A - wounded
DeRudio, 2nd Lt. Co. A - survivor Of The Battle
DeWolf, J. Acting Asst. Surgeon - killed
Dohman, A. Pvt. Co. F - killed
Donnelly, T. Pvt. Co. F - killed
Dorn, I. Pvt. Co. B - killed
Dorman, I. Interpreter - killed---only black man killed
Dose, H. Bugler - Co. G - killed
Downing, T. Pvt. Co. I - killed
Drinan, J. PVT. Co. A - killed
Driscoll, E. Pvt. Co. I - killed
Dugan, Pvt. Co. L - killed
Dye, W. Pvt. Co. L - killed
Egnen, T. Sgt. Co. E - killed
Eisman, G. Pvt. Co. C - killed
Engle, G. Pvt. Co. C - killed
Fanand, J. Pvt. Co. C - killed
Farley, W. Pvt. Co. H - wounded
Farrell, R. Pvt. Co. E - killed
Feeman, Capt. Co. F - killed
Finkle, G. Sgt. Co. C - killed
Finley, J. Sgt. Co. C - killed
Foley, J. Cpl. Co. C - killed
Forbes, J. Pvt. Co. E - killed
Foster, J. Pvt. Co. A - wounded

French, H. Cpl. Co. C - killed
Galvin, J. Pvt. Co. L - killed
Gardner, J. Pvt. Co. F - killed
George, W. Co. H - died of wounds afterwards
Gilbert, W. Cpl. Co. L - killed
Gillette, D. Pvt. Co. I - killed
Golden, P. Pvt. Co. D - killed
Gordon, H. Pvt. Co. M - killed
Graham, C. Pvt. Co. L - killed
Griffin, P. Pvt. Co. C - killed
Gross, C. Pvt. Co. I - killed
Gucker, J. Bugler Co. I - killed
Hackett, J. Pvt. Co. G - wounded
Hagan, Cpl. Co. E - killed
Hageman, O. Cpl. Co. G - killed
Hamel, Pvt. Co. C - killed
Hamilton, H. Pvt. Co. L - killed
Hammon, G. Pvt. Co. F - killed
Hansen, E. Pvt. Co. D - killed
Harnington, W. Pvt. Co. L - kiilled
Harrington, H. 2nd Lt. Co. C - killed
Harrison, Cpl. Co. L - killed
Hathersall, J. Pvt. Co. C - killed
Hauggi, L. Pvt. Co. L - killed
Heath, W. Farrier Co. F - killed
Helmer, J. Bugler Co. K - killed
Henderson, J. Pvt. Co. I - killed
Henderson, S. Pvt. Co. I - killed
Heyn, W. 1st Sgt. Co. A - wounded
Hiley, Pvt. Co. I - killed
Hime, J. Pvt. Co. I - killed
Hetesimer, A. Pvt. Co. I - killed
Hodgson, B. 2nd Lt. Co. B - killed
Hohmeyer, F. 1st Sgt. Co. E - killed
Holcomb,F. Pvt. Co. I - killed
Homsted, F. Co. A - wounded
Horn,M. Pvt. Co. I - killed
Housen, E. Pvt. Co. D - killed
Howell, G. Saddler Co. C - killed
Huber, W. Pvt. Co. E - killed
Hughes, T. Pvt. Co. H - wounded
Hughes, R. Sgt. Co. K - killed
Hughes, F. Pvt. Co. L - killed
James, Sgt. Co. E - killed
Jones, J. Pvt. Co. H - killed

Kavaugh, T. Pvt. Co. L - killed
Kellogg, M. Reporter For Bismarck Tribune - killed
Kelly, J. Pvt. Co. F - killed
Kelly, P. Pvt. Co. I - killed
Kenney, M.1st Sgt. Co. F - killed
Keogh, M. Col. Co. I - killed
Kidey, Pvt. Co. F - killed
Kiefer, Pvt. Co. L - killed
Killey, P. Pvt. Co. F - killed
King,G. Cpl. Co. A - wounded
King, J. Pvt. Co. C - killed
Kingsoutz, Pvt. Co. C - killed
Kline, Pvt. Co. F - killed
Klotzburscher, H. Pvt. Co. M - killed
Knecht, A. Pvt. Co. L - killed
Knight, Pvt. Co. I - killed
Kramer, W. Bugler Co. C - killed
Kretchmer, J. Pvt. Co. D - wounded
Knauth, H. Pvt. Co. F - killed
Lawrence, G. Pvt. Co. M - killed
Leddisson, Pvt. Co. I - killed
Lee, G. Cpl. Co. H - killed
Lehman, F. Pvt. Co. I - killed
Lehman, H. Pvt. Co. F - killed
Lell, G. Cpl. Co. H - wounded
Lerock, W. Pvt. Co. F - killed
Lewis, J. Pvt. Co. C - killed
Liddiard, H. Pvt. Co. E - killed
Little Brave, Indian Scout - killed
Lloyd, E. Pvt. Co. I - killed
Lobering, L. Pvt. Co. L - killed
Lord,G. Asst. Surgeon - killed
Losse, W. Pvt. Co. F - killed
Lieman, W. Pvt. Co. I - killed
Lunon, Pvt. Co. L - killed
Lymons, D. Pvt. Co. F - killed
Madden, M. Saddler Co. K - wounded
Madsen, Pvt. Co. F - killed
Mahoney, B. Pvt. Co. L - killed
Mann, F. Packer-Quartermaster - killed
Manning, F. Civilian - killed
Manning, J. Blacksmith Co. F - killed
Marshall, J. Co. L - wounded
Martin, J. Cpl. Co. G - kiilled

Mask,G. Pvt. Co. B - killed
Mason, Pvt. Co. I - killed
Mason, H. Cpl. Co. E - killed
Maxwell, T. Pvt. Co. L - killed
Mayer, Pvt. Co. C - killed
Mayer, Pvt. Co. C - killed
McCarthy, C. Pvt. Co.L - killed
McCurry, J. 1st Sgt. Co. H - wounded
McDonald, J. Pvt. Co. A - killed
McDonnall, P. Co. D - wounded
McElroy, T. Bugler Co. E - killed
McGinniss, J. Pvt. Co. G - killed
McGucker, J. Bugler Co. I - killed
McGue, P. Pvt. Co. L - killed
McGuire, J. Co. C - wounded
McLaughlin, T. Sgt. Co. H - wounded
McLchargey, A. Pvt. Co. I - killed
Mcintosh, D. 1st Lt. Co. G - killed
McVay, J. Pvt. Co. C - wounded
McVeigh, D. Bugler Co. A - missing
McWilliams, D. Co. H - wounded
Meador, T. Pvt. Co. H - killed
Meier, F. Pvt. Co. C - killed
Meirer, J. Pvt. Co.M - wounded
Meyer, A. Cpl. Co. E - killed
Meyer, A, Pvt. Co. C - killed
Meyer, W. Pvt. Co. M - killed
Mielke, M. Pvt. Co. K - wounded
Miller, J. Pvt. Co. L - killed
Milton, F. Pvt. Co. F - killed
Mitchell, J. Pvt. Co. I - killed
Moller, J. Pvt. Co. H - wounded
Monroe, J. Pvt. Co. F - killed
Moodie, W. Pvt. Co. A - killed
Moonie, Bugler Co. I - killed
Moore, A. Pvt. Co. G - killed
Morris, W. Pvt. Co. M - wounded
Morris, G. Cpl. Co. I - killed
Morrison, J. Pvt. Co. G - wounded
Muller, J. Co. H - wounded
Murray, J. Sgt. Co. B - wounded
Newell, D. Co. M - wounded
Noshaug, J. Pvt. Co. I - killed
Nursey, F. Sgt. Co. F - killed
O'Brien, J. Pvt. Co. I - killed
O'Bryan, J. Pvt. Co. F - killed

O'Connell, D. Pvt. Co. L - killed
O'Conner, Pvt. Co. E - killed
Ogden, J. Sgt. Co. E - killed
O' Hara, M. Sgt. Co. M - killed
Omeling, S. Pvt. Co. F - killed
Pahl, !. Sgt. Co. H - wounded
Pardee, O. Pvt. Co. L - killed
Parker, Pvt. Co. I - killed
Patton, Bugler Co. I - killed
Paul, J. Sgt. Co. H - wounded
Perkins, C. Pvt. Co. L - killed
Petring, H. Pvt. Co. G - wounded
Phillips, J. Pvt. Co. H - wounded
Phillips, E. Pvt. Co. C - killed
Pigford, E. Pvt. Co. M - wounded
Pitter, F. Pvt. Co. I - killed
Porter, J. Lt. Co. I - missing
Post, G. Pvt. Co. I - killed
Pym, J. Pvt. Co. B - wounded
Quinn, J. Pvt. Co. I - killed
Rauter, J. Pvt. Co. C - killed
Rapp, J. Pvt. Co. G - killed
Reed, A. Civilian - killed --- Nephew of Custer
Reed, W. Pvt. Co. I - killed
Reese, W. Pvt. Co. E - killed
Reeves, F. Pvt. Co. A - wounded
Reily, W. 2nd Lt. Co. F - killed
Reynolds, C. Civilian Scout--- killed
Riebold, C. Pvt. Co. L - killed
Riley, J. Sgt. Co. E - wounded
Riley, M. Sgt. Co. I --- Survivor Not Part Of The Battle
Rix, E. Pvt. Co. C - killed
Roberts, H. Pvt. Co. L - killed
Rodgers, B. Pvt. Co. G - killed
Rodgers, W. Pvt. Co. L - killed
Rood, E. Pvt. Co. I - killed
Rossbury, J. Pvt. Co. I - killed
Rollins, R. Pvt. Co. A - killed
Rudden, P. Pvt. Co. F - killed
Russell, J. Pvt. Co. C - killed
Rutten, R. Co. M - wounded
Ryan, D. Cpl. Co. C - killed
Saunders, R. Pvt. Co. F - killed
Shields, W. Saddler Co. E - wounded

Schmidt, C. Pvt. Co. L - killed
Schele,H. Pvt. Co. E - killed
Scollier, H. Cpl. Co. M - killed
Scott, C. Pvt. Co. L - killed
Seafferman, H. Pvt. Co. G - killed
Seiler, J. Cpl. Co. L - killed
Selby, C. Saddler Co. G - killed
Semenson, B. Pvt. Co. L - killed
Severs, S. Pvt. Co. H - wounded
Shade, S. Pvt. Co. C - killed
Sharrow, W. Sgt. Major - killed
Shea, J. Pvt. Co. C - killed
Sicfous, F. Pvt. Co. F - killed
Siemon, C. Blacksmith Co. L - killed
Smallwood, W. Pvt. Co. E - killed
Smith, A. 1st Pvt. Co. E - killed
Smith, A. 2nd Pvt. Co. E - killed
Smith, G. Pvt. Co. M - killed
Smith, W. Cpl. Co. B - wounded
Smith, A, 1st Lt.. Co. E - killed
Snow, A. Pvt. Co. L - killed
Somers, D. Pvt. Co. M - killed
St, John, L. Pvt. Co. C - killed
Stab, Indian Scout - killed
Stafford, B. Pvt. Co. E - killed
Stanley, E. Pvt. Co. G - killed
Staples, S. Cpl. Co. I - killed
Stella, A. Pvt. Co. E - killed
Stressinger, F. Cpl. Co. M - killed
Strode, E. Pvt. Co. A - wounded
Stuart, A. Pvt. Co. C - killed
Stungewitz, Y. Pvt. Co. C - killed
Sturgis, E. 2nd Lt. Co. E - missing
Sullivan, J. Pvt. Co. A - killed
Summers, D. Pvt. Co. M - killed
Sweetser, T. Pvt. Co. A - killed
Symms, D. Pvt. Co. I - killed
Tanner, J. Pvt. Co. M - killed
Tarbox, B. Pvt. Co. L - killed
Tarr, Pvt. Co. I - killed
Teeman, W. Cpl. Co. F - killed
Tenley, H. Pvt. Co. M - killed
Tessler, E. Pvt. Co. L - killed
Thadius, J. Pvt. Co. C - killed
Thomas, H. Pvt. Co. I - killed
Thompson, P. Co. C - wounded

Torrey, W. Pvt. Co. E - killed
Troy, J. Pvt. Co. I - killed
Turley, H. Pvt. Co. M - killed
Tweed, T. Pvt. Co. L - killed
Van Allen, G. Pvt. Co. C - killed
Van Bramer, C. Pvt. Co. I - killed
Van Rieley, W. 2nd Lt. Co. F - killed
Van Sant, C. Pvt. Co. E - killed
Varden, F. 1st Sgt. Co. I - killed
Varner,T. Pvt. Co. M - wounded
Varnum, C. 2nd Lt. Co. A - wounded
Vaugant, Pvt. Co. I - killed
Vetter, J. Pvt. Co. L - killed
Vickory, J. Sgt. Co. F - killed
Vincent, C. Co. D - killed
Voss, H. Chief Bugler - killed
Voight, H. Pvt. Co. M - killed
Volt, O. Saddler Co. H - wounded
Wagoner, J. Chief Packer-Quartermaster - wounded
Walker, G. Pvt. Co. E - killed
Walsh, F. Bugler Co. L - killed
Wanew, Pvt. Co. F - killed
Warner, O. Pvt. Co. C - killed
Warren, A. Sgt. Co. L - killed
Way, T. Bugler Co. F - killed
Wells, B. Farrier Co. G - killed
Whaley, W. Pvt. Co. I - killed
Whitaker, A. Blacksmith Co. C - wounded
White, C. Sgt. Co. M - wounded
White Swan, Indian Scout - wounded
Winney, D. 1st. Sgt. Co. K - killed
Wiedman, C. Pvt. Co. M - wounded
Wilbur, J. Co. M - wounded
Wild, J. Cpl. Co. M - killed
Wike, M. Co. K - wounded
Wilkinson, J. Sgt. Co. F - killed
Williams, W. Pvt. Co. H - wounded
Windham, Pvt. Co. C - killed
Windolph, C. Pvt. Co. H - wounded
Wright, W. Pvt. Co. C - killed
Wright, J. Bugler Co. H - wounded
Wyman, H. Pvt. Co. C - killed
Yates, G. Capt. Co. F - killed

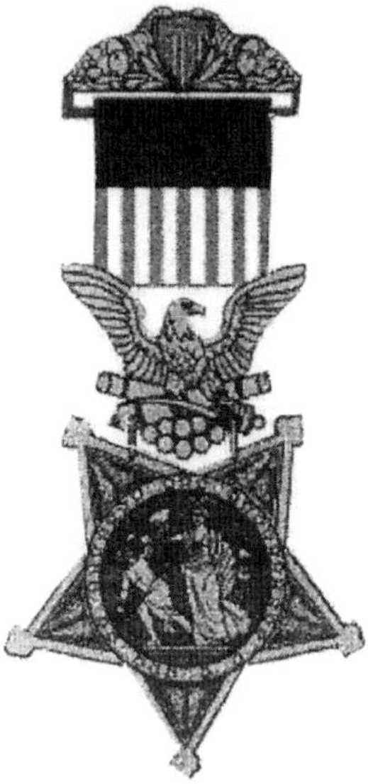

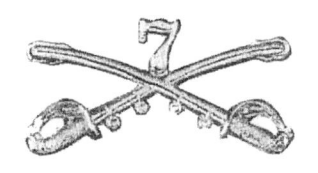

CHAPTER 19
Roster: Medal of Honor Winners at the Little Big Horn June, 1876

Abram B, Brant, Pvt. Co. D
Peter Thompson. Pvt. Co. C
Neil Bancroft, Pvt. Co. A
Frank Tolan, Pvt. Co. D
Thomas J. Callan, Pvt. Co. B
Charles H. Welch, Pvt. Co. D
Frederick Deetline, Blacksmith Co. D
Charles Windolph, Pvt. Co. H
Theodore W. Golden, PVT. Co. G
George Geiger, Pvt. Co. H
David W. Harris, Pvt. Co. A
Henry Mechlin, Pvt. Co. H
William M. Harris, Pvt. Co. D
Otto Voit, Pvt. Co. H
Rufus D. Hutchinson, Sgt. Co. B
Benjamine C. Criswell, Sgt. Co. B
James Pym, Pvt. Co. B
Henry Holden, Pvt. Co. D
Stanislaus Roy, Sgt. Co. A
Richard P. Hanley, Sgt. Co. C
George Scott, Pvt. Co. D
Charles Cunningham. Pvt. Co. B
Thomas W. Stivers, Pvt. Co. D
Thomas Murray, Sgt. Co. B

PVT. Charles Windolph was the last surviving member of the seventh cavalry who passed away in 1950.

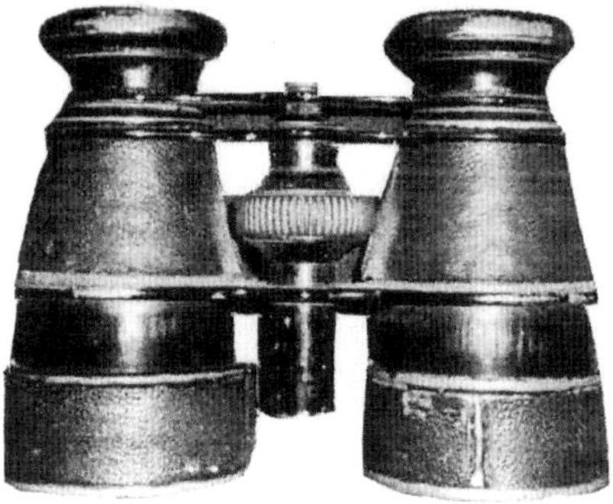

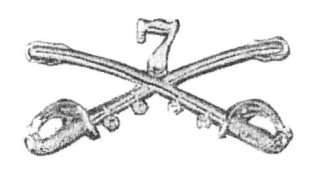

CHAPTER 20
Custer's Scouts

There was a total of forty-three scouts at the Little Big Horn that day of June, 1876 made up from Arikara's and Crows. There was a total of four civilian scouts present also, and two lost their lives. Custer had a total of six Crow Indian scouts with him and three of them died that day also. The Crows were hated by almost all the Indian tribes on the plains especially the Blackfeet and Lakota Sioux. The main reason for this dislike was the "horse". The Crow people breed horses for travel and mainly for hunting the buffalo. Many of the other tribes would raise raiding parties in pursuit of the four-legged animals and bad relations evolved from these raids. The Crow people greeted the whites with friendly gestures and they remained close allies. Many enlisted in the army and there they were recognized as valuable scouts for the military. There were six Crow scouts assigned to Custer's Seventh at the Little Big Horn and one hour before the battle Custer relieved all of them from duty basically because of anger!

When Custer didn't heed their warnings about the large Indian village, all the scouts took off their army issue uniforms and donned Crow war clothing. When asked by Custer for a reason, Half Yellow Face told him that if they were to die, they would rather die as warriors than as soldiers. Thus, Custer relieved them of their posts. All the Crows after leaving Custer made their way to Reno's position and that's where they remained for the rest of the battle yet to come. Besides the Crow scouts Custer also relied on the information from one Mitch Bouyer' 1837-1876. He was of French and Sioux ancestry and was Custer's reliable guide and interpreter. He too warned Custer of the large Indian camp. He told Custer, "General I've been with these Indians for thirty years and this is the largest village i have ever seen" Within two hours of the Crows leaving he would perish also with the Seventh. He knew that Sitting Bull had put a price on his head, but he chose to ride with Custer that day in June anyway.

The Crow scouts that where with the Seventh that day were as follows:

1. Half Yellow Face- Crow- 1837-1879. (Ishu-shi-dish) Was head of the Crow scouts at the Little Big Horn, and warned Custer along with the other scouts that his position had been observed by Sioux scouts and the Indians knew that Custer was coming, So much for a surprise attack from the Seventh! Custer wouldn't listen even after he was told of the enormous encampment the Indians had. He was the "pipe carrier" for the Crow's, because he was much older (forty) and he had more experience in war than the other scouts. He held the rank of Corporal and was said to have told Custer: "you and I are both going home tonight, down by a road we do not know".

*2. White Swan -Crow-*1850-1904. (Mee-nah-tree-us) Followed Reno and his men into the Indian village at the south end and engaged the Hunkpapa's. He was seriously wounded and suffered wounds to the head, right wrist and hand, leg, foot, and head. He was moved up to Reno hill early on, before the route began and that's where he remained for the rest of the battle.

*3. Hairy Moccasin- Crow-*1859-1922. (Esh-sup-pee-me-shish) Fought with other comrades on Reno Hill.

4. ***White Man Runs Him*-*Crow*-**1858-1929. (Mahr-itah-thee-dah-ka-roosh) Also joined his Crow brothers and fought at Reno Hill during the battle.

5. ***Goes Ahead*-*Crow*-**1851-1919. He also retired to Reno Hill to fight the Sioux.

6. ***Curly* or *Curley* - *Crow*-** 1856-1923. (Ash-ish-is-he) The most famous of the six that were relieved by Custer. When the Crows left Custer and his men, Curly followed the others for a shot time and then high tailed it for cover out of sight of the others who were headed for Reno Hill. After the battle he claimed he had out smarted the Sioux by hiding in the stomach of a dead horse that he cut out and eluded them. He claimed to have witnessed the death of Mitch Bouyer', and many of the troopers who were fighting for their lives. He had also stated that the Indian losses numbered well over six hundred or more. His story changed in every interview he gave, but he still contested that he escaped the battlefield by rapping a Sioux blanket (that he taken off a dead Sioux warrior) and made his way south along the river. He ended up down river where the steamboat "Far East" was docked and that's when the news about the defeat of Custer and his regiment was first told to the nation. In 1888 at the first Little Big Horn Reunion held, old enemies greeted one another as friends and recounted the battle of 1876.

Hands were shaking and presents were exchanged that day, but one individual got the surprise of his life, yes Curly! Attending the Reunion was Chief Gall and all those years after the battle and hearing of Curly's experiences during the battle, he was going to set things straight! Chief Gall approached Curly and told him point blank, "If you were at the battle with Yellow Hair, you would not be here today, you were like a bird with feathers and flew away from the battle, you are a liar"!

With that Gall turned around and left Curly standing by himself. There were a few other braves that fought with the Seventh that day. They were:

1. Little Brave, Arikara Tribe-1859-1876. Was with Reno's men when they rushed the Hunkpapa's village at the south end. Was shot and wounded at the west side of the river and died on the east side after being found by a Brule' Sioux warrior named "Red Feather" who shot him in the head.

2. Bobtail Bull, Ree Tribe-1831-1876. Was killed while under Reno's command, trying to retreat. While on horseback he encountered a Cheyenne suicide warrior named "Little Whirlwind" who chased Bobtail Bull into the river where they dueled and Bobtail lost his life.

3. Bloody Knife, Sioux-1840-1876. Was Custer's favorite scout. He followed the General on the Black Hills Expedition in 1874 where he and Custer hunted and fished together. Was assigned to Reno's column and was killed standing next to Reno down in the valley when they attacked the Hunkpapa's. Had his brains blown out that landed all over Reno's forehead, which some say contributed to Reno's mental health for the duration of the battle.

There were four civilian scouts at the Little Big Horn that day in June:

1. *Lonesome Charley Reynolds*, White man-1842-1876. Was a veteran of the civil war where he fought for the Union? After the war he became a drifter thus came the name "LONESOME". Met Custer in 1869 and was made a scout because of his marksmanship with weapons, a frontiersman, and a very good hunter. Stayed in the Seventh up to the Little Big Horn and was made Chief of guides and scouts by Custer. Was killed the first day on Reno Hill defending a doctor who was caring for the wounded.

2. *Isaiah Dorman, American negro*-1820-1876. Dorman was a former slave from the south and escaped in the early 1850's. He headed out west and became a friend of the Lakota Sioux. He stayed with one of the Hunkpapa tribes and became a trapper and trader for them. He learned their language and eventually wound up as a scout and interpreter for the army. He was assigned to the Seventh in late fall of 1875 and was liked by all, even Custer! He was with Reno's column the day of the battle and was shot in the wooded area as Reno attacked the village. He lay wounded and at one moment and found himself surrounded by six Sioux warriors. History takes over here for it was said that at that moment Sitting Bull rode onto the field of battle and stopped the warriors from killing the large black man. Dorman then spoke in the Lakota Sioux language and pleaded with Sitting Bull not to count coup on him and just wanted a drink of water. Sitting Bull got off his horse and walked over to Dorman and gave the man a cup of water. After refreshing Dorman Sitting Bull got on his horse and galloped away leaving the wounded man

to the warriors that were going to count coup anyway. Dorman died and the story is told that Sitting Bull and Dorman knew each other, but Sitting Bull had no control over the young warriors and the deed was done.

3. *Fred Gerard, white American*-1823-1923. Gerard was assigned to Reno's column and entered the village with the others. Couldn't get across the river when the troopers started to fall back, and spent the twenty fifth and part of the twenty sixth of June hiding in the woods along the Big Horn. When he got back to Reno Hill he helped Reno's surgeon Dr. Henry Porter care for the wounded.

4. *George Herendeen, white American*-1846-1919. Was General Alfred Terry's Chief scout assigned to Custer's column. Custer ordered Herendeen to Reno's command and accompanied Reno when he charged the southern end of the Indian village. Surprised by the soldiers, the Indians in due time massed and counter attacked the troopers who were now dismounted and in skirmish lines. During the fighting Herendeen said he could hear massive gun firing coming from the river above them. The Indians had him and ten other troopers pinned down in the wooded cottonwood area of the river, and he told them to listen to him. "He was an old frontiersman and he knew Indians, and he would get them out of the trouble they were in in due time". He surmised that the firing he had heard from the northern end of the river was Custer's column, and within an hour it ceased. Now was a good time to cross the river and make it to the hill that Reno had set up as a defense position. They all made it out safety and Herendeen later reflected that the Indians were to busy looting and mutilating the bodies of Custer's men and that gave him the edge on escaping. No sooner than Herendeen got to

Reno Hill, the Indians turned their attention on Reno and fierce fighting continued for the rest of the day and into the night. He made it out alive and lived to tell about the fight.

Scouts for the army earned every cent they worked for. During that period of time you had to be a more than a superman to survive. With danger around you all the time your senses had to be like an animal in the wild. One thing is for certain, the scouts for Custer's Seventh Regiment were experienced beyond the scope of the average scout.

?

CHAPTER 21
Myths and Truths About Custer's Last Stand

Truth- There was a real individual at the little big horn named Benjamin Franklin "Churchill" who was no relation to Norvell Churchill. He was a packer-quartermaster and was assigned to the pack train on the hilltop in back of Reno's position. He enlisted in the Army in April 1876 and was assigned to the seventh cavalry under Custer. I wonder if Custer made any advances towards Churchill to find out if he was related to Norvell Churchill, his good friend? Churchill's name popped up one night when I was researching the dead and wounded lists from the battle and that was when the idea for a story line and Orland was born.

Truth- Custer didn't have long yellow hair at the battle he sported a very short haircut because of the extremely hot weather.

Truth-Custer's troopers did not wear their field uniforms on the day of the battle. It was extremely hot and the men tied their blouses to their saddles and wore an array of different shirts and hats they mostly looked like a rag tag gang.

Truth-Custer's men did not carry their sabres at the little big horn. They were left back at fort Lincoln in storage.

Truth- sitting bull did not take part in the battle. He was in the village throughout the entire battle, though he was said to have been on last stand hill after the battle.

Truth-General Phillip Sheridan is given credit for the

phrase: 'The only good Indian, is a dead Indian!"

His real quote was: "The only good Indians I ever saw were dead!"

Truth-There were hundreds even thousands of survivors of Custer's last stand, they were the Indians.

Myth-Custer was first shot, down by the river when trying to find a place to ford it. It may have been mortal some experts have speculated. If it was, then why was his body found on last stand hill? All speculation, no one knows.

Truth-Over 300 books, 32 movies, 13 TV shows and 1500 paintings have been produced in telling the story about Custer.

Truth-Custer was disliked by his men.

Myth- Custer never had a successful engagement against the Indians. What about the Washita battle?

Myth-The Indians at the little big horn did not know Custer was coming to do battle.

Myth-The last stand did not take place on last stand hill, it ran it self-down the hill to the river in the ravine.

Myth-Tom Custer shot his brother before shooting himself! We don't know, and will never know

Truth-Custer was overconfident to the point of arrogance.

Truth-Many of the white markers on the battlefield are placed wrongly were a man fell.

Truth-The battle did not end with Custer's demise, it continued all night with Reno and Benteen defending their post position on Reno hill, accounts feel that the demise of Custer's companies took less than 30 minutes to an hour.

Truth-99% of what is written about Custer is false.

Truth-Reno and Benteen covered up for one another after the battle.

Truth-The seventh cavalry was out numbered 9 to 1 on the day of the battle.

Truth-The Indians used the tall grass and hilly terrain to hide form the troopers.

Truth-Custer did not have his whole command with him during the battle, he divided up into four separate commands.

Myth-Custer tried to rejoin Reno and his command.

Truth-The Indians did use bows and arrows, but most of the fighting was done with firearms. There were over 350 weapons used to include 100 Henry repeating rifles.

Truth-Bugler John Martin was the last man to see Custer alive.

Truth-The trail of cartridges found after the battle show that there was more of a running fight other than a standing defense from Custer's men.

Truth-Custer was the youngest general to serve in the U.S. army still to this day.

Truth-The little Big Horn was the last armed attempt to preserve the Sioux and Cheyenne way of life.

Truth-The Battle of the Little Big Horn was the greatest defeat in the history of the united states army.

Truth-the banks of the little big horn were high the day of the battle and many soldiers died in the river trying to escape death.

Myth-Custer went into battle with his own personal flag that was sewn by his wife Libby and which contained her initials in one of the corners of the flag.

Truth-There was one black trooper at the little big horn by the name of Isaiah Dorman, who was killed with Reno's men when the battle started down at the river, he was an interpreter.

Truth or myth-There is said that the Indians after the battle buried all the personal effects and weapons of the slain troopers in fear of retaliation from the U.S. government. Such a cache is still buried today.

Truth-In 1860 the Indian population was more than

500,000 by 1880 it had dropped to less than 250,000

Truth or Myth -George and Tom Custer were buried together in a single grave on top of Custer hill.

Truth-Custer had two bullet wounds to his body, one to his chest and one to his head. He also had his thigh slashed, and an arrow shoved up his penis. Both the marks of a Sioux warrior. One finger was missing the sign of a Cheyenne warrior, and a sewing awl was shoved into his ear by Cheyenne squaw.

Myth-The Indians did not ride in a circle around Custer on last stand hill. They were off their horses in tall grass bobbing up and down and taking pot shots at the soldiers defending the hill. The Indians though did divide Custer's ranks at least twice by running their horses through his lines, one such rush was led by Crazy Horse.

Truth-Reno and Benteen's detachments were only fifteen minutes away from Custer hill.

Truth-The first maps of The Little Big Horn were destroyed by the U.S. army

Truth-In nineteen ninety-one the Custer monument on Custer hill was renamed from "Custer battlefield" to "little big horn battlefield".

Truth-Sitting bull was quoted as saying that when the Indians in the valley saw the approaching soldiers, he said "we thought we were whipped"

Truth -The Indians had more weapons at the battle than the soldiers did. 350 - 400 weapons were documented to have been used.

Truth -When it came to burying the dead, the troops given the task, found in the Indian encampment all types of shovels, spades, and axes. These items aided the detail in burying their comrades. Not a lot, but it helped.

Truth-Reno instead of charging the Indian village as Custer ordered him to, dismounted his troops and fought on foot, before being forced to retreat across the little big horn river to Reno hill.

Truth -Reno could hear Custer's volleys from where he was. Scout George Heerden's statements in 1878 gave the account of hearing volley firing coming from the area where Custer was. After a while the firing stopped and died away.

Truth - Benteen was offered a promotion in 1866 as a major in 10th cavalry, but refused and took the position as captain with the 7th.

Truth - The Arapahoe were at the little Big Horn, but only in numbers counting no more than five young warriors. They were being held prisoners as the Sioux felt they may be spies for the white soldiers. During the battle one of the young men fought against Custer and saw him go down dead, his name was "left hand".

Truth-Reno and Benteen reported in 1876 the following: Reno - there were 2,000 warriors at the battle Benteen - there were 1,500 warriors at the battle Reno and Benteen reported in 1879 the following: Reno - there were 4,000 warriors at the battle Benteen - there were 9,000 warriors at the battle.

Truth - Mark Kellogg, correspondent for the N.Y. Herald. His body was found on the battlefield a few hundred yards from last stand hill.

Truth-Sage brush, prickly pear cactus, coarse grass, and timber made up a lot of the little big horn terrain on that day in 1876.

Truth- Charles Windholph Co. H, Medal of Honor winner 1876 was the last living survivor of the little big horn battle. He died in 1950.

Truth- The only way the surviving burial party could identify Tom Custer was by the tattoo on his right arm.

Truth - Custer command consisted of immigrants, nearly half from Ireland, Italy, Germany, and England

Truth - Custer received six brevet commissions during

the civil war and was always courted as 'General".

Myth-The seventh cavalry never wore yellow neckerchiefs. They were used by the movie companies.

Truth - Many of the troopers including the officers wore a knife from their waist belts. Extracting poor shells proved to be abundant that day in 1876.

Truth -Captain Thomas French Co. M and Sgt. John Ryan Co. M. were the last two soldiers to fire their weapons at the Indians on Reno hill. Ryan used his .45 cal. Sharps and French used his .50 Cal Springfield rifle.

Truth-Because the troopers 45/70's were jamming, captain French went around and used his cleaning rod from his Springfield to ram out the jammed shells.

Truth-Captain Thomas Weir was never asked any questions after the battle about his exploits on Reno hill and was never asked to give testimony at any of the government inquiries. He died six months later in 1876 due to PTSD: post-traumatic stress.

Truth - Major James Brisbins 2nd cavalry was turned down by General Terry to accompany the 7th to the little big horn. Custer said and I quote: the 7th can handle anything it meets" they he Custer and Brisbin loathed one another.

Truth - Custer's flanking moves on June the 26th were out of the Calvary manual "Calvary tactics and regulations of the united states army" regulation #561

Truth - Crazy Horses nickname growing up was "Curly", so was Custer's nickname "Curly" to his troopers during the civil war.

Truth - Custer wore a jockstrap! It was referred to as a "self adjusting U.S. army suspensory bandage". Exhibited in the museum at the Little Big Horn battlefield national monument located in eastern Montana.

Truth - Custer followed the protestant religion.

Truth - Custer was a democrat.

CHAPTER 22
Signs of the Times in America 1876

Alexander Graham Bell patents the telephone.
Mark Twain writes his novel, "Tom Sawyer".
8 baseball teams form the National League.
Rutherford B. Hayes won the presidential election in November and became the 19th president in 1877.
The population of the state of New York, 1 million.
The Brooklyn Bridge was being built.
"I'll take you home again Kathleen" was the song of the year.
Edison receives his patent for his mimeograph machine.
Jesse James and the Younger-James gang are almost wiped out trying to rob a bank in Northfield, Minnesota.
Texas A&M college opens.
Wyatt Earp starts his new job as a deputy sheriff in Dodge City, Kansas
First transcontinental express train arrives in San Francisco, California 83 hours and 39 minutes from New York city.
Colorado admitted as the 38th state to the union.
America celebrates the 100th anniversary of independence.
Heinz ketchup was introduced all these remarkable events took place in America in 1876 the year Custer died.

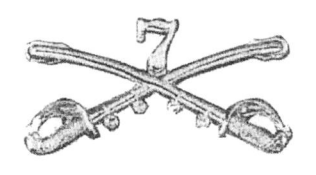

CHAPTER 23
Weapons of the little big horn 7th Calvary & Indian

"The battle of the little big horn", or "Custer's last stand", and now referred to as "the little big horn battlefield national monument" is one big question mark! When congress passed the legislation on renaming the battlefield in November of 1991 Custer lost another battle that year. But the debate still goes on! Who was better armed, who had the better advantage in numbers or weapons, and what did happen that day in June of 1876.

This chapter I hope will bring out more information about the battle to the general public that I discovered when doing the research on the book. Maybe the reader can go away learning new facts about the weapons used, and well I guess then I've done my job in writing this informative piece of work.

This chapter is on the weapons used, and how they may or may not have had an impact on the outcome of the battle. (Note: we will never know). From the start of this new nation, man wanted more room and he moved west. The movement started in the 1600's with the Pilgrims, then came the French and Indian War, which was followed by the American revolution, and then the war of 1812, which was followed again by the Mexican war, and finally the American civil war. All of these wars had an impact on firepower.

From the mere matchlock rifle to the musket. Hundreds of these weapons found their way into the Indian society and thus put both the white eyes and native Americans on an almost even keel. Fur trading companies, traders, post exchanges and yes wars changed the way of life of these tribes who still used the bow and arrow, but preferred the fire stick as a weapon.

Now getting back to the Little Big Horn battle, experts have said the Indians had close to 400 firearms amongst them when they went into battle. There were over 48 to 50 different types of weapons used by the tribes during the battle. I've even read accounts of the number being over 60 in the number of weapons. We'll never know! With all the wars that occurred on this continent, arms found their way to the Indian way of life. Immigration and expansion to the west also brought new weapons into the hands of the Indian. After Custer's demise hundreds of people have flocked to the battlefield and many artifacts disappeared. I've read reports on the calibers of the guns used and the cartridge cases found way, there were other arms used and the Indians used these to their advantage. A mere musket is as accurate as the henry rifle, in the right hands of a skilled shooter. A black powder gun can be deadly! Yes, the Indians did use the bow and arrow at the battle, but there were an awfully large number of black powder weapons used. With the migration of the tribes in America which include the following:

The Oto, Pawnee, Arikara, Cheyenne, Comanche, Sioux, Arapaho, Kansa, Bannock, Shoshone, Paiute, Nez Perce, Cayuse, Umatilla, Walla Walla, and the Wasco. These tribes had to have come into contact with the white eyes and weapons had to be bought, traded, stolen, or pried from the hands of a dead person.

These weapons found their way through out the west and their owners changed hands with these weapons many times. Miners, and homesteaders armed themselves with all types of pistols, muskets and carbines. Indians sought clothing, food, and weapons from these invaders that were encroaching on their lands. Now at the battle of the little big horn it has been proven that many types of weapons were used by the Indians. With the end of the civil war many arms were transported west, and wound up in the hands of the red man. Flintlocks, carbines, muskets, and all types of pistols were the new property of the Indian. The U.S. government disposed of many surplus arms and made them available to the Indian tribes at many army post exchanges. The Winchester and Henry Rimfire rifles were part of these offerings and yes, they were important at the battle. The only problem the Indian had was getting ammo for these arms.

Trading furs for ammo, and even ponies were generally the practice for Indians acquiring ammunition. It has been stated that the Indian tribes using firearms at the battle were low on ammo and was one of the reasons for Reno's troops surviving the battle. Yes, after defeating Custer and the rest of his command the Indians picked up many Springfield carbines, but the ammo situation was still at a premium. Most of the ammo for the troopers were in the saddlebags of the frantic horses that ran away when the battle started. Muzzle loaders were widely used and the owner could put anything that fit down the barrel and fire the weapon. A little far from being safe, but in a heated battle I guess anything went. Personal weapons were allowed on the army side and documented to have been used during the battle. There were accounts of heavy hand to hand combat during the battle and I'm sure many troopers also used the knives that were reported to have been carried by the men were used also. Custer and several officers were reported to have carried knives on their person on that day in June. Custer had with him his Remington .50 caliber sporting rifle and was reported to have taken a few pot shots at the Indian camp with it. Tom Custer had with him a Springfield officers model 45/70 carbine, and two members of company m, Captain French and Sgt. John Ryan had with them their personal weapons. Captain French sported a Springfield 45/70 trapdoor rifle "long tom" and Sgt. Ryan had a 15 lb. Sharps rifle with a telescopic sight attached. Both men with their sharpshooter abilities stopped the Indians from further deadly fire atop sharpshooter's ridge.

Many caliber cartridges and lead bullets have been found strewn all over the battlefield site. They range from .52 caliber, .50 caliber, .40 caliber, .44 caliber, 50/70 caliber, 45/70 caliber, .45 caliber, 56/50 caliber, .36 caliber, 44/55 caliber, .54 caliber, and .58 caliber. As I stated in the beginning, visitors to the battlefield picked up anything that wasn't tied down in the early years and who knows what other calibers or whatever type of cartridges wound up in some one's pocket or pocket book.

Weapons on the other hand are still a big question mark? Colt, Sharps, Henrys, Springfield, Evans, Remington, Ballard, Maynard, Starr, Hawkins, Savage, Enfield, Whitney, and Spencer are a few that have been documented. But what about the Josyln, Hall, Smith, Burnside, Werner, Richmond, harpers ferry, Smith & Wesson, Browning and numerous other carbines or rifles that may have been used during the battle. I've had the opportunity over the years to fire many types of the above-mentioned carbines or rifles and found them deadly accurate. Even the new reproductions that are available now to the shooter should show the novice historian what a horrific day it must have been on that hot June day in 1876. All types of arrow heads and tomahawk heads have been found on the battlefield which shows they were widely used also during the battle. When a trooper went down dead his weapon wound up in the hands of an Indian who may have had only a bow and arrow at the start of the battle. Recently I watched a movie on "TMC" titled "Escape from Fort Bravo" starring William Holden from the year 1953. In the movie the cavalry was surrounded by Apache warriors, who at the end gathered twenty or thirty of their braves and sent an onslaught of arrows into the air at the troopers. I've watched many movies were this was shown to have happened, namely "The Last Samurai" starring Tom Cruise, but not with the Indian tribes. To see the arrows shot into the air in great numbers was something to see, for the troopers had no place to hide from the death raining down on them from the sky. Hits in the back, leg, arm, neck and head were many. So, one can surmise that the bow and arrow did have an effect on the troopers on" last stand hill".

A war club or tomahawk, or even a war lance I'm sure would have been discarded by a warrior to retrieve a fire stick. There were many weapons used that day in June and the story has it that somewhere hidden in the hills or buried in the desert is a cache of the seventh cavalry's weapons, and who knows what else? Because the Indians didn't want any retribution from the us government they hid all that they captured. Somewhere there is a pot of gold to be found.

I find it very interesting when I observe a painting or print of Custer's last stand and take notice of the weapons being portrayed. Even a TV show or movie that recreates the battle often shows the lack or the fortitude of truth of the type of weapons which were used. I'm a purist and critique everything I see when watching something being shown, recreated, or displayed as being historical. Maybe that's why the battle of the little big horn is so etched in my mind.

Finally, again I would like to say with all the weapons out there, I'm sure we don't have a handle on what ones to a point were used during the battle, only the documented ones.

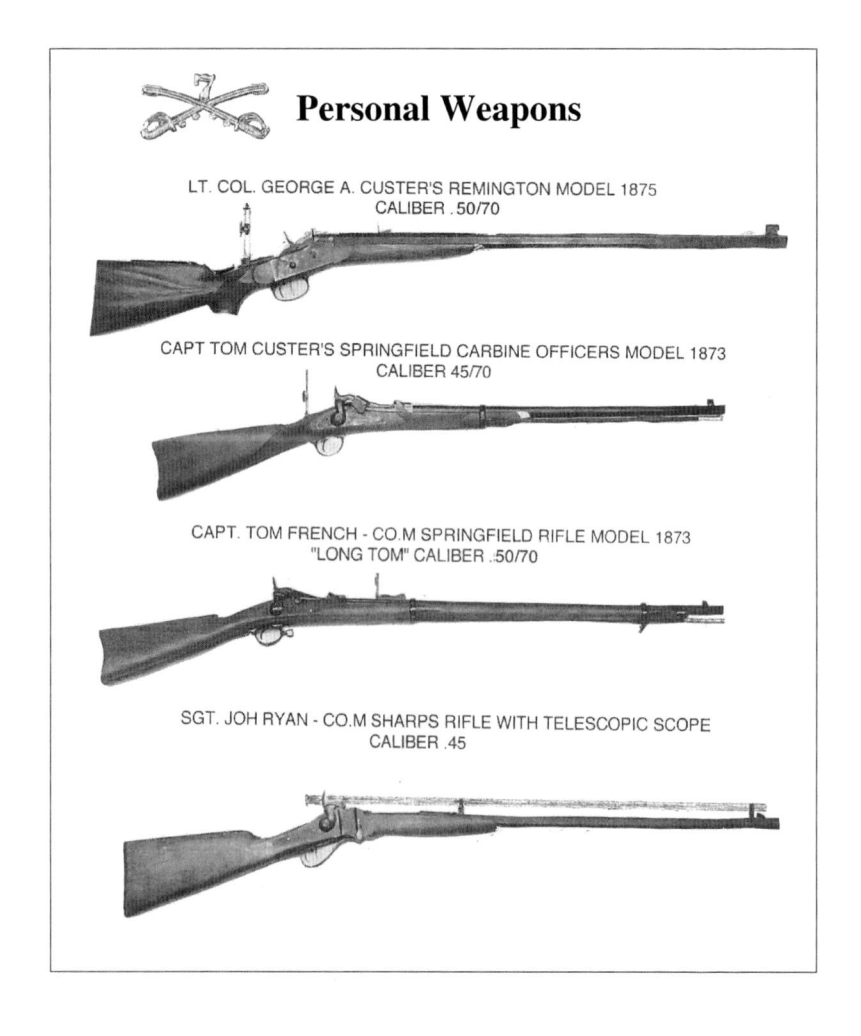

Personal Weapons

LT. COL. GEORGE A. CUSTER'S REMINGTON MODEL 1875
CALIBER .50/70

CAPT TOM CUSTER'S SPRINGFIELD CARBINE OFFICERS MODEL 1873
CALIBER 45/70

CAPT. TOM FRENCH - CO.M SPRINGFIELD RIFLE MODEL 1873
"LONG TOM" CALIBER .50/70

SGT. JOH RYAN - CO.M SHARPS RIFLE WITH TELESCOPIC SCOPE
CALIBER .45

Standard Issue

SPRINGFIELD TRAPDOOR CARBINE MODEL 1873
CALIBER .45/70-55

COLT ARMY MODEL P 1872 SINGLE ACTION REVOLVER
CALIBER .45

STANDARD WEAPONS FOR THE ARMY IN 1876 WERE THE
1873 SPRINGFIELD TRAPDOOR CARBINE & THE 1872 COLT
MODEL P SINGLE ACTION REVOLVER.

THE CARBINE WEIGHED 7LBS. AND WAS 41" IN LENGTH. IT WAS ACCURATE
AT 200-250 YARDS. 60,912 WERE MADE BETWEEN 1873 & 1893. SERIAL
#'S BELOW 43,700 ARE KNOWN AS CUSTER GUNS.

THE COLT REVOLVER WEIGHTED 2-50 LBS. AND HAD A LENGTH
OF 71/2". IT WAS ACCURATE AT 60 YARDS. 16,000 WERE MADE
BETWEEN 1872 & 1874.

Gatling Gun

DR. RICHARD GATLING PATENTED THE NEW FIREARM IN 1862 WITH THE INTENT TO SAVE LIVES ON THE BATTLEFIELD. A BATTERY OF GATLING GUNS WAS MANNED BY FOUR PERSONNEL.

CUSTER HAD WITH HIM IN HIS COLUM WHEN THEY LEFT FORT LINCOLN A BATTERY OF GATLING GUNS. HE LEFT THEM BEHIND WITH GENERAL TERRY AND BALKED AT THE IDEA OF TAKING THEM WITH HIM INTO BATTLE. HE FELT THEY WOULD HAMPER HIS MOVEMENTS AND SLOW DOWN HIS ADVANCE TO THE LITTLE BIG HORN.

THEY WERE 45/70 CALIBER GUNS EQUIPT WITH TEN BARRELS WHICH HAD THE CAPABILITY OF FIRING 1,200 ROUNDS PER MINUTE FROM EACH GUN! YOU CAN USE YOUR IMAGINATION ON THE OUTCOME OF THE BATTLE IF CUSTER HAD SET UP A MORE WELL PLANNED DEFENSE OR OFFENSE, WITH THE HELP OF THESE WHEELED WEAPONS OF DEATH. ANOTHER QUESTION MARK ON THAT DAY IN JUNE OF 1876 EMERGES.

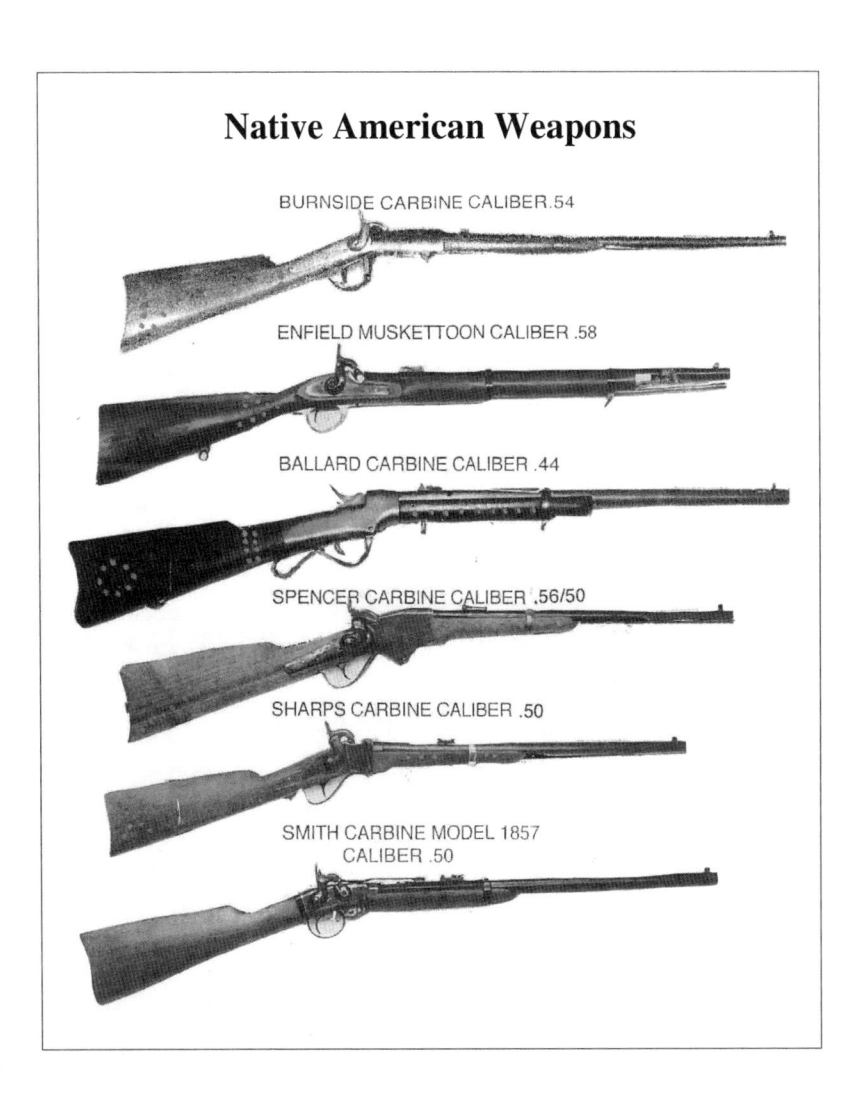

Native American Weapons

BURNSIDE CARBINE CALIBER .54

ENFIELD MUSKETTOON CALIBER .58

BALLARD CARBINE CALIBER .44

SPENCER CARBINE CALIBER .56/50

SHARPS CARBINE CALIBER .50

SMITH CARBINE MODEL 1857 CALIBER .50

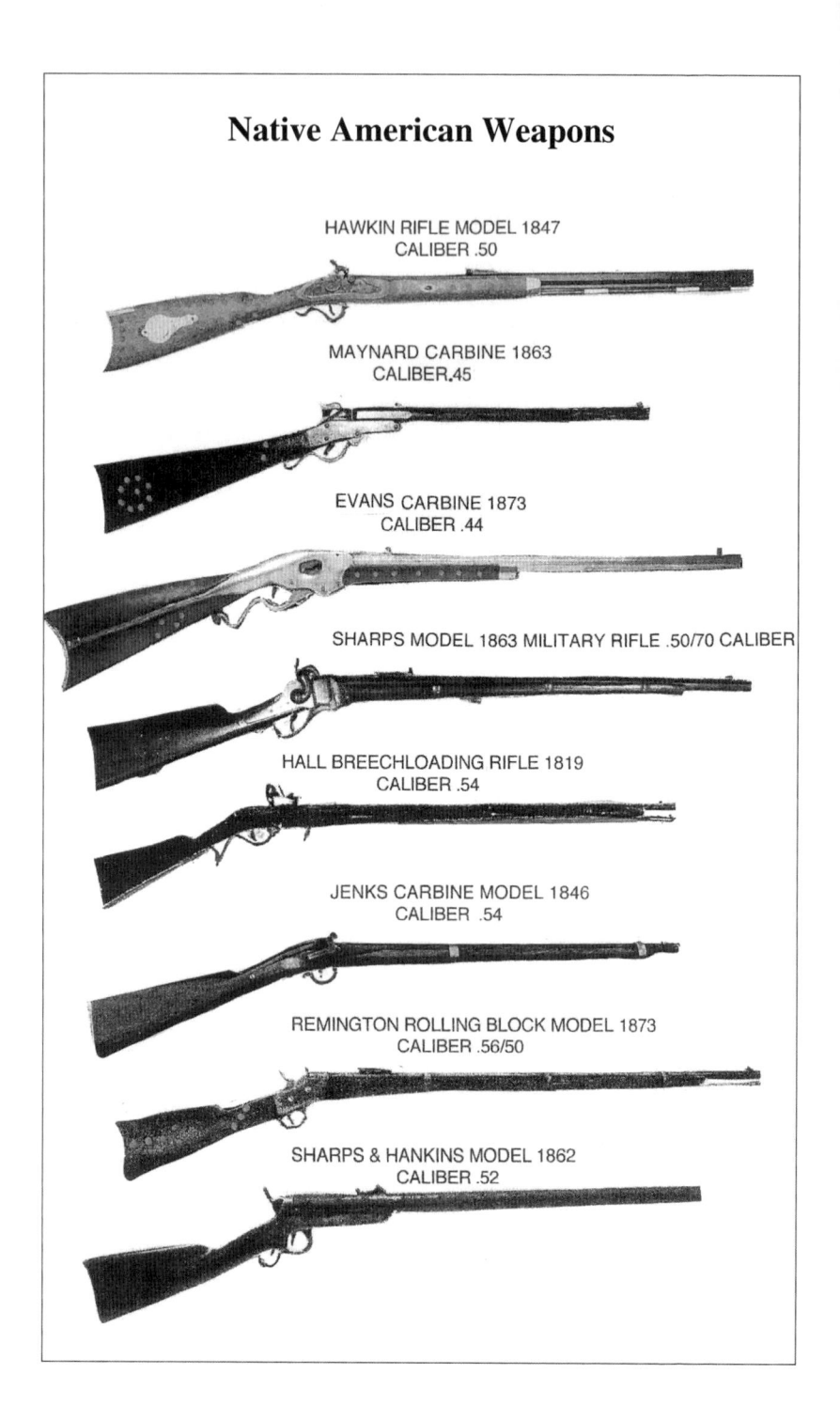

Native American Weapons

HAWKIN RIFLE MODEL 1847
CALIBER .50

MAYNARD CARBINE 1863
CALIBER .45

EVANS CARBINE 1873
CALIBER .44

SHARPS MODEL 1863 MILITARY RIFLE .50/70 CALIBER

HALL BREECHLOADING RIFLE 1819
CALIBER .54

JENKS CARBINE MODEL 1846
CALIBER .54

REMINGTON ROLLING BLOCK MODEL 1873
CALIBER .56/50

SHARPS & HANKINS MODEL 1862
CALIBER .52

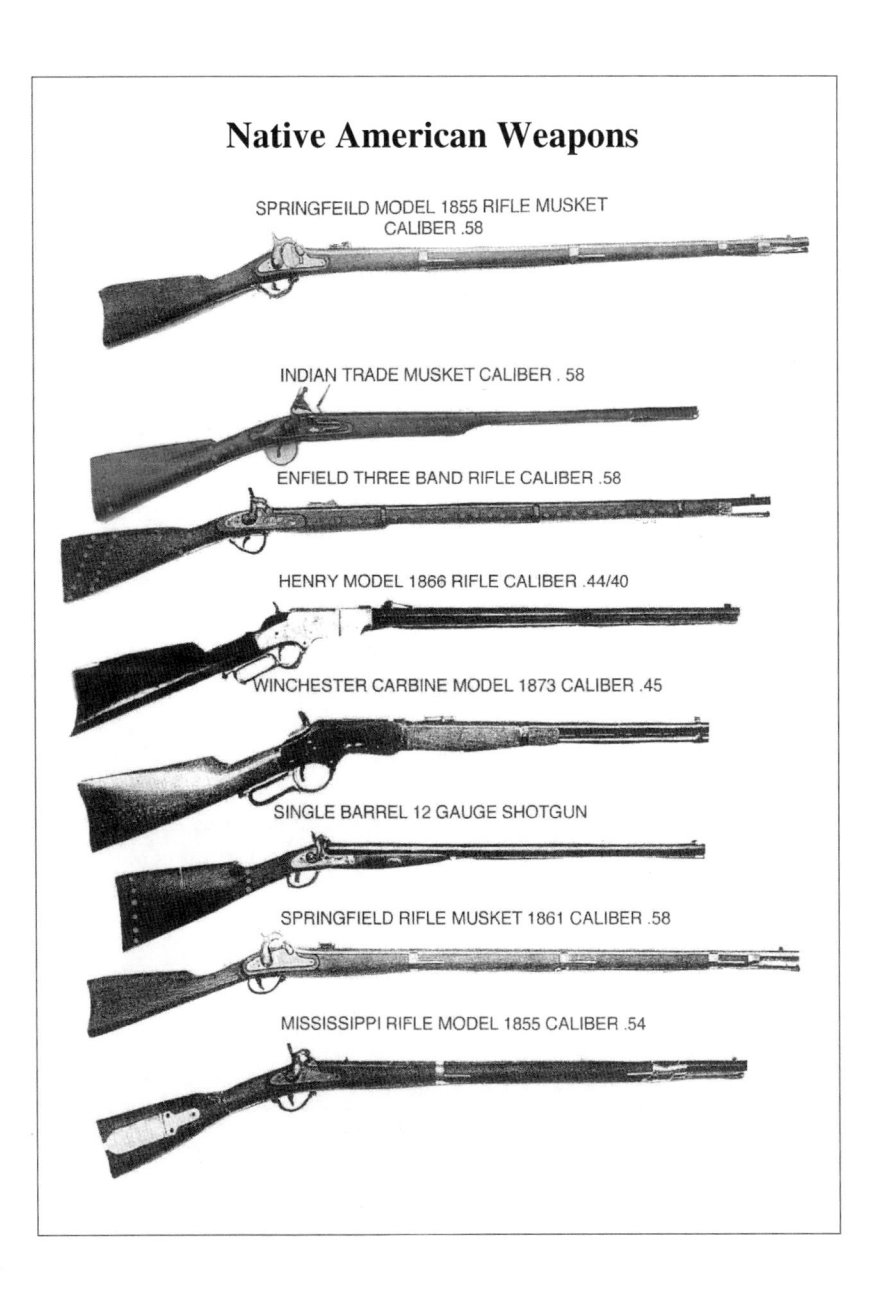

Native American Weapons

SPRINGFEILD MODEL 1855 RIFLE MUSKET CALIBER .58

INDIAN TRADE MUSKET CALIBER .58

ENFIELD THREE BAND RIFLE CALIBER .58

HENRY MODEL 1866 RIFLE CALIBER .44/40

WINCHESTER CARBINE MODEL 1873 CALIBER .45

SINGLE BARREL 12 GAUGE SHOTGUN

SPRINGFIELD RIFLE MUSKET 1861 CALIBER .58

MISSISSIPPI RIFLE MODEL 1855 CALIBER .54

Native American Weapons

LEECH & RIGDON REVOLVER MODEL 1864
CALIBER .36

SCHOFIELD REVOLVER MODEL 1875
BY SMITH & WESSON
CALIBER .44

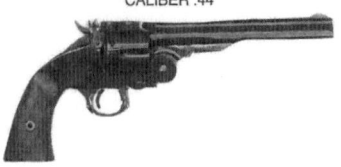

WALKER REVOLVER MODEL 1847
CALIBER .44

BACKWOODS PISTOL 1857
CALIBER .45

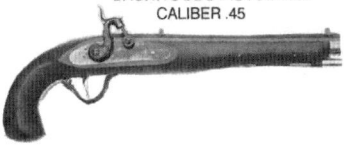

DRAGOON 2ND MODEL 1851
CALIBER .44

STARR REVOLVER MODEL 1858
CALIBER .44

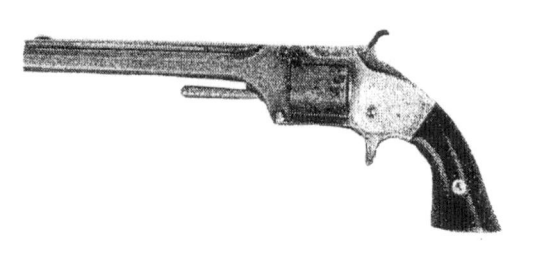

SMITH & WESSON MODEL 1861
CALIBER .32

Native American Weapons

DRAGOON PISTOL MODEL 1855
CALIBER .58

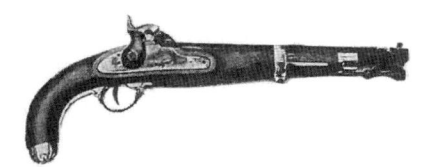

SIX SHOOTER REVOLVER MODEL 1873
CALIBER .44

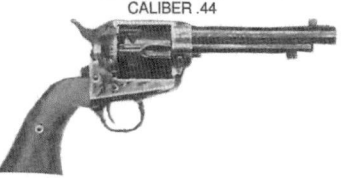

COLT PATERSON MODEL 1837
CALIBER .36

OPEN TOP COLT CONVERSION MODEL 1871
CALIBER .44 RIMFIRE

REMINGTON ARMY REVOLVER MODEL 1858
CALIBER .44

COLT ARMY REVOLVER MODEL 1860
CALIBER .44 PERCUSSION

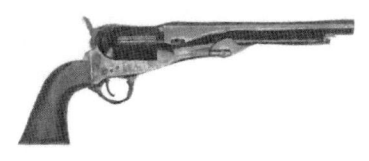

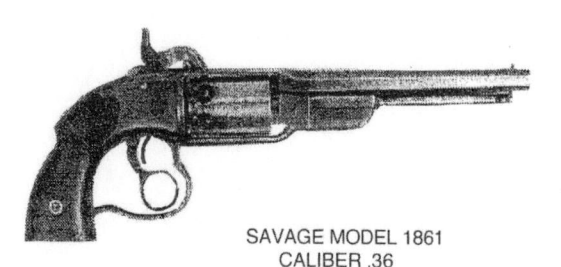

SAVAGE MODEL 1861
CALIBER .36

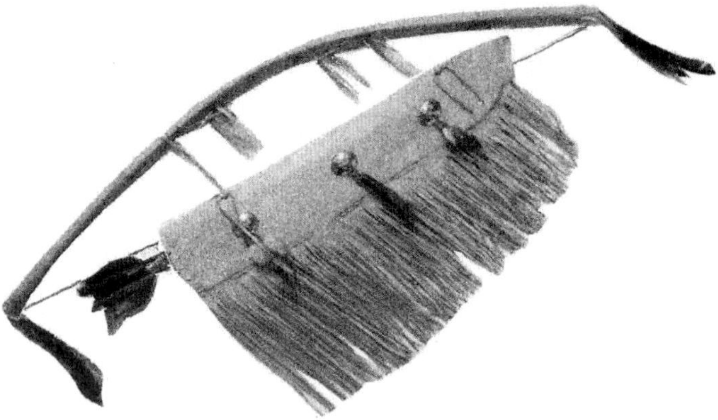

CHAPTER 24
Bows and Arrows and other Weapons

The tribes at the Little Big Horn not only had the white mans fire sticks to fight with. In addition, they also fought with the weapons that had been in their culture from the beginning. The Bow and Arrow, the lance, club, and tomahawk. I've read report after report of the battle being won by the Indians sending rains of arrows down onto Custer's men. Yes they were a winning factor in the battle, but I believe it was the rifle or carbine that won the day. The bow and arrow is an interesting weapon and each individual tribe used a specific color to designate it's owner. Red was used widely by the Sioux, and so was Black, Yellow, and White. Different symbols were used on the owner's arrows and this made it easier the tell who's arrows were who's. Arrows could range in length of 22 inches to 24 inches. I also read an article on how the women of the tribe would make each arrow for their warrior, and that when hunting or in battle the marked arrow would distinguish the owner from another.

I remember the movie" She Wore A Yellow Ribbon" and in the beginning a young Sgt. Tyree, (Ben Johnson) while out on patrol came upon the pay masters stagecoach and it was riddled with arrows! Later in the fort while showing the arrow to John Wayne, Tyree related that the arrow came from a Cheyenne dog soldier!

After the Big Horn Battle reports filtered in that the trooper's bodies looked like porcupines because of the large number of arrows sticking out of them. We know that the Indians went around and shot each trooper in the head with a pistol or rifle to make sure they were dead. Also, reports from the surviving Indians stated that many of their brethren were going around and shooting arrows into the bodies also. Feathers also designated a warrior's tribe. They were normally made from Turkey feathers, Goose feathers, Hawk feathers, duck feathers, Crow feathers, Eagle feathers, and Buzzard feathers! Lines and dots adorned many arrows as well as many symbols such as a Snake, Wolf, and Bird.

A really strong built bow with at least a ten inch draw length could fling an arrow a distance of 250 feet. Another story in the Indian way of life is what you're "rank" was in the village. Special markings on an arrow could tell someone how high up he was in a certain tribe.

The Sioux also died their bows green that they extracted from choke cherry berries. The colors scarlet blue and Red were common colors used on a tribe arrows. As far as the points on the arrows many iron points have been found on the battle field along with your common flint points. As stated earlier the arrows were 22 to 24 inches in length and the common bow would measure from 32 to 42 inches in length. Bows were made from a variety of woods such as Ash, Plum, Ironwood, Elm, Cedar, bone, or Hickory. There were reports that one trooper who had been shot twice in the back still hanging on to life and had to be tomahawked to death to kill him. I'm sure though that a skilled Indian could bring down the biggest of the big with one shot from a well constructed bow and arrow.

Most Indian's preferred the bow and arrow over a musket because you had to load every round and this was a difficult thing to do while riding hard and fast. The simple bow and arrow were light and easily handled. Hail the bow and arrow!

Other weapons the Indian tribes used were the war lance, war club, and the infamous tomahawk. Early fur traders came to the Indian country with wears to trade or sell, and one was the tomahawk. Many variations, and styles, but so deadly in combat. The war club was also used at the Little Big Horn and many a trooper went to his keeper after being brained with one of these horrific weapons. Lastly the war lance, and these too had many variations thru out the Indian nations. Not as deadly, but you had to get close to someone to do real harm or kill them. All these weapons as I said aided the Indians that day in June of 1876, and helped them win the victory that Sitting Bull foresaw in his dream.

****

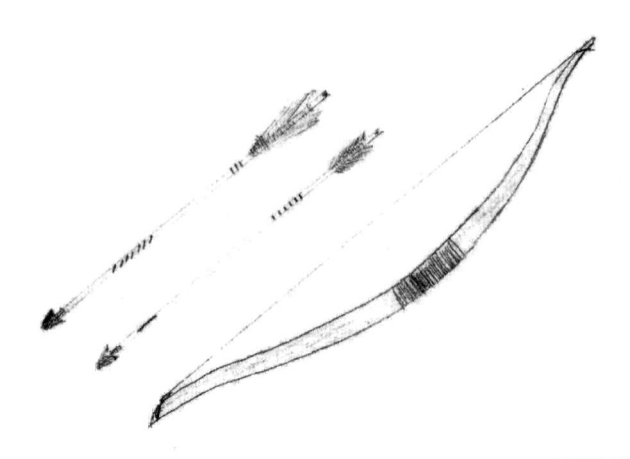

THE BOW & ARROW ALLOWED THE INDIANS TO LAUNCH THOUSANDS OF ARROWS UPON THE EXPOSED TROOPERS ON CUSTER HILL WHILE BEING OUT OF SIGHT IN THE TALL GRASS.

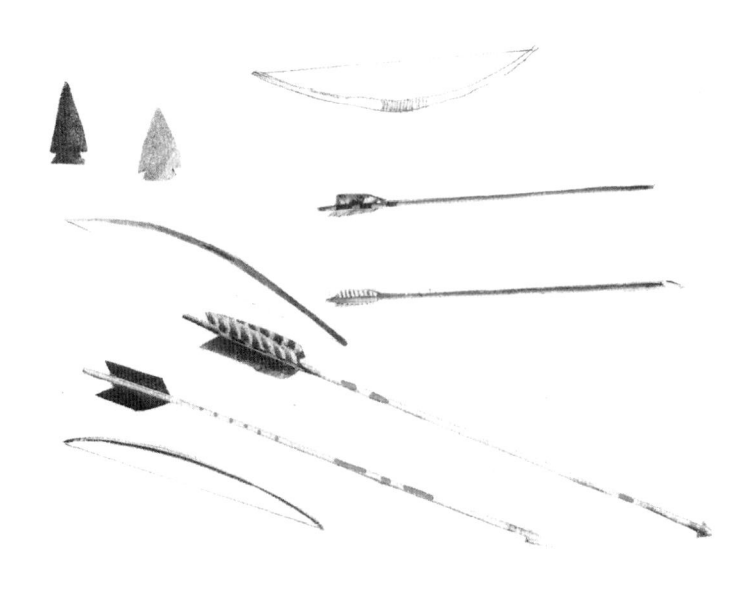

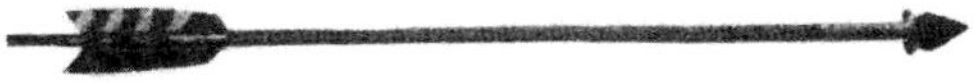

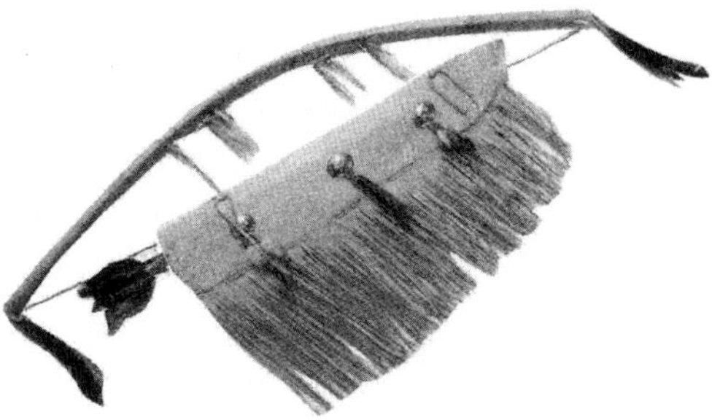

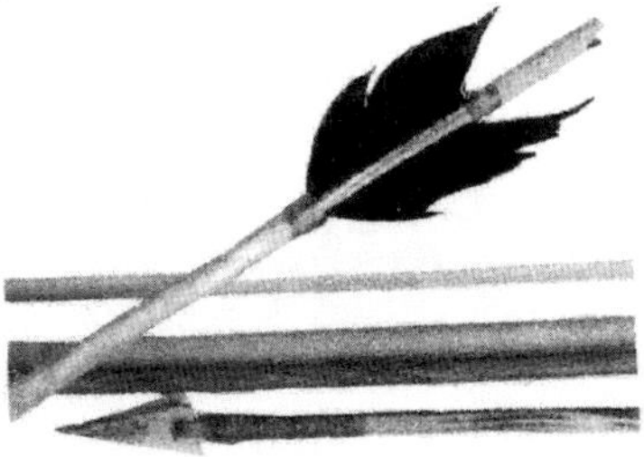

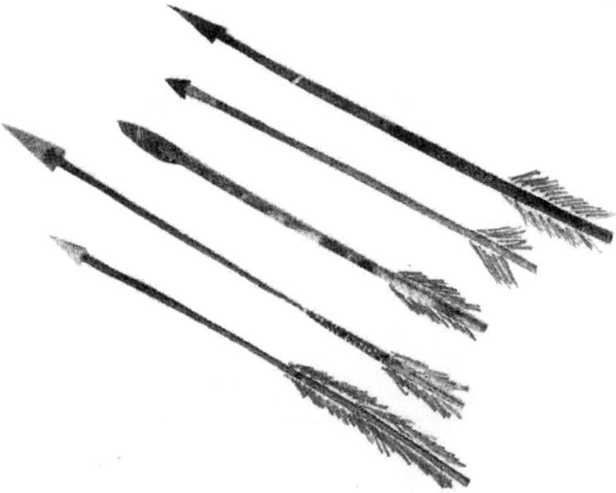

WHEN A GUN WAS FIRED AND ONLY HAD ONE SHOT THE TOMAHAWK WAS SECOND CHOICE AS A WEAPON

TOMAHAWKS WERE GIVEN AS GIFTS IN PEACE CEREMONIES AND WERE LAID WITH SILVER OR GOLD ON BOTH BLADE AND SHAFT

VARIOUS TOMAHAWKS & HATCHETS
CEREMONIAL, PEACE, WAR, THROWING

USED FOR CEREMONIAL, BATTLE, AND CAMPFIRE COMFORT

INDIANS AND FRONTIERSMEN PRIZED THE TOMAHAWK

THE TOMAHAWK OR ALSO CALLED THE HACHET WAS THE MOST PRIZED WEAPON DESIRED IN TRADE GOODS.

INDIAN WAR LANCES

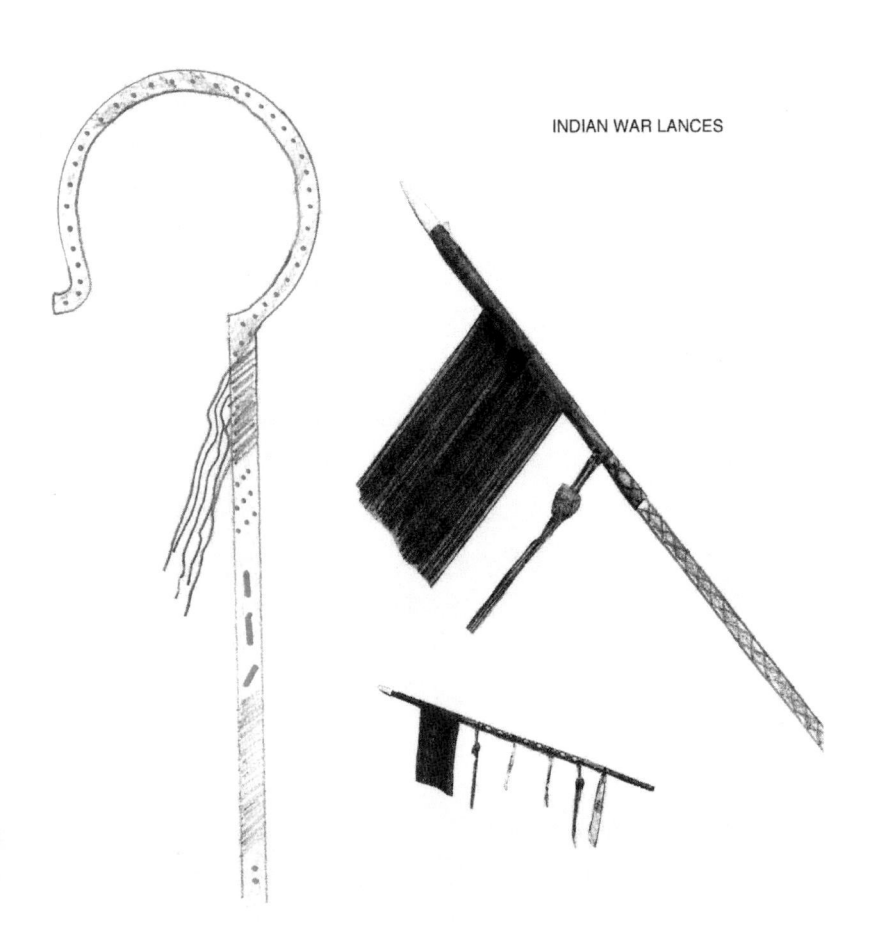

WAR CLUB / GUNSTOCK CLUB

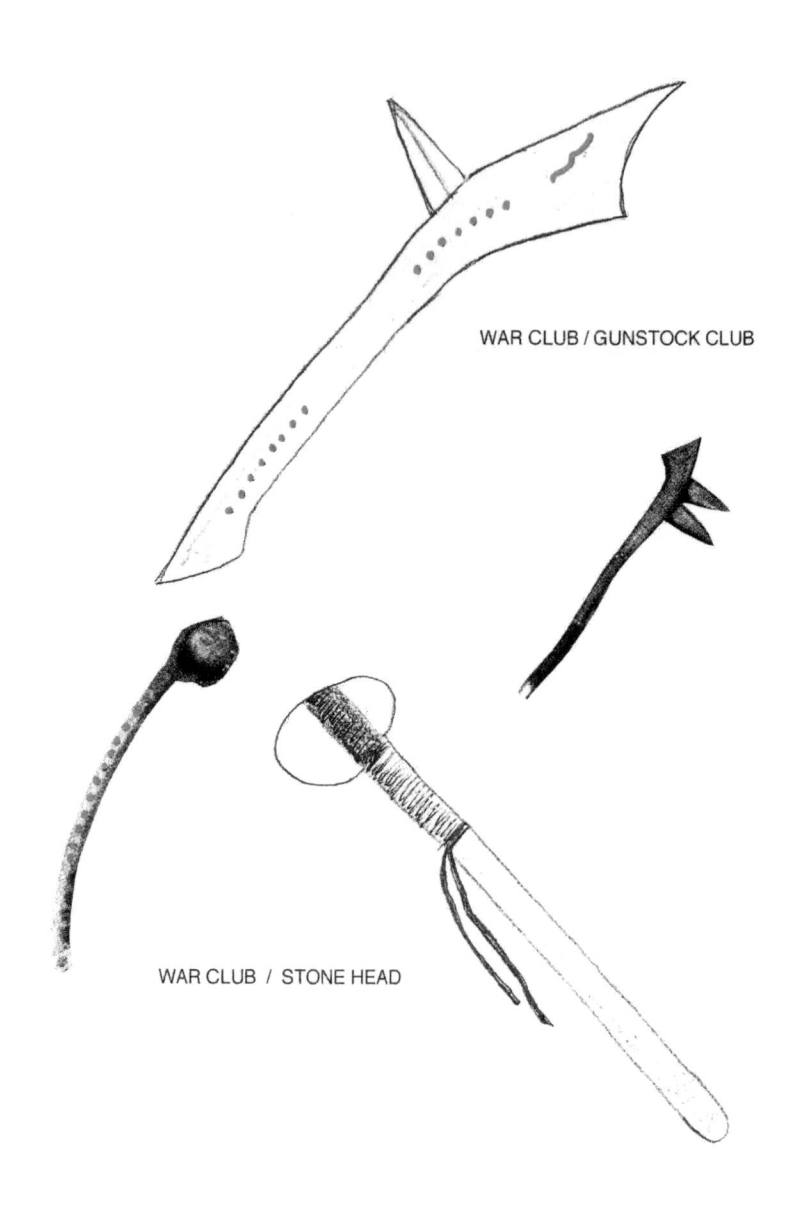

WAR CLUB / STONE HEAD

Acknowledgments

I would like to say thank you to Pat Churchill Hedgecoth Great Granddaughter of Norvell Churchill, hero of the Gettysburg campaign of 1863 during our Civil War. She made the pictures of Norvell come alive and possible plus the history of her Great grandfather. He was a true American hero not only during the Civil War, and the state of Michigan, but a true hero in the hearts of the people who looked up to him as a human being. He did walk this earth and he did make a difference.

I would like to thank Des Jean Bauer for bringing the likeness of Oraland and Waynoka to life. Also, Samantha Rapp for making the cover possible and very special. She brought out another of a long line of thoughts of what it was like after the battle of 1876. a special thanks to Rebecca Risenhoover at the Cheyenne and Arapahoe tribe's language program for helping me with the Cheyenne language translations. Many thanks also to Mary Burke and Renee Green at the Sid Richardson Museum in Texas for their timely help with the photo's used in the book.

Thanks also to the following people who gave me the inspiration on writing the book. Oraland and Deb Nelson, George Nelson, Owen Nelson, my late brother-in-law David Nelson and his wife Laurie. My son Wayne and his wife Kim, my daughter Donna Marie, my sister Diana and her husband Brad, my brother Walter and his wife Maria, my uncle, Dutch Treptow and my beautiful Aunt Joyce, and all those who urged me on to pursue the book idea.

Lastly, if it wasn't for my wonderful wife Marjorie this book would not have been written. She urged me on, and keep up the positive vibes for my ability to come up with a refreshing story line. Many hours were spent in the library to give her the quiet and privacy in our home for weeks from the rigors of a busy work week. This woman is my Waynoka in true life.

Bibliography

POWERS, THOMAS - "THE KILLING OF CRAZY HORSE":
RANDOM HOUSE 2010 PUBLISHED BY ALFRED A. KNOPF

MCMURTRY, LARRY - "OH WASHITA SLAUGHTER
" MASSACRES IN THE AMERICAN WEST 1846-1890":
SIMOM & SCHUSTER 2005

CONNELL, EVAN S. - "SON OF MORNING STAR":
CUSTER AND THE LITTLE BIG HORN NORTH POINT PRESS
1984

MCMURTRY, LARRY - "CUSTER":
SIMON & SCHUSTER 2012

LARSON, ROBERT - "GALL, LAKOTA WAR CHIEF":
UNIVERSITY OF OKLAHOMA 2007

COMMAGER, HENRY - "THE CIVIL WAR ARCHIVE":
BLACK DOG & LEVENTHAL 2000

BURNS, RICK & KEN - "THE CIVIL WAR"
KNOPF 1990

WISEHART, DAVID - 'ENCYCLOPEDIA OF THE GREAT
PLAINS"
UNIVERSITY OF NEBRASKA PRESS 2011

MARQUIS, THOMAS DR. - "WOODEN LEG, A WARRIOR WHO
FOUGHT CUSTER": UNIVERSITY OF NEBRASKA PRESS
2003,1927

EVANS, D. C. - 'CUSTER'S LAST FIGHT, VOL. 1 BATTLE OF
THE LITTLE BIG HORN": UPTON & SONS 1999

GRAHAM, W. - "THE CUSTER MYTH":
UNIVERSITY OF NEBRASKA PRESS 1986

AMBROSE, STEPHEN, - "CRAZY HORSE AND CUSTER":
RANDOM HOUSE 1996

HUTTON, PAUL A. - "THE CUSTER READER":
UNIVERSITY OF OKLAHOMA PRESS 1992

GRAHAM, WILLIAM A. COL.- "TRANSCRIPTS OF THE RENO COURT OF INQUIRY"
MILITARY AFFAIRS SECTION CHIEF OF THE JUDGE ADVOCATE GENERAL'S OFFICE 1879,1933

SHAPELL MANUSCRIPT FOUNDATION - FREDERICK BENTEEN'S OATH OF OFFICE AS CAPTAIN IN THE 7TH CAVALRY IN 1866

TURNER, DON - "CUSTER SURPRISES SLEEPING INDIANS IN THE BATTLE NEAR WASHITA". ARTICLE FROM THE AMARILLO NEWS GLOBE

HARRIS, EATHEN E.- "THE BARE BONES LIST"
WARRIORS QUILL 2012

HATCH, THOM - "CUSTER COMPANION"
STACKPOLE BOOKS 2002

THOMAS, RODNEY G. - "RUBBING OUT LONG HAIR"
ELK PLAIN PRESS 2009

GOBLE, PAUL - "CUSTER'S LAST BATTLE"
WISDOM TALES 2013

BRIZEE-BOWEN, SANDRA L. - "LITTLE BIG HORN BATTLE IN PLAINS INDIAN ART" A.H. CLARK 2013

HOOK, RICHARD - "WARRIORS AT THE LITTLE BIG HORN 1876" OSPREY 2004

CUSTER, ELIZABETH B. - "FOLLOWING THE GUIDON"
UNIVERSITY OF OKLAHOMA PRESS 1966

USCHAN, MICHAEL V. - "THE BATTLE OF THE LITTLE BIG HORN"
WORLD ALMANAC LIBRARY 2002

PHILBRICK, NATHANIEL - "THE LAST STAND"
WHEELER PUBLISHING 2010

WELCH, JAMES - "KILLING CUSTER"
PENGUIN BOOKS 1995

SKLENAR, LARRY - "TO HELL WITH HONOR"
UNIVERSITY OF OKLAHOMA PRESS 2000

GODFREY, EDWARD S. - "THE FIELD DIARY OF LT. EDWARD SETTLE GODFREY"
CHAMPOEG PRESS 1957

BRUST, JAMES- POHANKA- BRIAN, BARNARD, SANDY - "WHERE CUSTER FELL"
UNIVERSITY OF OKLAHOMA PRESS 2005

BISHOP, CHRIS- DRURY, IAN- GIBBONS, TONY- "1400 DAYS THE CIVIL WAR DAY BY DAY"
GALLERY BOOKS 1990

BRAUN, ERIC- EDITED BY COMMAGER, HENRY S. - "THE CIVIL WAR ARCHIVE"
BLACK DOG & LEVENTHAL 2000

ANDERSON, GARY CLAYTON - "SITTING BULL AND THE PARADOX OF LAKOTA NATIONHOOD"
PEARSON/LONGMAN 2007

WEIL, ANN - "SITTING BULL"
HEINEMANN LIBRARY 2013

PENNER, LUCILE RETCH - "SITTING BULL"
GROSSET & DUNLOP 1995

DU BOIS, CHARLES G. - "KICK THE DEAD LION"
DU BOIS 1961

CHICAGO TIMES ACCOUNT "THE RENO COURT OF INQUIRY"
THE OLD ARMY PRESS 1972

DAVIS, WILLIAM C. - "THE CIVIL WAR, BROTHER AGAINST BROTHER"
TIME- LIFE BOOKS 1983

LAWSON, MICHAEL L. - LITTLE BIG HORN: "WINNING THE BATTLE, LOSING THE WAR"
CHELSEA HOUSE 2007

"CUSTER AT THE LITTLE BIG HORN" DONOVAN, JAMES - THE MAN, THE MYTH, THE MYSTERY
VOYAGEUR PRESS 2001

NEVIN, DAVID - "THE OLD WEST"
TIME LIFE BOOKS 1974

COLEMAN, NICK - JOURNALIST
MONTANA STAR TRIBUNE

MEDICINE CROW, JOSEPH - "FROM THE HEART OF THE CROW COUNTRY, THE CROW INDIANS OWN STORY"
BISON BOOKS   2000

LEMAN, WAYNE - "A REFERENCE GRAMMAR OF THE CHEYENNE LANGUAGE"
CHEYENNE TRANSLATION PROJECT   1991

WINDOLPH, CHARLES - "I FOUGHT WITH CUSTER, THE STORY OF SGT. WINDOLPH, LAST SURVIVOR OF THE BATTLE OF THE LITTLE BIG HORN"
UNIVERSITY OF NEBRASKA PRESS   198W

RAISOVICH, ELI - "CUSTER LIVES.COM"

UTLEY, ROBERT - "CUSTER AND THE GREAT CONTROVERSY"
WESTERN LORE PRESS 1962

TERRELL, JOHN UPTON - "FAINT THE TRUMPET SOUNDS: LIFE AND TRIAL OF MAJOR MARCUS RENO"
N.Y. N.Y. D . MCKAY CO. 1966

CONRADT, STACY - "THE QUICK 10: 10 FACTS ABOUT THE MEN OF THE LITTLE BIG HORN
MENTAL-FLOSS ARTICLE- 2008

NIGHTENGALE, ROBERT- "BATTLE OF THE LITTLE BIG HORN"
TRUE WEST MAGAZINE-HISTORY NET JUNE 1996

ALLEN, MARK - DAILY MAIL. COM ARTICLE - JUNE 2010

HUTCHENSON, WILL- "ARTIFACT OF THE BATTLE OF THE LITTLE BIG HORN"
SHIFFER PRESS 2016

MOVIES

WELCH, JAMES & STEKLER, PAUL - "THE AMERICAN EXPERIENCE LAST STAND AT THE LITTLE BIG HORN"
COPRODUCTION OF WGBH/BOSTON- THIRTEEN/WNET & KCET/ LA 199W

ARMSTRONG, BILL- "THE LEGEND OF CUSTER"
SIMTAR ENTERTAINMENT 1992

COFFEE, LENORE J. - KLINE, WALLY & MACKENZIE, AENEAS- "THEY DIED WITH THEIR BOOTS ON"
WARNER BROS. 1941

DEWITT, JACK - SCREENPLAY BY SALKOW, SIDNEY- "SITTING BULL"
UNITED ARTISTS 1954

BERGER, THOMAS - SCREENPLAY BY WILLINGHAM, CALDER "LITTLE BIG MAN"
NATIONAL GENERAL PICTURES 1970

PACKER, PETER - SCREENPLAY BY SWARTHOUT, GLENDON "7TH CAVALRY"
COLUMBIA PICTURES 1956

DEWITT, JACK - SCREENPLAY BY JOHNSON, DOROTHY M.
"A MAN CALLED HORSE"
NATIONAL GENERAL PICTURES 1970

BERNARD, GORDON - JIMET, JULIAN
"CUSTER OF THE WEST"
ALPHA (WEST GERMANY) 1967

CONNELL, EVAN S. - TELEPLAY BY MATHISON, MELLISSA
"SON OF MORNING STAR"
AMERICAN BROADCASTING COMPANY 1991

APEL, DAVID- HAYWARD, LILLIE- FOSTER, LEWIS- "TONKA"
BUENA VISTA DISTRIBUTION
WALT DISNEY FILMS 1958

BLAKE, MICHAEL- "DANCES WITH WOLVES"
ORION HOME VIDEO 1990

BLANFORT, MICHAEL - "THE PLAINSMAN"
UNIVERSAL PICTURES 1966

BRUCKNER, ROBERT - "SANTA FE TRAIL"
WARNER BROS. 1940

PECKINPAH, SAM - "THE GLORY GUYS"
UNITED ARTISTS 1965

SCREENPLAY BY- NUGENT, FRANK S. - "FORT APACHE"
WRITTEN BY BELLAH, JAMES W. RKO RADIO 1948

SCREENPLAY BY-NUGENT, FRANK S. - "SHE WORE A YELLOW RIBBON"
WRITTEN BY- BELLAH, JAMES W. RKO PICTURES 1949

SCREENPLAY BY- MCGUINESS, JAMES K. - "RIO GRANDE"
WRITTEN BY- BELLAH, JAMES W. REPUBLIC PICTURES 1950
SCREENPLAY BY- MAHIN, JOHN L. - "THE HORSE SOLDIERS"
WRITTEN BY- SINCLAIR, HAROLD UNITED ARTISTS 1959

SCREENPLAY BY- NUGENT, FRANK S. - "THE SEARCHERS"
WRITTEN BY- LEMAY, ALAN WARNER BROS. 1956

DAN DALTON - "THE GREAT INDIAN WARS 1840-1890"
SIMITAR ENTERTAINMENT INC. 1991

ROD SERLING - "THE 7TH IS MADE UP OF PHANTOMS"
"THE TWILIGHT ZONE" EPISODE #10 1963
WRITEN BY - FRANK GRUBER - "WARPATH" PARAMOUNT PICTURES 1951

Lithographs used for research

BECKER,OTTO - "CUSTER'S LAST FIGHT"
ANHEUSER-BUSH 1896

VON SCHMIDT, HAROLD- "CUSTER'S LAST STAND" 1950

PAXSON, EDGAR S. - "CUSTER'S LAST STAND" 1899

MULVANY, JOHN - "CUSTER'S LAST RALLY"   1881

LORENZ RICHARD - "CUSTER'S LAST COMMAND" 1914

RUSSELL, CHARLES M. - "THE CUSTER FIGHT" 1903

MARDON, ALLAN - "THE BATTLE OF GREASY GRASS" 1996

LORENZA, RICHARD - "CUSTER'S LAST STAND"   1914

STIRNWEIS, KIRK - "THE LAST COMMAND" 2014

REUSSWIG, WILLIAM - "CUSTER'S LAST STAND" 1950

REMINGTON, FREDERICK - "THE LAST STAND" 1889

HEINZ, RALPH - "SGT. JOHN RYAN CO. M 7TH CAVALRY"

Reference Outlets

KIDPORT REFERENCE LIBRARY
CHIEF DULL KNIFE COLLEGE
AKTA LAKOTA MUSEUM CULTURAL CENTER- LAKOTA PHRASE ARCHIVES
CHEYENNE LANGUAGE WEB
CHEYENNE & ARAPAHO TRIBE'S LANGUAGE PROGRAM (REBECCA RISENHOOVER)
ARNOLD MARCUS CHERNOFF -COLLECTION OF INDIAN ARTIFACTS
OMNIGLOT ON CHEYENNE ENCYCLOPEDIA
OMNIGLOT ON SIOUX ENCYCLOPEDIA
CHEYENNE KEYBOARD PROGRAM
LITTLE BIG HORN COLLEGE
LIBERTY UNIVERSITY ONLINE CROW LANGUAGE
GIVING BACK TO WOUNDED KNEE FOUNDATION INC. LAKOTA LANGUAGE
RED NATION -CHEROKEE LANGUAGE
BARNS & NOBLE
PHOENIX LIBRARY
HEARD MUSEUM -PHOENIX- ARIZONA
CUSTER BATTLEFIELD NATIONAL MONUMENT
WIKIPEDIA
RPG FORUM
LAST CHANCE SALOON
FRAZIER HISTORY MUSEUM,LOUISVILLE-KY.
WEST POINT ACADEMY-N.Y.
GETTYSBURG VISITORS CENTER-MUSEUM
UNIVERSITY OF VIRGINIA LIBRARY
ARCHIVE ON THE INTERNET
ONLINE BOOK PAGE
BIBLIO.COM
DIXIE GUN WORKS
LODGE WOOD MFG. -DANIELLE STAVLO (PICTURES)
LEROY MERZ ANTIQUE FIREARMS
WWW.AMERICAN-INDIAN-ART.COM (ED HAYDEN)
JOURNEY MUSEUM - CONNOR MCMAHON CHIEF CURATOR
CRAZY HORSE MUSEUM - MARGARETE CULLUM
NEW YORK CITY PUBLIC LIBRARY

MESQUITE LIBRARY- PHOENIX ARIZONA
PUTNAM VALLEY PUBLIC LIBRARY
NYACK PUBLIC LIBRARY
BISMARCK TRIBUNE
NATIONAL PARK SERVICE/ FORT LARAMIE NATIONAL HISTORIC SITE
ENCYCLOPEDIA BRITANNICA
ARIZONA FLUTES & NATIVE ARTS- CAROL BUCKLEY (CAMP VERDE, AZ
LARRYGOTKINHANDMADE - LARRY GOTKIN (TUCSON, AZ
CAMP VERDE MILITARY POST - CAMP VERDE, ARIZONA
N-SSA
TRUE WEST MAGAZINE
HISTORY CHANNEL
CIVIL WAR ANTIQUE SHOP

Illustration and Photo Credits

Photos:
Custer, Reno, Benteen, Sitting Bull, Gall, Crazy Horse, Black Kettle, Tom Custer, Boston Custer, Libbie Custer, Autie Custer, James Calhoun, Norvell Churchill.

Photos obtained from:
Pat Churchill Hedgecoth
Library of Congress
Mathew Brady
Wikipedia
Marjorie G. Treptow

Cover:
Original painting contracted work by Samantha Rapp

Sketch of Oraland Churchill & Waynoka:
Original sketch contracted work by Des Jean Bauer

Map:
Little Big Horn Battle:
Wayne F. Treptow

About the Author

Wayne was born in 1947 in Goshen N.Y. to a second generation German Family. His father was a district manager for the Prudential Life Insurance Company, and his mother was a housewife to three children. After graduating from Nyack High School in upstate N.Y. he continued his education at the University of Arkansas and majored in history and industrial education. He was enrolled in the ROTC program and was a member of Company D 7th Regiment of the National Society of Pershing Rifles.

For the next 43 years he was a professional salesman dealing in the construction industry and covered all the nuclear job sites along the east coast from Philadelphia to Maine. In his spare time he was involved with Civil War living history. He started in 1962 during the centennial of the war and was involved for over 33 years as a hobby. He did an impression of his Great Great grandfather (Bodwin Cortwright Lee) who was a Sgt. In the 124th N.Y.V. who were mustered into the Army of the Republic from Goshen N.Y. They were referred to as the "Orange Blossoms".

Wayne has been involved in many things during his life time including being an ordained minister, a well known music DJ from the upstate N.Y. area and the father of two children and grandfather of three grandchildren. He now resides in historic Camp Verde, Arizona with his wife and four dogs. He is very active in the local history of the town and is engaged in local events.

The Author started writing in 1960 and his first short story won him a $500 cash prize. From then on he was hooked on the pen and paper and has four books published. The first book "Dog Tags" was published in 2009. It is about time travel shadowing the Civil War and Vietnam War. It has over 3ooo copies sold it is in its second printing.

The second book "The Other Side" published in 2013 captures out of body experiences and the characters in the book visit famous and well known people. This book was inspired by the loss of a family member and a personl out the body experience which the author experienced.

The third book "The Fam-Damliy Cooks Cookbook" is a compilation of historical family recipes. The Author loves to cook and has cooked for 2000 people and a family of two.

Now introducing "Hok A Hey". It is a result of years of detailed study of the Battle of the little Big Horn in 1876. It all started in 1958 when his father brought home a print of the 1896 Otto Becker's painting "Custers Last Fight". The print has been in the author's head all these years and he has written fantastic story line for the reader, enjoy!

To Order Books

Contact Wayne Treptow directly at
vikwayaz@hotmail.com

To Order Books
Glorybound Publishing
www.gloryboundpublishing.com
439 S. 6th St. Camp Verde, AZ 86322
928-567-3340